THE ENEMY

AMELIA SHEA

Amelia Shea

This book is a work of fiction. The names, characters, places and incidents are products of the writer's imagination, or have been used fictitiously and are not to be construed as real. Any resemblance to real persons, living or dead, actual events or organizations is entirely coincidental.

Copyright © 2020 by Amelia Shea
All rights reserved.

The unauthorized reproduction or distribution of this copyright work is illegal. No part of this book may be distributed, reproduced, or stored in a retrieval system, or transmitted in any form or by any means, electronic, mechanical, photocopying, recording, or otherwise, without express written permission of the publisher.

Dedication

For Tricia, my favorite Nebraskan.

Chapter 1

Welcome to Ghosttown.

Phoebe eyed the dented brown sign with a small smile playing on her lips as she drove past. It was old and beat-up, some of the lettering scuffed. *God, I've missed that sign.* She drew in a deep breath and let it out with a slow release. It had been too long. Six months since the same sign had been in her rearview mirror. She gripped her steering wheel and rolled her neck, fighting against her nerves.

Relax, you're home.

She was. Her small shack on four acres in the middle of nowhere was the only home she had been able to afford to keep once the debt was paid off. *Well, almost paid off.* She was still forty thousand dollars in the hole for her deceased husband's extracurricular expenses. Vacations, five-star dinners, jet-setting around the world to places Phoebe had never been. Those luxuries were reserved for his lovers. Not his wife. *Christ, Jared, really?* A year and a half after his death she was still paying off his sins. *'Til death do us part, and then some.*

She shook the memory of Jared from her head. Nothing good ever came from rehashing the past and playing the blame game. If she did, she'd be forced to take a long hard look at everything she'd been blind to. Every lie she had believed and every gut instinct she'd ignored. She had to own her part in their marriage—the unsuspecting wife. *A role I'll never play again.* Neither unsuspecting nor wife.

She had given him everything, all of her, and in the end, was left with nothing.

"Past is in the past," she muttered.

She entered Main Street, and a budding warmth filled her blood. *Ghosttown.* The only place she ever truly felt at home. There was just something about the town that put her at ease, with the exception of the dark cloud currently looming over her head. She sighed, ignoring the anxiety building in her chest. It had been over six months since she'd been back. Considering how she left, her reception would be interesting.

The town had closed down for the night. The businesses occupying the three-block center of town usually closed by five, including the only gas station for twenty miles. It was what kept it quaint. As she drove down the empty street, she gradually pressed on the brakes until she came to a dead stop in the middle of the empty road.

"What the…" She was shell-shocked from her view, unable to even finish her sentence.

She jerked her head toward the passenger side window and leaned over the seat to get a better look.

"We have a tattoo parlor?" Her eyes widened. "And a coffee shop?"

When she had left six months ago, the only businesses open were the market, the diner, and the antique store. All the other buildings sat vacant.

She settled into her seat and slowly angled her head to the left. GHOSTTOWN AUTO PARTS. She arched her brow and smirked. It could only mean one thing. The new residents had arrived and settled in. She had left town before they had officially moved in. The Ghosttown Riders MC. While the mayor sang their praises, others didn't seem quite as sold on the motorcycle club taking up residency.

She remained neutral on the Ghosttown Riders. She wasn't currently in a position to judge anyone. Even if her circumstances had been different, it wasn't Phoebe's style. She believed everyone was decent until they proved her wrong. A prime example would be her deceased husband. *Asshole.*

Phoebe continued down the road, eyeing the new look of Main Street. Some people, the old-timers, or originals as they liked to call themselves, wouldn't be happy with the expansion. One in particular.

She snorted and shook her head. She'd bet money, she and the MC would have at least one common enemy.

She turned left at the gas station, driving a quarter mile before the townhall came in view. It was fitting her homecoming would be at a town meeting.

She had wanted to come back quietly. The townspeople had other plans. Once word got out that Phoebe was coming home, she received calls demanding her presence at the meeting.

My town, my people.

She widened her eyes as she neared the lot for the town hall.

"And those must be the new neighbors." She eyed the motorcycles lined up along the edge of the road and on the side of the building. There had to be about thirty of them. She wasn't privy to exactly how many members had moved to their small town. From the looks of the lot, the population had doubled with the arrival of the club.

Phoebe slowed down, bringing the car to a roll as she turned into the graveled driveway. It had been quite some time since she'd been to a town meeting. She couldn't remember ever seeing this much action. Most residents showed up, mostly for the pastries, free coffee, and the drama.

Arnett.

She eyed his blue truck as she passed the entrance. *First spot taken by the resident pain in the ass.* She rolled her eyes with an amused smirk as she made her way around back.

Tonight would mark her first face-to-face with him since the incident that drove her out of town for half the year. While she wasn't proud of how she handled herself with their altercation, she couldn't strum up regret. She could only be pushed so far before she snapped. For all her thirty-two years on the earth, she'd never laid her hands on anyone. Until six months ago.

Move forward, not backward. At the suggestion of her court-mandated anger management counselor, she reached out to Arnett a few months ago. It was important to make amends and take ownership for her part. Arnett refused to accept her apology. He called her a handful of colorful names, and then he continued to berate her until she struck back with a sarcastic rant. Thankfully, they were separated by three hundred miles at the time.

Phoebe scanned the back edge of the lot and pulled into the only available spot.

She climbed out of the car and took in her surroundings. The gravel lot looked like a motorcycle convention. Before the club moved in, even a packed meeting wouldn't have filled half the lot.

She tucked her keys in her back pocket and started through the lot.

The town hall was a converted barn. Some renovations had been done outside, mainly the roof and siding. The last she heard from Bailey, an anonymous healthy donation had been given to restore the inside.

She slowed her steps as she grew closer to the entrance. Her heart beat faster on her approach to the double side doors. She dragged her sweaty palms down her jeans. It was the first time seeing everyone since her abrupt departure. She didn't doubt she'd get a warm welcome from most, but there were a select few who would have been happy to never see her face again. *I'm back, Arnett.* She drew in a breath and walked up the stairs.

From the platform deck, she got a peek inside. Even through the throngs of people, she immediately noticed the walls had been repainted a lighter warm beige. The floors were either refinished or completely replaced. Either way, they looked amazing.

She stopped at the entrance, taking in the scene. The meeting hall was packed, beyond capacity if she had to guess. There were many familiar faces, and even more unfamiliar. Her gaze skated around the room as she remained unnoticed tucked away close to the entrance. She flattened her lips, keeping her amusement at bay.

There was an obvious divide. To her right, lined against the wall were a slew of men dressed similarly in jeans, work boots, and their obvious cuts, naming them as part of the club. On the opposite side of the room were *her* people. The front half of the seating was occupied by all the familiar faces. When she glanced to the back, the Ghosttown Riders took up the entire three rows of chairs. It was dominated by men, only a few women mixed into their crowd.

Bikers. The corner of her mouth curled. There was an even mixture of old and young, though they shared a similar rugged and rough appearance. The bad boy persona had never been her thing. Then again, *her type* had led her to a man who had betrayed her. Jared had been the polar opposite of every man sitting in the back of the room. Where Jared had been charming and handsome, he lacked the virile sex appeal and intrigue of the men sitting five feet away from her.

A warm heat flashed over her cheeks. *And I'm intrigued.*

She leaned over slightly to get a better angle of her view. Her gaze drifted through the rows, catching a few glances her way. She continued her perusal until she locked eyes on a man sitting at the end of the aisle.

I'm really intrigued now.

He was living up to every stereotype she had in her head. His long, light brown hair weaved down his back, falling just past his shoulders. His hard features were outlined by a light-colored beard. It wasn't quite the length of a mountain man who'd been living in the wild for a year, yet it was too unruly for the average

Joe jumping on the latest *beards are in* trend. She muffled her snort. Nothing about him was average.

His thick arms were folded, resting over his chest. The cuffs of his shirt were hiked to his elbows, showing off his intricate black and gray tattoos. Even from twenty feet away, she noticed the bulging outline of his muscles. *Sweet!* She flicked her gaze to his hard face. Deep lines imbedded between his thick brows, a darker shade of brown than his hair. She tilted her head and bit her lip.

All the while as she openly checked him out, he watched her. His dark stare was sending a shock to her system and awakening her lower region. She shifted on her feet but refused to glance away. *It almost feels like foreplay.*

Since Jared, she'd dated quite a few men, keeping everything casual, including the sex. It was a rule she'd set up for herself, and one she strictly followed. She wasn't interested in a relationship, or anything more than a good time. The corner of her mouth curled. *He looks like fun.*

She quirked her brow and smiled. The faint hitch in his cheek was the only reaction she got. It was enough for her. A warm swirl circled in her belly. This man was not her type, yet something sexy and sinister had her fascinated. *I bet he has wall sex. Yeah, definitely the guy who presses you against the wall, rips down your panties, and fucks you until you can't remember your own name. And counter sex, from behind, gripping your ass as he pounds inside you until you're riding the longest orgasm of your life.* She smirked. *And the positions this man must do. Him on top, me on top, doggy style, reverse cowgirl, legs thrown over his broad shoulders with my heels digging into his sweaty back. I would definitely keep my stilettos on.* A burst of heat trailed from her belly to her core. *This man definitely 69s.* She drew in a deep breath trying to combat her beating heart. Her nipples beaded into sharp points, and she swore her panties would be drenched if this eye-fucking continued. *I bet he's amazing with his tongue.* She clamped her thighs together.

"Can we get on with this?"

She released a small whimpered moan at the interruption to

her fantasy. *Asshole.* Her shoulders sagged, and Phoebe closed her eyes. *His fucking voice.* There were so many things she missed about Ghosttown. Arnett's voice was not one of them.

She blinked her eyes open to find the biker's gaze still on her. She licked her lips, watching his eyes drop to her mouth. *Is he imagining my lips around his cock, my tongue licking him from root to crown? Are we in his bed or my bed? Are we naked? Oh God, I hope we're friggin' naked.*

"I have issues that need to be discussed." Arnett's nasally voice echoed through the room, sucking every sexual vibe out of her dazed fantasy.

Oh hell. She sighed and regrettably turned away. She stepped into the room, lining up with the bikers on the wall. All of whom turned to look in her direction.

"Didn't you get the memo, darlin'?" The familiar voice was music to her ears. She glanced across the room at Bill. "Meeting starts at seven." His boisterous chuckle was definitely one of the many things she'd missed in Ghosttown.

Bill, like most of the residents, was friendly and warm, with a fabulous sense of humor. He, like her and so many others, showed up mostly to enjoy the comic relief of Arnett and to watch him lose his shit. Nothing set him off more than people showing up late.

The sound of chairs shifting was her warning. Her presence was now known to the whole room. She was greeted with short waves and smiles from the front half of the room, including the men lined up next to Bill.

My people.

She chuckled and shrugged. "Well, it's seven," she glanced around the room, "-ish." Her comment garnered an uproar of laughter from most.

Arnett shot up from his seat in the front row and scowled at her.

Here we go...

She slowly moved past the bikers lined up on the side, offering a welcoming smile. She received some glances and perusals of her body. One in particular, a dark-haired handsome man with a goatee, raised his brows and smiled. She winked as she passed and heard the soft chuckle from behind. He didn't quite rank as high as the man with the dark eyes, but he was a close second when it came to sex appeal.

When she reached the front of the room, her greeting to her friend was interrupted.

"You're late!" Arnett shouted.

Phoebe turned. "I'm here now." She tilted her head with a grin, watching his face turn a dark shade of red. "Have you been counting down the days until my arrival, Arnett?" She clicked her tongue and waved her finger. "I knew it. Deep down inside, I think you missed me."

He scoffed and his eyes went wild. She had anticipated and prepared for her first face-to-face with Arnett. His sharp tongue would not get the best of her again. Calm and cool was how she'd handle him, no matter what he threw at her this time.

She made her way to the large oak desk. It had replaced their old folding table. Phoebe slid her hand across the wood, stopping in front of Bailey who was flanked by the councilmen. Like most of the people, she was greeted with welcoming smiles.

"Look at you guys, all fancy at your new desk. It's starting to look like a real legit town." She winked at Gerry, who chuckled. She reached out and grabbed Bailey's hand. "Good to see you, girl." Bailey tightened her grip and nodded.

"Welcome home, Feebs." Bailey leaned forward and wrapped her arm around Phoebe's shoulders. They had a lot of catching up to do. Phoebe closed her eyes, taking in the warm embrace. *God, I've missed her.*

It was only a matter of time before Arnett and his snarky mouth ruined their reunion. She wouldn't give him the satisfaction. Phoebe stepped away from the desk, smiling back at her friend. They'd get together soon. For now, the meeting was top priority. She turned around, sending smiles to those who were watching her. She made her way down the end aisle toward the snack table.

The only saving grace to these meetings was the food. Six months was too long to wait for her favorite. She glanced down searching for them. *I've waited six months. Where the hell are they?* She glanced over her shoulder, realizing most people were watching her.

"No apple turnovers?" Her mouth watered just saying it. They'd always been her favorite homemade dessert. She glanced around the seats. "Where's Karen?" She was a goddess with baked treats.

"She and Charlie moved six weeks ago," Marley said.

They moved? Karen, Charlie, and their children had been one of the first families to introduce themselves when Phoebe had bought her house seven years ago. They were one of Ghosttown's original families. They couldn't move. Some changes were acceptable. This one was not.

"What? Why?"

"They moved out to California, be closer to their son." Marley smiled and rested her hand on her belly. "He just had a baby."

She eyed Marley suspiciously. Phoebe wasn't struck so much with the news of Karen and Charlie moving as she was with Marley's hand placement and how she slowly caressed her belly. Phoebe gasped as she began to put two and two together. She and her husband, Coop, had been trying to get pregnant for years. It had been a struggle, some of which Marley had shared with her. She glanced up to see Marley grinning with pride. *Holy shit!*

She turned around to Coop, who was leaning up against the wall and smiling.

My town, my people.

She shook her head. "You sly son of a bitch, you knocked up your wife."

Couth had never played a big part in Phoebe's life. Most days, she repeated her thoughts. Thankfully, the townspeople appreciated it. The room as a whole echoed with laughter.

"Oh my God, congratulations, this is the best news." She reached out, grabbing Coop's hands and tightening her hold. They were going to make awesome parents. "We should be celebrating with apple turnovers." She turned and playfully pouted at Marley.

"I'm available for babysitting as soon as he or she is potty trained."

Marley laughed along with a few other residents.

Phoebe grabbed a cookie. "So, they sold their house?" She glanced back at Bailey, who was shaking her head.

"Nope, saving it for Trista. She's coming back after she graduates." Bailey raised her brow with a small smirk playing on her lips.

Phoebe chuckled. Trista had been so eager to get out of the small town six years ago. She remembered the teen going on and on about wanting to be free and see the world. *Now, she's coming home.*

"It's good," Marty said. "Need some young blood here."

Phoebe playfully narrowed her gaze. "Is that a dig at my age, Marty?"

He chuckled. "No, darlin, it's a dig at mine."

Ahh, I've missed these people. My people.

"Oh, for hell's sake, we have a meeting to start." Arnett stood and shouted across the room. "We're not here to discuss babies or food." He whipped around to face Bailey and snapped, "As mayor, I demand you do something."

His outbursts and rants were nothing new. However, Phoebe wasn't sure the Ghosttown Riders would be giving as much leeway as the rest of them. Phoebe glanced across the room.

Bailey's face paled when a curse from the back of the room sounded. From the corner of her eye, she saw a figure straighten and step forward, only to be stopped by another man. *Oh, Arnett's pissing off the bikers.* She had not been formally introduced, but if she had to guess from the narrowed sharp gaze, the tall handsome biker who was giving a silent warning to Arnett must be Saint,

The Enemy

Bailey's man. *Damn, good for you, Bailey.* Beyond his twisted lips and tense, jagged features, the man was gorgeous. Phoebe glanced back at Bailey, who seemed nervous, with a small shake to her head. The last thing her friend needed was a brawl breaking out.

Phoebe took a bite of her cookie and inched to the edge of the row where Arnett was holding court.

"Calm. Down." He flinched and she snickered. "You gotta relax, Arnett. It's not good to get all worked up, all right?" She popped the last of her cookie in her mouth and licked her lips.

His glare went straight through her, which only intensified her desire to laugh. He was wired up so tight his head was about to burst.

"How about this? I'm gonna go and grab another cookie from the table, maybe a cup of coffee, and Bailey can start the meeting. I know there are pressing issues, like," she shrugged, "feral cats and who toilet papered Main Street."

The room erupted in laughter. Her comment had only fueled Arnett's anger, and it was solely directed at her. *Some things never change.* She held up her hands and backed up from him. She turned to Bailey and waved her hand. "Take it away, Bails."

"I'll have you know we got illegal pressing issues in this town. And if you showed on time or even at all, you'd know that."

Phoebe halted and slowly turned around, trapping him with her glare. He knew damn well why she couldn't show up. As per his usual angry bitter self, Arnett was being an asshole. Why couldn't he just let shit go? She eyed his face. He had healed, she'd been punished. It was over.

Bailey cleared her throat. "Uh... let's start and focus on the agenda."

"Is the illegal activity in this town on the agenda?" he snapped.

Phoebe groaned. "What illegal activity, Arnett? We live in friggin' Mayberry." She snorted, rolling her eyes.

The snickers from the crowd intensified Arnett's anger, and his face brightened to a deep shade of red. He jerked his chin toward the back of the room. She followed his gaze to where the all Ghosttown Riders members resided. She flattened her lips. They didn't seem too happy with how they were being referenced.

"What have you got to say to them, *Mayor*?" The snide tone resting on his last word hadn't gone unnoticed. *Bitter, bitter, bitter, Arnett.*

"Mr. Collins…" Bailey said, lifting her hand. She was about to act as peacemaker, a role Bailey was born to play. However, Phoebe felt the strong desire to intervene. Any opportunity to piss Arnett off, she'd gladly take.

"Bailey, if you don't mind, I'll handle this." She was aware of all the eyes on her, and she scanned the room, taking in the club members. Again, she was caught by one particular stare from the sexy, gruff stranger at the end of the aisle. He watched her through hooded eyes.

"This is a small, tight-knit community." She noticed his jaw lock in anticipation of her next words. "On behalf of myself and the fine, law-abiding people of Ghosttown…" She glanced around the residents, who seemed thoroughly amused by her display of theatrics. Well, almost all. Arnett was not amused, though he did seem curious as to what she'd say next.

She grinned. "We'd like to welcome you to our little town." She clasped her hands. "We hope you enjoy your time here as much we do. And?" She raised her hand, noticing everyone's attention was hanging on her last words. "If any of you have a desire to bring apple turnovers to the next meeting, we would surely appreciate it."

It caused the exact reaction she knew it would. Of course, her attention was focused solely on the long-haired, dark-eyed biker. The corner of his mouth jutted up slightly. Not much of a reaction, but she'd take it. *God, he's sexy.*

"You are not our goddamn Welcome Wagon, so you need to shut your trap," Arnett shouted. The laughter died down, and the tension grew. She had no doubt his comment had put the residents on edge waiting on her reaction.

No one in the room, including Phoebe, was looking for a repeat performance from six months ago. Arnett, on the other hand, had no issue with resorting to nastiness and antagonizing any situation. It seemed Arnett had learned nothing from their altercation. Phoebe had no problem giving him a verbal reminder.

"Shut my trap?" She raised her brows, seemingly calm. It was all for show. Inside her blood was boiling. She drew in a breath and stepped toward him. "Why don't you come over here and *make me shut my trap*, Arnett?"

In a room full of people who would surely step in if she took another step closer, Arnett seemed hellbent on pushing her. He sneered. It was a challenge; one she knew he wouldn't take if not for their audience.

"You are an unstable, crazy, psychotic, delinquent criminal."

Phoebe grinned. "With a hell of a right hook, wouldn't ya say?"

Aside from the hushed gasps, the room fell silent. She refused to look at anyone except Arnett.

"All right everybody, just calm down. Arnett, have a seat so we can continue." Gerry said.

The councilmen seated next to Bailey, shifted in his seat uncomfortably. She could understand why. Being a small town, especially as small as Ghosttown, word of her altercation had travelled from every house to those who hadn't witnessed it. The residents knew what happened to the most minor detail. No one wanted Phoebe set off again.

Gerry cleared his throat, eyeing her and Arnett. "We've got a lot to cover tonight, so let's get started. Bailey, why don't you take over?"

Arnett glared back at Phoebe. She winked, and his brows furrowed in a tight squeeze. He'd hit her with the lowest of blows, a virtual sucker punch, setting her off six months ago. It was her own fault, she allowed him to get in deep. A mistake she had learned from. From now on, everything he said would roll off her shoulders. She wouldn't give his words power. *Thank you, therapy!*

"Oh, for Christ's sake, Arnett, sit down. Ya over there throwing daggers at her, delaying the meeting even more." Coop, who was standing next to her, sighed heavily when Arnett remained standing. He leaned closer and whispered, "I get to punch him this time."

She laughed, playfully slapping his arm. The few people closest to where they were standing by the snack table also joined in.

"I want a turn too," Carla said from her seat two rows back.

"We should have one of those town carnivals, ya know, where they have the dunk tanks. Except, instead of water, we could all line up for a punch at him." Mary, who had to be pushing eighty, laughed. "I'd spend my social security for the chance to make the old goat see stars."

These are my people.

Phoebe had done her best to meet all the members of Ghosttown when they bought their small property seven years ago. Being part of the town and getting to know everyone had been important to her. They made it easy. Everyone had been welcoming and friendly, minus a few grumpy assholes.

Finally, Arnett took a seat, and Bailey started the meeting. It would be a long night. Most meetings ranged from an hour to ninety minutes. With the arrival of the new residents, it was sure to take longer.

Phoebe peeked past Coop to the back of the room. According to Bailey and a few others, the MC was going to revitalize the small town. The plans were set to have all the storefronts occupied with new business, and they even offered their services to revamp the existing. From the looks of Main Street, they had stayed true to their word. They'd made it clear they wanted to be part of the town, not take it over. A concept Arnett and a few of the other older folks couldn't quite grasp. Not everybody was on board with the changes.

Phoebe was all for it. Especially since Ghosttown would become her permanent residence as of today.

She shifted on her feet. After five hours of driving, she would have thought standing would have been a welcomed reprieve. Her legs disagreed. She surveyed the room for open seats. She sighed when she spotted the only vacant chair. Right next to Arnett. His jacket lay on top with a folder. The room was packed with half the people standing, even some women, including herself, and he was hogging a chair for his stuff? *Bullshit!*

She cleared her throat and raised her hand, gaining the attention of Bailey.

"Can I just say something?" Before she could finish, Arnett was on his feet.

"No, you can't. You got no say in anything that goes on in this town, seeing as how you aren't even a full-time resident."

While Ghosttown may not have been her permanent residence in the past seven years, it was very much her home, same as everyone else in the room. Unlike Arnett, she didn't spend her time bitching about what was wrong. She met her neighbors, she interacted with the people, and made a life, though not full time, in Ghosttown. She was as much invested there as he was, and unfortunately for him, his statement was actually false.

Her excitement was bubbling over, and she was seconds away from blurting out the truth. *I can't wait to see the look on his face.* It wasn't the right time, though.

She raised her brows and smiled. "Oh yeah? My tax bill says different, Arnett. I am very much a resident of this town." She tilted her head. "You're more than welcome to come on over to my place and check it out." She squinted. She couldn't resist pulling the tiger's tail. "How about it, Arnett? Wanna come over? Or are ya scared?" The corner of her mouth curled.

"The whole town should be scared of your kind of crazy," he spouted.

"Nope, got no problem with anyone else." She waggled her brows. "Just you."

The loud bang from the back of the room had everyone turning in their seats. She leaned forward past Marty, who was standing next to her. In the back corner, a small girl was on the floor. From the looks of it, she dropped her book.

"Children aren't allowed at the meeting. I won't have it!" Arnett shouted, and she watched the girl jerk her head as her lips tugged downward. *Oh God, this man.* As if it wasn't bad enough, he was an asshole to adults, now with a child?

No fucking way!

She whipped her head around and stepped out into the aisle. "That little girl has made less noise in the past hour than you have in the last ten seconds. So if you won't have it, let's take a vote." Phoebe glanced around the room. "Arnett or the little cutie in the back. My vote's going for her to stay." She raised her hand and enjoyed not only the snickers but the many people raising their hands.

She clucked her tongue. "It's like the mayoral election all over again." She smirked and leaned forward, staring at Arnett. "You lose."

PHOEBE SHAW.

He clasped his hand over his mouth, raking his fingers over his beard.

So, this is her?

Kase had remained neutral throughout the hour of antics playing out in front of him. Other members hadn't been able to table their amusement. He couldn't fault them. The meeting as a whole was a fucking train wreck. The back and forth between her and the old man hadn't slowed the fuck down since it started. It was a shit show with the two of them as the main attraction. Highly entertaining for most. Not him.

She would be a problem.

The club had been trying to purchase her property for the last year. Each offer, one higher than the other, presented by their representative, had been denied. She'd made it clear she had no intention of selling.

He'd originally scoffed at her declaration. If he wanted it, he'd get it.

Kase had come up with a new angle to work. He could manipulate anyone into doing anything he wanted. Being ruthless and cunning had always been second nature for Kase. His main objective for attending this specific meeting was to get a first look at his new neighbor. He considered a low-key introduction. He wasn't opposed to using the MC presence as a silent intimidation strategy. He wouldn't strong arm her. He wouldn't have to. A recent widow licking her wounds from the loss of her husband would be an easy target. He had no problem using her vulnerability for his gain.

Before walking in tonight, he had no doubt they'd be taking ownership of her property within the month.

He snorted, eyeing the blonde. He had her all fucking wrong.

Phoebe Shaw was not who he expected.

A hell of a right hook?

Why don't you come over here and make me shut my trap?

Are ya scared?

What the fuck? She had spewed out quite a few blatant threats to the old guy. All of which seemed to be ignored by the townspeople. It was interesting the way they seemed to turn a blind eye to everything she said, with some even agreeing with her. He had underestimated her pull in the town and how she was received by the people.

This is a big fucking problem.

He didn't have the full story on Phoebe or her absence for the past six months. He'd asked Bailey where she was after months of the property being vacant. All she would say was there was an incident a few months back and Phoebe was staying away. He heard a few references of an altercation. However, the residents were tight lipped about what had happened. It appeared she had the whole town backing her on an incident no one was willing to talk about.

If he had to guess, the incident had involved the asshole in the front row. Arnett was no stranger to Kase. He lived across the road from the new clubhouse, making him Phoebe's neighbor too.

It seemed odd she'd leave town due to an issue with him, seeing as how she was handling him now. If anything, Arnett seemed to be intimidated, though he was trying to mask it. Kase knew people, knew their mannerisms, and had a keen sense for fear. Arnett may not have been backing down, but Phoebe's presence had him uneasy.

Kase folded his arms, focusing on the blonde against the wall. There was no hiding the bond she had with the majority of people. She was filtering around, holding side conversations with half a dozen people as the meeting continued. They liked her, engaged with her, and seemed genuinely happy she was back. *Big fucking problem.*

Kase's chair shifted forward, and he felt Gage at his back. "I think I'm looking at my future ex-wife."

Kase remained silent. Apparently, he wasn't the only man watching her. There was no doubt Phoebe was on half his brothers' radar. His gaze travelled over her body. A gray tank, plunging low into her cleavage, molded over her tits. Her shirt alone had gotten half the males' attention in the room. Her waist dipped and her hips flared with her tight jeans curved over her ass and down her long legs. Cherry on the fucking cake? Red stilettos. He wasn't fucking blind; he saw the appeal. Half the men in the room were concocting seven different ways to take her if they could get her in their bed. They hadn't even been treated to the sultry eye fucking he got when she walked in. It was all the reason to keep his distance. This one was fucking trouble.

He drew in a breath and slowly angled his head, pinning Phoebe with his stare. Unlike most women, she didn't shy away when he looked back at her. He ground his teeth, watching the corner of her lips curl slightly in a playful hitch. This was new territory for him. He was usually approached in two ways, unsure or all in. Phoebe was neither. He hardened his jaw in hopes of making his message clear. *Not fucking interested, sweetheart.*

He turned his attention back to the meeting and ignored her gaze. She only served one purpose for him and bedding her wasn't it. The MC and their interests always came before pussy.

Since he took the gavel years ago, he vowed to put his brothers and the club before anyone. He'd made good on his promise.

Her feminine giggle caught his attention again.

"I swear, I stopped in the middle of the road and thought I was in the wrong town," she whispered, making her way toward the back, putting her a few feet away from him. "I can't wait to go to Main Street. I'm gonna hit the cute little boutique first and stock up on candles, then grab a slice of pizza, stop in at the coffee shop for a latte and pastry, and end my day with a tattoo." She bounced on her toes and grabbed Coop's arm. "I love this new Ghosttown."

Coop snorted. "Woulda thought you'd get a tattoo while you were serving time."

Kase jerked his head before he could control his reaction. Doing time? *What the fuck?* Coop was holding back a smile, and he winked at her.

Phoebe shook her head. "Not enough time." She held up her hand and raised her brows. "And no, I wasn't somebody's bitch."

Kase furrowed *his* brows. He heard the snickering coming from behind him. Gage must have been listening too.

"Do ya got *any* good prison stories?" Bill teased, coming up behind her.

"Not enough time to cause too much trouble."

"Six hours?"

Phoebe scoffed. "Try twenty-seven."

"Twenty-seven?" He whistled. "Thought you would have been out in a few hours."

She leaned forward. "They lost my paperwork, so there was a

delay on my release. But at least I get to claim two days as my sentence. So much more badass than just a day, don't ya think?"

The older guy chuckled, and Kase noticed him wrap his arm around Phoebe, pulling her into his side. She went willingly and curled her arm around his waist.

"Missed you," he whispered. "These meetings have lacked the entertainment value for the past six months. You good, sweetheart?"

"I'm good, and don't worry, Bill." She glanced up, smirking. "Prison hasn't changed me." She backed away and turned. She moved closer to the back of the room where he and the club had settled in at the beginning of the meeting.

The prison comment caught his attention, though it was said in jest. What the fuck was he missing here?

He kept his head forward and remained acutely aware of his surroundings. Kase watched as she quietly angled her body next to a guy who stood a foot away from his seat. She curled her arm through his and smiled. The guy, who he'd tag as old enough to be her father, weaved his arm around her shoulders and tugged her into his side. He'd met Phil and his wife, Delores, at his store. They were both retired, and he was currently in the process of rebuilding an old beat up Porsche.

"Good to have ya back, sweetheart."

"Yeah, well, every town needs a bad apple. Looks like I'm Ghosttown's." Kase heard the shared snicker. They were obviously close. "Need a favor."

"Name it."

"I have to bring my car in for repair. Do you think you can give me a ride home if they need to keep it?"

"Take it to the one on Truman?"

Kase watched her confused reaction. Before she could speak, Phil jerked his chin toward the back of the room. "The MC opened up a repair shop right on Truman." Phil smiled. "No more driving over to Turnersville for us. They replaced my carburetor a few weeks ago. Good price."

The Enemy

"Yeah?"

Kase turned his attention toward the front of the room but caught her movement from the corner of his eye. Her steps were soft and headed in his direction. He would have preferred his first encounter with her to be on his terms. When she stopped a few inches away, he glanced up at her, keeping his features hard and uninviting.

She slowly bent down, resting her hands on her knees, putting them at eye level. And dangerously close. Her long blonde hair swung past her shoulders, inches away from touching his thigh. Most people shied away from getting too close to him, but Phoebe didn't seem concerned or intimidated. If anything, she appeared interested.

No fucking way, sweetheart.

She drew in a breath and angled her head. "Hi there."

Kase cocked his brow and remained silent.

"I heard you guys have a garage? I was hoping you could help me out." Her gaze flickered past him, landing on Rourke seated beside him. Phoebe smiled. "I was driving in, and my sailboat light came on."

Gage snickered, along with a few other brothers in the surrounding area. It didn't seem to faze her. She giggled. "Why the hell do I even have a sailboat light?" She shifted her gaze back at him, and the corner of her mouth curled.

Kase stared back. "It's your temperature gauge."

She widened her eyes with amusement. "That's my sailboat?"

Trax and Rourke laughed. She glanced over at them and then set her sights back on Kase. With his close-up view, he noticed the small light freckles peppering over her nose.

"It's a fucking temperature gauge, not a fucking sailboat."

Her brow cocked, and she smirked, leaning closer. "But it looks like a sailboat, am I right?"

Her effort to flirt with a playful banter would be lost on him. He wouldn't play into anything with her. More experienced women, versed in sexual seduction and flirtation, had tried and failed.

Kase locked his jaw and jerked his chin toward Trax and Rourke. "Bring it in, they'll check it out."

She jerked her gaze past him to Trax and Rourke and then smiled and leaned a bit closer to Kase. She was so fucking close her sweet vanilla scent swirled over him. *Fucking vanilla?*

"Thanks. Can I bring it by tomorrow?"

He ground his teeth, ignoring her scent. Vanilla? He was accustomed to women who bathed in flowered scented shit that stung his eyes when they got too close. Hers was faint and sweet. *Oh fuck me.* The woman wasn't sweet, she wasn't innocent, and she wasn't beautiful. She was his fucking enemy.

Her breath fanned his face. It was deliberate, and he refused to take her bait. Phoebe had no clue who she was going up against.

"I'm Phoebe Shaw."

Kase drew in a breath, and for the first time since they interacted, he smirked. *Get ready, sweetheart.*

"Kase Reilly."

It took a second. Her expression changed as recognition flashed across her face. They'd never formally met, but he'd made plenty of offers on her property. She knew his name. In fact, if he had to guess, she probably loathed the mere uttering of it. His lawyer, who was on retainer, had aggressively made a move on the club's behalf to purchase the property. Twelve offers, all declined. After the last one, his lawyer came back to him defeated, with a message from Phoebe herself. His lawyer's direct quote was, "I'm not selling. Back off."

He expected anger, annoyance, possible aggravation. He got nothing except cherry pink lips spreading in a wide smile.

"Kase Reilly," she whispered in a low sexy purr. "We finally meet." Her tone was laced with humor and something else he couldn't quite place. Phoebe drew in a breath and glanced up through her lashes. "Rumor has it I got something you want." It was a seductress's tease. The corner of her mouth curled as she slowly straightened. Even as she turned around, she kept her eyes on him.

Not much caught him off guard, but her brazen, bold comment was unexpected. He clenched his jaw, watching her, mainly her tight ass, saunter back toward Phil. *A little too much confidence, sweetheart.* He wanted her property, not access to her bed.

The meeting ended ten minutes later. Once Bailey hit the gavel on the desk, it was a mad dash for the door. Kase stood, stretching out his legs when he felt a hand on his back. He glanced over his shoulder.

"Kase, I'm begging, do not pull the *off-limits* bullshit with her," Gage said.

Kase didn't need to ask who he was referring to. All the single brothers had Phoebe tagged the second she walked through the door. Kase didn't bother responding as she approached. When she glanced up, her stare was on him. Not Gage. Her face softened, and her lips pursed. She had no clue who she was dealing with.

Too much fucking trouble.

She was a few feet away when an older lady, who he noticed stayed close with Arnett, ambled forward, halting in front of Phoebe and blocking her path. She was flanked by two older guys who were glaring at Phoebe. He'd seen the same tactic used on Bailey.

Had it been the mayor, he would have stepped in. With Phoebe, he would merely observe.

She sighed and raised her brows, waiting as if she knew exactly what was coming. The confrontation garnered quite a few onlookers since they were now blocking the passage to the exit. Some members who'd been walking out stopped and turned around.

"Hello, Elsa. How are you?" Phoebe asked.

The older lady ignored her greeting and stepped closer. "I hope you have learned your lesson," she sneered, shaking her head.

Kase watched as Phoebe drew in a breath, but he remained silent. She still possessed her same confidence, but it was evident she didn't want to engage with the old bitch, clearly looking for an argument, or at the very least, to shame Phoebe, for reasons unbeknownst to him. He folded his arms and waited. Hopefully, another argument would grant him more insight to what the town refused to talk about.

"Do you know what I think?"

Phoebe folded her arms and smiled. "Nope. But I'm sure you're going to tell me."

"I think you need the Lord."

Phoebe nodded, licking her lips, seemingly amused. "So ya think there's still hope, huh? Good to know."

"I think you've lost your way. If you spent more time praying and less time trying to hurt people, God would reward you with a happy heart. Maybe a new life." She sighed, and her condescending tone was even pissing off Kase. He'd always despised the holier than thou attitude.

He watched Phoebe. Had he looked away, he might have missed it. While her reaction wasn't overtly obvious, he caught the slight tightening of her lips, and her excessive blinking was a cue the old lady had swung hard and Phoebe felt it.

She narrowed her gaze. "My heart is just fine, but I appreciate your concern."

"My concern is for this town." She shook her head. "I think you're broken, set to rain down your self-loathing and fury on those around you. Violence has no place in Ghosttown."

Phoebe eyed her, and he noticed a few residents also taking in the conversation. A few of the men seemed on guard. Phil stepped closer, resting his hand on her back.

Phoebe jerked her chin. "But antagonizing and hate do?"

Elsa flinched and remained silent.

"I'll take responsibility for my part. I have taken my punishment." Phoebe narrowed her gaze but kept a smirk on her face. "I apologized, I spent over twenty-four hours in prison, paid my fines, and even completed my community service and anger management. Got a big fat gold star on my certificate to prove it. The restraining order was lifted." Phoebe lost her smile. "That's it. It's all I got." She shrugged. "And if that's not good enough for you," she paused and glanced over Elsa's shoulder, "or anyone else in this town, then it's your problem. Not mine." She forced a smile. "Have a nice night, Elsa."

Prison, fines, community service, and anger management?

He watched as she sauntered through the crowd, making her way to the front of the hall to the mayor. He'd known Bailey was friends with her, close friends by Bailey's admission. Their greeting earlier and the one he was witnessing now confirmed it.

Bailey threw her arms around Phoebe's shoulders as if she'd just returned from war. Or prison.

He held back, waiting on the remaining residents and his brothers to usher out the door before starting toward the front of the room.

Once Bailey had released Phoebe from her clutches, she seemed to have been introducing Saint. Kase was too far away to hear the exchange, though it didn't matter. From their facial features, Phoebe appeared just as excited to meet Saint as Bailey was to introduce him.

He slowed his approach and leaned against the wall a few feet away.

"I'll see you this week, maybe a pizza date?"

Bailey nodded as her gaze shifted over Phoebe's shoulder and landed on Kase.

"Phoebe, have you met Kase?"

She slowly turned around, and the corner of her mouth curled when she locked eyes on him. Her light blue gaze staring back at him. It came off as innocent, and if he was a naïve man, he might even fall for it. Kase wasn't buying it. Her record alone proved Phoebe was far from innocent.

"I've had the pleasure." She winked.

Kase remained stone cold and unaffected with her attempts at being cute. Men would fall for it, maybe even a member or two, like Gage or Dobbs. *Not me, sweetheart, move the fuck along.* She didn't seem fazed from his lack of response. She waved to Bailey and sauntered out past him.

"Isn't she sweet? I told ya, right?"

Kase shook his head and snickered. "Yeah, nicest ex-con I ever met."

Bailey flattened her lips.

"When were you gonna mention we got a violent psycho bitch living next door to the clubhouse?"

Bailey frowned. "Phoebe's not violent or psycho," she snapped, and immediately her cheeks flushed. Bailey was showing her protective side. She swallowed a breath. "And she's only a bitch when the situation calls for it. We're all bitches sometimes. Even me. Ask Saint."

Saint snorted. "You're never a bitch."

Bailey rolled her eyes and then glanced over at Kase.

"A heads up woulda been nice."

She sighed, eyeing Kase. "She's not dangerous, and if you're nice to her, ya got nothing to be worried about."

He wasn't particularly concerned for his safety. He just didn't want any bullshit from her. He was going to use this to his advantage. Bailey had been tight lipped when it came to Phoebe. Not anymore. He wanted answers.

"Need you to give the fucking story, Bailey."

She shrugged and twisted her hands. "Not mine to tell."

He decided to change tactics to one he knew would work.

"We family?" Kase asked, getting the exact reaction he knew he would. She tightened her lips and shifted her gaze to Saint, who seemed to be taking Kase's side. The club had taken Bailey on as one of their own. They'd done for her what most people wouldn't have.

"It doesn't leave this room, and I'm not going into detail."

Kase nodded. It wouldn't be hard to find out once he knew what he was looking into.

Bailey sighed, and her gaze darted around the room. "A little over six months ago, Arnett and Phoebe were arguing. I can't remember exactly why." She widened her eyes and pointed her finger at him. "I do know he started it, and when she tried walking away, he continued to badger her, Kase."

Kase curled his lip. Sweet mayor defending her friend. "Okay."

Her shoulders sagged. "It escalated really quick, and Arnett just kept going after her verbally until she snapped." Bailey gritted her teeth and rested her hand on her chest. "I would have snapped too."

Bullshit... Bailey didn't have an aggressive bone in her body.

"Then what, sweetheart?" Saint asked.

Bailey glanced between the men. They were forcing her hand, and she wasn't happy. She grabbed her papers and kept her gaze on the table. "She grabbed a bat from her car and stormed after him. Before anyone could break it up, she had taken a few punches, mainly to Arnett's face."

Saint hushed a curse. It was the exact response Kase was thinking. Bailey's head whipped between both men.

She spread out her hands, gauging their reactions, and stammered, "L-look, the incident was isolated and completely out of character for her. A person can only take so much before they snap, and I'd think you, of all people, would understand." *Well played, Mayor.* Kase was notorious for his short fuse.

"Sweetheart." Kase smiled when Bailey narrowed her gaze. "She came after the old man with a fucking bat." He raised his brows.

"She didn't use it," Bailey blurted.

Saint laughed, and Kase shook his head. "No, she used her hands." Kase teasingly shrugged. "But ya know, she didn't use the bat, so that was nice of her."

He could tell while he and Saint were amused, Bailey was not.

"I don't condone what she did. But I don't condone what he did, either. It wasn't unprovoked, and while Arnett didn't physically attack her, he struck first and second and third, and however many more times before she lost it. He had a weapon, his words, and sometimes, like this one, it may have been a knife stabbing into her heart." Her bottom lip trembled, and she glanced away. He could tell she was shaken by the incident and not by Phoebe's actions.

Her statement sobered up his lingering humor. "What did he say?"

Bailey shook her head. "Nothing I'm willing to repeat." She got up from the desk and walked around, heading to the back of the room.

When she was out of hearing range, he stepped closer to Saint. "Think she'll tell ya?"

Saint turned slowly. "Probably, if I pushed her."

Kase raised his brows.

"Which I won't do, brother."

Kase sighed and started out through the doors. The lot had cleared out with the exception of his bike and Saint's truck. He started through the gravel lot, examining the abandoned area. He stopped when he got to his bike and stood silently.

The only sound he could hear was a small breeze ruffling the leaves. A warning.

Calm before the storm.

Chapter 2

She glanced over at the clock. Her delivery should have been there an hour ago. Her dad was able to get her a deal if she was willing to be flexible. Her bank account insisted she was. She had a hard enough time convincing the company to do her move, a small load of a few end tables and her boxes.

Her one-bedroom shack on four acres was officially home. Her *only* home. She had bought the land with Jared seven years ago. It was nothing more than a hunting shack. It was her dream, not Jared's. The only selling point for him was the small lake the property backed up to. They had a condo on the east coast and a house on the west. She loved the idea of a weekend getaway somewhere in the middle. Jared had pushed for a beach house; he'd been relentless at times. Phoebe refused to budge, and she held the upper hand as it was her savings that had made the down payment for it.

It may not have been his dream, but it was hers. She had spent more time at the cabin by herself than with Jared. Oddly enough, it never bothered her.

It wasn't much, but it was all she had. They had always lived a little beyond their means. She'd been guilty of it too. They had two mortgages, a few credit cards, and car payments. Or so she thought. Nothing prepared her for the sit-down with her accountant after his death. It seemed Jared had more debt than she was aware of, and upon his death, solely responsible for. Hundreds of thousands of dollars. Jared had also stopped making payments on his life insurance a year earlier. It was a nightmare. She demanded an audit; in complete disbelief they had racked up their credit so poorly. It was then the hard, ugly truth was exposed. Thousands of dollars spent with other women.

Fuck you, Jared.

With thoughts of her past infiltrating her present, she decided she needed a change of scenery. Even if it was just to check on the mail.

She started out her door and down her driveway. She glanced over at her new neighbor's property. Their lot doubled her size. She hadn't been around for the construction. It had been done while she was away. Though before she left, the property had been leveled on the large hill, the driveway had been paved, and the building markers had been set up. At the time, she had no clue it was going to be home to a motorcycle club.

She made her way to the end of the lot, swinging open the wide metal gate.

She glanced down the road to find several motorcycles lined up. She walked closer to get a better look, and her heartbeat spiked. She was wondering when she'd see him next.

Hi, neighbor. Kase's back was to her, and from the roar of the engines, she assumed he wouldn't hear her. It wasn't necessarily a sneak attack. Although she did like the idea of creeping up on him. If he saw her coming, he probably would have walked away. She had the distinct feeling he wasn't quite as amused by her *rumor has it* comment as she was.

She was three feet away when he turned. His brows knitted together as he eyed her with a harsh scowl. God, even angry and pissy was a good look on him. Had she known she'd be seeing him, she might have put a little more effort into her outfit. But for a biker, she was sure cutoff shorts and a tank top were acceptable.

The Enemy

"Hey, neighbor." She grinned with a coy wave. The lines between his brows deepened. She usually got a similar reaction from Arnett. Phoebe stopped a few feet away. If she was waiting on him to speak, they might be there all day.

"Having a party?" When he didn't respond, she inched a foot closer and cocked her head. "You do know about the noise ordinances in town, right?" She pointed across the street. "Arnett is all over that. He's a stickler for the rules."

She drew in a breath and twitched her lips when he didn't respond. She must have hit a nerve the other night. She smiled in hopes of breaking his hard shell. It didn't. He lowered his eyes. She could almost feel his gaze as if it were a soft touch over her skin. Her nipples beaded, and she shifted on her feet.

"But you're not." He cocked a brow and turned around to face her. His tone was challenging. She glanced up through her lashes. He had to be about six-three. Tall, brooding, and sexy. He folded his arms, which seemed to magnify his height. "How ya think I should handle him? Bat or my fists?"

She sucked in a deep breath. She was caught off guard with his comment. However, letting on was not an option. She couldn't be sure how much he knew about her. Any one of the residents could have shared her altercation with Arnett. It was, after all, the biggest thing to happen in their small town—until the arrival of the MC.

She clucked her tongue. "Looks like somebody's been asking about me, huh?" She glanced down at the ground and peeked up through her lashes, striding closer. "Did ya get all the juicy details, or ya need me to fill in the holes?"

He didn't budge. *No reaction*. She was going to have to step up her game for her new neighbor.

"Got enough to know you're fucking trouble."

Her jaw dropped in amusement. The biker in a gang was calling her trouble? *Oh, the irony.* She tilted her head, squinting her eyes playfully. Still no reaction from him. He was stone faced, masking any emotion. He slowly turned, giving her his back, and started up his driveway.

"Is it 'cause I'm an ex-con?" she shouted.

When he slowly glanced over his shoulder, she waggled her brows. "You scared?"

His gaze travelled over her body, sending a shiver down her spine. It was an odd reaction to a man who was not her usual type. She had always gravitated to pretty boys. And Kase was definitely not pretty; he was too gruff and hard. The tattoos alone were usually a turnoff. Strangely, they had the opposite effect and heightened her attraction for him. For the first time since she spoke, she caught a glimpse of heat in his stare, and his lips twitched. *Here's my in, and I'm gonna take it.*

She strolled forward, leaving a small gap between them. "Don't be scared, Kase." She purposely paused and whispered, "I won't hurt you." She shrugged. "Unless that's what you're into?"

He cocked his brow. "You always come on this fucking strong?"

She fought against the blush on her cheeks and snorted. "You think I'm flirting with you?" She scoffed and waved her hand. "This is just me being neighborly." It was a lie. She was flirting, and enjoying every second of it. Kase was a challenge. Little did he know, she thrived on challenges.

He raised his brows. He was a hard read.

"You can't have them bikes blocking the goddamn road."

Ugh, are you serious? She had been enjoying her attempt at flirting too much. Of course, Arnett would be the one to ruin it. She jerked her head and glared in his direction.

"Now, this is my road and I..."

Phoebe cleared her throat, and Arnett whipped his head in her direction, shooting daggers from his beady eyes. "You don't own the road."

His face turned red, and he lunged forward. She held her ground. She'd been dealing with him for seven years. Arnett was all bark. Phoebe was not. She folded her arms and stepped forward. It seemed to serve as a reminder.

"I been living here for…"

Phoebe moaned dramatically and spread her arms. "For forty-two years, we know, *we all know,* Arnett." He did not appreciate her cutting him off, and his nostrils flared. She snickered, shaking her head.

Phoebe hadn't realized Kase had moved closer to her until she saw his boots lined up near her flipflops. She glanced up. He was glaring at Arnett, and a warm swirl twisted in her belly. She'd always been one to handle herself, but seeing the badass biker next to her taking what seemed to be a protective stance? *Holy shit, it's sexy as hell.*

"I been here longer than you been alive. Gives me seniority on this road. And I don't care to see you carrying on and seducing bikers while blocking up my road. The whole town has turned to crap since you came here."

She usually paid no mind to Arnett and his barking rants. However, this one piqued her curiosity.

She slowly turned to Kase and lowered her voice. "Was it working? Was I seducing you?"

He arched his brow, and she noticed the small twitch in his lips. Her stomach plummeted. *Fuck, was it working, and Arnett totally ruined it?*

"Move those goddamn bikes, or I'll call the police," Arnett threatened. Phoebe rolled her eyes. Even if the cops were called, it would take at the very least an hour before they showed. It was on the tip of her tongue to say something until she heard the venomous snarl.

"I'll move them," Kase paused, "when I'm ready to fucking move them."

Phoebe clamped her lips. It was her only defense against laughing in Arnett's face. His aggressive verbal spouts might work on other residents, but not on the president of the Ghost-town Riders.

Kase glared at Arnett, and she took immense joy in watching the old bully retreating a step. Watching Kase from the corner of her eye, her belly fluttered. There was no fake, all-talk bravado with him. He was the real fucking deal and so damn sexy. He steeled his eyes and turned toward his driveway without uttering another word.

"Bye, neighbor."

His steps never faltered, and he gave no reaction to hearing her. Maybe he had and chose to ignore her.

The rumbling engine distracted her from watching his retreat up the driveway. In the distance, she saw someone coming down the road. With only one headlight, it appeared to be another motorcycle. *Damn, they are having a party.*

"Carrying on as a two-dime whore for a gang."

Her muscles tightened, and she slowly turned her gaze, glancing across the street. Arnett stood, glaring at her. For all his bullshit and nastiness, this was a new low, even for Arnett.

"Say it again, I dare you." She balled her fists, ignoring the engine roaring toward her. She had taken a lot from him, but this crossed the line.

"I call it like I see it. Jared deserved better than you." Arnett's lip curled in a disgusted sneer. "And thankfully he had better than the likes of you." His eyes darkened. "Whore."

He barely got the word out and Phoebe was halfway across the street directly in the crosshairs of the motorcycle.

Motherfucker.

BYE, neighbor.

The sound of her soft, sultry voice echoed in his fucking head. Kase clenched his jaw, driving a shooting pain into his molars. He'd underestimated her. Phoebe was coming on strong. Not something Kase wasn't used to. The club girls threw themselves at him on a daily basis. Phoebe was different. His defenses seemed to be weakening slightly for his neighbor. *Motherfucker.*

With an abundance of pussy at his disposal, it was senseless to think Phoebe was affecting him. If he was smart, he'd find a woman and take her in the back. With all the willing participants, he could be balls deep in one of the girls in a second.

He shifted forward, resting his elbows on the bar trying to focus. He couldn't remember the last time, if ever, anyone had irritated the fuck out of him as much as his new neighbor. She'd fucking lost her mind if she thought for a second, he was falling for her flirting bullshit, sweet, tight curves, and her innocent, blue *fuck me* eyes. He'd gone up against far more experienced women and hadn't fallen for their bullshit. Phoebe would be no different.

Kase had never fallen prey to a female, and he had no intentions of ever letting it happen. Especially *her. Then why the fuck can't I stop thinking about her?*

"Who we waiting on?" Trax said.

"Saint," Kase muttered, and then downed his glass of bourbon. He slammed the glass on the bar and signaled to Nadia for a refill. He had planned the meeting a few weeks ago. With all the deliveries, he wanted to touch base with the club. Some members, including Trax, wanted to request scaling back on their out of town nights. Kase understood it. Trax and his wife were expecting a baby, and Trax hadn't wanted to leave her overnight. It was a fair request that Kase would grant. Too many people missed the most important aspects of the club. They were family. They took care of each other.

Kase checked his phone for the time. Five minutes late. It wasn't much, but for Saint, who was always on time or earlier, it struck Kase as odd. He turned toward the door when he heard the scrambling.

"What?"

Joe, one of their oldest prospects who was slated for membership at the end of the month, stumbled over his words. He glanced over his shoulder and then turned to the brothers.

"Fucking speak, asshole," Rourke snapped.

"Saint needs you. I think."

Kase stood and moved swiftly toward the door. "Where?"

"Down at the end of the driveway. I don't know what the fuck happened. I think the chick from next door went after the old guy from across the street. Saint's holding her back now."

Kase balled his fists and rushed through the door with his brothers at his back. *Motherfucking psychotic bitch. What the fuck?* He'd just left her ten minutes ago, and she was on the attack again. He double timed it down the long drive. Saint had, in fact, been holding Phoebe back with Arnett inching forward. Brazen motherfucker was showing his set when someone was holding her back. He rushed down toward them, eyeing Saint, who was fighting against Phoebe, who was shouting over his shoulder.

"Say it again, spineless fucking asshole. You are so fucking lucky he's holding me back!" Phoebe screamed. It was pure rage and on the verge of incoherent. She jerked her arms, but Saint had her bound, trying to calm her.

She halted for a brief second before turning on Saint. "Because of my absolute adoration and love for Bailey, I'm giving you a fair warning. Let me go before I kick you in the balls."

Oh hell. Kase rushed forward and gripped her arm, yanking her against his chest and wrapping his arms around her waist. She thrashed in his arms, and Saint glared at her.

Kase lowered his mouth to her ear. "Settle the fuck down."

"I'm calling the cops. You need to be locked up," Arnett spouted from across the street and made no move to retreat. He was baiting her, and Kase was half tempted to let Phoebe go.

"Do it, Arnett, call the cops. You are a weak, poor excuse for a real man who hides behind a nasty tongue and hate." She jerked her body. It was a useless effort. Kase had her locked in a vise grip.

"You belong locked up, you whore."

Kase tightened his hold on Phoebe as she reacted to Arnett's words. *What the fuck did he just say?*

The Enemy

"It's no wonder Jared left you."

Kase loosened his grip, and she pulled from his hold. He would make it to Arnett before her. He could almost see his fist throttling Arnett's jaw. He drew in a deep breath and gripped her hips, pulling her against his chest and making his way into her driveway. She continued to thrash under his hold, shouting over his shoulder.

"Whore? Is that what you said, you deranged clueless bastard?"

He made it halfway up her driveway, far enough away from Arnett. He didn't release her, tightening his grip around her waist. He could feel her heart pumping with her anger on the verge of exploding.

"Calm the fuck down."

"Fuck him."

"Yeah, fuck him." Kase sighed and wrapped his hands over her arms, holding her in place with her back against his chest. "You got a record with this asshole. You don't need the cops here. And *I* don't need the cops here." She pulled away, and he tightened his grip. "Settle the fuck down."

Surprisingly, she did. He had only caught the tail end of their argument, but he'd heard enough. The old man was baiting her with the whore comment, and throwing her dead husband in her face. Arnett knew what would set her off, and he used it.

Phoebe relaxed slightly into his chest, resting her head back. Without the distraction of her thrashing, he was aware of how easily she fit into his arms. He could have let her go but remained with his arms clasped around her.

She scoffed. "Ironic, right? Jared fucked every piece of ass he ever came into contact with, and that bastard is calling me a whore."

The new admission struck Kase. Her dead husband had been fucking around behind her back? It was a vantage point. Leverage he could use. Why the fuck wasn't he saying anything, using it against her? He caressed her arms, calming her in the most unlike-

Kase Reilly move. Had she been any other woman, he would have walked away minutes ago. Why the fuck was he still there?

He cleared his throat. "Who the fuck cares what he says."

Her silence caused an uneasy shift in his blood.

"Kase?"

He glanced down at her to find her soft blue eyes peering up at him. "What?"

She sucked in a breath and turned her head, glancing over her shoulder. The corner of her mouth curled. "Is there any chance you'd let me just take one shot? Just one hit, my fist, his jaw, please."

Kase smirked and fought against his chuckle. She was a fighter. He jerked his chin over his shoulder. "He ain't worth it."

She sighed and collapsed against his chest. "I know. I'd still like to hit him."

"You already got your shot."

She bowed her head and snorted.

He released his hold, confident that if she tried to make a break down the driveway, he would beat her. She stood silent and then slowly made her way toward her house without looking back. Whatever the old man had said hit her hard. He felt an unnatural possessive instinct. He shouldn't be feeling anything for her. Yet his blood rushed through his veins and his anger simmered. He watched as she made her way into her house. As soon as the door closed, he turned started down the driveway with his target in his sights.

"Kase, man."

"Fuck, Kase."

He couldn't decipher which of his brothers had spoken. They all surrounded him as he made his way across the street. Rourke, the biggest of the members, butted up against his chest, grasping his shoulder. "Do not do this, man. We're gonna let Saint handle this shit."

Kase drew in a breath, unsure where his possession had come from. He was never one to take up for someone he didn't know.

Bringing unnecessary attention to the club was something Kase avoided at all costs. This was different. This altercation was different. Kase pushed forward, bringing Rourke, and now Trax, with him. "Kase, man, calm down," Trax barked.

No, Kase wasn't having anyone else handle this except for himself. He lunged forward with his men close at his side. It was for the old man's protection, not his own.

"The next fucking time she goes after your crazy ass? I'm gonna let her, and I'm gonna provide the bat so she can use it this time, you hear me?" Kase tore his arm from Rourke's grip. "You wanna say something to her? You say it to me, motherfucker." He lunged forward, and Rourke set himself in front of Kase.

"Brother, settle."

Who the fuck was this asshole to take a shot at her? By her own admission, her husband was the one fucking around on her.

Saint shielded his advance and turned to their neighbor. "I'm giving you fair warning. You walk back inside your house and never speak another word to her again." He paused, and Arnett shuffled backward. "If I ever hear you speak to her that way again, you will deal with me." Saint stepped closer. "And Kase." One step closer sent Arnett three steps back. "And the club. Am I making myself clear?"

Arnett didn't answer. He turned quickly and rushed inside. The whole scene, and Kase's own reaction, seemed to throw his brothers off. Each man stared back at Kase in question. Rourke released his hold.

He turned his back, glancing up at Phoebe's place. His chest expanded in deep breaths with his heartbeat raging. She was having an unnatural effect on him, and he didn't like it. The possession and need to have her back was angering the hell out of him. He clenched his jaw, grinding his teeth to the point of pain.

"Kase," Saint said.

He turned and found his VP. The others were making their way up the hill.

"You good?"

Kase eyed Saint. They'd been close forever. Aside from his own brother, no one knew Kase the way Saint did. For as close as they were, Kase wasn't about to admit any kind of claim on Phoebe. His actions would need an explanation since they were out of character for him.

"Not gonna have that asshole setting off her kind of fucking crazy. Shit like that will bring cops swarming around. It puts us on their radar. The shit we moved away from, and I ain't gonna have it here."

The majority of the club's ventures and businesses were legal. Most. However, they continued to dabble in some activities that teetered on the line.

Saint nodded. "I agree. It was actually the reason I stopped and stepped in when it went down. Had it handled." The corner of his mouth curled. "A little surprised to see you coming to her aid."

Kase exhaled deeply through his nose.

"If either of those two dipshits were in need of aid, it wouldn't be her."

Saint remained silent with a smirk playing on his lips. Kase halted, resting his forearm on Saint's chest. "The only thing I'm interested in is her acreage, not her pussy."

Saint arched a brow.

Fucking Saint with his silent bullshit.

"Don't fucking read into it, Saint. Nothing there."

Saint nodded, which fueled the fire in his veins. *Who the hell was he trying to convince?*

It meant fucking nothing.

Chapter 3

What a fucked up day.

Phoebe tapped her nails on the glass cupped between her hands and stared out into the field behind her house. She refused to revisit the events from earlier in the afternoon. Giving Arnett any more thought or head space was not happening. One simple word had sent her over the edge. *Whore.* She snorted at the irony. She was being accused of the very same thing Jared had done. He was the whore who had cheated on her. She had been faithful throughout their whole marriage. She hadn't even considered other men. *That makes me the fool.*

She closed her eyes. *The good, Feebs, focus on that.* She fluttered her lids and smiled.

From her back porch she had the best view of the sunset. It was what sold her on the property. The seclusion and quiet had been the second selling point. *I love it here.*

She glanced to her right, watching the party next door filter into the yard. From the distance, she couldn't make out who was there. Based on the movement, it was apparent they were having a good time. She lifted her glass, keeping her gaze locked on the yard of the clubhouse, and sipped her drink. She'd be lying to herself if she didn't admit to seeking out Kase. She had, with no luck.

When her phone lying next to her rang, she glanced down and immediately answered.

"Hey, Dad."

"Hi, sweetheart. How's it going?"

It was an interesting question. How was it going? *I almost landed my ass back in jail.* She shook her head, ridding Arnett from her mind, and keeping the small piece of information to herself. Her dad had worried about her enough. She wouldn't add to it.

She drew in a deep breath. "Going great, Dad."

He chuckled. Her dad knew her better than anyone. It would be easy for him to read through her bullshit. "Starting over is always hard, baby. Keep your head up. Good times are waiting for you."

She smiled without response. *My dad.* Forever the optimist. It was a shame it hadn't rubbed off on her. She drove her fingers through her hair, brushing it over her shoulder.

"Have you cleaned out the house yet?"

Phoebe snorted. "Six boxes all set to be donated."

Aside from moving all her stuff in, she was moving Jared's out. She hadn't realized how much of his shit had accumulated until she opened drawers and the closets. It was a strange feeling tossing his belongings in a box without a second glance. It was almost sad how much she didn't want to hold onto anything from a man she had shared her life with for so long. The man she was supposed to grow old with. *Motherfucker.*

"Good news. I haven't attacked anyone since I got here, though I came close with Arnett at the town meeting." And two hours ago. "Don't worry, Dad, I've banned all bats and weapons from my possession."

She pressed her lips together when she heard the heavy sigh. "Too soon, sweetheart."

Phoebe laughed and pushed off the porch, pacing through the yard.

This place. It was handpicked by her. She craned her neck and stared up through the giant pines. *Exactly where I'm supposed to be.* This place was heaven.

My place. Jared had been against the purchase, but she'd fought hard for it and never backed down. There was something about the small town. Phoebe had refused to budge and insisted they buy the small shack. Where had that girl gone?

Jared stole her. Then, he erased her. *And I let it happen.*

"Phoebe?"

She blinked, bringing herself back to present day.

"I'm here."

"Yes, you are. In the place that makes you happy."

She sighed with a soft smile. She inhaled a deep breath through her nose, taking in the pine scent. It had always been her favorite. It was Ghosttown.

"I'm good, Dad." Her reassurance was for herself as much as it was for her father. They both needed to hear it. The last year had been a rollercoaster of ups and downs. Moments where she truly wanted to throw in the towel.

"I don't doubt it, sweetheart. Strongest woman I know, second to your mom, of course."

She chuckled. "Those are big shoes to fill."

"Yes, they are." He paused. "You've got it in you, Phoebe." The small silence echoed on the line. "You lost your way, kiddo. I have confidence you'll find your way back." He snickered. "Everyone falls from grace, Phoebe. You just have to get back up."

She sighed. Even as a child, he gave the best speeches. She wasn't sure she deserved the pep talk after the path she had chosen with Jared.

"I should have seen it, Dad. I look back, and I can't believe I didn't see Jared for the man he really was." Her eyes teared, and she inhaled a deep breath. For everyone around her, Phoebe gave the strong, hard front. A front, that's what it was. The only person alive she'd ever let her guard down with was her father. "How did I not see it?"

"Because love blinds us. There's nothing to be ashamed of, Phoebe. You loved a man who was unworthy. The fault lies on him, not you."

"Well," she laughed through her fallen tears, "won't be making that mistake again."

"You can't give up on love because someone hurt you, Phoebe."

She scoffed. "Love is bullshit, Dad."

It was.

Her dad sighed. "I had twenty-seven years with your mom, and I can say with one hundred percent positivity, it wasn't bullshit, kid."

She tightened her hand, silently scolding her black heart. She may have had a bullshit marriage, a sham of a partnership. Her parents hadn't. She was being an asshole by diminishing it.

"You guys had something special, Dad. I didn't mean you and Mom."

His soft chuckle put her heart at ease.

"We had a lot of years of true love. We weren't special, sweetheart, it exists. You gave your heart to the wrong man. He didn't deserve you. Someday, you will find someone who does. Maybe not now, but someday this conversation will playback in your head, and you'll say, 'the old man knew what he was talking about'. That I can guarantee, Phoebe."

Ah, this man. She smiled. "Guarantee, huh?"

"Yes."

She laughed and kicked the pebbles under her feet. There was always something special about her dad. He was imperfect, he'd made mistakes, she'd been there to witness them. He had faults, yet he was perfect in her eyes. No man, not even Jared when she'd been blinded by love, could hold a candle to the first man in her life.

"I'm thinking about going skinny dipping in the lake behind the house."

He groaned and she laughed.

"Could always count on you for the inappropriate stuff." He laughed. "Do what makes ya happy, sweetheart. Just don't tell your old man about it. Talk to ya soon."

She smiled, a genuine muscle shaking, all in, smile. Maybe her first in months. "Love you, Dad." She hung up and felt a weight lift from her shoulders. Her dad had always had a way of making her see the positive, even in the worst of times. She strolled through the woods, heading down toward the lake. It was her own private oasis.

Just the escape I need.

THE LEAVES and brush crunched under his heavy boots as he made his way down the path. The prospects had made a clearing for easier access to the small lake behind the property. It was state land, but nobody monitored it. The only access available was from the club's property and hers.

The day had been completely fucked. His new neighbor was proving to be more of a distraction and liability than he'd anticipated. Too much shit hanging over his head and on his shoulders. He needed some fucking give and to just relax. He stopped at the edge of the lake, leaning up against an old oak. He'd come down here plenty of times by himself. It was quiet, and a short getaway from all the responsibilities with the club. *So fucking quiet when I don't have to share it.*

His peace was short lived. The voices echoing through the trees announced the arrival of a few members. He should have expected it.

The others had breached the opening, and a few of the girls were already half naked. Kase had seen them and fucked them enough to not bother taking in the scene unfolding. He hadn't necessarily become immune to the girls in the club, but he'd grown tired of them. Each one vying for his attention with the end goal of becoming his old lady. No fucking way. Thirty-eight years without one and he was completely content.

As president of the club, he had enough responsibility taking care of his brothers and their families without adding on another. He'd never even considered settling down with a woman or becoming a father. Some men were built for it. Kase was not.

"You coming in Kase?" one of the girls asked.

He ignored her. The sole purpose of coming down to the lake was for a bit of peace. That was shot to shit a few minutes ago. Time to head back to the house.

Kase drew in a deep breath and glanced out at the lake, noticing the rippling water near the north end. The moon shining over the water gave a natural lighting effect. It took a second for his eyes to adjust.

He squinted and sucked in a breath. *You gotta be fucking kidding me?* He'd spent the day trying to rid her from his mind. Now she was fucking here?

He caught her a few yards out in the middle of the lake.

"Who's that?" Val asked, pointing to the lake. The girls were topless and ready to dive in, but the addition already in the water had everyone taking notice.

Dobbs stood next to him. "You know?"

Kase kept his gaze on her and lifted his cigarette, taking a drag before answering. "The neighbor." His tone gave nothing away. Phoebe.

He watched as she swam up to shore, stopping only when she realized she was being watched. He was far enough away to stay in the shadows, but Phoebe saw them and waded in the water, staring up at the small group.

"Hey."

Gage moved closer to the shoreline. "I was just thinking we haven't seen enough of our new neighbor." He hadn't been around for the brawl earlier.

Kase gritted his teeth when she laughed. All the women were

taken in by Gage. Usually it didn't bother him. For some reason, right here and now with Phoebe, it did. She wasn't one of them. She was an outsider, and Gage was fucking with her. Or was he trying to find an in with Phoebe? It irritated him more than he was willing to admit.

Phoebe glanced up at the group. "You guys going for a swim? Water's nice."

"Yeah?" Gage said, grasping the hem on his shirt and lifting it over his head. "Gonna have to join you, then."

Kase furrowed his brows, watching her smile brighten.

"Actually, I was just getting out." Only her head was above water. She raised her brows and smirked. "Think you can be a gentleman and turn around while I get out?"

Kase took another drag from his cigarette and watched her. Was she fucking naked?

Gage laughed. There wasn't a gentleman in the bunch, or a man who hadn't already seen a naked women a thousand times over. He was almost surprised at Gage's response.

"Yeah, we can do that." One by one the members turned around, giving Phoebe their backs. Not Kase. He leaned against the tree, smoking his cigarette, staring back at her. He noticed her shift in the water and her gaze wander over the group who had turned around.

As she breeched the water, her tits came into sight. It was a chore fighting against his raging hard on. He'd seen topless women every damn day of his life for the past eighteen years. It made no sense for him to respond to her with such a deep desire. He was tempted to look away for his own self-preservation. He didn't.

He made no movement, but Phoebe caught his stare as she glanced across the brush. He expected her to duck back into the water.

Phoebe stared back at him, and the corner of her mouth curled. She slowly emerged from the lake, water droplets dripping off her tight nipples. *Fuck me.* She walked as though she owned the fucking lake. There wasn't an ounce of uncertainty in the sway of her hips.

He'd seen thousands of women naked in front of him. Yet nothing as sexy, revving him up as much as the one coming his way.

Her hair was slicked back, and beads of water peppered her face and skin. A slow perusal of her body was enough for Kase to harden to a steel rod, painfully straining in his jeans. His cock stretched against the seam. *Fuck!* She wasn't anything special. His body would respond naturally to any naked woman. He sucked in a breath and gritted his teeth.

As she neared him, he narrowed his gaze. She knew exactly what the fuck she was doing. It was impossible not to peruse her body. Perfect handful of tits and her waist dipping, giving her the sexiest hourglass figure. Too many he fucked thought the skinnier the better. Not Kase. He wanted his women soft, something to hold onto while he fucked her hard.

She reached down, grabbing her shirt and shorts. He steeled his natural response to her. As she closed in next to him, she glanced over her shoulder at the other men, who had shown her the decency to turn around. Something Kase hadn't.

She smirked and strolled forward with her gaze locked on him. She had yet to cover her breasts, and his gaze lingered down to her tight nipples. The pointy peaks begging to be sucked.

"Hey, neighbor," she whispered.

Fucking trouble. He'd called it the second he saw her at the meeting.

She passed by, and he side-glanced her ass in soaked panties with the hem riding up her crease. He gritted his teeth and turned back to the water. He was never one to get distracted by a piece of ass.

Then came Phoebe.

What the fuck?

Chapter 4

Free!

She had been held captive by boxes of her own shit for the past few days, a prisoner in her own home. For someone who sold everything she had owned supposedly, she had a lot of boxes. By definition she was a hoarder, packrat, or as she liked to think of it, memento-keeper.

For now, she was set on human interaction and looking at anything outside her house. She pulled up in front of the new boutique. She'd heard about it through Bailey. Two wives from the club had opened up a few months back. As she strolled on the sidewalk, she peeked in. She recognized one of the girls from the meeting and waved. She would stop in eventually, but right now, her stomach was dictating her next destination.

She grabbed the handle and opened the door to the next building over. Once the scent wafted her nostrils, she closed her eyes and inhaled the aroma. *God, I've missed you.* The pizzeria had been her favorite spot in Ghosttown before they closed their doors a few years back. It was a mom and pop eatery, and they made the best pizza. Like most places in Ghosttown, they didn't have the revenue to stay open. With only forty full-time residents, and a handful of tourists, the odds were stacked against them from the start.

When Bailey had told her, a silent investor offered to help them reopen, she almost cried.

It was still early, and the place was quiet, with only one other customer. His back was facing her, giving her the perfect view of his jeans contouring his ass. They weren't tight, just enough to curve around his butt. Her gaze travelled up over his patched leather vest. *Ghosttown Riders.* His light brown hair was clipped at the back of his neck.

She hadn't ever been overly drawn to men with long hair, but on him? She was having seconds thoughts. She couldn't quite figure out what attracted her so much to him. There was something, though. She'd never been a girl with a bad boy fetish. Throughout high school and college, she veered toward the athletic and fun as opposed to the rebel. Now, here she was, thirty-two years old, and finally looking to take a walk on the wild side.

She inched closer, but he had yet to notice her.

The attraction was mutual. *Right?* It had to be. She couldn't have been reading it all on her end. The other night at the lake she'd read through his harsh glare. Behind the façade, she caught the heated desire in his eyes. She spared a quick glance down at her body and twisted her lips with a quirky shake of her head. She was pretty even though she'd lost the youthful glow of her twenties. Her body was toned, with extra baggage from her love of chocolate, chips, and ice cream. She bit her lip. She had nothing to lose. Flirting with him had become a mini obsession for her, along with nighttime fantasizing. And apparently, daytime too.

I bet he's a hair puller. She smirked.

Kase was resting against the center column with the phone up to his ear. "I'll call and make sure he fucking does it." Phoebe widened her eyes. Whoever was on the receiving end of Kase Reilly's call was fucked.

His shoulders bunched. "Talk to Riss about Pop?"

The Enemy

While she didn't actually know Riss, Bailey had mentioned her enough times for her to be familiar with the name.

Kase laughed. "I ain't gonna fucking upset her, ya pussy." He stopped and straightened, sending Phoebe a step back. "She needs the break. I'll take him for a week, give her some downtime."

Phoebe cocked her head, staring at his back. It was another side to him she hadn't seen. There was almost a twinge of empathy in his graveled voice.

"Later." He clicked his phone and folded his arms.

Time to make my presence known. She sidled up beside him.

"Hey, neighbor."

His movement halted, and his shoulders tightened. *Interesting effect I have on him.* She half wondered if he was going to pretend he didn't hear and simply ignore her. However, Kase didn't strike her as the type of man who would shy away from uncomfortable encounters. If anything, she figured he'd go head to head. He slowly glanced over his shoulder with his usual scowl locked in place. The corners of his eyes crinkled.

"Phoebe."

She giggled and shook her head. "It's hard, right?"

He furrowed his brows, sending a shiver down her spine. His side-eyed glance was forcing her to tighten her thighs together. The sexual chemistry had to be two sided. *Or maybe it's just me?*

"My name. Phoebe." She smirked. "It's sweet and feminine, almost impossible to snarl the two syllables." She shifted closer and lowered her voice. "Though you do give it a good try, Kase."

Nope, not one sided at all. His eyes hooded, and she didn't miss the heated glare he was sending her. It could have been strictly irritation. She didn't think so. Kase might not *want* to be interested, but he was. She craned her neck, getting an eyeful of his rough, gorgeous face. The pads of her fingers tingled with a strong urge to touch his beard.

"How was your party?" She stepped closer. "I never got my

invite. Probably got lost in the mail." She playfully rolled her eyes. "It was a nice surprise seeing you all at the lake."

If he had been the least bit affected, Kase hadn't shown it. He showed no emotion or after effect of her naked play. It hadn't been planned, but when she saw he was the only one who hadn't turned their back, she played into it.

"We don't invite outsiders," he said in an even tone. He had blatantly ignored her comment about the lake.

"Outsider? Me?" She rested her hand on her chest. "Is it because I've done time? It is, isn't it? My stint in the big house makes you wary of my kind."

His gaze lingered over her face, his lip pulling up at the corner. She was going to take her opportunity.

"We would probably become real good friends if you just gave me a chance." She batted her lashes. "This whole 'you want my land, I'm the enemy', it's so early eighteen hundreds." She winked. "How about you come over to my place? I'll cook, we'll have some drinks." She shrugged. "And ya know, we'll see where the night takes us." She curled her lip. "Or we could go for a swim at the lake? I showed you mine, now you can show me yours, Kase."

It was a bold statement.

"Here ya go, Kase," Maria said. His stare hesitated on Phoebe before turning to walk to the counter and retrieve his four pizzas.

She watched him spare a chin nod to Maria, who was smiling back at him. He turned, glancing over at Phoebe. She assumed he'd walk past her, but instead he stopped next to her.

"I got a full-stocked bar at my place, women on hand to make me a meal. Don't need nothing from ya, *neighbor*." He sneered his last word. It was a huge indicator she was getting under his skin.

Not the only thing I'm looking to get under.

She chuckled. "Except my property, right, Kase?"

His stone-cold masked exterior only chilled more from her dig. He obviously wasn't amused with her playful banter. Serious people had always been a downfall for her. She lacked resistance in letting them be, as her father used to say. Aside from the obvious outward appearance, Kase reminded her of her brother. Too serious for his own good.

This was not how she intended her run in to go. She grappled with her next words.

"Wait, Kase." She started toward him even before he turned.

She didn't have an exact plan of what she was going to say. She silently groaned. Winging it had never been her strong point. When she made it near him by the door, his annoyance was evident. He scowled and glared down at her.

She clasped her hands, cracking her knuckles. It was a stall tactic. She glanced up through her lashes. He wouldn't give her much more time. Whatever she wanted to say had to be done in the next few seconds before he bolted. Urgency to keep him there had her spurting her next words.

"Thanks."

He furrowed his brows but hadn't made a move to leave.

She licked her lips. "The other day, with Arnett." Her voice tapered off, unable to finish the sentence. She had come dangerously close to having a repeat performance from six months ago. It would have landed her in jail again with a much harsher penalty. She sighed. "I'm working on my anger management."

"Yeah, you need to work fucking harder."

She clenched her jaw and was preparing for a sarcastic retort. What could she say? Kase was right. She nodded.

"I wasn't really going to hit him." It was a half-truth. She wasn't actually one hundred percent confident she wouldn't have taken a swing if the MC hadn't stepped in.

Kase raised his brows. He wasn't buying it.

"I *probably* wouldn't have hit him." She paused. "He knows what buttons to push."

Kase inched closer, catching her off guard. "And you fucking feed into it."

She couldn't dispute his accusation. She did. Arnett hit a

nerve, and her first reaction was to go after him. Again. She simply nodded and lowered her gaze to the floor.

"Stop playing into his hand," Kase growled, and she glanced up through her lashes. His features tightened, his jaw squared, and the lines in his forehead deepened. "Next time, you walk the fuck away."

It was beyond strange for a member of a motorcycle club to give her advice on walking away. She doubted Kase had ever taken his own advice on standing down. She refrained from pointing out the obvious.

"I will."

He scanned her face, his gaze softening slightly, Along with his jaw. *God, this man is gorgeous.* He inched closer and leaned forward, pinning her in his stare. "You do that." He paused. "Don't want to lose your gold fucking star for good behavior."

It took her a second to comprehend. A gold star was what she had earned for her anger management. She had mentioned it at the town meeting to Elsa. And he remembered. Her mouth spread into a wide smile.

Kase straightened, taking another second before turning to walk out the door. *Holy shit, was that a moment with Kase Reilly?*

Bailey was just walking up past the window. He said something she couldn't hear. It made Bailey laugh and rest her hand on her small protruding belly. Even at four and a half months pregnant, she just looked bloated. Kase hooked his boot around the bottom of the door, holding it open for her. As Bailey passed through, she reached out, gliding her hand against his arm. It was impossible not to notice the familiarity of those two.

Bailey waved and rushed toward her, wrapping her arms around Phoebe. "You're home."

Phoebe smiled, embracing her in a tight hug. She'd missed Bailey. She smiled and glanced up to catch Kase through the window. He was walking across the street heading back to his shop, glancing over his shoulder and staring directly at her. She drew in a breath, keeping her gaze locked on him.

"C'mon." Bailey stepped back and tugged her arm, forcing her to look away from Kase. She was tempted to look back. *It was totally a moment.*

When they settled into their table near the front window, she searched the empty street with no sight of Kase. She sighed and focused all her attention on Bailey.

So much had happened in their small town while she'd been away. She'd kept tabs on everyone, but Bailey was giving her all the details, including those of her and Saint. Phoebe sat for an hour listening to her friend. Bailey had given her the condensed version of life in Ghosttown while strategically leaving out information on the newest residents.

"So, what's going on with you? Are you seeing anyone?"

It was a fair question. In the past year, she had shared with Bailey all her illicit dates. It was the perfect segue into her immediate thought.

"Nope, but let me ask you something? Kase? Taken, available, what?" Phoebe rested her elbows on the table and waited eagerly on Bailey's answer.

Her excessive blinking was the start of Phoebe's fascination with her friend's response. It continued to get more amusing by the second. Her brows hiked up to her hairline, and then her head tilted in an awkward motion, followed by her lips opening and closing. She remained silent during her entire display. Phoebe chuckled and grasped her hand resting on the table.

"I don't even know how to go about interpreting your facial responses."

Bailey shook her head and flickered her lashes. "I-I don't even know..." She clamped her lips. "You're interested in," she gulped, "Kase?"

Phoebe burst out laughing. Was it really so strange? The man was sexy, rough, and gorgeous, so why wouldn't she be?

"Is it that weird?"

"Yes," she blurted, and her cheeks shaded to pink. She shook her head. "I mean, I just didn't see Kase as your type."

Phoebe sat back in her chair. It made sense. Kase was the polar opposite of Jared. *Thank God.*

"Kase is single."

Phoebe glanced up with a smirk.

"He's *always* single, Phoebe." She widened her eyes, and Phoebe could see her hesitation. "He doesn't date. Or if he does, he doesn't do it well because he's always with a different girl from the club." She glanced up at the ceiling and furrowed her brows. "Actually, I don't really think you could call what Kase does, dating. He, um..." Bailey blushed.

He fucks them. Though Phoebe would bet her life savings, currently pennies, those words would never come out of her friend's mouth.

Phoebe snickered. "Why should you be the only one who gets to bang a biker?"

Bailey smirked, shaking her head.

"Not looking to marry him, Bails." Phoebe snorted. The last thing on earth she wanted was to be strapped down again. It was a long, hard, painful lesson. Love was for suckers.

Phoebe settled into her seat. "Just looking for a good time, girl. Nothing more, I promise."

She sighed. "Okay. I just don't want you to get hurt. Ya know, some people can be the best at one thing and the worst at another. Kase is a great leader to the club, he's awesome with the guys, he's loyal and protective." She shrugged with a soft smile. There was no doubt Bailey loved him and thought highly of him, "When you're in with him, he's got you." Bailey smiled warmly. "Kase has moments when he's better than most." She paused, and Phoebe wondered what she wasn't telling her. Whatever it was, Bailey was keeping it to herself. She glanced up, and her lips pursed. "But he never struck me as the type of man who would be a great partner."

"Really? Too bossy in bed, ya think?" Phoebe teased.

She twisted her lips at Phoebe's teasing. "I only think of Saint when it comes to sex."

"I don't blame ya." Phoebe waggled her brows.

Bailey blushed and ignored the comment. "I don't want you hurt, Feebs."

There were not enough Baileys in the world. *Government scientists should clone her DNA. The world would be a better place.* Phoebe smiled, keeping her thoughts to herself.

"Look, Kase won't hurt me, I promise. Hurt is reserved for those who invest their hearts." She chuckled. "And there's no way any man will ever get a piece of mine again."

Bailey's smile faltered. "There are good guys out there." She shrugged. "I found one."

Phoebe nodded. "And you deserve him. I'm not interested in anything but a little fun." She winked. It was the truth. As callous as it may have sounded, Phoebe wasn't looking for anything more than a good time and a mind-blowing orgasm that ended with her partner leaving shortly after.

Bailey shifted forward, resting her elbows on the table with a somber smile. "Can I ask you something?"

Their lunch had taken a turn to a serious note. Phoebe geared up for it.

"Sure."

"It's personal."

Phoebe snorted. "Oh, even better."

"How come you've never talked about Jared and everything he put you through? I mean, it's none of my business, and you can tell me to shut up and never bring up his name again and I will, but umm..." Bailey bit her bottom lip. "You can talk to me." She shook her head and raised her hands defensively. "Or not. No pressure from me. But you've always been there for me and listened when I needed to vent." Bailey snorted. "Let me cry in front of you without judgement. You've seen me at my worst." Bailey reached out and grasped her hand. "I want to be that for you if you need it, okay?"

Phoebe stared back, overcome with emotion. It had nothing to do with Jared. It was all for her. Phoebe had shared with Bailey but hadn't gone into detail. She kept it all to herself. Even her father, her closest ally, was left in the dark when it came to her feelings regarding Jared. *I'll take it to my grave.*

Phoebe cleared her throat and squeezed Bailey's hand. "I don't talk about him because I don't want to give him any more of my time. Not an hour, not a minute, not even a friggin' breath. He got enough of me." Phoebe licked her lips and inhaled a deep breath. Her tears were balancing at her eyes, and the last thing she wanted was to cry. "But if I did need to talk, to scream, to cry," Phoebe paused with a slow nod, "you'd be my go-to, Bailey."

There was a long silence between them. Phoebe released her hand and grabbed her soda, taking a sip, and glanced out the window. The pizzeria was situated diagonally from the parts store. She watched as two men straddled their bikes and talked to the man in the doorway. *The perfect distraction.* When he stepped out onto the sidewalk, the corner of her mouth lifted. *God, he's sexy.*

"I feel like I ruined lunch by bringing him up. Let's talk about something good."

Phoebe laughed and turned to Bailey. "Okay. How *good* do you think Kase is in bed?"

Bailey's cheeks burned red, and she covered her face with her hands while Phoebe burst out laughing. It was good to be home with Bailey, making her blush.

KASE WAS GROWING INCREASINGLY annoyed by the second. Watching his brother pussyfoot around his wife for the last hour was pissing him off.

Kase and Caden had agreed last week. Marissa needed a break. With the new baby, a teenager, and Caden's workload, Marissa had taken it all on, including their dad. While she never complained, it was obviously taking a toll on her. When Caden approached him about taking their dad for a week, Kase didn't hesitate. Caden and Marissa had done their part and then some. It was Kase's turn to man the fuck up and do his.

Caden insisted he be the one to tell Marissa, which made sense as her husband. Kase had no problem with it until about an hour ago. Caden was skirting around it in hopes of gently breaking the news to her.

Kase rested his hip against the counter and folded his arms. *Time to rip off the band-aid.*

"I'm gonna take him to the clubhouse for a week," Kase blurted. When she turned to him, he raised his brows. "Cade and I talked about it. You need a break."

He watched Marissa widen her eyes and immediately turn on Caden. "You think I can't handle everything?"

She had handled everything for a long time. She was so far in with his family she couldn't even see she needed a break. Kase rolled his eyes and ignored Caden's glare.

"No, that's not what I said."

It was exactly what Caden had said, and he was right. Kase lifted his beer, watching the showdown between husband and wife. It would have amused him if not for the tears in her eyes. *Fuck me.* He flattened his lips trying to keep himself out of their domestic disagreement.

"Riss, stop," Caden said with a tone meant to be comforting. His wife wasn't having it. When he stepped closer, she backed away.

"I can do this." She sniffled, wiping her sleeve across her cheeks. "I have a routine with Jack, and I've got Cora on his sleep schedule. I'm caught up on all the paperwork from the shop and-and," she inhaled a shaky breath and turned to Caden. "Do I not make goddamn dinner every night?"

Kase clamped his lips. Not many people had ever gotten inside and settled deep in his heart. Marissa was one of the select few. While he wasn't vocal, he had more respect and love for her than any woman he knew.

"What about you, Riss?" Kase asked. "Where's your fucking time?"

She dropped her stare to the ground. She avoided the answer because she didn't have one. She was dedicating everything to everyone around her. She was forgetting about herself.

"No one is saying you can't handle it, baby." Caden sighed and inched closer, carefully timing his approach.

She jerked her head up and squinted her eyes. "You are." She turned to Kase. "And you." Her lips pouted down to a frown.

Kase shifted off the counter and pulled her into his side, sliding his arm over her shoulder. She resisted, but he was stronger and more persistent at the moment.

"You been carrying this family for over a fucking year now, okay? You do more for that crazy fucker than any of us." It was true. Marissa had devoted all her time and effort to not only Caden and Trevor, but to their father.

"I don't mind." She whimpered. Kase glanced up at Caden, who was watching Marissa. He drew in a breath. Cade had found the perfect partner, someone who would forever give. They weren't worthy of her, not a single Reilly. He smiled.

"I know ya don't, but I do."

She slowly looked up with tears threatening her eyes.

"And Cade does." He narrowed his gaze. "Ya got the baby now. You need a fucking break." She shook her head, and he tightened his hold. "I'm gonna tell you what your pussy husband won't 'cause he doesn't want ya upset. You need this, and we're giving it to you. Jack is coming to stay with me at the club for a week."

She sniffled and remained silent. It would sink in eventually. "You better bring him back." It was a sweet, weepy demand. He tightened his hold.

Kase smiled and leaned closer, whispering in her ear, "I will. Trust me, a week with his ass will be enough. I'll be the one needing a fucking break."

Kase glanced up to Caden who stood across the room

watching him. He nodded and released Marissa. He'd give them a minute to get their shit back on track.

Kase lit a cigarette as he walked out on the porch and gazed off the property. His brother had a good set up, one he worked his ass for through the years. He'd always been hard on Caden, as their Pop had been hard on him. *It's what made a man.*

The screen door opened, but Kase kept his stare trained on the front yard.

"She's packing up his things." Cade cleared his throat. "Thanks for stepping in back there. Hard to do what I know is right when I got her crying in front of me."

Kase glanced over.

Caden shrugged. "She's my weak spot."

Most women were, especially the good ones. Marissa had come in a year ago and changed the Reilly men, including himself. She brought a softness they desperately needed, even if he wasn't willing to verbally admit it. Marissa was good for them, all of them. She took care of them. It was time to return the favor.

"He's getting worse, Kase."

Kase clenched his jaw. "I know."

"Do you?"

Kase grasped the railing of the porch and turned to his brother. "Yeah, I fucking know, Cade. He lives here, but I know my own fucking dad." It was his own guilt speaking. He hadn't been there for Jack or Caden as he should have been. Caden had taken on the burden of caring for his father while Kase had run the club.

Caden held up his hands. "Just want you prepared."

Kase scoffed. "For what? His death? Pop's been losing his mind for the past few years. I know what the outcome will be." He did. As much as he refused to admit it, Jack's impending demise was weighing heavy on his shoulders. It had been the last few years. It was hard watching the man he'd idolized during his entire childhood become a shell of the man he once was.

As a kid, Jack seemed larger than life. He lived for the club, with Kase and Caden coming up a close second. He didn't fully understand the devotion until he turned eighteen and prospected. He knew he wanted to be a member, and he'd do what it took. He had visions of it being easier than it was. Jack made him earn it. He'd been harder on Kase than any other prospect.

It had been worth it. All of it, to be sitting at the head of the table, taking over the gavel when his Pop stepped down.

"How much time ya think we got?" Kase asked.

Caden sighed, strolling up next to him. "He's had a few bad weeks, Kase." It was a warning.

Kase nodded and drew in a breath. Caden handled mostly everything with his father. It had been a mutual understanding and agreement. Kase's lifestyle didn't allow the same flexibility as Caden's. *Fuck you and your fucking copout.* He turned to Caden. His brother had stepped up when he didn't. When he should have.

"Whores and booze, he'll have a good time for the week," Kase said, which got the tension draining from his brother's shoulders. Caden glanced up, grinning.

"Not a bad way to go."

"Fucking best way," Kase said, slapping Caden's back and gripping his shoulder. Someday soon it would be just the two of them. It was a realization that weighed heavy on Kase.

Chapter 5

It was odd for someone to knock on her door. With so few neighbors, random surprise visits were rare, aside from Mary across the street. She started out of her bedroom and stopped near the kitchen counter, glancing up at the time. Ten-fifteen was too late for Mary to be stopping by. She inched closer to the door. Through the small part in the curtain she saw a tall figure in a black leather vest. Her heart spiked, and she angled her head to get a better look.

An abrupt sharp knock pounded on the door, shifting the curtains. It wasn't enough to get a full visual of the man on the other side of the door. It could be any member of the club. The black leather was a dead giveaway. Phoebe had a sneaking suspicion it was Kase. Her belly swirled with excitement as she closed in on her door.

She grabbed the doorknob and yanked it open with a smile. *Too eager, settle down.*

"Hey there, neighbor." The sultry tone was done with purpose.

Kase stood two feet away, donning his signature glare. "Got a proposition."

She leaned her head against the door. "Well, my day just got interesting." She was teasing. The only reason Kase would show up with a proposition would be solely for acquiring her land.

He reached into his pocket, pulled out a piece of paper, and handed it to her. She grasped the small square, and her fingers grazed over the calluses of his knuckles. Rough hands.

It didn't take superhuman powers to know he was giving her another offer. She slid the small paper between her fingers. She arched her brow. "How about we have drinks by the fire, and I'll listen to your proposal?"

His jaw squared, and his glare sharpened. "I don't have a fucking proposal. I got a fucking number. A better offer than you'll ever get for this property." He released a disgusted snarl. "I ain't gonna waste my time trying to convince you to do shit. You either take it, or you fucking don't."

She widened her eyes. That was not the response she had been expecting. She was learning quick Kase wasn't the usual type of man she interacted with. The man had a chip on his shoulder and a short fuse. Surprisingly, she wasn't turned off. It was refreshing to see a man be upfront, honest, cutting out all the bullshit. She pushed off the door and inhaled a deep breath.

"Okay, forget the proposal. Just have a drink with me." She stepped closer.

"What?"

"Come hang by the fire, share my whiskey." She shrugged. "I owe you, remember? Had you not stepped in with Arnett, I could be serving twenty to life right now." It was a desperate attempt at a joke.

He shook his head and glanced across her lawn. She noted he didn't immediately take off. The deep lines between his brows eased slightly. *I need to make my move before he bolts.*

She reached out, sliding her fingers over the back of his hand. He jerked his gaze back to her but didn't pull away. She could read his face. He wanted to.

Before she lost her nerve, she started back in the house and reached up on her top shelf to get the glasses. The bottle had been on her counter, and she grabbed the neck, walking back to Kase standing on the porch.

"C'mon." She didn't wait for a response and started down the steps. All she could hope for was that he followed. Her lips curled when she heard his boots crunch into the concrete step stones.

She had attempted to start the fire. It only lasted a minute before he aggressively took over. He nudged her aside and bent down, grabbing the logs and setting them up. The fire was always Jared's thing, and she hadn't quite gotten the hang of the stacking process. She settled in a chair, pouring the whiskey, and watching Kase. He reached over, grabbed a handful of newspaper she had stacked near the ring, and shredded strips, tossing them onto the logs. Once he'd gotten the fire started, he settled into the seat across from her, much to her dismay. There was a seat directly next to her.

He sipped from his glass, taking a larger mouthful than she did. It wasn't the flavor she enjoyed. It was the heat and slow burn down her throat. The warming of her belly and the ease only whiskey could deliver. Kase drank as though it was water.

"So," she said, staring across the flames. "What should we talk about?"

The sharp edges of his cheekbones protruded from his face, and his gaze narrowed. "The offer." He jerked his chin to her hand.

She'd almost forgotten about the slip of paper in her hand. She glanced down and opened it, acutely aware he was watching her. She flattened her lips and held back her surprise at the number staring back at her. *Holy shit!* It was the highest offer she'd been given from the club. *Too bad I'm not moving.*

She glanced up, hoping she was pulling off her poker face "If I turn down the offer, will you leave?"

He raised his brows. She wasn't sure how to interpret the response. Would he leave? Probably. It was his only reason for being at her place. Without her selling, he had no interest in her. Or did he? She wasn't willing to take the chance.

She curved the corner of her lip. "Okay. I'll think about the offer."

Kase snorted, and the corner of his mouth curled. "You're so full of shit."

Did he just smile? Not a full-fledged committed grin, but a smile. She internally celebrated her small breakthrough.

"Ya ain't gonna take anything I offer, are you?"

She blinked and glanced up at him. She slowly shook her head. "It's nothing personal. I just don't want to sell. It's home."

His dark gaze travelled over her face, sending a shiver down her spine. He leaned forward, and her heart skipped thinking he was leaving. When he grabbed his glass from the ground and brought it up to his lips, she sighed in relief. He kept his gaze locked on hers. Her heart picked up its pace, and a flash of heat spread across her chest and neck. Any flirting done in the past was mere child's play when up against Kase. She watched his throat bob and could almost taste his salty skin on her lips as if she were licking his neck. She tightened her thighs together.

"Can I ask you something?"

"Are we fucking sharing?"

A blustering bubble built in her belly. He had to be the grumpiest man she'd ever come into contact with. It seemed strange for a man of his age to be so pissed off all the time. *Why the hell am I so turned on?* She sipped her drink and licked her lips. His dark eyes had yet to look away, sending a small tingle over her skin, mainly across her breasts, shooting straight to her core.

"Let me ask *you* something." It was a command rather than a request.

It was enough to knock her out of her sex-hazed trance and she blinked. She scooted up in her seat and turned her body toward him. "Yes. Let's share. I'll ask first, then you."

She noticed a change in his eyes. A suspicious glimmer. "No."

"Okay, you go first. What do you wanna know?" She waggled her brows. "Open book, Kase."

The anticipation was too much. Her mind was riddled with

potential questions. *What's my favorite position? Can I come from sex alone, or do I need clit play? Am I willing to get naked right now? Yes, I am.* She bit her lip and cocked her brow.

He sipped from his cup, eyeing her over the rim of his glass. "Your old man?"

She flinched before she could register her reaction. She was caught off guard. Of all the questions he'd ask, the subject of her husband hadn't even peaked her radar. Purposely bringing up a deceased spouse was usually a major *faux pas*. Although, Kase didn't strike her as the type to follow rules of etiquette. The last thing she wanted to discuss with him would he Jared. In fact, she rarely discussed him with anyone. She furrowed her brows and glanced at the sky. "Finally get to hang out with a biker, and he wants know about my deceased husband?" She side-glanced him. "I thought for sure you would ask me something scandalous, like my favorite position."

Kase arched his brow, allowing his gaze to drop to her tight fitted T-shirt. He glanced up and smirked. "Reverse cowgirl, 'cause you get off on being in control." He slowly lifted his cigarette to his mouth and lit it. "Sixty-nine as a fucking second."

Her eyes widened, and for a brief second, she was frozen with a plastered smile on her face. The man had nailed her favorite positions by just a scan over her body. Her howling laughter ripped through the valley. He shook his head, pursing his lips. If she had to guess, he was holding back his own laughter. This was good. It made him seem more human.

"Oh my God, that's awesome." She scooted up in her chair, resting her elbows on her knees. "Can you do that with anyone? Because seriously, if so, we need to go to a bar right now. I totally wanna see this."

Kase stared back for a few seconds before the corner of his mouth lifted slightly. She blinked, caught off guard. This was a breakthrough of sorts. *Did I really just make Kase Reilly smile, sort of?* It was the most emotion she'd gotten out of him. Even the lines in his forehead eased slightly. She sucked in a deep breath. His features, when not brooding and stern, were…handsome.

"Your husband?" he asked.

If she wanted *this* Kase to stick around, she'd have to continue with one of her least favorite subjects. It was a decision of what she wanted more.

She shrugged and sipped from her glass. "Dead."

Kase snorted and shook his head. It wasn't much. At least he wasn't leaving.

"Fucking smartass."

She smirked and lifted her glass to her lips, prolonging the sip far longer than it should have lasted. He stood up, adding another log to the fire before taking his seat. Kase was showing no signs of leaving. She leaned forward over the arm of her chair and pointed in his direction.

"You get laid a lot, don't ya?"

It was her turn to be amused. His hand froze as he was lifting his cigarette to his lips, and he glanced up. She was sure Kase wasn't caught off guard often. Her question definitely threw him off his game.

"I do all right."

She nodded. "I bet you do." She tilted her head. "I bet women get off on the motorcycle, the tats, the whole bad boy biker thing, huh?"

He eyed her suspiciously. His stare darkened and took on a heated, dangerous vibe. It only made her more intrigued.

"You getting off on it?"

Yes! A burn heat flashed over her entire body.

"I'd answer that, but it's my turn to ask a question." She licked her lips. "When was the last time you had sex?"

He cocked a brow. "You gonna share your last fuck?"

It was a challenging tone. He didn't think she would, and on any given day, he'd be right. Something in her didn't care. *It's called liquid courage, jackass.* She ignored the voice in her head. If Kase wanted to share, she was game.

She shrugged. "Last month." She shimmied in her seat and dropped her feet to the ground. "Lucas." She sighed just remembering him. "He was so hot, and I mean, I know women say that all the time, they are forever pledging the man they had was the best thing ever. This guy was incredible to look at. Completely ripped, dark hair, dark eyes, had a deep raspy voice." She glanced up and lifted her brows. "Kase, he was hot."

"Yeah, I got that."

Phoebe rested her head against the back of her chair. "Twenty-six." She arched her brow. "The young ones are so damn eager to please." She lifted her glass, pointing at him. "See, you and me have a lot more in common than ya think. We're both fans of the twentysomethings." It was an assumption on her part, and a valid one. Phoebe had seen quite a few girls next door, and not one appeared over the age of thirty.

She winked, expecting him to appreciate her comment. His jaw clenched tightly for unknown reasons, and he drew in a breath. *Get on with it before he ditches our drunk ass.*

"It was a blind date. The conversation wasn't anything amazing. It was the first date, which is always awkward. I invite him in, and he kinda hesitated saying he wanted to take things slow." She rolled her eyes. "The next thing I know, I'm up against a wall and he's giving me an orgasm." She widened her eyes and knew her speech was slurred slightly. She didn't care. "Like five minutes in, I'm screaming his name, biting his chest, and coming." She sat back in her seat, released a heavy built up sigh, and grinned. "It was glorious."

It had been. Each and every time. She never understood women who balked at great sex. Maybe they did because they never had any, or maybe they were too ashamed at coming off dirty. Whatever their own case was, Phoebe enjoyed it. The passion, the hunger, the damn orgasm.

The silence lingered between them. She didn't mind. She was still basking in sex memories of Lucas to care.

"Ya still with him?"

"We went out a few more times, ended the night in positions I didn't even know were possible." She burst out laughing. "But no, I don't see him anymore."

"Why?"

She gazed up at Kase. He was wholeheartedly invested in her story, which was sweet. But the reason she and Lucas never lasted wasn't something she wanted to think about. It would sober her up in seconds. She desperately needed a change of subject, a diversion.

"I screw twenty-six-year olds, I don't date them."

He spit out his whiskey and wiped his mouth with his sleeve. "God, you're so fucking unpredictable."

Was that a good thing?

"Your turn, Kase. You promised."

He stared at her, prolonging the silence. Then he jerked his chin. "Finish yours."

She scoffed and frowned. "I did. We went out, we banged, end of story."

He arched his brow. "This guy gives you the fuck of your life, and then you end it?" He paused. "Sounds like bullshit to me."

Fuck! Why was he so damn insistent on digging deeper? Why wouldn't he just leave it alone? It was almost methodical the way his mind worked. She had a suspicion these were calculated questions. Of course, they were. Kase had an agenda that had nothing to do with getting to know her. But why? Had she been in a less alcohol- induced state, she may have been able to figure it out.

"He a dick, stop calling, fucking around on ya?"

"No." She straightened her shoulders. Lucas had been the complete opposite.

The corner of his mouth curved in a sinister smirk. "We done sharing?"

She cocked her brow. "So far, you've shared nothing."

"Never claimed to be an open book." He took a drag from his cigarette. "That's on you, sweetheart."

Sweetheart. It wasn't said with the usual endearing tone, but it did seem to roll off his tongue without hesitation. She was probably reading into it too much. For all she knew, he called everyone sweetheart, though he didn't seem the type.

She smiled. "Sweetheart, huh? We've evolved to pet names now?"

His eyes darkened, sending a heated rush from her stomach to her core.

"Finish."

Why couldn't they go back to flirting? She swallowed back the knot in her throat. Just talking about it was sobering her up.

"Honestly?"

"No, fucking lie to me."

She snickered and inhaled a deep breath. *Here goes…*

"I have trust issues." Trusting the wrong people to be exact. When the truth came to light about Jared, it had rocked her world; she had been blindsided. A man she'd loved, devoted her life to, had turned on her in the ultimate betrayal.

"Fuck." He snorted. "Who doesn't?" He leaned forward, grabbed the bottle from the ground, and filled his glass. He glanced up at her glass, pausing a second before dropping it back to the ground. She furrowed her brows and opened her mouth, but he cut her off.

"What happened with the guy?"

Oh, just tell him. The quicker she ended the subject, the quicker they could move on.

She sighed. "He wanted more than I was willing to give."

"Anal?"

She burst out laughing, spitting out a mouthful of whiskey. It took a minute to recover, and oddly enough she wasn't embarrassed he'd witnessed her drunken display.

"Kase, we gotta hang out more." She sighed, reached for the bottle, and poured another glass.

"Finish."

She darted her eyes in his direction. Even without looking, she could feel the weight of his stare. He wouldn't let it go. Maybe it was the whiskey, or just having another person to hang out with. Maybe her loneliness was catching up to her. Kase would be the last person she'd expect to open up to.

"Lucas invited me to dinner with his friends. He wanted everyone to meet me. He wanted to come over to my house, order takeout, and binge watch this series we were both addicted to." She forced a smile and watched his head cock to the side. He was waiting on a horrific confession, like he beat her, got drunk, and turned crazy. But none of that happened. "He wanted to take me away to the beach for the weekend. His family owned a boat, and he talked about wanting to watch the sunset with me."

She snorted, and then finished off her drink and closed her eyes. Lucas had been a nice guy. Weren't they all at the beginning? Seeing a man's true colors wouldn't come out in a few dates. She would have to open herself up, let a man in. *No fucking way.*

She jerked her gaze to find Kase intently watching her. Kase was invested in hearing the whole story. She shook her head with a soft chuckle. The irony wasn't lost on her. The one thing she was trying to avoid with men was unfolding in front of her.

"He wanted a relationship." Phoebe paused.

Kase's brows furrowed. "I thought women loved that shit?"

She shook her head, dazed. "Not this one."

Lucas had been a sweet guy, fantastic in bed, and would make some girl very happy. *That girl isn't me. I was ruined. He deserved more than someone who couldn't give everything.* She didn't have anything to give.

"Some asshole fucked you over good, huh?"

She stared down at the fire.

Jared dug into my soul and gripped my heart into an agonizing hold, twisted it through a torturous pain, and ripped the fucking thing out of my chest.

She sipped her drink and rested her head against the back of the chair. "Yeah, he did."

HE WATCHED her for the next minute as she remained silent. The mood had taken a drastic turn. Her glow had dimmed, and she seemed lost in the silence. It should have been his cue to head out. The heart to heart deep talks were never his thing. He wasn't built to handle weepy women. Though, Phoebe didn't seem on the verge of a female heartbreaking meltdown. He'd been witness to a few in his time, mostly with members and their old ladies. She wasn't displaying anything more than regret if he had to guess.

Phoebe remained silently focused on the fire. Her openness had caught him off guard. It was rare for most people to share anything in depth with him other than those closest to him. It took trust, which Phoebe should not have with him. Even being the bastard that he was, he knew the guts it took to share intimate details with a virtual stranger. Unknowingly, she was giving him ammunition to use against her. A weakness.

For the first time in his life, he wasn't sure about using it.

He should have made her the new offer and left. Hanging out with her hadn't been a consideration—until she started in with her clever banter. In his head, he knew to the get hell out of there, but he stayed. Just as he was doing now. *Why the hell am I still fucking here?*

She shifted in her seat, bending her knees and settling her feet on the chair. With her arm wrapped around her legs, she rested her chin on her knees. She seemed almost vulnerable as she stared back at the fire. It was a far cry from the Phoebe he'd seen previously. When she licked her lips, his gaze was drawn to her mouth, which was tugged into a small somber frown.

He wasn't sure what bothered him more. Her sadness or his unrelenting desire to console her.

Do not fucking touch her.

He clasped his mouth, dragging his hand down over his beard and eyeing her.

"You all right?" *No, she isn't fucking all right, asshole.* Phoebe didn't come across as the type to wear her heart on her sleeve. She had revealed more than he expected and probably more than she did. It seemed to have set her back in time of sorts. He clenched his jaw, staring back at her.

"Yeah, sorry." Her head was bowed.

Look at me. He wanted those blue eyes on him. Even in the dark, they glowed, and he wanted them staring back at him.

"Hey." He sounded harsher than he intended. She needed a distraction. When she glanced up, he sighed. *Fuck!* He licked his lips. "Last fuck was a foursome."

His admission could go one of two ways. Disgusted or impressed. It took her a second, and her eyes darted up, and the corner of her lip curled. The air around them shifted.

"You had a foursome? As in four people having sex? With each other? At the same time?" She shifted in her seat, practically hanging over the arm.

It fucking worked.

Her expression was worth the risk. He slowly nodded and sipped his whiskey.

She widened her eyes. "Two couples?"

He twisted his lips. "Fuck, no. Me and three women."

Her bottom lip fell open, and she shifted in her chair again, putting only a foot of distance between them. His plan had worked and backfired at the same time. She was no longer upset. In fact, she seemed to be bubbling over with excitement and intrigue. His distraction had worked. However, it also sent her closer to him. Dangerously close. While he tried his best to ignore the attraction, he wanted her. Physical distance was imperative to keep his hands off her.

Her next move only tested his control. She grasped his wrist. Her grip was tight, but he felt her soft caress sweep across his skin. *Fuck. Not good.*

"How does that even work?" She leaned closer and eyed his jeans, and then trailed up to his mouth. She was mentally counting how he could please three women at once. When she glanced up, catching his stare, he waggled his fingers, which were wrapped around his glass.

"Shut up!" She fell back in her chair, laughing. "Oh my God, Kase." She covered her mouth and curled her feet up under her ass in the seat. "You win. Even hot sex with Lucas can't top a foursome." She laughed, the sound of her giggle echoing in the trees.

Her blonde streaks swept across her forehead, shadowing one eye. Those fucking eyes. Without thinking, he reached out, swiping her hair behind her ear for no other reason than wanting to see both her eyes. His fingers caressed down the side of her face, and she nestled her cheek against the pads of his fingers.

Get the fuck up and leave, asshole. He dropped his hand to the arm of the chair.

"Kase." She leaned closer, her voice low and breathy. "We should have sex."

He was lifting his glass when she spoke and stopped in mid-air.

"What the hell did you just say?"

She smirked. "I think it'll solidify our bond as neighbors, don't ya think?"

He turned his head and furrowed his brows.

"What the fuck is in that glass?"

She was drunk, and she had been for the past hour. However, she hadn't been off the fucking rails. Hell, she wasn't even slurring her words or falling over herself. She must have been able to contain it better than most. It was the only reasonable conclusion.

"C'mon. Aren't you tired of all those young beautiful girls with huge boobs and round asses and legs that go on for days?" She smirked playfully. "When was the last time you had sex with a middle-aged woman with decent looks and a killer sense of humor?" She winked. "Aren't you even curious?"

This was fucked. Not the proposition, but how she just described herself. *Decent looks?* Fuck, this was probably one of the most beautiful women he'd set eyes on. And he'd stared at her enough to know that her tits were a perfect handful, and her ass, while slightly larger than he was used to, he liked it. A lot. Now, she was offering it up to him. He clenched his jaw. *Walk the fuck away.*

She sat up in her seat, practically bouncing on her knees. She had to be teasing him. He eyed her carefully. Was she testing him? She had to be. Phoebe wasn't the type to go around offering sex to men she barely knew. He'd had countless encounters with women from the club who had been virtual strangers. It was a common occurrence in his lifestyle. Not Phoebe's. *She's fucking with me.*

"Okay, let me set up the scenario, and you tell me if you'd follow through, okay?"

At this point he was humoring her. He knew she was full of shit, but curious to see how far she'd take it. He'd play her game.

"All right."

She smiled and pushed off her chair, standing up. Just the view of her body was enough to get him hard. And it did. His cock jutted forward, pressing against his zipper. He sucked in a breath and grinded his teeth.

"If I strip down, right now, right here, would you fuck me?"

Bullshit. She was bluffing. Even in her drunken state, she didn't have the balls to do it.

He snorted. "I'd tell ya to lay off the fucking booze."

She gripped the hem of her shirt and lifted it over her head. She tossed her shirt to the side without even losing his stare. *Fuck! Middle-aged, my fucking ass.* Her toned stomach led up to her breasts pouring out of her hot pink bra. From the cleavage alone, his breath labored. She smiled and reached behind her back. *Oh hell, no.* If she took off her bra, he wouldn't be able to control himself. Not when he knew exactly what was underneath. He'd seen the move enough times to know she was unsnapping her bra. He'd called it wrong; she wasn't bluffing. *Shit.*

He swiftly reached out and grabbed her wrist. It was meant to halt the striptease. Like most things that night, it backfired. Phoebe lost her balance and fell forward into his lap. Her hands grasped his chest, and he circled her waist to keep her from falling to the ground. The move propped her ass directly against his cock and her lips a breath away from his mouth. Her hands curved over his chest, hooking around his neck. It was slow motion, plenty of time to pull away or turn his head. Unfortunately, Kase didn't have the restraint.

He clawed his hands into her ass, yanking her closer. *Fuck, don't do it.* It was too late. She pressed her lips against his mouth. He was done. He angled his head as her lips parted, and he felt her warm breath filter into his mouth. His tongue slid past her soft lips, sliding into her mouth. He'd kissed thousands; it was an act as common as washing his hands. Something was different with Phoebe. He felt her need, her desire—he felt everything.

Her teeth grazed over his bottom lip as her ass pressed against his cock. The combination set him off, and he dug his fingers into her ass, pulling her closer. Her hands were everywhere, as if she couldn't get enough of him. His reaction was no different. He gripped her jaw, gaining a better access, a closer connection to deepen the kiss. Her tongue tangled over his in a silky caress, setting a fire through his chest.

A loud rumbling echo in the background was all it took for reality to strike. It was a sharp whip to his chest and a siren of warning bells blasting in his ears. *What the fuck am I doing?* He was seconds away from stripping her down and fucking her in her back yard.

He tightened his hand on her ass and jerked his head to the side. "Stop."

Her lips grazed the shell of his ear. "No." Her nails bit into his neck. He was at the brink, the point of no return. If she didn't stop, he'd have her naked in record time.

He grabbed her waist with both hands, finding it next to impossible to push her away. "We do this, you'll regret it in the morning."

"Not if you make me come, I won't." She giggled, sending the soft vibration shooting straight to his dick.

Kase closed his eyes, fighting against the feel of her mouth on his neck, and he drew in a harsh breath. "I will."

Her mouth froze against his neck. It was a brief second before she slowly released his chest and sat back, staring at him. The heated glaze was shadowed by something he couldn't pinpoint. Shock? Disappointment? Her entire face shaded to a deep pink. *That would be embarrassment, asshole.* Before he could say anything else, she climbed off his lap.

She rushed to the ground, grabbing her shirt and turning away from him as she slid it back on.

He waited with her back to him. Why the hell was he feeling guilty? He was saving her ass from morning regret.

What the fuck was he supposed to do now? The seconds felt like hours as he stared at her back with her hair falling forward. She jerked around, but kept her gaze on the ground with her head slightly bowed.

"You're seriously turning me down?" She forced a laugh, but he knew it was fake.

Fuuuuuuck! This night had turned to shit in five fucking seconds.

Kase cleared his throat and leaned forward, resting his elbows on his knees. "Yeah, I am."

She nodded but refused to meet his stare. *Fucking look at me.* She didn't and curled her hair around her ear.

"I'm gonna go, but thanks for hanging with me." Through her thin shirt he could see her heart pounding in her chest. "Bye." She turned so quickly she stumbled, but caught herself.

He shot up from his chair. "Phoebe," he snapped with an edge, demanding she look at him. She ignored him and increased her pace until she disappeared around the house.

He drove his hand through his hair, tugging hard at the ends. "Fuck!"

He waited longer than necessary. The lights were still gleaming in her house, but he knew she wasn't coming back out. He broke down the fire and walked back to the clubhouse. The party was going strong, but he wasn't feeling it.

"Hey, Kase." Nadia sidled up next to him as he started down the hall. "You okay?"

"Not fucking now, Nad." He continued down the hall to his room, ignoring everyone.

He slammed the door shut and locked it behind him. He didn't need anyone coming in behind him. Kase paced around his room like a caged animal. He did the right thing. If he'd fucking taken her, it would only end with regret on both their parts.

She'd regret having him in her bed.

He'd regret getting a taste of something he couldn't have.

Chapter 6

She stood over the sink washing her hands, taking quick glances in the mirror. Two days later, she was still finding it hard to look at herself without shuddering in embarrassment. For all the humiliating acts she'd done in her past, her night with Kase would teeter as number one on her list.

She dried her hands and stared at her reflection in the mirror. She shook her head in utter disgust. "You are never to drink whiskey with him again. You hear me?"

Yep, loud and clear. I heard you yesterday morning, heard you after lunch, heard you last night, heard you in bed, in the yard, at the desk.

She cringed at her obsessive chants. If she reminded herself enough times, she was sure history would not repeat itself. She closed her eyes and groaned. Embarrassment had a funny way of shifting the brain to two personalities. The drunk free spirit and the sober reality-minded one. If she could go back to that night, she wouldn't have even opened the door. How does one person make so many mistakes in one night?

Whiskey.

"Whiskey," she muttered, and pried open her eyes. She pursed her lips and drove her hand through her hair.

She had been avoiding Kase since their last encounter. The

morning after her failed attempt at seduction, she was nursing her excruciating hangover and, on her couch, licking her wounded ego. The man had probably bedded hundreds of women, and he flat out turned her down. It was a hard rejection. So hard that when her doorbell rang the next morning, she slithered into her couch, muted the TV, and covered her head with her blanket. Thirty-fucking-two years old and she was hiding. *Pathetic.*

She couldn't be sure it was him, but she wasn't taking any chances. The second day had been equally cowardly. She was grabbing her mail when she heard the motorcycles coming down the road. She practically ran up her driveway, never looking back, even when she thought she heard the faint yell of her name.

Her hiding came to a quick end. The town meeting was a place she knew she'd have to see him. Not going wasn't an option. A vote always required a majority of residents' attendance, and Bailey made her promise to show so they could pass the new park. She purposely stalled on leaving. If she walked in late, as usual, she'd avoid Kase.

When she pulled up at seven-ten, her anxious energy escalated into a fire in her belly. It was mortifying to have to face him. She hadn't been this embarrassed since she struck up the nerve to ask Drew Cole to dance at the spring fling. He laughed in her face.

She grabbed her coat and walked through the lot, intentionally slow. As she approached, she noticed a few men standing in the doorway with their cuts. *Just fucking great.* She was hoping to hang by the entrance, keep a low profile. That plan had been foiled. Now, she'd actually have to enter the building.

As she started up the steps, one of the men, who she recognized from the garage, turned. His brusque disposition was off putting. For most people, they'd shy away, but for Phoebe, she saw him as a bit of a challenge. She'd spent a half hour at the garage forcing him to talk to her. He seemed slightly more open when she discovered his sweet spot. His wife, Macy.

She forced a smile. "Hey, Rourke. I miss anything?" She raised her brows. "Tell me we're getting a water park!"

The corner of his mouth curved. "Same shit from the old guy." He stepped aside, allowing her to pass through the wall of bikers.

Phoebe sighed. "He's fun, isn't he?"

She heard the low rumble of a few masculine chuckles.

She was relieved to see the place was packed. She did a quick inspection of the front of the room. She knew the Ghosttown Riders usually took up the back half, so Kase would be easily avoidable. She just had to make sure there was no eye contact. *What am I, twelve?*

"The noise. We need to address the noise ordinance."

She groaned and rolled her eyes. She started past the front half of the room. A cool chill spread over her neck. A clear sign she was being watched. She refused to look over at the MC. She wedged herself between Marty and the snack table. She kept her focus on Arnett, until she felt a tug on her leg.

"I made banana bread. I knocked yesterday, but you musta been out." Mary smiled and reached down in her bag, pulling out a rectangular loaf covered in foil. "It's not warm, but I hope it's good."

My people. "Thank you, Mary."

"No side talk," Arnett snapped, and Phoebe jumped back from the aisle.

She straightened and glared his way. The last thing she needed tonight was his mouth. She grinned dramatically, and he turned away, starting up again about the bullshit noise curfew. She turned to Marty.

"His end has to be coming soon, right? He's like ninety thousand years old."

Marty snickered, lowered his head, and wrapped his arm over her shoulders. Phoebe fell into his side.

My people.

The vote for the park was taken. Most of the residents were in favor, with only six opposed. It would go through, much to the dismay of Arnett and the old geezer posse.

The meeting lasted another thirty minutes. She passed the time engaging in one-liners with Marty and Coop and munching from the snack table. She was pleasantly surprised to see a tray of apple turnovers among the food. Even though they weren't quite as good as Karen's, they were appreciated. At the end of the meeting, Maria and her husband were invited up to the front of the room at Bailey's request.

Maria smiled. "I just wanted to thank everyone who has come in. We're so happy to be back and in business. It was a hard loss closing down a few years ago, and we appreciate the town supporting us." She smiled brightly, aiming her stare to the back of the room. "I know part of the deal was no public acknowledgement, so I won't out those who helped us." Her smile grew as she stared at the back of the room where the Ghosttown Riders sat. "We just want to thank you."

Phoebe jerked her head for the first time of the night to the back of the room. Maria was thanking the club? Most stayed even keeled, but a few, including the women, smiled back at Maria.

Marty leaned closer and whispered in her ear, "Heard the biker club threw in cash for the renovations and the start-up."

She whipped her head and widened her eyes. "Are you serious?"

He nodded with a small shrug.

"Heard that too."

She turned to find Coop next to her with Marley tucked into his side.

"Thanks, Maria, and the anonymous contributors," Bailey said. She was about to hit the gavel when Arnett shot up from his seat.

Arnett stood facing Bailey and the councilmen. "I oppose the park and demand another vote. I think we could use our town money more wisely than on a park which will encourage delinquency."

Town parks encouraged delinquency? She sighed and grabbed a pastry from the tray. With her body shifted to the back of the room, it gave her full view of all the attendees.

She bit into her chocolate éclair at the precise moment she locked eyes with Kase. He was seated in the same position as he'd been the first night she set eyes on him. With her recent rejection, it should have been easy to turn away. She had made a complete fool of herself. She got drunk, divulged information about herself, and threw herself at the president of a biker club.

Heat rose from her chest, up her neck, and spread across her face.

"Anyone?" The familiar voice yanked her from her daze, thankfully. For some reason unknown to even her, Phoebe raised her hand.

"Thank you, Phoebe." Bailey said.

She spun around to face the mayor. From Bailey's expression, whatever Phoebe just did made her excited. She eyed the folks seated near the front. She furrowed her brows. *Why was Mary giving me the thumbs up?*

"Oh hell, what did I do?"

Coop snorted. "You just offered to be the chairperson for the parks committee."

She groaned and rolled her eyes at the ensuing snickers. At least she was fighting for a cause Arnett was against. That alone made it worthwhile.

A loud, sharp crack sounded through the room.

"Meeting is over," Bailey said.

The meeting ended abruptly, and everyone began filing outside. Phoebe made a point of blending in with the crowd as she walked out the door and into the parking lot. As luck would have it, she was directly behind Arnett.

As if he felt her presence, he spun around, narrowing his gaze. "Don't trust you behind me."

Phoebe couldn't resist. He was making it too easy. "You shouldn't, Arnett." She raised her brows and smiled.

"You threatening me?" He straightened to his full height, which towered over her. "Could have you arrested again."

"For what?" She snorted. "Walking? Is that a crime now in Ghosttown?"

"You shouldn't be here. No one wants you here."

She burst out laughing. It was his own delusional bullshit, or wishful thinking. If there was any resident the town would love to see go far away, it was him, not her.

"No, *you* don't want me here." She sighed. It had all gone too far. As neighbors, they needed to call a truce. However, Arnett was impossible.

"I apologized, Arnett. I said I was sorry for everything that happened six months ago." She inhaled a breath. "You don't want to accept it, there's not much more I can do." She smirked and cocked her head. "I was an asshole who went to extremes with an *asshole* who baited me." She shrugged.

Fuck you, Arnett. He needed to own his part in what went down.

His face transformed, and she wasn't sure she'd ever seen anyone turn that bright shade of red. She tightened her lips to keep from smiling.

"Being an asshole ain't no crime," the graveled voice spouted from behind her. Phoebe turned to find an unfamiliar older man standing two feet away. "I been all over this goddamn country, been an asshole in every single state, and never did time for it." His brow arched, reminding her of someone she couldn't seem to place. "Other shit, though. Assault, attempted murder, but never for being an asshole."

Phoebe bit back her chuckle and eyed the older man.

"Then you two have a lot in common," Arnett sneered. "Criminals of both your kind aren't welcome here."

Phoebe balled her hands and sent Arnett a heated glare.

"I never assaulted a man who didn't deserve it." The gruff man stepped closer.

Phoebe aimed her amused grin at Arnett. "Me neither."

Arnett turned quickly, eyeing her with a harsh scowl. If he

made a move, she'd be ready, though she doubted he had it in him. Arnett was all talk.

"You," the man snapped, gaining Phoebe's and Arnett's attention. "Get the fuck out of here and leave her alone." He squinted. "I know your type. Pussy, going after someone you think you can intimidate. Makes you a weak fucker."

Phoebe's mouth dropped open. Her immediate thought was *why am I not filming this?*

"And I know your type, Jack." Arnett shook his head and curled his lip in disgust. "Years later and you still haven't changed."

Phoebe flicked her gaze between the men. Arnett spoke with familiarity, leading her to believe they knew each other. She glanced over at Jack, whose brows furrowed, scowling at Arnett.

"I know you?"

Arnett curled his lip. "Same old arrogant son of a bitch."

Phoebe widened her eyes in shock. Apparently, there was a history between these two. There were certainly bitter memories on Arnett's side.

Jack barked out a laugh, which caught Phoebe off guard.

"I can't remember ya, but I figure I kicked the shit outta ya at one time or fucked your woman. Either way, it don't matter. You probably deserved whatever punishment I handed ya." Jack turned to Phoebe and shook his head. "Weak fuckers piss me off."

Arnett sputtered while stepping back. "Who the hell do you think you are, speaking to me..." Whatever he was going to say was interrupted.

"I don't think, I know. I'm the man who's gonna beat your ass from here to fucking Main Street then piss on your grave, you don't get the fuck outta my sight in two seconds. You hear me, motherfucker." His face burned red and his lips contorted, leaving no doubt it wasn't an idle threat.

He held up his finger and barked. "One..."

Phoebe had no idea what Arnett was doing since her eyes were trained on the snarling man next to her. While she wasn't opposed to seeing Arnett get his ass kicked down Main Street, having these two seniors fist fight in the parking lot would not do the town any good. She stepped in front of him and held up her hands.

"Let's all calm down."

"Pussy," the man muttered, shaking his head. Phoebe glanced over to catch Arnett speed walking through the parking lot. She was actually impressed. She'd never seen Arnett move so fast.

She turned back to the find the man a step closer with his lip curling as his gaze trailed down her body. "Assault, huh?"

She nodded. "I'm a lot more dangerous than I look."

His gaze shot up, and he grinned. "Back in my day, we'd a called you a spitfire."

Phoebe laughed. "Which is so much better than now where I'm considered a psycho bitch."

The man burst out laughing, catching the attention of the entire parking lot. Or maybe he had had it the whole time when she was in the middle of her confrontation with Arnett. Either way, she'd just made a new friend.

KASE STOOD next to the exit of the town hall, taking a drag from his cigarette and watching. He'd clocked her the second she walked through the doors, and had eyes on her the entire time. She was different tonight, quieter and more reserved. He didn't like it.

She was avoiding him. However, it seemed another Reilly man was getting in with her. He stepped forward on the edge of the landing, watching his old man taking Phoebe's back. His Pop had always been protective when it came to women. Little did Jack know, she was fully capable of handling Arnett.

His dad bellowed out a laugh and leaned closer to Phoebe, who was smiling. He was too far away to hear them, but his old man seemed in his element flirting with her.

The Enemy

Kase carried a lot of Jack's traits. Flirting wasn't one of them. Where his father had always been sweet on the girls, Kase had a harder approach. If he wanted her, she naturally submitted. He couldn't remember a time when he sweet talked anyone. It wasn't how he was built. Kindness came in short and rare spouts for him. His brother had inherited the softer side of Jack, Kase got all the piss and vinegar.

"Jack's fucking up my chances with her."

Kase snorted and glanced over to Gage, who was smirking. *As if you'd get a fucking shot with her, asshole.* She made it clear exactly where her interests lay the other night. On Kase. He fought against sharing a smug smile.

"Why don't you go over and tell him to back off?"

Gage chuckled. "'Cause I enjoy breathing. Jack would slit my throat if I go in and mess with his game." He paused. "She still up for grabs, or are you claiming that sweet ass?"

Kase clenched his jaw, dropping his gaze to her tight pants. Her round ass curved perfectly in the tight denim. Her taste, warm whiskey, and her soft fucking lips. Kase didn't have many regrets in life, but there were a few. He was currently staring at one.

Phoebe cocked her head with a soft smile aimed at his father, listening to whatever the old man was saying. *Fucking beautiful.*

He could feel Gage's stare and was relieved not to have to answer him when his phone rang. He jutted his chin and started off down the steps toward his bike.

"Yeah."

"No, we don't fucking miss you."

Kase snorted. While bikers and cops usually didn't mix, he had a mutual respect for Carter Ross. He'd helped him out on some intel in the past. While Kase was a firm believer in staying loyal to the brothers and never snitching or working with law enforcement, there were certain people the rules didn't apply to. Those who preyed on women and children didn't get respect of the club. When Carter had reached out to him a few times, Kase had used his underground connections to help out. In turn, Carter had become an ally to the club.

Kase had reached out to Carter a few days before Phoebe arrived in town.

"Sorry it took me so long to get back to you, been swamped here. How's it going, man?"

"Good. Getting settled."

Carter laughed. "Still can't believe the club moved."

Blacksburg had been home to the Ghosttown Riders for quite a few years. There were aspects of living in a bigger city Kase missed. The trade-off was worth it.

"Need something from you."

Carter's heavy sigh echoed through the receiver. "Ah fuck, I knew this wasn't a social call."

Kase smirked. "Just need information on a woman."

"Kase," Carter warned.

"You know me fucking better than that. Just need details."

Kase eyed Phoebe, who was walking toward her car with Jack following closely. Originally, he'd reached out to Carter for more information when he needed an angle to work and force her hand at selling her property. *Originally*. Now, it was personal. He wanted everything on her for the sole purpose of knowing more about her.

"I got your word, nothing happens to her?"

"Yeah."

There was a long pause and sigh. "Give me her name."

Kase licked his lips, watching as she waved to Jack and got into her car. "Phoebe Shaw."

"Wait, who?" Carter cleared his throat. "What's the name?"

Kase tore his gaze from her and furrowed his brows. Carter's response seemed off. "Phoebe Shaw. Lives in Ghosttown but didn't move in permanently until a few weeks ago. I need everything. Arrest record, court documents, financials. I want it all."

The silence struck him as odd.

He watched as his dad made his way over to the brothers

gathered by the entrance. Bailey offered to drive him back to the clubhouse, and they were waiting on him. There was a long, silent pause on the line, and Kase checked his phone to see if he'd hung up.

"Carter," he snapped when he didn't receive a response.

"Uh yeah."

Something was off.

"I'll uh, work on it and get back to you in a few days."

"Okay. Later." He hung up and shoved his phone in his pocket.

Chapter 7

A week had passed since her last encounter with Kase. It proved harder than she expected to avoid him as neighbors living in an extremely small town. With all the members riding around town. she found herself on high alert every time a motorcycle drove down Main Street.

Today, however, there was nothing she could do about a run in. She would be spending some time on his territory. A run in was almost inevitable. If not for Bailey and her unwavering love and affection, she wouldn't be stepping foot on the Ghosttown Riders' property.

Unfortunately, she accepted the invitation before the incident with Kase. Phoebe sighed, grabbing her jacket from the arm of the couch while shoving her phone in her back pocket. Maybe if she'd mentioned her slight indiscretion to Bailey, things would have been different. The idea of raining on anything Bailey planned wasn't doable. She'd take her licks and motor on through. *Not the first time I've embarrassed myself, won't be the last.*

She yanked the door closed before crossing over the large patch of grass up to the fence. She weaved her body through, getting hung up on a piece of wood. A swift struggle and she was on enemy territory. She rolled her eyes and straightened her shoulders, prepping herself to see Kase. Hopefully, he'd ignore her, and they could forget their encounter ever happened. She snorted. *I won't be forgetting that kiss any time soon.* Their moment, though brief, had played over and over in her head, especially at night.

As she approached, she noticed Bailey and a few others circled in front of the house, off to the side in the yard. When Bailey caught sight of her, her face lit up, and she extended her hand for an enthusiastic wave. Phoebe smiled and started toward the group. She'd seen two of the them at the town meeting. The older woman and the one holding the baby she didn't recognize.

"I live the closest, and I'm the last one here." She snickered.

"I thought maybe you got lost." Bailey pulled her in for a hug. While she'd had plenty of friends from her old life, some remained, other friendships had run their course. Hers and Bailey's was special. Mostly because of who Bailey was.

Phoebe stepped back and waved to the women eyeing her. "Hey there."

Bailey grasped her hand, tugging her forward. "Everyone, this is Phoebe." Bailey pointed and did introductions down the line. "This is Meg, Marissa, and baby Cora. Macy and Cheyenne."

Macy stepped forward. "Can I just thank you for your entertaining performance at the town meeting?" She giggled. "I told Rourke I'm only going back if you're there." She side-glanced Bailey and smirked. "No offense, Bails."

Bailey chuckled. "None taken, I always enjoy them more when Phoebe shows up."

Cheyenne smiled and extended her hand. "Ditto to Macy's sentiment. You should charge admission." She winked. "I'd pay."

Phoebe felt an instant ease and shrugged. "Just doing my part to keep the town amused. Plus, I just can't seem to help myself with Arnett."

Meg stepped closer and eyed Phoebe. "From what I hear, he's an asshole. I might have to make it to one of these meetings." She smirked. "It's all Mace and Chey talk about."

The group laughed, and Phoebe let all her tension go as Macy walked them through the set up around the yard. Both she and Cheyenne seemed to have everything set with food, drinks, and decorations. Phoebe hung back, watching Bailey gleam with all the details. She considered Bailey one of her closest friends but loved seeing her with the other women. It seemed every one of them appreciated the true beauty of Bailey.

They were rounding the back yard near the fire pit when Marissa dropped back, evening her strides with Phoebe. Her baby girl curled into her chest was adorable. She hadn't spent much time around babies though she'd always loved kids.

"Bailey said you're moving here permanently?"

Phoebe nodded. "Yeah. I've had the house for about seven years, using it as a weekend getaway every few months." She sighed. "Just moved all my stuff a few weeks ago."

"I live in Turnersville." She raised her brows in thought and grinned. "Bailey comes down once a week." She gestured to her baby. "My husband insists I get some time away. Bailey and I do lunch, some shopping. Come along with her next time."

Phoebe smiled. "Absolutely, I'd love that. Caden's wife, right?" Bailey had mentioned Marissa quite a bit. It seemed they'd become very close. "That makes you Kase's sister-in-law?"

She seemed taken aback by the question, almost on edge. It wavered, and Marissa smirked. "He's not as bad as he seems."

It was a funny response. Phoebe pressed her lips together and nodded. "Really?"

Marissa grinned and then burst out laughing. "Okay, so maybe he is what he seems." She paused, and her features relaxed into a solemn smile. "He's an amazing uncle."

Phoebe laughed as they continued to follow the women in through the back door. She held the door open for Marissa and followed her inside. *Finally, I'm getting a look.* She glanced to her right, which was empty, with several closed doors. A look to the left revealed the same, though at the end, double doors were opened, giving her a glimpse of what seemed to be a game room.

She caught the edge of a pool table, and from her stance, she saw two dart boards on the wall next to a small bar.

She started forward, realizing most of the group had continued on while Marissa was standing a few feet ahead waiting on her.

"Never been here?"

Phoebe shook her head.

She pointed to where Phoebe had been looking. "That's basically a hang-out room with pool tables, pub tables, and a bar." She arched a brow. "And a stripper pole with a tiny stage."

Phoebe laughed. "I'd expect nothing less from an MC."

Marissa chuckled and jerked her chin to the room. "Want to have a look?"

It was a loaded question. How could she say no? She nodded before she could even think, and Marissa was walking her into the open room. There were a few members who stopped what they were doing and glanced up.

"Hope we're not bothering you guys," Marissa said.

Phoebe peered through the room, noticing a few familiar faces. One in particular. Gage had been a man she'd seen before. Beyond sexy in the bad boy sense and unbelievably flirty. He hopped off his stool and advanced toward them.

"Hot women are always welcome, you know that, Riss." He may have been talking to Marissa, but his gaze was zoned in on Phoebe. The man did wonders for her ego. His stare bore through her, making her feel as though she was the only woman in the room. She wasn't. In fact, there was a topless dancer with fabulous boobs swinging on the pole in the corner of the room.

Phoebe smiled coyly at Gage and walked around the pub tables lined up against the wall. It was giving her a better view of the gorgeous brunette sliding down the pole. Phoebe stopped a few feet away, and when the dancer glanced over, she smiled.

"You wanna give it a shot, honey?"

Marissa slowly angled her head, glancing over her shoulder at Gage, who was standing near the makeshift bar. *Yum*. Long blond hair tied back at the nape of his neck, striking blue eyes gleaming back at her with a mischievous smirk. Gage was a good time, she guessed. *And mine for the taking, if I want.*

Do I want him? She ducked her head, giving her attention to the woman on the pole. Her moves were graceful and seductive, her technique was flawless, but her grip was off. She was obviously not a professional, though she did work the pole as though she'd been trained. Phoebe moved closer.

"Can I give you a helpful hint? It'll make your spin smoother and your thighs and ass will thank me for it."

She cocked her head in slight confusion. "Okay."

"If you hook your ankle on the pole, you'll glide easier and the flow will be more natural."

She wasn't sure what she had expected. A possible backlash? The woman remained silent for a brief second before stepping back, grasping her hands on the pole above her head, and forming a spin, taking Phoebe's instructions. The move was effortless as she rounded the metal bar in a sensual dance.

She stopped once her foot hit the ground and glanced over her shoulder, winking at Phoebe. "Thank you."

Phoebe nodded and turned back to the small group. All eyes were on her, including a new pair at the door. It was inevitable she'd see him. It was his house. She had expected his presence, but the intensity in his dark eyes and his harsh features aimed in her direction was unexpected.

"Well, now, I wouldn't have pegged you as a stripper."

The comment tugged her out of her heated eye fucking with Kase. She turned to face Gage. He was thoroughly amused.

She licked her lips. "I'm not. I took a few classes, though. It's an amazing workout."

Gage's gaze travelled down her body, appreciating her hard-earned classes. "I can see that."

Phoebe chuckled, glancing over at Kase who was staring back at her. He lacked the carefree desire Gage was sending her. Kase seemed as though he was at a crossroads between wanting to kick her ass out or bending her over and fucking her with reckless abandon. Her stomach flipped and her breathing grew heavy.

"I should get going," Marissa said, and Phoebe rushed forward.

"Me too, let's walk out together."

Marissa nodded, and Phoebe noticed her gaze shift to Kase.

Phoebe turned and waved to the men and shuffled through the doorway following Marissa. As she passed Kase, the smoke from his cigarette drifted in front of her. She only got two feet into the hall before Kase stalked forward, advancing in front of her and halting Marissa.

"I'll follow you. Gotta pick up Pop," he said with his gaze stuck on Marissa. "Gimme five, and we'll head out."

She nodded and glanced over her shoulder, smiling. "Phoebe, I'll get your number from Bailey? Maybe we can all get together soon? You guys can come over to the house."

"Yes. I'd love that." She held up her finger, pointing at Marissa. "But promise me you'll let me hold that baby."

Marissa chuckled. "Absolutely. I'll even let ya change a diaper." She winked and headed down the hall. She had just turned the corner when Phoebe moved forward to follow. Kase grasped her forearm. It all happened so fast. One second, she was in the hall and the next she was ushered into a room and the door was slamming behind her. Her back was forced against the wall and Kase loomed over her. He gripped her arms, making it impossible for her to move.

"What the fuck are you doing?"

Phoebe tried to yank her arm, but his grip remained tight. "Bailey invited me. You got a problem, take it up with her. Now get your hands off me. Unless you're looking to be my next assault victim." She snarled her last sentence.

She wasn't even sure where her voice had come from.

He growled, pulling her closer, and her breasts grazed his chest. This was a far cry from the man who bailed on her when she offered a night in her bed. The heat rose on her cheeks, and she glanced down at his chest. His president patch stared back at her.

"Don't got a problem with you in my house," he growled. "Got a problem with you not saying shit to me while you're in it."

She glanced up through her lashes. "What do you want me to say, Kase?" She raised her brows.

His dark eyes blackened, and she felt the air between them thicken. She drew in a breath, needing more oxygen. His head curved slightly, and for a brief second, she could envision him leaning closer and kissing her. She licked her lips with anticipation, and his gaze dropped, following her tongue circling over her upper lip.

He leaned closer. *Kiss me.* "You'd regret getting in bed with me," he snarled with an angered tone. She lowered her hand over his chest and felt the spike in his heart under the pads of her fingers.

"You'll regret it, Kase. Not me," she whispered.

He scoffed, and she expected him to push away. Instead he tugged her closer, and his body slid into hers. He was doing a shit job concealing his attraction to her, and she shifted closer, gripping his shirt. What the hell was she doing?

His warm breath fanned over her face, and she jutted her chin upward. *Kiss me.* She was silently begging him. Her hands wandered over his chest feeling the outline of his muscles through the thin cotton.

"You like it from behind, Phoebe?" His voice rumbled and her panties moistened.

He jerked her around, pressing her chest into the door as she gasped for a breath. His body flattened against her back, and she was sandwiched between the door and his body. His hands were rough as he draped over her waist and up her chest to cup her breasts into a tight squeeze. Gentle was not what she'd expect from him nor would she get. *Fine by me.* His fingers sifted over her shirt and bra, pinching her hard nipples through the material. Even with layers between them, she felt the need and desire.

She rolled her hips, pressing against his cock. The hardened member pushing against her ass. He wanted this as much as she did. They were both crossing enemy lines.

Her hands gripped the wood beneath her fingertips, and she rocked her backside into his growing cock. His hands gripped her hips in a tight hold, his fingers digging into her flesh through her T-shirt.

"Don't be a tease, Kase," she panted.

He growled in her ear, sending shivers down her spine and a moisture seeping into her panties. He remained silent, and another snarky retort was on her lips, but his hand flitting around her and dipping into her jeans had her gasping for a breath. *Lower, lower, lower.* As if he heard her silent command, his hand wedged between the seam of her denim and trailed down her pelvic flesh. She wiggled her hips, making room for his hand. The man needed no help. His finger skimmed over her clit, and she jolted forward.

It was as if she hadn't been touched in years. She rested her forehead against the wood door, savoring the feel of the pad of his finger over her clit. His motions were lazy and teasing. She arched her hips for a deeper contact.

"No," he snapped in a harsh whisper. He gripped her hair, pulling her head to lay across his shoulder. She moaned in a whisper when she felt the direct contact on her clit. Her eyes rolled into the back of her head from the friction and electric tension. He circled her bundle of nerves, and her breathing labored. It was a delicious warping sensation. It was almost too much to take. Too much feeling; she was a live wire set to burst into flames.

"Kase." She hadn't meant to call for him. She hadn't meant for any of this. She swiveled her hips wanting more. He took her cue and lowered his finger, slowly dipping between her folds.

She turned her head, bumping against his chin. He wouldn't deny her a kiss. Right?

His mouth descended on hers with a hurried, desperate need,

his tongue tangled with hers, and his hot breath filtered past her lips. *Yes. Fuck, yes.* Her fingernails scraped down the wood.

The harsh knock from the door set her back against his chest.

"Kase, prospects are here."

His finger stilled inside her, and she clamped her core, tightening her hold and trapping him inside her. She was being greedy and aggressive. *I don't care, I wanna come, dammit.*

"They gotta head out in five, man, if they wanna make the delivery time." She pried her eyes open, staring back at the wood door. Her heartbeat drummed erratically. His hand slowly pulled from inside her, slipping out of her pants. So much built up sexual tension, it was cruel to end this way. She turned, bumping her arm into his chest. With Kase standing so close, there left little room to maneuver.

She glanced up through her lashes, settling back against the door.

"Gimme five." Kase growled and gripped the hem of her jeans, ripping open the snap and the zipper in a flash. It happened so quick she wasn't even sure what he was doing until his warm, rough palm slid against her pelvis and deep between her thighs. She gasped at the sudden intrusion. He was knuckles deep, two fingers, straight into her pussy.

He thrust inside her in deep and long, even strokes. *God, yes.* Kissing him was off the table. She was panting too hard. She gripped his forearms, pinching her nails through his skin, and arched her hips.

She knocked her head against the wall, closing her eyes and riding the longest, hottest, toe-curling orgasm of her life. Her legs threatened to give out and began to shake.

She wasn't sure if it was the built-up sexual desire for him or just him alone, but she was spent.

She tried to gain control of her breathing and opened her eyes to find him staring at her. His hard face showed no softness, no crack in his hard exterior. Nothing.

Well, of course, he didn't get to come.

Phoebe glanced down at his jeans, a bulge straining against his zipper. She reached out, but his fingers wrapped around her wrist in a binding hold. She jerked her head and watched as he pulled his hand from her pants and backed up. He let go of her wrist and jerked his chin for her to move.

It's over? Surely, he would want to finish what he started. Right? The scene was a first for her. She'd never had a man turn her down. Except Kase. Twice now. His gaze narrowed when she remained blocking his exit.

"It's a power thing with you, isn't it?"

His brow arched, and a slight twitch in his lip was his answer.

Asshole.

She shifted to the side and watched him leave the room, not even sparing her a glance. The door closed behind him, and she balled her fists.

She closed her eyes. What the hell was this ridiculous attraction to him? Yeah, looks-wise he was sexy, rugged, dangerous. Everything she was never attracted to. Maybe it was the chase. Whatever it had been, she needed to steer clear of him. Her only interaction might happen when the party happened. Other than that, she was staying as far away from Kase Reilly as humanly possible.

Asshole.

WATCHING her walk away was harder than he'd thought it would be. He waited a brief moment for the relief to sink in. It didn't. It was a moment of weakness. Having her in his space, among his club, in her tight, curve hugging jeans. *Fuck.* He'd shut it down before it could go any further, but he was teetering on the edge. Getting too involved with her was not an option. Yet he couldn't seem to stay away. She interpreted it as a power thing, and he'd let her think that. The last thing he needed was her knowing she got to him.

Kase dragged his hand over his face. She was his biggest enemy of all. The more time spent with her and he'd lose himself, and he wasn't willing to risk it. Thirty-eight years on this earth and he'd never fallen under a woman's spell. *Fuck me.* He needed to get laid. He needed a whore to suck his dick, and then fuck her faceless body and find an empty release. It was who he was, what he'd always been. *Until a gorgeous blonde-haired, blue-eyed vixen showed up at the town meeting.*

He stalked through the clubhouse and ignored the stares from Gage and Dobbs. It would have been easier if not for Gage's fucking mouth.

"Her unclaimed status change yet?"

Kase gritted his teeth and spun around. The heat rose from his chest. He had no claim over her. If Gage wanted a shot, he could take it. "Fuck off, Gage." He eyed his men, who seemed caught off guard. Dobbs raised his brows while Gage sported a smirk that Kase wanted to swipe off his mouth with his goddamn fist.

"I'll take that as a no." Gage snickered and glanced over at Dobbs, who seemed as though he wanted no part of this conversation. He was the smarter of the two apparently.

Kase opened his mouth and caught movement from down the hall. She'd exited his room, and he watched, expecting her to exit from the main entrance. Once she breached the hall, she turned left and snuck out the back.

"I'm just gonna go and make sure she gets home." Gage shifted forward, and Kase reacted without even thinking. He gripped his arm.

"Why the fuck aren't you down at the junkyard?"

"Got the prospects working it."

"No!" Kase snapped, his anger spiking to a level that tightened his grasp on Gage's arm. "Ain't gonna watch the yard go under just so you can get your dick wet." He snarled and moved closer. "You want her pussy, you get that shit on your time, not fucking club time."

It was a fair statement; however, his tone had been the dead giveaway. There was no denying he was holding Gage back. It was evident to all of them, though neither Gage nor Dobbs had the balls to call him out on it. It didn't stop Gage from laughing. He yanked his arm from Kase's hold.

Kase headed toward the back door when he heard his name. He glanced over his shoulder, staring at Gage, who raised his brows and curled his lips. *I'm gonna fucking punch this bastard.*

He jerked his chin toward Phoebe's house. "You're showing your hand, motherfucker." He grinned. "All your fucking cards."

Kase balled his hands and cracked his neck, turning away without another word.

The ride to Caden's house had been too long. Twenty minutes to stew in his bullshit with Phoebe had him itching to get out of the confines of his own mind.

He pulled in next to Marissa's truck and got out. She grabbed the bag from the trunk as he was walking around her bumper.

"Let me help," he said, not bothering to wait on her response. He ignored the bag she thrust toward him and angled between her and the door. She chuckled and stepped back. Marissa knew exactly how he was going to help. He leaned forward and unbuckled the latch, sliding his hand under her padded butt and stretching his forearm to scoop Cora out of her car seat. It was one fluid motion that came naturally. While some men hesitated, Kase was comfortable with babies.

He cradled her into the crook of his arm and straightened. When he turned, Marissa was smiling and shaking her head.

"You're a good uncle."

He arched his brow and slammed the door before walking up the front yard.

"You'd make a good dad too, Kase."

He sighed and opened the door, jerking his chin for her to go inside. Marissa was a pain in the ass. He loved her, though he'd never mentioned it to her. She knew. Since her arrival to Turnersville, she was able to get inside with him. Not an easy task for anyone who wasn't family or part of his club.

"Ever think maybe you'll have kids?"

"No." His response was quick, void of any emotion. Children weren't part of his life. As the son of a president, he knew what his childhood entailed. He wasn't looking to strap that on anyone.

"I think you will," she whispered and passed by, dropping her bag onto the floor. "I'd make a really good aunt."

Kase ignored the comment.

Caden was in the kitchen and turned when he heard them come in. Marissa immediately circled her arms around his stomach and lifted, kissing him. Kase pulled out a chair and sat, hoisting Cora in his arm. He glanced down but held back his smile. Too much affection witnessed by Marissa and she'd be thinking more baby thoughts about him. He was getting enough shit from his brothers about Phoebe.

He started a slow, steady rock, and she opened her mouth, yawning before turning to the side and closing her eyes with her tiny face curling into his chest.

"I'll take her, man."

He furrowed his brows and looked up to Caden, who was standing next to him. "You fucking live with her. You hold her all the time." He rolled his eyes when Caden smirked and held his hand up. "Wanna be useful, get me a beer."

Rissa laughed and took a seat across from him.

"Phoebe seems really nice."

Oh fuck me.

"Who's Phoebe?" Caden asked while in the fridge.

"Kase's neighbor. She's helping plan Bailey's party, so you'll get to meet her soon." Marissa meshed her lips with a playful gleam in her eye. "It's weird. I expected to see her walk out when I was waiting at the car for you. I never did."

Kase grabbed the beer Caden handed him and pinned his glare on his little brother.

"She pretty?" Caden was asking him, but it was Marissa who answered with an amused chuckle.

"Very pretty." Marissa smirked. "Don't you think, Kase?"

Kase knew where this was going and refused to feed into it.

He jerked his gaze to Caden. "Where the fuck is Pop?"

Caden snorted, shaking his head, and started toward the hallway. When he caught his sister-in-law's gleaming smile, he scowled.

"What?"

She shrugged. "Nothing, Kase." She bit her lip and lowered her gaze to the baby, smiling. "Nothing at all."

"Hey, Fruity Fucking Pebbles, whatever you're thinking, ya got it wrong."

Most women would have been offended by the nickname. Marissa took it as a term of endearment, and although Kase would never admit it, it was intended to be with Riss. She folded her elbows and leaned on the table, smiling. "Okay, Kase."

He heard his father coming, barreling down the steps. Kase inhaled, prepping himself to handle Jack.

"Gimme that baby," Jack snapped from behind him. Kase sighed and stood up to face his father.

No greeting. Kase maneuvered Cora into his father's arms. It always struck Kase as odd, as he was sure it did for Caden, how truly gentle and soft their old man was with her. Jack stroked her head lightly and shifted on his feet, rocking her. He'd never seen this side of his dad. Even when Trevor was a baby, his father had still been president of the club. He was good to Trevor, showed him more attention than Kase or Cade had ever seen growing up, but he'd never been soft. Not as Jack was with Cora.

His dad bent closer, swiping his lips across her forehead, and smiled. Even though Kase and Caden were standing on either side of him, he walked to Marissa and handed her over. When Jack turned, all the softness was gone, and he widened his eyes.

"Are we going or what?" He pushed through Kase and Caden. He reached down, grabbed his bag, and started to the door. "See ya later, Coll." It was his only goodbye, just for Marissa.

"Deep down he really does love you both."

Kase jerked his head to Marissa in unison with Caden. Kase

was well aware Marissa held some guilt that their dad had been kinder to her than them. His brother snorted and rolled his eyes.

"Yeah, sweetheart, we're really feeling the love."

Kase chuckled and slapped his brother's shoulder. "See you in a week."

Kase started out the door. It was time to bring Pop home to the clubhouse.

Chapter 8

It had been a long and stressful couple of days. Mostly it had been self-induced. She was late on her deadline. Her mind had been out of whack, too much weighing on it, she supposed. She'd thrown herself into her project the last few days. It seemed her ideas and creativity had taken a turn, and thoughts were coming slower than they once had. *I suck.* Self-loathing had never been part of her work, but it seemed it had reared its ugly head.

She'd spent the last two days working on her project for the design company. She wasn't exactly sure if she'd even slept. The assignment wasn't a specifically large job, but she found herself second guessing all her decisions. A lot was riding on this. If the client didn't like it, she wouldn't get more contracts. Lack of confidence was new for her.

Too much.

The soft knock at her door had her lifting her head with her gaze darting around the room. *Am I hallucinating now?* Her door rumbled, and she glanced over. What time was it? She glanced down at her phone. It was half past nine, not exactly an ungodly hour, though she rarely got announced guests past six.

She got up and made her way to the door. "Who is it?"

"An ex-con who swiped a bottle of whiskey. Top shelf, darlin', so open the fucking door."

She grabbed the knob, smiling. *I know that voice.* When she opened the door, Jack was standing on her porch, living up to his word, his right hand strapped around the neck of a bottle of whiskey and his other lifting to his mouth and taking a drag from his cigarette.

He might as well have had a halo and wings. Jack was saving her day. Her finances wouldn't solve themselves, but the whiskey was sure to help her forget, even if just for the night. She widened the door and gestured.

"Get in here. I love when guests come bearing gifts."

He laughed, tossing his cigarette off her deck and bustling through the door. He held up the whiskey.

"Jack, I think we're kindred spirits."

He chuckled. "Get your sweet ass into the cabinet and get us some glasses. We'll celebrate."

She sauntered to her small kitchen. The living area was open and connected. She glanced back, watching Jack check out her place. She had unpacked most of her things. It wasn't where she wanted it to be for visitors just yet. By the look on Jack, he didn't seem to mind. She reached up and grabbed two glasses.

"What are we celebrating?"

He turned with a smirk. "Fucking breathing, darlin'."

She walked over with a grin. Jack's spirit was exactly what she needed tonight. "I'll drink to that."

He snorted. "At my age, ya drink to anything."

She placed the glasses on the table, and Jack poured a hefty fill to each. He wasn't lying about the top shelf. She smiled and grabbed a glass, lifting it for a short clink against his and taking a sip.

"So, Jack?"

He was glancing around her house and then stopped at her.

"You live around here?" She sipped her drink and licked her lips. "I thought I knew everyone in this town."

He jerked his head to the left. "Staying at the clubhouse."

She raised her brows. It didn't shock her he'd be associated, though he did seem older than most of the members she'd met. "Are you an ex-biker?"

His face turned red, and his brows dipped in a harsh scowl. "No fucking ex about it, and I'm gonna let that go 'cause I'm thinking ya don't know shit about the life."

Shit! She had pissed off Jack. She held up her hands in defense and offered a warm smile.

"You're right, don't know shit, Jack. Sorry."

He eyed her, and the corner of his lip curled. He squinted and angled his glass in her direction. "Gonna let it slide. You got a great ass, it works for ya." He winked and strolled through her living room.

She bit back her laugh. She always thought of her ass as too big, but it seemed to save her this time.

"You're a member, Jack, of the Ghosttown Riders?"

"President for nineteen years."

"Thought Kase was president?"

Jack coughed a graveled laugh. "Only 'cause I stepped down. That fucker is lucky I handed him the gavel." He sighed. "Left it in good hands with another Reilly."

She furrowed her brows. "Are you related?"

"He's my boy."

What. The. Fuck. Jack was Kase's dad. She eyed him carefully. It was hard to see any resemblance. He stared back at her and scowled. *There it is.* It was all in the eyes.

Jack jerked his chin. "Let's do a fire. Grab the whiskey, sweets."

For reasons unknown to her, she smiled and followed Jack Reilly out the door.

WHILE THE REST of the guys were partying in the bar, drinking and fucking, he was holed up in the conference room with schedules splayed out over the table. The legitimate businesses seemed to need more time dedicated to them. The truck runs for deliveries and parts pick-up had been doled out each month, and it was a pain in the ass. The money wasn't anything to scoff at, though. As predicted, the club was pulling in a lot of cash. The members had sacrificed a lot when his vision of heading back to Ghosttown began. It was finally paying off.

They still weren't one hundred percent legit, and probably never would be. They continued their cash lending endeavor, which proved lucrative and low risk. Not all members participated. Rourke and Trax had opted out, but remained as muscle when they were needed. He understood it. They had their women and planned on families.

He tossed his pen down on the table and gripped the arms of his chair.

"Need a fucking drink." He got up and walked down the hall.

He scanned the room in search of his dad. Jack would be heading back to Caden's tomorrow night. It had been a fairly good week without many upsets. The members respected his father, as they should as a fucking president. Spending the week with Jack had given Kase a real-time view of his demise.

He sucked in a deep breath. *Fuck.*

It was a quieter night at the club. He halted at the bar entrance and glanced around the room. The last he'd seen Jack, he was at the bar bullshitting with Dobbs.

"Where the fuck is he?" Kase shouted, sending everyone at the bar jerking toward the doorway.

Joe, one of the prospects, perked up and almost dropped one of the girls who had been sitting on his lap. He turned, searching the bar for Jack. "He was here before."

Kase balled his fists. "I don't give a shit where he was before. Where the hell is he *now*?"

Nadia sauntered over with her head lowered and her eyes

glancing up through her lashes. "He snagged a bottle from the bar a few hours ago. Let me check his room. He's probably just hanging there or passed out." Her hand grazed his arm as she passed. It wasn't done in her usual sexual advancement. She was strictly trying to calm him.

She'd always been one of his favorites. Nadia was different, and even a cold bastard like himself could recognize it. Of all the girls, he'd spent the most time with her, but never getting too close.

Kase jerked his gaze to Joe, who was standing around looking like he was about to piss his pants.

"Go fucking find him," he barked, gaining the attention of the whole room. His glare followed all the faces of his brothers, including Gage, who was headed toward him.

"Kase?"

Her turned to find Nadia at the edge of the hallway. "He's not there."

"Motherfucker." He pushed past Gage and started to the door. He didn't look back, but he snapped at the room. "Fucking find him." With everyone looking, they were bound to find him, but if he'd taken off by foot, God only knows how far he could have gotten. Walking to town was feasible, but for an old man who didn't know his bearings, it was a dangerous situation.

Kase stormed out of the house, making his way across the lot to his bike. *How the fuck do you lose a hundred seventy-pound adult man?* Once Jack was found, he had plans to return and beat the shit out of Joe. He pounded the gravel and was a foot away from his bike when the orange glow from next door caught his gaze.

He'd purposely kept his distance. He had watched her place. Too much. She wasn't a creature of habit, some nights shutting down the lights at ten and other nights up until two in the morning.

He stretched his neck, catching two silhouettes outlined by the fire beyond her house. He clamped down on his teeth, feeling the shift in his molars. It was a good distance, but he could make out Phoebe and an unknown male figure by the fire.

"Motherfucker."

He may have held back with her, but somebody didn't. He narrowed his gaze, squinting his eyes. "Gotta be fucking kidding me."

He started through the high grass separating the properties. He gripped the top of the fence and swung his legs over effortlessly.

His steps slowed as he rounded her house.

Leave it to his old man to swipe *his* liquor and share it with the fucking enemy.

They were seated next to one another. His father's profile was lit up from the flames. He was resting back with his legs kicked out in front of him. Kase was having flashbacks to childhood. Sitting around the fire as a kid with Caden, his Pop, and all the club brothers. He'd always watched Jack, trying to replicate everything about him. He had hero worship back then.

As he got closer, he slowed his steps. Kase had obviously walked in mid conversation.

"Write her a letter."

His dad scoffed and waved his hand. "She ain't even a few months." She laughed, and Jack held up his phone. "This one right here, she's smarter than the rest of us, but she can't read."

He was always bragging on Caden's little girl. *Cora.* With good reason, she was something special. It seemed the whole fucking lot of Reilly men had bowed down to the newest member, including Kase himself.

Phoebe angled on her seat, tucking her feet underneath her. "No, not now. But," through the fiery glow, he saw her face soften, "someday."

"What the hell do I know about writing?"

"Write what ya feel. Tell her about all the things you want to do with her, stuff you want to teach her or show her." Phoebe smiled. "That way, if you're not here, she'll know all the big plans you had for you and her. It gives her something of you, let's her feel you, Jack." Phoebe took a sip from her glass and settled into the chair. "I think you should do it."

Kase watched the silent exchange between his Pop and Phoebe. He drew in a deep breath. Knowing the end was coming for his father was something Kase tried to block as much as possible. It would be a hard loss, especially for Riss, Trevor, and Cade. *And me.* Being the patriarch of their fucked-up, dysfunctional family, life would be different without Jack.

For as much as all of them knew Jack's days were numbered, Kase hadn't given much thought to Jack realizing it himself. But from the conversation he was hearing, he did. He knew he wasn't going to be around to watch Caden's baby grow up. Kase grasped the back of his neck, relieving some tension in his shoulders. They'd need a small fucking miracle for his dad to see Cora say her first word, which most likely would turn out to be *fuck*. The corner of his mouth curled thinking of how Riss would probably lose her shit and come for all of them, not knowing which one she overheard. *And Pop will miss that too.*

He eyed his father resting against the seat with the glow of the fire reflecting off his face. It had been a good day, and by the looks of it, it was going to end good for him.

Some days he was Pop, pissing insults, swearing at any man who was in his way, and showing the sweet side to Riss. Other days, the hard to watch ones, he didn't even know who he was or anyone around him. Kase hated those days. He preferred listening to Jack spew venomous rants on how Kase had made the Ghost-town Riders soft pussies, and back in his day, they raised hell, not fucking fundraisers. *At least he knows who I am on those days.*

Jack shook his head, laughing. "Back in my day, I would have tried to get you in my bed."

Kase smirked, shaking his head. Seventy years old, losing half his mind and on the verge of the end, and the old man was still making a play for the ladies. He glanced over at Phoebe, who was clearly amused. She cocked her head and smiled at his dad.

"Back in your day, I probably would have gone willingly, Jack."

Jack burst out laughing, followed by a soft giggle. He shifted his gaze to catch his dad lifting his glass above his head.

"Toast to you. To hot women with great asses and whiskey."

Phoebe raised her glass. "And to badass bikers with foul mouths and whiskey."

There was no denying the ease these two felt with one another. *My father drinking with the fucking enemy.*

Kase clenched his jaw and felt the tightness in his chest. The scene had taken an abrupt turn and pissed him off. How had she swindled herself into Jack's good graces? Something he hadn't managed to do in thirty-eight years. Jack had always been hard on him and Caden. Kase more so. It was rare they agreed on anything.

Kase couldn't remember the last time he'd sat around a fire, drinking whiskey and shooting the shit with his old man.

He stepped out from the side of the house, and he caught Phoebe glance over her shoulder. He was probably the last person she expected to see at her house. Her expression confirmed it.

He ambled forward and stopped a foot away from his father's seat. "Been looking for you."

He kept his gaze locked on Phoebe. He clenched his jaw when Jack glanced over his shoulder and shook his head. Dealing with his dad in front of her wasn't something he looked forward to.

Jack surprised him and stood without saying a word and stumbled closer to her chair.

"We'll do this again, darlin."

Phoebe gazed up with a grin. "I look forward to it, Jack." She winked, which sent his old man walking off with a puffed-up chest and an ornery strut to the fence.

He watched him until he got to the fence and then whipped his head, glaring at Phoebe. "What the fuck do you think you're doing?"

Her mouth gaped, and she winced as if she'd been struck. He

was being an asshole. Yet he couldn't stop himself. Something about the exchange between her and his dad had set him off.

"Having whiskey by the fire with your dad." She arched her brow. "He's very friendly."

He stalked forward as she rose and side-stepped her chair.

"Stay the fuck away from my dad, you hear me?"

She flinched. "Kase, I just had a drink with him. You really think I'd hurt Jack?"

Don't do it. He was being such a bastard he couldn't even listen to himself.

"I know ya got a violent streak against the seniors around here, so stay the fuck away from him."

She gasped. "He came here, Kase."

"Yeah, and it's the last fucking time." He closed in on her. "You stay away from me, my family, and the fucking club, or you will have a problem."

"Don't you come over here and threaten me, asshole." She stopped herself, but Kase knew he'd struck a nerve. She drew in a breath. "I didn't do anything wrong. Jack came here, remember that." She held up her hands and shook her head. "Why are you so upset?"

"I'm not upset, I'm fucking pissed. I got my old man wandering out of the fucking house and coming over to hang out with your crazy ass. Don't need that shit."

She cocked her head. "My crazy ass?"

"Yeah," he barked. "Don't need you taking a swing at the old man if he says shit to set you off." It was a low blow. His anger was heating every word that came out of his mouth. He clenched his jaw. "Want nothing from you." He gazed down her body and cocked his brow. "Fucking nothing." It was a lie. Possibly the biggest he'd ever told.

He was sending a harsh, untrue message, and Phoebe was receiving it. She clamped her mouth with a pink blush crossing over her cheeks. She twisted her lips and glanced up with a devilish glare.

"Except my property, Kase. That you want." She had him there, and from the sinister spark in her eye, she knew it. "I suggest you get going before I'm forced to call the police. Trespassing is against the law, ya know. And I'm sure I'm not the only one standing here with a record for a *violent* past." She winked.

He was seething as he stepped back. His anger—for what, he didn't know—was being put on her, and she was feeling it. He was being himself. A bastard. He walked away and reached down to swipe the bottle, but it disappeared before he could grab it. He spun around and watched as she tossed it into the fire, and the flames shot up a few feet. He narrowed his gaze, and she smiled.

"It slipped." She sneered, and her eyes heated in anger. "Now, get the fuck off *my* property."

If she hadn't already been the enemy, he'd solidified their stance. He slowly walked away with her heated glare ripping through his back.

Chapter 9

Could it get any worse?

A looming deadline had her on edge, along with her fight with Kase. *Don't forget solely in charge of the parks committee.*

At least she had one bright spot at the moment. Phoebe sighed listening to her father on the other line. If ever a man had set a bar so high no other could reach, it was her dad. All positivity even at her lowest points.

"Got a deadline I'm not sure I'll meet." She drove her hand through her hair.

"You'll get it done, honey."

This man. Even at her lowest, when she knew she'd been an utter disappointment, he'd rallied her through the hard times. *My biggest hero I might not deserve.*

She sighed. "I'll talk to you soon."

"Hold up, honey."

She furrowed her brows. "What's wrong?"

"Nothing, just uh, wanna know if there's a reason you're not taking your brother's calls. Says he's been trying to get ya for a week."

"Really?" She feigned shock. Her dad saw through it.

"Phoebe."

She tightened her lips and punched the air, having a silent tantrum. What kind of grown man bitches to his dad to get his sister to call back? *My brother.*

"I'll call him back. Bye, Dad." She hung up and tossed her phone on the table.

She twisted her lips, staring down at her phone. She didn't say when she'd call him back.

At thirty-two years old, she shouldn't be calling her dad for advice, guidance, and a friggin' pep talk. What the hell had happened to her? Jared. It was an easy excuse, but truthfully, she'd allowed herself to get lost. It had been good for so long; she had missed when the tide had turned. It was easy to see it after the fact. During their marriage, she'd been clueless.

She peeked up when she heard the phone ring.

Phoebe glanced down at her cell. *Oh, hell no.* He was the last person on the planet she wanted to talk to. She closed her eyes and groaned. It was the same knee jerk reaction she always had when he called. How they were born from the same cloth boggled her mind. She eyed the phone and considered her options. He rarely called, as in once a year for her birthday. However, that had changed a week ago when he began blowing up her phone every day. If she didn't answer, she'd be fielding calls from her dad wondering why she was ignoring his calls. She grabbed the phone, walking over to the couch. Anytime they spoke, she felt the need to be comfortable.

"Like this wasn't planned," she muttered, inhaling a calm breath. She was going to need it. She curled into the sofa and answered.

"I was just thinking we don't talk enough."

"Shut up."

Typical Carter, always the asshole.

Phoebe laughed and settled into the couch. "And this is why. I just can't compete with your sunny disposition."

"Wanna explain to me how the hell you end up on a motorcycle gang's radar?"

He'd gotten her attention, and she shifted against the cushions. There was only one MC's radar she could have gotten on. Giving him the upper hand of confusion wouldn't fare well in her best interest. Neither would feigning naïveté.

"Well, we are neighbors."

"What?" he snapped.

She rolled her eyes. "Carter, I live in Ghosttown. You know this, it's not top secret." She snorted. "And even if it was classified information, I would think you, being a grade A detective, would have known." She smirked and tilted her head. "Maybe you're not as great as you think you are, big brother."

She knew of quite a few siblings who were best friends. It was the polar opposite of her and Carter. Separated by almost seven years, they were as opposite as anyone could imagine. Though he'd never admit it, she believed Carter resented her since birth.

"Yeah, in the same fucking town, not next door."

Why the hell did he care? Hell, it had been six months since they'd last spoken. It would have been longer had their dad not interfered.

"Hey, I was here first. I have no control where they build their house."

"You never learn, do you?" She heard the heavy condescending sigh. "Thirty-two years old and you still can't read people."

Son of a...

It was typical Carter. He was always the golden child in their family. It was sickening what a perfect asshole he was. He lived for showing off, and their parents fed off of it. In fairness, he'd always done well in school, he had goals, and for outward appearances, he was a model son. *Asshole.* She had to put up with him for her first eleven years of life. When he went off to college, her life enhanced. With the exception of holidays and summer breaks when he came home.

"I'm hanging up 'cause, as always, you're being a dick. And unlike when we were kids, I don't have to take it." She pulled the phone from her ear but was drawn back.

"No, you're gonna listen because I need to know what the hell you've gotten yourself into and try to bail you out *again*."

She would forever hold a secret grudge against her father for calling Carter after her altercation with Arnett. She would have preferred jail time than to be indebted to her brother.

"I didn't do anything."

"Then why is the president of the Ghosttown Riders blowing up my goddamn phone wanting me to check into you?"

She flicked her gaze across the room and held her breath. Why was Kase calling Carter about her?

"Kase called you?"

"Oh fuck, you're on a first name basis?"

"Uh, it sounds like you are too, hypocrite. Why the hell does a president of a *gang* call a lead detective for intel on someone? Huh, Carter? Maybe this isn't the first time you've helped him out?" She sneered. "Playing dirty cop, are you?"

He scoffed. "Judging me, Phoebe, are you fucking serious? How the fuck did playing the naïve, enabling wife work out for you? While I was working my ass off, you sat around collecting mounds of fucking debt, courtesy of your piece of shit husband."

She tightened her grip on the phone and gritted her teeth. He knew exactly what to say to get under her skin.

"Fuck you, Carter. I paid back my debts. All of them."

"And you borrowed money from Dad to do it."

How the hell did he know that? She would have thought her dad would have kept her loan between the two of them.

"They weren't mine to begin with, and I'm paying Dad back."

"That's right, Jared was fucking wining and dining all over the fucking country." He laughed. "Bastard even got the last laugh on you, dropping dead in another woman's bed. And still it's not enough for you to grow up."

A cold chill rushed through her blood. It was true, but for

Carter to throw it in her face, knowing the humiliation she'd gone through when she found out, made him an even bigger asshole than she gave him credit for.

"Y-you are..." She licked her lips as her anger built. All her anger management skills were out the door. If Carter was standing in front of her, she'd punch him in the face.

"I'm cleaning up your mess, like always. Christ, Phoebe."

"I didn't ask you to help me, asshole. I've never asked you for anything."

"No, you haven't, but I'm forced to clean up your messes outta family obligation. You really think I'm going to allow my own father to go into debt for you?"

What? Why would her father go into debt? When she explained to her dad that the debt Jared had left her with had her drowning, he stepped up, suggesting a loan. He offered to give her the money and she would pay him back. She resisted at first, but he assured her he had plenty in his savings. He basically demanded she do it. *I'm forced to clean up your messes outta family obligation. You really think I'm going to allow my own father to go into debt for you?* Her stomach dropped and twisted in a painful ache with the realization the money wasn't her father's, it was Carter's.

She closed her eyes and cupped her mouth. Of course, it was. Her dad had to know she'd go bankrupt and die of hunger before taking money from Carter. *Goddammit. Isn't there one man on this earth she could wholeheartedly trust?*

"Fuck." It was a hushed curse, probably in response to her silence.

"I'll pay you back immediately."

"Christ, you don't have the money. Now, calm the fuck down and listen."

She ended the call and tossed the phone on the bed. Her phone rang again, and she shut it down. Forty thousand dollars. Where the hell was she going to come up with that kind of money? Even if she got another job or two, it would still take years to pay him back. She lowered her face into the palm of her hands.

"I have nothing," she muttered, and then her heart sank. She did have something. The one thing that would make it go away. In fact, it was all she had, and she was sitting in it. She peeked between her fingers. Her tears welled immediately, and she sucked in a deep breath.

The only viable option to pay Carter back would be to lose the one thing she loved the most.

After Jared's death and his debt had come to light, she didn't hesitate to sell everything, the property they shared, the toys they acquired, his cars, and her own. She sold all her jewelry, most of her possessions of value. She would have sold the shirt on her back just to keep her Ghosttown shack. Now, she'd have to give it up.

Her chest tightened, and a sharp ache ripped through her chest.

"Bastard is fucking me over from the grave." She grabbed the throw pillow beside her and whipped it across the room. She shot up and paced through the room.

Her mind was going in a million different directions. She needed a distraction before she did something impulsive. As if on cue, she heard the rumbling of the engines from next door.

Kase.

After the argument they had a few days ago, Kase would probably jump at the chance to buy her property and be rid of her. *Asshole.* She could sell to the club, probably get more than if she went through a realtor. She could have Carter paid back by the end of the month.

She walked to the door and crossed her porch, standing at the edge facing the clubhouse. There were only two viable options to get her out of debt, pay back Carter, and finally move on. She bit her lip and eyed the clubhouse. There were a flurry of people walking inside and out. She refused to admit it, but she was searching for him in the mix of people.

She clenched her teeth and breathed heavily through her nose when she spotted him. He was walking out to his bike but stopped midway. She shifted her gaze a few feet back and watched as the club girl in barely-there shorts and a cutoff shirt sauntered his way. Just watching them together was giving her flashbacks to the other day. Her body pressed against his, her tongue deep inside his mouth while his fingers invaded her in the most delicious way.

When the girl reached out, grasped his arm, and slid up next to him, Phoebe felt the surge of jealously rip through her chest. She spun around and focused her attention on the woods in front of her.

Kase had the power. She wasn't going to grant him more. She stomped across the porch and into the house, slamming the door behind her.

No fucking way.

It was petty, and though she really didn't have too many options, selling to Kase and the club would be her last choice. *My crazy ass isn't selling to him.* Going through a realtor wouldn't give her the quick result she needed, but at least she wouldn't have to see Kase's smug face take possession of her home.

She should have taken a day or two to think about it, but it would have been pointless. Phoebe had always worked off her adrenaline. Some days it prevailed, other times it backfired.

Screw him. She'd get out of this dilemma without his assistance. She dialed the familiar number and waited as it rang.

Initially, she and Tory had been business acquaintances. She was the agent who sold the shack to her seven years ago. But as with most people Phoebe liked, she extended her friendship.

"Hey, girl, you back?"

"Yeah but not for long."

"What? Why?"

Phoebe closed her eyes and pinched the crown of her nose, trying to ease the tension racing through her body.

Ghosttown was the only place where she felt truly at home. When the fiasco with Jared happened, his death, the lies revealed, the compounding debt he'd left behind, his betrayal? All she wanted was to come home. Here.

Being away for six months had been torturous. She had patiently bided her time, knowing she'd be back for good in no time. Now, a few weeks later, she was set on leaving again. This time, forever.

"Phoebe?"

She licked her lips and inhaled a deep breath, staring up at her cracked ceiling. She refused to give in to her threatening tears. "I need to sell. Fresh start, Tory."

The silence lingered.

"Can you make time for me today?"

"Uh yeah, I just finished with a showing in Turnersville. Give me thirty minutes, and I'll come by."

Phoebe hung up and fell back into the couch. For the next half hour, she sat in silence, pondering. As she glanced around the room, her eyes welled. *You're mine.*

SHE WALKED DOWN HER DRIVEWAY, following Tory, who drove down and parked at the end. She slowed her steps, watching the agent pop her trunk and pull out the sign.

"I could hold the paperwork, Phoebe." She shrugged. "Just a week, and if you still want to sell, I can put it through and come back with the sign."

"No, I'm ready."

Tory sighed and started down to the corner. It seemed to happen in slow motion. She spiked the sign into the earth and stepped back. *Déjà vu.* Except it was bringing her back to a time when Tory was removing the sign after the closing. *Bittersweet.*

She folded her arms and watched as Tory drove down the street. It was the same time Kase drove toward her. His bike slowed, and even from behind his sunglasses, she knew he was looking at her. Or maybe it was the sign? She turned and started up her driveway when the engine sounded closer. She glanced over her shoulder to find Kase at the edge of her drive. He ripped off his sunglasses and glared.

"What the fuck is that?"

She snorted. "My crazy ass decided to sell." Her lip curled as his brows furrowed. "Looks like you'll be getting some new neighbors, Kase." She may not have won the war, but she sure as hell was winning this battle. "Oh, and just to be clear, I won't be fielding any offers from the club, so don't waste your time."

Now who's got the power, asshole? She smirked and waggled her brows. She turned before their conversation could go any further. It was a small victory, but she'd take it.

I WANT to wring her fucking neck.

If he wasn't scheduled for a meeting, he might have. He wasn't sure what got under his skin more, seeing the sign or her smug smile. What had he expected? He came at her with low blows and insults that cut deep. He wasn't willing to apologize. *Fuck her.* He was dealing with shit, the latest being this one-on-one meeting at Saint's. The last thing he needed was a distraction.

He drove through Main Street, the warm breeze sifting over his face and through his hair. The private meeting was at Saint's house. When Saint requested it, he found it strange he didn't want it at the clubhouse. All meetings, even between the two of them, happened at the club. He turned onto his street, catching sight of the sprinkler on the front lawn and a small girl running through it.

She was too small to be Cia, Saint's daughter. A closer assessment, and he smirked. He pulled into the driveway of the two-story home. Saint had done renovations a year ago and had plans to add on two rooms off the back after the baby was born. Kase had offered him the list of open properties to find a better house, bigger or possibly more land, but Bailey was set on living there.

The club offered to buy her out of her house, but she refused. She wanted to keep it.

He turned off the engine and swung his leg over his seat. He noticed two bikes in the driveway next to Bailey's car. One was Saint's and the other must belong to the reason for this private meeting.

Ambush from the Monroe brothers?

Kase walked down the drive and headed to the back door when he saw the little girl waddling down the concrete, struggling with her towel. Saint was in the process of getting the driveway repaved since it was beat to hell. He watched as she stumbled a bit. He took wide strides, making it to her before she did more damage to her feet. When he stopped in front of her, she craned her head looking up, grinning.

"Hi."

"Hey, Allie."

"My feet hurt."

He reached down, tucking his forearm under her butt, and hoisted her up against his chest. She reached her arm out of her towel and wrapped her tiny arm over his shoulder as he made his way to the back door. He opened the screen and walked through the mudroom, which opened to the kitchen. Saint and Hades were at the table while Bailey was leaning up against the sink. Her small belly was poking out with her hand resting over top.

"Uncle Kase is here!" Allie shouted, possibly puncturing his eardrum.

"Hey, man." Hades nodded.

"I'm moving." He turned his head to catch Allie smiling. "And I'm gonna live in Aunt Bailey's house, and I get my own room."

"Really?" Kase said. He'd feign it for the kid, but his glare was set on Saint. As usual, the fucker wasn't remotely affected. He could strike the fear in any man alive. Except Saint.

"Uh-huh, and I get a new bed too."

He glanced over at Hades, Allie's dad, who didn't bother

hiding his arrogant grin. Kase bent down, setting Allie's feet on the floor, and watched her make her way to Hades.

"You done outside?"

She nodded, gave him her wet towel, and skipped out the door. The product of a junkie whore and a man who'd been more dangerous and deadly than most, Allie was probably one of the sweetest kids in the club family.

Kase lifted his chin. "What the fuck is going on? Or do I gotta get Allie back in here to tell me the rest?"

Saint snorted.

Hades rested his elbows on the table, eyeing Saint. "Gonna rent Bailey's house for me and the kid."

"Yeah, I got that part, now tell me something she didn't. Like why the fuck you're settling down two hours from your club?"

Hades had approached him a couple of months back about renting property. His explanation of having a place close to Saint and Bailey to watch Allie for him made sense, but Kase knew there was more to it. He didn't push or question Saint on the idea. He knew eventually they'd come to him. *And here we fucking are.*

Hades sat back in his chair. "You know why."

He did. Hades was the VP to their charter club, which dealt primarily in illegal activities. At one time, his own club rivalled their criminal background. They were going down a road where they'd spend their lives in and out of prison. None of his brothers wanted it. The reward was hefty but not worth the risk.

Kase balled his fists. "Fuck me, Hades."

He knew what it meant. Hades wanted to settle in with his chapter. Plant roots in Ghosttown, which made sense since it put him close to his brother and Bailey. It may have made sense, but it wouldn't be easy. Not by a fucking long shot. They were a harder crew who never abandoned the criminal element when the split happened. Neither did his club originally, but they were never as hardcore as Ghosttown East.

"It's doable," Saint said.

Kase slowly turned his head. "Yeah, if he's a fucking nomad, but as VP? They're gonna fucking lose it he comes over with us." He turned to Hades. "You talk to Mack?"

Mack was the president of Ghosttown East. He was a solid guy who made no apologies, a lot like Kase. However, he wasn't interested in going legit. He hadn't had the same vision Kase had when they split clubs. The illegal bullshit was never in his long-term plan, whereas Mack was all in. The same reason none of Kase's guys had done time in the last five years, and all of Mack's had done a stint, including the man sitting across from him.

"Yeah."

"And?"

Hades shrugged. "Wants a sit-down with you."

Kase muttered. "I bet he fucking does." Kase sighed. "You got the votes?"

In order for Hades to switch charters, he'd need to be voted out by his own club and voted in by Kase's.

Hades nodded. "I gotta a few I need to work on, but they're pretty solid. And I got them with you."

He did. Kase couldn't think of one brother who wouldn't openly welcome Hades into the club. Aside from being Saint's blood brother, he'd always been a standup, ruthless when needed, member of the club. Even Kase could see him as a viable asset.

"You don't bring shit into my club, Hades."

Saint stepped forward, and Kase raised his hand. Saint rarely listened to Kase, but he was respectful, and he would listen. "Just making myself clear." He raised his brows. "You come to us, you fucking work with us, and nothing on the fucking side with East. Took a long fucking time to get us outta that shit, and I'm not letting any motherfucker come in and take that. Not from my brothers."

Hades eyed him with a slow nod. "Looking to get out of that shit, not bring it over." Hades sighed. "Spent over a year away, man." Hades gritted his teeth, and he watched as his gaze transformed into a deadly stare. It wasn't for show. It was all Hades. He could be the meanest motherfucker when he wanted. "A year away from my kid, leaving her with her mom. I get out, still on parole, and the courts give Allie to me. What the fuck does that say about the cunt who was supposed to be watching her for a year?"

Kase folded his arms and remained silent. He knew exactly what it meant. He didn't know Allie's mom, some club whore Hades knocked up, but he knew women like her. Shit women.

"I'm fucking doing it for Allie, and I ain't going back. You have my word, Kase."

Kase glanced over at Saint. Years back when they made the split, Saint wanted Hades with him, but they had different agendas at the time. This would be big for Saint, and their club as a whole.

"All right. Set up a meet with Mack. Want him at our house, not his."

Holding court on his own territory was an advantage. While they ran with the same club, the ideals behind each charter were different, and so were their rules. Kase had trust for his brother charter, but not one hundred percent, especially considering the reasoning for the meeting.

Hades nodded.

Three glasses hit the table along with an aged bottle of bourbon. It was a reason to celebrate. Having Hades part of their club would be an asset as long as he could leave the shit behind.

They drank and talked over the shop and the runs for the parts. Hades had his CDL and would be ready to go once the vote was made official. Hades was as smart as he was deadly. He'd talked about some plans and ideas he'd had for getting the revenue to Ghosttown.

If they could make it happen with Mack, it would be a good thing having him a member of the Ghosttown Riders.

"I'm heading out," Kase said, and stood.

"I'll call when I get a day for the meet. Sooner than later, that work for you?" Hades asked. He was reading Saint's brother as if he were his own. He wanted out of the element. Kase had no doubt, if not for the little girl upstairs, this conversation wouldn't even be happening.

"You tell me when, and I'll make it happen."

They lingered in the kitchen but halted conversation when Bailey entered the room. This was the reason they handled club business at the club. No interruptions. Kase understood why this needed to happen here, though.

Saint and Hades left the room, and he turned toward the door.

He passed Bailey, who was looking in the fridge. He grasped her back gently.

"I'm heading out."

She turned her head. "You don't wanna stay for dinner?"

"Got shit to catch up with at the shop."

"Okay." She leaned over and kissed his cheek. Bailey was the only one who did that every time he saw her. Most of the women stayed away and greeted him with a simple wave.

He walked to the door and halted in the doorway.

The meeting had been a small distraction from what had been playing over in his head all afternoon. If anyone could give him answers, it was the woman standing a few feet away.

"Why's she selling now?"

Bailey turned in apparent confusion. She cocked her head. "Who?"

He could read people better than anyone. He wasn't seeing any deceit or cover up; Bailey genuinely had no idea who he was referring to. That fact struck him hard. Of all the people in town, Phoebe was closest to Bailey. Why the fuck wouldn't she mention she was moving? Something wasn't right.

"Phoebe."

Her eyes widened. "Phoebe's not selling."

Kase raised his brows and caught Saint lingering in the living room doorway. He glanced over to Bailey. "She's got a for sale sign in her yard."

Bailey darted her stare between him and Saint, finally landing on Kase. She squinted and shook her head. "She loves her place and this town. She wouldn't sell."

He sighed and cocked his brow. "I know what I fucking saw and heard, Bailey." Something definitely wasn't right with this whole thing. From her year-long refusal, and now Bailey not even having a clue. What the fuck was she hiding?

"She got debt?"

Bailey's brows knitted together, and her lips flattened. She knew something. Maybe not the move, but something he didn't know.

"Sweetheart?" Saint said.

"I'm not discussing Phoebe's personal finances with anyone, so don't ask."

Kase snorted. "I think you just gave us the answer."

He walked out without another word. He had been waiting on Carter to get back to him. A few messages had been returned with a quick, "I'm working on it". Kase had a keen sense when shit didn't sit right, and everything with Phoebe was off.

Chapter 10

"And that pretty much sums up the logistics of how it works. I think you'll agree it's an extremely lucrative investment, Miss Shaw."

Phoebe inhaled a deep breath. With her house newly listed, she had people coming out of the woodwork to purchase. She had flat-out refused to deal with a development company. She had made that clear to Tory. Somehow, they had gotten her number. This was the second call she had fielded in the last few days.

She had just spent the last twenty minutes speaking to the guy from the leasing company. At her father's insistence, she heard him out. Two minutes into his spiel she was ready to hang up. While it was a viable option, a good one for someone in her predicament, it wasn't right for her. Not right for Ghosttown. Even if she had to sell and move away, she wouldn't jeopardize the town for her own gain.

"Do you have any questions?"

Phoebe shook her head and leaned against her car, parked in front of the diner. "No, you pretty much answered everything." The quicker she ended the call the better. Hearing his sales pitch left her feeling dirty. It was business, and she could respect it, but not at the expense of a town she loved.

"Great. I can have a rep come to you at your convenience and have a proposal written and move forth."

Absolutely not.

"I really don't think this is for me, but I appreciate your time. I'm going to…"

"I'd like to set up a meeting, have a rep come down and show you the actual proposal. On paper is always most efficient."

She groaned. *Salespeople.*

"Yeah, but I'm not…" She rolled her eyes when he cut her off again. The guy was good.

"Excellent. I'll have a rep reach out and find a good time to set up a formal meeting."

"Okay." She smiled, knowing she was never picking up the phone and would spend the rest of her life dodging his company's calls.

"Looking forward to it."

She hung up and started to the diner. A wave of chrome caught her eye, and she glanced down the street. A few members were standing out front greeting a man who'd just pulled up on his bike. She watched the small group. As her gaze travelled across their faces, she locked eyes with one in particular.

"Waste of a hot man," she muttered and watched his brows furrow.

The enemy. It was how she referred to Kase in her head. She jerked her gaze and straightened her shoulders. She purposefully walked into the diner, slow and methodical. She wasn't rushing away from him, and he better know it. She took her usual booth at the window and settled into her seat.

"Does your place even have a kitchen?"

Phoebe smirked, glancing up through her lashes. "Yes, it does. In fact, since it's rarely used, it's gloriously clean, which is how I intend to keep it, Carla."

The waitress burst out laughing and slid into the booth seat across from her. "We've missed you, honey." She was smiling, shaking her head. "Not quite the same without you."

"Well, I had to do my penance before returning to the scene of the crime."

"Ain't no crime in standing up for yourself."

Phoebe snorted. "Don't think Arnett would agree with you."

Carla scoffed, waving her hand in front of her face. "I've known that man over twenty-five years. Not a damn thing we've ever agreed on." She raised her brows. "I don't trust anyone who sides with his grumpy ass." Her gaze lifted over Phoebe's shoulder, and she furrowed her brows. She got up from the table and turned toward the counter when the bell sounded.

"When I retire, I'm gonna shove that bell up his ass." She straightened and walked away. "Give me a few, Feebs."

She nodded and opened her menu. She flinched when she heard a knock from the window. Jack was peering inside with a scowl. She watched him hurry down the sidewalk and turn into the diner, coming toward her table.

"Why the hell ya eating alone?"

She chuckled and shrugged, putting down the menu. "I got stood up."

Jack slid into the seat across from her and slapped his hands on the table. "The fuck you say?"

"I'm just kidding. I usually eat alone, but since you're here, my luck is changing." *Kase isn't going to like this.* She grinned at Jack.

He winked, glanced around the small dining room, and raised his hand to get Carla's attention. She shook her head and strolled toward them, rolling her eyes.

"Glad to see ya learned your lesson."

Jack laughed. "Well, I like my balls, darlin'." They enjoyed a chuckle while Phoebe remained clueless. Her confusion was caught by Carla, who hooked her thumb at Jack.

"First time he came in, he snapped his fingers to get my attention."

Phoebe widened her eyes.

"Told him he ever did it again, not only would I kick his ass out, I'd slice off his testicles with the butcher knife from the kitchen."

Jack burst out laughing and turned to Phoebe. "The sexy women are always the craziest."

Carla smirked. "What'll it be?"

Phoebe opened her mouth, but she was cut off by Jack. "Two burgers, rare, double fries, and make 'em well done. None of the green shit on mine." He turned his head. "You want anything else?"

Yeah, I want my salad. She glanced up at Carla. "I'll take the green shit with mine."

Carla snickered, writing it down on her pad. She grabbed the menus and turned to the counter.

"Double fries, huh?"

He grabbed his water, taking a sip and twisting his lips. "Ya ain't gonna keep your ass eating salads."

"You've got a point, Jack."

He eyed her and furrowed his brows, setting his glass down. "Ya got a great ass, you wanna keep it."

She curved her lips and nodded.

Lunch was amusing and enjoyable, as she knew it would be with Jack. He had stories upon stories, most she didn't quite understand, but the way his face lit up as he told them, she wouldn't ask questions.

Jack reached for his wallet and opened it up. His face turned a bright shade of red. His temple pulsed, and the lines in his forehead thickened. "Son of a bitch," he shouted, gaining the attention of the whole diner. He tossed his wallet on the table.

"What's wrong?" Carla rushed over, darting her gaze between them.

"Someone's been swiping twenties from my wallet. Motherfuckers, bet it's my boys. Those little shits." His anger was increasing by the second.

Phoebe reached out and grasped his hand. He attempted to

yank it away, but she gripped him tight, forcing him to look at her.

"I got money, Jack, it's no big deal." Her plan to calm him backfired. He ripped his hand from her hold, and his face hardened.

"I'm fucking paying," he shouted with a menacing glare.

Carla inched closer. "Kase set up a tab, remember? It's covered."

"I pay for myself, don't need a little fucker paying for my meal," he snapped, and the rage built in his eyes.

Phoebe clamped her lips and tossed down a twenty and a ten. When Jack eyed her, she shrugged. "Not often I get to buy lunch for a biker. Let me do this." She smiled, which only seemed to flame his fire. *Shit.*

Jack's condition was easier to read. Phoebe had yet to see an aggressive side with Jack. It all changed a minute ago. Diffusing the situation was necessary, though she had no clue how to. A quick glance to Carla showed she wouldn't be much help either.

He jerked his head to Phoebe. "Let's go," he ordered, and for reasons unknown to her, she followed. It was a feat to keep up with him as he stormed down the street. Leaving him alone in his irate state was not an option. She softly jogged, catching up to him.

He turned and swung open the glass door. "Get inside."

She hurried in and glanced around. She hadn't been inside the MC's parts store, but she'd seen it from outside. Jack stalked forward, grasping her wrist tightly, and she was forced deeper into the store. The last thing she needed was a confrontation with Kase. She glanced around, noticing a few members rally at the counter. When she locked eyes with Gage, she smiled and raised her brows. He seemed confused and started toward Jack.

"What's up, Prez?"

Jack whipped around at the smiling blonde and glared. "Where the fuck is Kase?"

Phoebe drew in a deep breath, prepping herself for the shit

show that was about to happen. Gage straightened, eyeing Jack with a thoughtful smile. It was obviously not the first time he'd dealt with Jack's outbursts. Gage lifted his chin over his shoulder and called out to the back.

"Kase, man, need ya out here." Gage sighed and cocked his lip, smiling at Jack, but she read the hesitation in his demeanor.

Kase walked out from the back flanked by Rourke and Dobbs. He slowed his steps when he caught sight of Jack, and then his gaze locked on Phoebe. His eyes darkened, and his cheek twitched, but he kept his steady pace, stopping at the counter.

"What's going on, Pop?"

Jack lunged forward, and Phoebe gasped. He didn't make contact with Kase, who hadn't even wavered.

"You been lifting cash from my wallet again?"

Oh, this is bad. She had seen the signs when speaking with Jack, but she was getting a full-eye view of how bad off he was. For Jack, he was set in another time, in years past. It was heartbreaking. She shifted on her feet, glancing down at the linoleum. It was incredibly awkward, and her face heated, wanting to be anywhere but there.

"No," Kase answered in a calm and neutral tone.

She glanced up through her lashes. Kase was intently watching his father with a strained tightening of his features. She couldn't even imagine going through this with her own father.

"Fucking liar," he snapped and reached back, grabbing her wrist and pulling her next to him. "Had to have her pay for my fucking meal 'cause of you lying degenerate thieves."

She bit her lip, refusing to look at the men. She curved her neck and whispered, "Jack?" He turned with rage blazing in his eyes. She forced a smile. "It was my treat."

His brows twitched, and his lips turned down. "I pay for you, that's the way it is." He tightened his grip on her wrist and turned to Kase. "Give her the fucking money you stole from me." It was a command.

She dared a glance through her lashes and saw the heated

anger in Kase's eyes. She was prepared for him to shout and yell at Jack. Instead he reached to his back pocket and pulled out his wallet, tossing two twenties on the counter. He remained silent.

Jack watched him and shook his head, giving her a reprieve on her aching wrist. He slapped his hand on the counter and grabbed the cash before placing it in her palm. He turned, not saying another word, and walked out of the shop.

She waited until Jack breeched the door. The air in the room was thick. She didn't have much experience with the disease, but she figured she was getting a first-hand look at one of the side effects. It was a horrible scene all around. It was sad and frustrating for Jack as much as it was for Kase, she assumed. She didn't bother looking at him. She stepped to the counter and put down the money. Even across the counter his heated anger resonated. She needed to get out from his crosshairs. She turned and started to the door.

"Take the money."

She glanced over her shoulder. "It's fine, I don't mind paying."

His brows dented, and the lines in his forehead deepened. "Take the fucking money."

She swallowed the lump in her throat. "Kase, it's fine."

His jaw clenched. Maybe she should have just taken it and left. While she enjoyed her banter with him, it was not the time or place.

He grabbed the cash and circled past the counter, charging over to her. He grabbed her hand and shoved the bills into her palm. "Take it. Made it fucking clear, want nothing from you. From what I hear, you fucking need the money." His sneer was intended to hurt. He'd succeeded. He stepped back and pointed over her head. "Told ya to keep your ass clear of my old man."

Phoebe bit back a harsh retort. She drew in a deep breath and silently counted. It was a ridiculous tool she'd learned from the anger management class. For Kase's sake, she needed all the help she could get from not exploding on him. His aggression stemmed from Jack's condition. She needed to focus on it and calm the hell down.

She swallowed a breath. "I was sitting at the diner, and he sat down with me. I didn't invite him, but I certainly wasn't about to send him away." She glanced around his men, who were solely focused on her. "I tried to help when he got upset at the diner, but..."

She flinched when he stormed forward, leaving a small gap separating them. He leaned closer. "I don't need your help. Don't need your land. And I sure as fuck don't need you in my bed." His lips curved in a sinister smirk. "Take your help, your property, and your offer to fuck you, and get the hell outta my store."

She gasped. A burning, prickled heat rose from her neck to her face. Humiliation had its own special blush. It was a horrific combination of twisting belly, pounding heart, and crimson heat spreading over her entire body. She breathed solely through her nose, flaring her nostrils because her teeth clenched down so hard it would have taken a crowbar to part her lips.

It was Arnett all over again. *Punch him in his fucking mouth.* She squeezed her eyes shut and forced her fingers to stretch. She hadn't realized they had balled into tight painful fists. While she had compassion for Kase's situation with his father, he took it to extremes in his efforts to not only embarrass her in front of half his club but strike her with his sharp tongue.

Unleashing on him would have been easy. Walking away took maturity. She was a thirty-two-year-old woman who had learned her lesson. *If Arnett could see me now.* She turned and slowly walked toward the door, aware of everyone looking at her. An awkward chill raced over her flesh. Then she heard him.

"Cunt."

She halted in mid-stride a few feet from her escape. Had she not heard the hushed remark, she'd be halfway to her car. *I heard it.* It was too much to let go. She turned and slowly walked back to the counter. Kase had stood on the opposite side, glaring at her through his hooded gaze. She slapped her hand on the counter.

The Enemy

"I don't need your money, Kase, and I certainly don't need you or anyone airing my business. You think you know about me?" She raised her brows. "You don't know shit, but feel free to fucking ask 'cause as I've mentioned..." She leaned closer and squinted. "I am an open fucking book."

His brows knitted, and his nostrils flared. He may not like the scene she was stirring. Then he shouldn't have started it. She cocked her head.

"All ya gotta do is ask." She pointed to her chest. "Me. Ask me, Kase." She snorted and glared around the room, receiving harsh scowls from the members. *Fuck them.*

"I got everything I need to know." He sneered. "You get the fuck outta here."

She scoffed. "You don't have shit, Kase. The only thing you have is you turned me down for sex." She cocked her head and smiled. "But not for a little finger-banging in the back room." If he wanted to out their shit, she would lay it all out for their audience. "That's the best you got? I'm drunk on whiskey and come on to you and you turn me down. Am I supposed to be upset?" She had been, but after his two outbursts, she considered it a blessing in disguise. She pressed her hands on the counter and raised up on her toes. "Newsflash, sweetie, I'm not." She snorted and was damn proud it came out as confident as it sounded. *I wasn't sure I could pull that off.* She leaned closer. "Let's put everything out there. Sound good?" she snapped and stepped back, smiling. "I'm Phoebe Shaw, thirty-two-year-old widow. I'm currently over forty thousand dollars in debt with a horrendous credit rating." She cocked a brow. "Not my debt. That came courtesy of my husband. Apparently, he had a flare for wining and dining women before he fucked them. Son of a bitch even died in the bed of one of his whores." She snickered. "It's like a freaking Greek tragedy, huh?" She drew in a deep manic breath. "That's what I'm paying for, Kase." She laughed. "Yep, I'm the stupid, gullible, unknowing wife who was at home working her ass off while her husband was out racking up credit and fucking anything with two legs." She glared at the brothers, aiming her stare on Kase. "I'm sure you all have mad respect for him." She caught the small shift in his features. *Surprise?* She huffed a breath and shrugged. "Here's another fun fact, Kase." She pinned him with her stare. "Shaw is my married name." She cocked her brow. "I used to be Phoebe Ross. Ring a fucking bell, asshole?"

She watched him intently for clarity to strike. Had she blinked, she would have missed it. Luckily, she was focused on Kase, and when his lids lowered and the corner of his eyes crinkled, she knew he understood fully.

"You wanna know something about me, Kase? Ask me." She drew in a breath and raised her brows. "Don't be a little *bitch* and ask my brother." She turned quickly and stormed out in complete silence.

NEVER IN HIS life had anyone dared to call him a little bitch. It took every ounce of restraint and two brothers not to go after Phoebe. Gage grasped his stomach and pulled him toward the back. It was all too much at one time, first his dad, then Phoebe. He was on the edge of losing his shit. Who the fuck did she think she was coming at him? And fucking Carter? He pulled away from Gage's hold and stormed to the warehouse, heading toward the back door. He threw his shoulder into the steel door, sending it flying open wide. He yanked his phone and hit speed dial.

Motherfucker.

It rang twice. "Ross."

Kase gripped the phone in his hand. It would take a miracle for the plastic not to break. "Your fucking sister?"

There was a moment of silence. "You stay the hell away from her." The warning was sharp, however, not firm enough to cover the wavering concern in his tone.

Kase sneered and grinned with a manic snarl. "She lives next door, brother. I got easy access. Maybe you should have mentioned she was your sister from the start."

"You lay one finger on her, Kase, and I will come for you."

Kase laughed with zero ounce of humor. "You threatening me, Carter?" He sneered and gripped the phone. "You knew exactly who she was when I asked you, motherfucker. Putting your own in my hands, that's on you, asshole."

"You stay the fuck away, Kase." It was a threat.

Kase smirked and mounted his bike. "Maybe I will. Maybe I won't." He hung up before Carter could say another word. He started his engine and headed back to the clubhouse.

The ride seemed longer than ten minutes, and did nothing to calm his nerves. Phoebe was Carter's sister. How the fuck did this get past him? He'd known Carter for years, and never once did he mention any family. Hell, Kase thought the asshole might be raised by wolves. He gripped his handlebars and started up the driveway. It took great effort not to glance over at Phoebe's property. Who the fuck cared if she was home? He pulled into his spot in the front, and his gaze was drawn to her house. There was a small light in the front of the house, and her car was parked in the driveway out front. He slammed his helmet down and started to the doors.

The hallway was quiet with a low sound of music playing in the background. He stopped at the doors and glanced around the bar.

"Where's Jack?" he asked.

Nadia glanced up from the bar. "Dobbs built him a fire out back."

He eyed the brothers, who were watching him. Kase nodded and glanced back at the hall. He rolled his neck and gripped the edge of the bar. He was feeling way too fucking old. The scene with his dad had been a disastrous clusterfuck. He should have handled it better. And Phoebe? Fuck her and that fucking mouth.

He dragged his hand through his hair, feeling the stress of everything take over. Finally settled in Ghosttown, his stress level should have decreased. He pulled out a cigarette, setting it between his lips, and glanced around the room. A few brothers were scattered around the bar and the tables near the stage. One of the girls was working the pole, grinding her ass against the metal, and had slipped off her top. *I need a distraction.* How long had it been? For a man like Kase, a few weeks without sex was unheard of, especially when his house was crawling with eager and available pussy. The redhead on stage smiled and locked her gaze on him. One flick of his head and he'd be balls deep in minutes. All he had to do was give her the sign to approach.

He jerked his head away and stared down at the bar. From the corner of his eye, he watched as Nadia placed a glass in front of him. He glanced down.

"Go hang with your dad, Kase."

He gritted his teeth and glared at Nadia. Most of the women knew better than to tell anything to him. Nadia had a way of making it sound as a suggestion. Her small smile was warm. She lifted her chin to the back hall, and then she turned away, making her way back to the other end of the bar. How she wasn't someone's old lady, he didn't know. Actually, he did. Nadia wasn't interested in being tied down to one man. At least none of the men in the club. He didn't have many conversations with the women in the club, but he recalled Nadia mentioning something that had stuck with him.

"For now, I love being here, but I know one day I'll wake up, and I won't love it anymore. And when that day comes, I'll pack up and head out."

Kase eyed her carefully. Of all the women to pass through the club, Nadia had been the most beautiful. She came with no strings attached. She was a perfect club whore. She winked and set her smile on him before turning around and sauntering down the bar.

He swiped his glass and headed toward the back. When he got outside, he found his Pop sitting on one of the stumps, Dobbs standing with a beer across from him. He glanced up and lifted his chin.

Her jerked his head toward the house. "Think Nad was looking for you." It was bullshit, but Dobbs read through it.

"Later, Jack." Dobbs slapped Kase's back while he passed.

Kase moved closer to the fire, staring at the orange flames. He drew in a deep breath, calming his body. It hadn't worked. He was still full on enraged adrenaline from everything that had gone down in his shop. He glanced over at his father, taking in his serene smile. For his Pop, that moment Kase was dwelling on had long passed.

"You remember the fire we built in the woods camping down by the river?" He rested his head back and stared up at the sky. "Flames were twenty feet high. You and Cade were small, maybe eight and ten. Begged me to let you night fish." His throaty laugh turned quickly into a cough. "Swore the fish would be biting then."

Kase took a sip from his drink, feeling the burn down his throat. "Cade."

"Yeah, it was Caden." Jack snorted and then paused for a few seconds. "Think he'll take Cora fishing?"

Kase glanced up to see his dad staring at the pit. Caden would, same as he'd done with Trevor all those years. A few times Kase had tagged along. A few with Jack too. Little did they know it would be their last.

"Had some good times. Just us boys."

They were few and far between, but memorable when they happened. Growing up in the club with Jack as president left little family time. There was some, though.

"You take your pills?" Kase asked.

Jack stared down at the fire, lifting his glass in silence. If not for Marissa's text reminding him, he would have forgotten too.

"Later."

Kase sighed. "Pop, ya gotta fucking take 'em."

Jack smirked and side glanced Kase. "They ain't the good ones. Back in my day, we had good shit." He shifted in his seat, slinking down. "Better women, better club."

Kase cracked his neck.

"You remember that game, football. It was the last fucking game of the season, playoffs or some shit. Whole fucking town closed down. You remember that?"

Kase cocked his brow with a slow nod. "Cade's senior year."

Jack smiled. "That boy could play."

Kase sighed and sipped his whiskey. Cade was a star on the field. No one could touch him. Set records in their old high school, only to be broken by Trevor years later. It was where the two of them shined. He'd been a full-fledged member at the time. A huge party, one of their biggest. Women, fights, drinking, fucking; some members still talked about it.

Not me. Kase had opted to go to Caden's last game with his Pop.

Jack shot up in his seat and slapped his leg. "The next night, we went on a run. Stopped at that little bar." He grinned. "Locals thought they'd stretch their fucking muscle. One of us took on three guys that night, showed 'em who we were." Jack laughed, settling in his seat. "Then we took the ride out by the canyon. Camped out. That was a good night, Kase."

"Yeah." Kase smirked. *That was me.* He'd taken on three guys, beat the shit out of all of them single- handedly. It had been forever since he thought of that night. He'd been trying to impress the club, mainly his dad. The assholes had gotten a few good shots at him, but he'd taken care of them. He set them straight. No one fucked with the Ghosttown Riders.

The silence lingered. It was welcomed for Kase.

"You didn't swipe my cash, did ya?"

Kase angled his head toward Jack, who was staring back at him. Some days when his father looked at him, it was as though he was looking into the eyes of a stranger. Tonight? It was his Pop at present day, recognizing his own demise.

"I did it enough times as a kid, I was overdue you calling me out for it today. We're good, Pop."

Pop nodded slowly, his lips tugging into a frown, and the lines between his brows creased. His father may not have won any award for Father of the Year, but he gave it his best, even when his best was shitty. He stayed. When his mother left, Jack stepped in. He was away a lot, left Kase to watch over Caden, but both brothers became independent fairly quick. Jack wasn't always the best, but he never deserted them.

"I like that one."

Kase glanced over and found Jack resting back in the chair, staring down at the flames in the pit. A serene and soft glow shadowed his face. This was Jack now. One minute he was raising hell, the next he was being taken over by his past, and finally, he was just Pop. Kase didn't bother asking who he was referring to. Kase suspected he knew who.

"Great ass on her."

The corner of Kase's mouth perked up. Now, he definitely knew who his Pop was talking about. It was apparently the consensus. Phoebe had a great ass.

"Sexy as hell."

"You had a lot of women, Pop."

"Yeah." He sighed. "Something about her, though. Met her years back, would have done my hardest to get her to stay, I think."

There was something about Phoebe even Kase couldn't shake. It went beyond his virile need to fuck her. She proved to be the first woman he'd had a connection with outside of anything sexual. He couldn't remember a time when he'd voluntarily hung out with a female with no plans to bed her. Until Phoebe.

"You got something with her?"

Kase drew in a breath, tightening his grip on his glass. "No."

Jack snorted. "Bet ya wish you did." He shook his head. "The good ones, Kase. You don't let them get away 'cause you spend the rest of your fucking life wondering how different it all woulda been if you had kept her."

"She ain't mine to keep." He gritted his teeth, wondering why the admission pissed him off.

Jack laughed and settled into his seat, staring at the orange glow of the flames. "Yeah, a woman like that, a little wild, speaks her mind, you gotta be something to be her man," Jack paused with a somber sigh. "Gotta know what ya got, respect it, and have the strength to be who she needs. That girl's a little broken, probably 'cause of a man. She ain't tell me nothing, but I can see it."

His dad may not be all there all the time, but he still had the gift of reading people. He'd nailed it with Phoebe. A man had broken her, yet she kept on going. Even today in the store, he'd struck hard with purpose. The anger from seeing his father breaking in front of him, he'd turned on Phoebe. She was giving him an out, but Kase, doing what he does, kept pushing and pushing, delivering a nasty blow. Then she came out swinging, calling him out.

Jack chuckled, catching Kase's attention once again.

"But a fighter. The strong ones are always the hardest to keep but worth it. They'll test ya, make ya see fucking red at every corner, and hell, ya can't tame 'em. You gotta let them be who they are, gotta go all in and ride the waves 'cause there's sure gonna be a fucking lot with someone like her." Jack smiled softly. "Worth it, though, I think." It was as if his dad had gotten inside his head.

"Regret is a shitty thing to live with, Kase." Jack scooted up from his seat and stood, stretching his arms over his head.

It was. Kase had very few regrets, but one shined brighter than most. He should have let her walk out with a word. Instead, he was a motherfucker, cutting her every fucking chance he had.

"I'm heading in."

"Take the pills, Pop."

Jack snapped. "I'll take the fucking pills."

Kase lifted his beer to his lips, hiding his smile as he watched his dad toss the bottle in the trash and circle the fire.

"Wanna a good woman, ya gotta be a good man." Jack walked past him and whispered, "'Night." He headed back inside without another word. There was nothing left to say. Jack had laid it all out for Kase whether he realized it or not.

The problem was, Kase wasn't a good man, never had been. He wasn't built to be what Phoebe wanted or needed. It was cut and dry, black and white. That fact alone should have him never thinking of her again. Yet he sat at the fire, alone, with all his thoughts on her.

Chapter 11

The last night had been a blur. Everything that had gone down with Kase and Jack at the store mounted, as her need to pay back her asshole brother and sell the house had catapulted into a stress-induced somber two days where she vegged on her couch feeling sorry for herself. It was pitiful.

I showered and I brushed my teeth, as good as I'm gonna get. Peace out, motherfuckers. When had she fallen so low and so damn fast? *I'm better than this.* Was she? At the moment she was feeling fairly comfortable at rock bottom. It was ironic. She would have sworn at Jared's funeral and the days following they would have been her lowest point. *But here I am at the bottom of the barrel, killing it.*

The harsh knock sounded and startled her from her self-loathing. She angled her head at her open bedroom door. Again, it was rare for anyone to come over unannounced. She sat up, resting on her elbows as the knock became hurried and aggressive.

"Go away!"

The response was immediate and ear deafening. The pounding was constant, and she pushed off her bed, glaring as she stumbled to the door. Through the sheer curtain there was no mistaking who it was. She gripped the knob tightly and opened it wide. She should have left his ass standing at her door. She cocked her head to the side.

"What do ya want?"

Kase's brow cocked, and his eyes gazed down her body. He was certainly getting an eyeful. Since she wasn't expecting company, she was dressed in tiny athletic shorts and a one-size-too-small tank top. She clucked her tongue, gaining his attention. She smirked.

"I got nothing you want, remember?" She grinned and slowly twisted her lips into a hateful glare. "Besides, I'm just a cunt, right?" She swiftly closed the door but wasn't quick enough. His foot shot out, blocking the closure, and he pushed it back open.

His eyes darkened, and his cheeks hollowed. "Need to talk."

She eyed him carefully. Whatever he had to say had Kase on edge. It was a different look on him. She licked her lips and dropped her own gaze to peruse his body. *God, the man was fit.* She had caught a glimpse of him without a shirt and knew his sculpted abs and defined chest remained hidden by his shirt. If he didn't open his mouth, he'd be perfect.

"Fuck. No." She smiled.

"Phoebe," he growled. She ignored the spike in her chest when he said her name. The man was an asshole, no matter how sexy her name on his lips sounded. She sucked in a breath and shook her head.

"You have nothing to say I want to hear." She sighed and glanced over her shoulder into her tiny living room and then back to him. "I don't have a desire to hear ya speak. In fact, if I go the rest of my life without your voice? I'll die happy." She grasped the door to close it again, but he grabbed wood pane.

"I'm coming in, and you're gonna sit your ass down and listen."

She laughed and stepped back away from the door. "If you step one foot in this house, I will get my gun and shoot you."

He stepped forward, and she spun around. "You were warned."

"Get your ass over here."

She turned and twisted her lips. "You suck with the opposite sex. Do you even grasp how much you suck? Don't you dare come into my house and start barking orders. Your power is shit in my domain, Kase."

"Why the fuck didn't you tell me Carter was your brother?"

This is what he wants to talk about? If ever there was a subject off limits, it would be her brother. Even the sound of his name was a buzzkill.

She scoffed. "I don't have to tell you shit about me or my family, Kase. I don't owe you anything." It was true, she didn't. But a thought popped in her head, and she smirked. "But I am willing to listen if you've got dirt on my big brother."

He remained stoic.

"Your property. Why ya need to sell now?"

She snorted and shook her head. "Nope, none of your business. I've moved on to other avenues."

"Phoebe," he snarled.

She squeezed her eyes together and burst. "No!" she shouted. She whipped around and pointed at him. "You don't get to come in my house and demand anything. Unless you're here to apologize, get the fuck out."

He remained silent as his shoulders bunched and his jaw locked.

"You yelled at me, called me a cunt, then outed me for wanting to have sex with you." Just repeating it all made her cheeks burn. "You purposely tried to hurt and embarrass me when all I did was have lunch with Jack, pay for his meal, then try to calm him when he started to lose it. I deserved a thank you," she paused, "not a fuck you."

His chest rose, and he folded his arms over his chest, staring back at her. She snorted and turned her back, heading toward the kitchen. It was so faint she almost didn't hear him.

"I fucked up."

She slowly turned, facing him again.

Kase dragged his hand over the top of his head. She expected him to glance away, but he didn't. His eyes remained locked on her.

"I got a lot of shit going on, and then I got Jack. Took that out on you. It wasn't right." He drove his hand through his hair and sighed. "I'm sorry."

Did he just sincerely apologize? She didn't think he had it in him to admit any kind of fault. She snorted and arched her brow. "I don't know what to say. I didn't think you'd actually apologize." Her lips curled, and she moved forward with only inches separating them.

"I fucked up. I own my shit."

She nodded in a slight daze. "I was just trying to help, Kase."

He cleared his throat and sighed. "I know."

She licked her lips. "Okay, so where does that leave us, then?"

He stared at her with an intense, uncertain gaze. He seemed caught in an internal struggle. She bit her lip, and his gaze dropped to her mouth, his eyes darkening.

"Fuck it." He took two long strides, and he was towering over her.

When his hands curled under her arms, she gasped, stepping back. She didn't get very far. His grip tightened, and he lifted her off the ground, tugging her body against his. She widened her eyes as he curved his neck and pressed his lips against hers.

It wasn't sweet or gentle, it was exactly what she'd expect from him. It was hard and rough and demanding and had her wrapping her legs around his waist and knotting her feet together. His tongue breached her lips and tangled against hers. She was slightly aware of her body moving, but she kept her eyes closed, completely entranced in their kiss. His tongue penetrated her lips, and she opened for him. Between his hands gripping her ass and his tongue sliding into her mouth, she heard the faint slam of her door closing.

Yes! It was better than any fantasy she'd ever had. The anger and feuding from minutes ago were a memory. *What fight?* All she wanted was him.

"Kase," she breathed. "I want you inside me."

A soft growl vibrating through his chest was the only response she'd gotten.

His grip tightened over her hips with his fingers digging into her flesh. She was completely lost in the kiss to comprehend anything beyond their lips fused together. She wrapped her arms around his broad shoulders, tightening her own grip over him. This moment had been weeks in the making. She grasped his shoulders, digging her fingers into him, and angled her head to get closer. She slid her tongue over his lips in a tracing motion. He stilled his movement, and she continued, all the while feeling his heated breath filter into her mouth.

She had no concept of time or where he was taking her. Her house was too small to pose many options. When she felt her soft mattress brush against her back, she sighed. She had no objections to him taking her anywhere. Her counter, her couch, hell, he could have taken her against her kitchen wall, and she wouldn't have cared. All she wanted was him.

His body pressed against hers, sending her back into the mattress. She was slightly aware of his hands caressing down her, though, and easing her strong grip. Her shaky hands slid down his chest and gripped the buckle of his jeans, tearing it open and not bothering with the zipper. She plunged her hand down his pants. He wanted this as much as her. She gripped his hard cock in her palm and felt his groan against her lips.

"Too many clothes, Kase," she whispered.

Phoebe felt the loss of his heat and flicked her gaze open. Kase stood at the edge of the bed, ripping off his shirt and lowering the zipper of his jeans. She eyed his cock when it came into full view. Her urge to reach out and touch him was obstructed by his hand tugging at her shorts. Had he even taken off his jeans, or were they hanging out at his ankles? She curled her lips when she caught his heated stare.

"Want you naked. Now," he snarled, and she shimmied out of her shorts. She hitched forward, ripping off her shirt, leaving her red bra the only piece of clothing on her body. He eyed her breasts.

"You like it?"

His eyes darted up and caught her gaze. She smirked, and for the first time she could remember, Kase's eyes softened. It changed his face. Without a sharp glare and scowl, his features were accentuated into a smooth, handsome face. How had she not seen him this way before? She brushed her hand against his cheek, and he curled his face into her palm. There was a connection between them. Maybe it was purely sexual, but it seemed almost hypnotic on both sides.

He leaned forward, taking her lips, and slid his hand around her back. She gripped his shoulders, pressing her breasts against his chest. His hand bunched against her back, and she felt the release of her bra and his hand skimming her stomach before palming her breast. His lips fused against hers.

She'd been with other men since Jared, but none of them came close to the desire Kase evoked from her. She grasped at his hips, wanting him inside her. He shifted his body and wrapped his hand around her waist, tugging her up on the mattress.

For as spontaneous as it was, she wasn't so out of sorts as to not demand he wear something. His tongue curled against hers, and she almost forgot her last thought. *God, he can kiss.* She grazed her teeth against his lip, tugging at his bottom lip with a small bite. His growl rumbled through his chest, and his hand locked into her hair, pulling her away and stretching her neck against the pillow. His mouth suctioned onto her neck as she dug her nails into his ribs.

"Kase." It sounded like a plea, though she wasn't sure what she was asking for. She needed some relief to the building pressure at her core. His cock lined up with her pussy, and her breath hitched from wanting him to slide inside her.

Then she felt the cool air breeze over her lower region, and she blinked, finding him leaning over the bed with his cock as hard as a rod. She reached out, grasped his dick, and smirked when she heard the gasp in his breath. His hand balled into a fist as he clenched his pants pulling out a foil square between his fingers. She continued to palm his cock in a slow methodical jerk. She was throwing him off his game. He ripped open the condom, swatted her hand away, and then sheathed himself. She snuggled into the mattress waiting on him. She didn't have to wait long. His body folded over hers, his cock at her entrance. There was no foreplay or hesitation. The crown of his cock nudged at her lips and pushed inside with wet welcome. He gripped her thighs, spreading her open, and plunged deep inside her body. She clutched his shoulders as the thick intrusion penetrated her core. She jolted forward and arched her back.

"Ah, God," she breathed, resting her head against the curve of his shoulder. Had it been too long, or was he just that big? She sucked in a breath and prepared for him to move. To her shock, Kase kissed her neck, trailing his lips over her throat, and shifted slightly.

"So fucking tight." He licked her neck, tracing up to her lips. His tongue licked at her bottom lip, and she opened for him. He rocked forward slowly, which seemed out of character. "You need me slow?"

She nodded and blinked. His dark stare pinned her against her pillows. She bit her bottom lip, drawing his gaze to her. He leaned closer, licking her lip and taking it between his with a soft bite.

"Slow, Kase."

"As slow as you want it, Phoebe."

Phoebe. He rarely used her name, which made it sound that much sweeter in a soft whisper.

He moved forward, and her head arched into the pillow. He was definitely larger than the last man she'd been with. He kissed her neck, rocking his hips into her and starting a rhythm. She swiveled her hips, adjusting to his length.

So much for her brazen *fuck me* attitude. All she wanted was to feel every inch of him. She curved her hand around his waist and jutted her hips, gasping from his full tilt. She grinded her hips closer, wanting him to move. He took her hint and pulled back, easing into her slowly with an even thrust. She gripped his back and dug her nails into his skin.

"Kase." She curled her face into his neck, sucking on his skin and nibbling the soft flesh. It must have turned him on because he stroked deeper into her core, his hips rising and plummeting deep inside. She wrapped her legs around his thighs, tightening her grip. The tremor started slow, then exploded, and she rocked her hips forward as she felt the shiver course through her blood, gripping with sheer intensity.

"Right there," she begged, and he swiveled his hips, pounding deep inside her exactly where she needed him to be. She scraped her nails down his back, and he cupped her jaw, angling her head to take her lips. She was breathing so heavy, his tongue pierced through her lips, and she moaned her breath into his mouth. *Holy hell.*

She'd never come so hard in her life. She panted and tore her mouth from his. Well, she tried, but he forced her lips against his, and his tongue glided across hers. Her body was giving out, but she felt him harden in her core and jerk inside her. *Fucking perfect.* His lips grazed over her slowly, his tongue gliding against hers in a sensual kiss.

This man had destroyed her for anyone in the future.

Her body slumped into the warm sheets, and she closed her eyes. The only indication he had moved was the cool air wafting her body. She missed his heat and pried her eyes open. His ass was the view she got, and she curled her lips. Perfection. She fell to her side, taking in the view. With the shadowy light streaming in from the kitchen, she watched as he made his way through the door. She blinked hazily, waiting on his return. Then he did.

She curled into her pillow, not knowing what would come next. Kase lifted the covers and got into the bed. Without hesitation, she shifted into his side, and his hand drew her closer. He was resting against her headboard, and she didn't bother glancing up. She smelled the cigarette and curled deeper into his chest with a small smile playing on her lips.

"Make up sex is the best." she whispered.

A low rumbling chuckle was his only response.

Sleeping with the enemy. *Hell yeah!*

SLEEPING with her was not what he intended when he'd come over. He wasn't complaining. He knew she'd be impossible to resist. Lying in her bed was proof. He should have gotten dressed and gotten his ass out of her place. Yet, there he was.

She burst out laughing, and Kase glanced over his shoulder at her shaking in her sheets.

"What?" he snapped.

She shook her head and continued to giggle, wiping her eyes. She was having a hell of a good time at his expense.

"What the fuck?"

She glanced up at him through her hooded lids, which seemed sexier than anything he'd ever seen in his life, which said a lot considering all the women he had bedded.

"Just thinking of you doing the walk of shame out my door." She winked. "I might have to take a picture for Bailey's newsletter. The town won't believe it without proof."

"You ever getting tired of being a smartass?"

She grinned and crawled over the bed, reaching out and grabbing his hips and tugging his body against her. "Nope. My dad always said if ya find something you're good at, go with it."

He clasped his hand over her jaw and kissed her. Her tongue slid past his lips as she moaned softly. She would be his downfall if he let her. Her nails slid down his back, and he felt himself growing hard. *Fuck.* He tore his mouth away from her. They needed a distraction. Otherwise, he'd never fucking leave.

"How come you never told me about Carter?" Kase asked,

gliding his hand down her chest and hooking around her hips. He knew her brother was a sensitive subject, which wouldn't sit well with her.

She groaned and rolled her eyes. "You are totally ruining the mood with bringing up my brother, you realize that, right?" She snorted.

When she tried to pull away, he tightened his hold and narrowed his gaze. "Carter."

"Why would I tell you, Kase?" She gasped and twisted in his arms, nailing her elbow into his ribs. He sucked in a harsh breath. He had no time to curse. She grabbed his chest and pressed her tits against him. "We should take a selfie and send it to him." She grinned and lunged across his body. He gripped her waist before she could reach for her phone on the nightstand.

"Was this a revenge fuck against Carter?"

"Maybe." She grazed his lips. "Why? Are you offended I used you, Kase?"

He snorted while pulling her closer to deepen their kiss. Cuddling and kissing after fucking was an anomaly for him. He rarely shared a bed for the night, with the exception of Nadia. Even when he did, she was gone when he woke, and cuddling next to her was never an option.

His hand caressed her back, cupping her ass and pulling her over his body. Her leg swung over his thighs, and she straddled him, never breaking away from the kiss.

She pulled away slightly, her warm sweet breath fanning over his face. "You staying the night, 'cause if you do, I'll expect you to take me to the diner for breakfast in the morning."

He leaned closer, taking her lips again much to her surprise. She gasped and melted her naked body against his.

"Gotta head out soon."

"Okay." She swept her lips across his. Soft lips. He gripped her hips, dragging her pussy against his cock. The wetness was evident when she swiveled her hips against him. Once was not going to be enough. She turned her head, dragging her lips across his stubbled cheek and over to his neck. He bit back a shiver from her tongue circling his ear.

"You weren't a revenge fuck, Kase." She kissed his neck, skimming her nose against the crook of his shoulder.

It was a shy admission, setting something off inside him. His heart pounded in his chest. It shouldn't have mattered to him either way. It did. He didn't want to be something she'd done out of an obligation as a *fuck you* to her brother. The thought unnerved him, and he felt a sense of closeness he'd never felt before. The raw honesty was more than he could take or give back. He weaved his hand through her hair, angling her head to take her lips. He needed to kiss her. He may not have been capable of being open, but he could show her. He gripped her tightly and flipped her over. She gasped at his quick move and settled against the mattress. He trailed his lips over her neck, down to her breast. He sucked the sharp point between his lips with a strong pull. She arched and moaned.

"Kase." His name on a breathy whisper had him trailing his lips over her stomach, sliding his tongue along her skin.

He dipped between her lips, tasting her and getting off on her moaning his name again. He hiked her thighs over his shoulder to get the perfect angle for all he wanted to do to her. Tasting her had run through his mind since she walked into the town meeting. His first thought might have been getting her naked and splayed out for him, but the close second would be how she felt on his tongue. She arched her back when he swiped his tongue over her clit. He gripped her hips, forcing her to stay in place for him. He'd waited too long for this, and he was having her. She swiveled her hips in motion with his tongue.

Going down on a woman was nothing new for him, but somehow it felt different with her. He wanted to get her off, wanted to bring her to orgasm. Kase *wanted* to be the best she'd ever had. He brushed his mouth against her lips, glancing up past her beaded nipples and watching the pure ecstasy on her face. Her lips quirked, and he swiped her clit again. Her hand blindly reached toward his head. He closed his eyes as her hand threaded through his hair, massaging his scalp. Even when she was taking, she was giving.

It didn't take long to find her sweet spot. He angled his shoulders, hoisting up her thighs and resting his fingers at her opening. She needed two to get off. He slipped his fingers in her entrance and slid right in. She was so fucking wet.

"God, Kase," she breathed, and he maneuvered inside her, fucking her with his fingers and assaulting her clit to the point of her panting breathlessly.

She moaned, spreading her legs, and he glanced up, loving her body shivering from his touch. Usually, he was concerned about his own pleasure, but seeing Phoebe wither under his touch, he wanted to get her off more than his own pleasure. He slowly fucked her with his fingers and tongued her tight bead until her back arched and her core tightened over his hand. She rocked her hips forward, and he followed her lead until she screamed and her body tremored, shaking uncontrollably until it was fully sated. He licked her clit softly, and her thighs constricted. He smirked, wiping his mouth over her stomach and crawling up her body. He hadn't even reached her breasts when she grasped his shoulders, pulling her on top of him and rubbing her moist core against his aching cock.

He could slip inside and be in heaven in less than five seconds. He wouldn't, though. Going bareback inside her was a hard tease, and one he wouldn't indulge in. He'd hadn't been with anyone without wrapping up, but he'd been with too many to risk Phoebe.

Her lips grazed his neck, and he fell over her body, tightening his grip in her sheets. He was seconds from sliding inside her. He pulled away quickly, wrapping himself up in record time.

She curled her arms around his waist, pulling, and he dropped his chest against her body. He angled his hips to the right and slid inside her. She was so fucking tight. He drove inside her slowly, feeling the constricted walls tighten around him. He wondered if she was purposely doing it. He didn't care. He just didn't want her to stop. He pushed off the mattress and swiveled his hips, opening his eyes and taking in his view. Her tits swayed with every jolt to her body as her hands trailed over his back.

He'd been with hundreds of women in his lifetime, but never one as sexy and beautiful as Phoebe underneath him. He stroked his cock slowly inside her, feeling every inch close in on him, getting off on her breathy moans. Her nails dug into his back in an erotic pinch. The slow fuck had been overrated, at least for him. He'd always taken pleasure in the hard and fast, but Phoebe had him rethinking it. Or maybe it was her. He melted against her breasts and kissed her neck, thrusting deep inside her. He was so fucking close.

Her leg hooked over his ass, giving him full access, and he pumped inside her, his body straining to get as deep as he could. Her walls constricted in a tightening grip, and he thrust forward, feeling his body drain and his orgasm at its peak. He hitched forward and grazed his teeth over her throat as he came deep inside her body. His cock pulsated, lasting longer than he could ever remember. *Fuck.* He gripped her shoulder, thrusting deep inside her. It took a few seconds for his body to settle into her welcoming soft body. His breathing labored as she caressed the pads of her fingers over his back.

It took all his strength to hold himself up. He was completely shot. She tugged on his back, but he resisted. He outweighed her by about one hundred pounds and didn't want to crush her. She wasn't having any resistance. She pulled on his back until he dropped onto her chest. In a swift move, he turned, pulling her alongside his chest. He rested his head back, his eyes lowering, and trailed his hand over her arm, curling her deep into his side.

Do not fall asleep, asshole.

Sleeping with a woman, in her bed, was not an option. Especially cuddling up next to her. It went against everything he'd ever done. As he felt himself fade into a deep sleep, her lips pressed against his neck. It was over, he didn't have it in him to fight it. And he didn't have the desire to fight it off. *Fuck!*

His sleepover was confirmed when the sunlight breeched the curtain. He squinted and turned his head, taking in the sweet cherries and vanilla scent as she circled into his chest. He pried one eye open and saw Phoebe's blonde hair against his shoulder. He stretched his legs, which were tangled with hers.

He reached over and grabbed his phone to check the time. *Shit!* Another first, he'd overslept, and it was past nine. He was scheduled to be in the shop by ten.

She pulled away, turning in his arms, and he immediately pulled her back against his chest. Where the fuck was she going? She came willingly and flickered her eyes open, brushing her face against his chest.

"Morning." It was a groggy greeting, and the corner of his mouth curled.

"Gotta get to work."

He expected her to pull away again. Instead she curled against his chest and circled her fingers over his pec. The small touch was working its way to his lower region. For all their fucking the night before, he was ready to take her again. He sighed, running his hand over his face. No time.

She crushed her face against his chest. He watched as she pushed up on her elbow and yawned. Fucking beautiful. *Too beautiful.*

"You want coffee?"

He rubbed her back and hitched forward to sit up. "I'll get it at the house."

She nodded, and he turned away. It was his only chance to get away. Seeing her dazed and dreamy was fucking with him. It had him wanting to stay in her bed. He heaved his legs over the side of the bed and stretched his back. He heard the crack. *I'm getting too fucking old.* Forty was knocking on his door, and he was feeling the effects.

He forced himself out of her bed and got dressed. He hadn't

looked over at her, assuming she had passed out again. He'd gotten dressed quickly and heard the shuffling behind him, which he assumed was Phoebe settling back into her bed. He walked through the door, heading to the counter to retrieve his phone. Then he heard her giggle and glanced over his shoulder.

Too fucking sexy.

"Something's missing," she teased.

She snapped her fingers and leaned against the doorway, dressed only in her tank top and panties, looking sexier than anything he'd ever seen.

"You need a walk of shame theme song." She smirked.

He stalked over to her quickly and wrapped his hand around the back of her neck. She perched up on her toes, leaning in for a kiss. Kase wasn't having any of that. He held her in place when she shifted forward, and he leveled her with his eyes. Her eyes searched his face in confusion, and he waited until those blue eyes met his again. Fantastic fucking clear blue eyes.

"I spent the night in your bed," he lowered his voice. "In you." He paused, watching her cheeks heat, which seemed almost rare for Phoebe. "There ain't no fucking shame in that." He pulled her an inch closer, kissing her.

"Better be careful, Kase. You may not realize it, but you're being sweet." She angled her head and crushed her breasts against his chest. "I didn't know you had it in you."

"I don't."

"Yes, you do, and I like it," she whispered. The soft tone had him gripping her tighter. Her voice was proving to be a downfall for him. Her lips grazed his chest, and she glanced up through her lashes. "You should come back."

His hands cupped her jaw, strumming his thumbs over her cheeks. He'd be back.

It would take a natural disaster to keep him away. *Fuck it.* It would take death to keep him away. He gripped her neck, pulling her in for a kiss. His tongue swirled against hers, and her body strained against him. If he didn't pull back, he'd be inside her again.

His lips swept against hers, and he gripped her jaw setting her back an inch. "I'll see you tonight." He kissed her again and released her from his hold. He purposely didn't look back. Kase didn't trust himself not to climb in her bed again.

Kase walked out her door, squinting from the sun. He needed to shower and get down to the shop. It wasn't rare for him to oversleep, but it was for him to stay in bed bullshitting. He dredged through the lawn, hopped over the fence, and made his way to the front door. He caught Gage smirking by his bike.

Kase motored up toward the clubhouse, waiting on his brother's snide remark. He was surprised when Gage remained quiet, simply eyeing him. Kase turned as he passed, pinning Gage in his stare.

"Now she's fucking off limits."

Gage burst out laughing as Kase walked up to the door with a small smile playing on his lips. No one would go near Phoebe. He was staking a claim, and it would be followed. He made his way through the bar, which was empty except for Nadia at the bar. He glanced over, and she smiled with a quick wink.

"Another one goes down." She giggled, and he ignored the comment.

His day was busy with time at the shop and reaching out to charters setting up the deliveries. They were making bank, but they needed to continue on with the cash flow. He'd be in her bed tonight, though. He'd make sure of it.

Chapter 12

Fourth night in a row.

Her fingers dug into his bare chest, tracing the outline of his muscles. It was hard to concentrate on anything when he was kissing her. His tongue dipped between her lips, and she moaned softly, heaving her breasts against his chest and deepening the kiss.

His hand dipped between her legs and shifted to allow better access. Round Two.

The pads of his fingers slid over her clit, and she arched into his hand. "Two days is too long." She moaned, dropping her mouth to his chest and licking his nipple. His finger curled against her nub, and her breathing labored.

She didn't expect a response to her statement. If she'd learned anything from Kase, it was that he was stingy with his words unless he was barking orders. While his hand worked her core, his other reached into her locks, threading his fingers through her hair.

The sharp knock on her door had Phoebe bolting up from the bed and skittering away from Kase. She never got unexpected visitors. Well, except one. He grunted and shifted up on the bed.

She glanced back at Kase, who was reaching for his cigarettes.

He didn't seem even the least bit concerned about who might be at her door.

The loud knock got her attention again. "Who do you think it is?"

Kase sucked in a drag of his cigarette. "Only one way to find out."

She leaned to the floor, grabbing her shirt and whipping it over her head. She flipped her hair from the collar and reached across the bed for her pants. She turned to Kase, who was staring at her with a smirk.

"What?"

"Your tits look fucking great without a bra."

"Are you seriously talking about my tits while I have someone pounding on my door at eleven thirty at night?" She grabbed her jeans, yanking them off the bed and awkwardly trying to get them on without giving Kase a show. Asshole didn't deserve one.

She jerked her head and glared at him. "It could be a serial killer at my door, and all you're concerned with are my breasts."

Kase chuckled, and his chest shook. "Psychos don't knock."

She raised her brows and smirked. "You do."

He scowled. "You're lucky I like your pussy."

Phoebe widened her eyes and nodded. "Oh yeah, biggest honor of my life, asshole." She gave him the finger and walked out the door.

The knocking intensified, and a few options passed through her mind. One of the members looking for Kase. She was pretty sure his sneak-overs hadn't gone unnoticed by Saint or Rourke. She had caught the three men gathered in a group in the club's yard before he came over.

She tiptoed to the door and slid the curtain. *What the...* She quickly flicked the lock and opened the door. Her heart raced. Something had to be wrong. She never showed up announced. It was completely out of character.

"Hey, you okay?"

Bailey drew in a breath and grinned. "I hope I'm not bothering you." She held up a yellow folder. "I've got the information on the park, guidelines and suggestions. It's a hard copy, and I'll email you everything too."

"Great." The visit had caught her off guard and seemed completely suspicious. Bailey's demeanor only added to it. She glanced over her shoulder, her eyes looking around the interior the best she could from her angle in the doorway. Was Bailey spying?

Phoebe bit back her chuckle and smiled. "You want to come in?"

"Oh no, I just wanted to drop off the papers." She bit on her lip. Was she stalling?

"All right."

Bailey jerked her gaze to Phoebe. "You're coming to the party, right?"

Phoebe raised her brows. "You know I'm coming." She laughed. "Bails, what's going on?"

"Nothing, just confirming," Bailey said and stepped back. She grinned and waggled her brows. "Tell Kase I said hi."

Phoebe froze and clamped her lips tightly.

She waited until the door closed before heading back into her room. When she opened the door, she found Kase staring at her.

She grabbed the hem of her shirt and lifted it off her body. His eyes heated.

Kase leaned over to her nightstand, never taking his eyes off her. He stumped out his cigarette.

"Get your ass over here."

Phoebe reached for the snap on her jeans and unzipped her pants, slowly dropping them down her legs. Once they hit the floor, she toed them away from her feet and brought her knees to the mattress. She dropped her hand to the bed and crawled closer. Kase watched her through his darkened gaze. Her hand caressed his ankle and moved up his thigh past the sheet. Even through the material, she could make out his hardening cock. Her hand drifted up his thigh and grasped the sheet, yanking it away.

"I was thinking about sucking you off, but where does that leave me?" she said, draping her breasts over his chest and reaching for the condom on the nightstand. Before she could tear it open, he ripped it out of her hand and glared at her.

"Touch yourself."

She straddled his thighs as he ripped open the condom with his teeth. Her hands slid over her neck, down to her breasts as his eyes watched her very move.

"You're being lazy, Kase, making me do all the work. Ya know, I can come without you."

His soft growl was the only warning she got. He grabbed her hips just as her fingers grazed over her pussy. She gasped as her body was pulled over his. Her hands gripped the edge of the headboard as she eased over the crown of his cock. It was a tease, and if she hadn't wanted to get off so badly, she would have continued. She slowly lowered, sending his cock sinking into her core.

She meshed her breasts against his chest, and his hands circled her waist, dropping to her ass. She moved slowly, knowing Kase may not admit it, but he loved the slow fuck. She tightened her core, squeezing his cock. Another move she knew he was a fan of, and one which hit her g-spot. She moaned, sliding over his dick. His hands were everywhere, over her back, gliding into her hair, and forcing her head toward him. His mouth locked on her hers, and his tongue slipped past her lips, swirling against her own tongue. His kiss alone had her swiveling her hips and thrusting over his length. Among many things, Kase had been the biggest man she'd ever been with. She pulled away slightly from his lips to inhale, but he was relentless, taking her lips and plunging his tongue inside her mouth. *God, this man can kiss.* She gripped his shoulders and rocked over him, slightly engaging her rhythm and speed. She sat back, gripping his thighs and dropping her head on her shoulders.

His fingers caressed up her stomach and slid over her breasts. For as rough and reckless as his exterior, the pads of his fingers feathered over her nipples with a tease, and she tightened her core.

"Kase." She squeezed his thighs and arched her back, driving her pussy over his cock. His soft, hushed curse made her smile. It was good to know she was affecting him as much as he affected her. His hand slipped down her stomach, sliding onto her clit, and curled the sensitive nub. Fuck! She fell forward against his chest, locking his hand between them. She curled into his neck, her mouth breathing heavy against him as his hips jutted forward, stroking his cock deep inside her. She felt him everywhere. It was too much.

She reached between their bodies and gripped his wrist. She was caught between too much feeling and being on the verge of orgasm. Her mind was spinning, and she moaned again. His finger relentlessly flicked her clit, and she gasped.

"Oh God, that's so good."

He growled, grazing his teeth over her neck and thrusting his cock inside her. Her free hand gripped his shoulder as her thighs tightened and her toes curled while rocking her hips against his, her entire being lit with a fiery tingle over her skin. The rise to her orgasm was almost as good as when she finally came. Almost. She dug her nails into his skin and screamed out when she reached her peak. *Oh fuck*. His continual thrusts inside her only prolonged her orgasm to the point of pure exhaustion. She collapsed against his chest, swiveling her hips until his strokes deepened and he was seated so deep inside her core, she could feel him coming inside her. His finger flicked against her clit, and she tightened her grip.

"Please stop, you're gonna kill me if you keep doing that."

His hand stilled, and she shook under his rumbling chest. He pulled his arm from between them. She was no help. She could barely lift her body. She dropped her head to his neck and completely settled into his chest.

She closed her eyes and panted heavily, ignoring the fact that he was still inside her and probably needed her to move to clean up. *He can wait.* And he did. In a surprising move, she felt her sheets glide over her back and his hands rest over her.

"I know I gotta get up, but I need a minute."

"I'm in no rush."

She pried her eyes open. This was nice. Settling in with a lover after fucking. Her nose skimmed his neck, and his arms tightened around her back. Who knew Kase Reilly was capable of cuddling? She closed her eyes and drifted. The soft caress on her back was rocking her to sleep.

FOUR NIGHTS in a row with the same woman. The only *woman*. It was a record for him. Phoebe had changed everything for him. Here he was, sleeping with her again.

It was a general rule he'd made for himself years ago. Yet, with Phoebe, he seemed to be breaking all of them. *Fuck, she feels good.* His hand rose up her back, threading his hand through her hair. She turned her head with her eyes at half-mast.

"That feels good, Kase."

He threaded his fingers, massaging her scalp. The way she was curling into him kept him going. She angled her head and pushed off the mattress, pressing her lips against his. This was new territory for him. Phoebe was new territory. He'd had women come in and out of his life for most of his adult life. Some stayed longer than others, but he'd never felt any kind of connection. They were club girls, and being brought up in the club life, he knew what to expect. He'd seen his brothers settle down with women from the life. For some it worked, for others it fucking failed. He never had an interest in a woman for more than a night.

Kase had an agenda when it came to the club, which always came first. As it should. He'd built his life around the Ghosttown Riders, a decision he never regretted. Had he been missing something? She nestled her ass against his cock. A move hundreds of women had done in the past. However, his reaction was different.

He dropped his hand to her hip and tugged her against his body, molding her into him, and dropped his mouth to her ear. Her hair tickled against his nose, and he closed his eyes taking in her scent.

"Bailey said to say hi." She inched closer, and he tightened his hold. "Forgot to mention it before. I was distracted."

Kase smirked, brushing his nose against the back of her head. Her scent should be fucking bottled up. He settled in next to her and the warmth of her body.

"You got nothing to say?"

He flicked his eyes open. "About what?"

"Bailey knows you were here. The house is small, Kase, only one place you could be."

"What the fuck are you talking about?"

She groaned and turned in his arms. He jerked back to make room for the ungraceful spin. She glared up at him. "She knows you were in here." Her eyes widened. "My bedroom."

"Yeah, and?"

Her brows knitted together, and she eyed him suspiciously.

"Why don't you seem shocked she knew you were here?" She squinted with a playful smirk donning her lips. "Tell me."

"Are we fucking sharing again?" His tone was laced with sarcasm, which seemed to amuse her. Making a woman laugh was not his usual MO.

"Yeah, let's. No sex-escapades, though. My stories aren't nearly as exciting as yours." She clucked her tongue, and the corner of her mouth curled into a sexy half smile. "Actually, I do have a few that might impress you."

"Phoebe." He gripped her neck and scowled harshly. The last thing to come from her mouth should be speaking of another man she'd been with. Kase was rarely jealous of anyone, but his possession over Phoebe was bringing out new sides to him.

She giggled. "Fine, no sex stories." She nestled against his chest. "Tell me about Jack."

"What's to tell, you know him."

"Was he a good president?"

"Yeah." He wasn't sure where the question was going. He'd always been suspicious of anyone outside the club, especially those who took an interest in his club.

"Better than you?"

He scoffed and furrowed his brows. "If you ask him? Yeah."

She smiled. "His stories true, or is he exaggerating?"

"He been telling you about the life?"

"A little."

"He's old and losing his fucking mind, but he doesn't lie. All he's told ya, yeah, it's true."

She arched her brow. "He told me you're an asshole."

"I am."

She grinned, swiping her lips under his ear.

"He likes you."

Phoebe stilled with her lips grazing his neck. She pushed away, leaving only a few inches.

"Jack don't like a lot of people." He snorted. "I can probably count them on one fucking hand. But you?" He raised his brows. "He likes."

She grinned. "Does it bother you I'm one of your dad's favorites?" She was teasing. He could easily play it off. He chose not to.

"It did. That night you were drinking whiskey by the fire. I hung back listening to you guys. He ain't open like that with a lot of people. But with you, it was like he'd known you forever."

She licked her lips and shifted her hips. He knew her well enough. Phoebe was growing increasingly uncomfortable with the conversation. She was taking it the wrong way, and he needed to rectify that.

"I said it did bother me. It doesn't anymore. Me and Jack, we're too much alike to ever get close. Knew that a long time ago. Seeing him bond with someone else, it hits old wounds." Kase paused. "Makes me the asshole who talks shit to a woman who was showing the old man some fucking kindness."

He wasn't about to rehash all the shit he'd done wrong with

her. The diner and store scene were fucked up, but she'd forgiven him. He wasn't looking to revisit it again.

She curled her lip and twitched her nose. "I think Jack likes me more because I got a better ass than you."

Kase shook his head and laughed. She was making him laugh, naked in bed. She thrust forward, planting her hands on his chest.

"I'm loving our sharing. I want more."

He dipped his chin. "Ask."

"Did you always wanna be a biker?"

He sighed, spreading his hand over her back. "I grew up in it. It's part of who I am. Don't remember wanting to do anything else."

"Did your mom approve?"

He gritted his teeth. It was a reactionary response every time she was brought up, which was rare. With exception to the ranting about her, his Pop never mentioned her. Neither did Caden. She had always been a taboo subject among the Reilly men with good reason. He could blow off the question, but why the fuck would he? If she wanted to know, he'd tell her.

"She was a cunt."

Phoebe stilled in his arms and slowly lifted her head, angling up on her elbow and staring back at him with a glazed shocked scowl. "Don't think I've ever heard someone refer to their own mother as a cunt." She raised her brows. "Kinda harsh, don't ya think?"

Kase clenched his jaw. "She left before I turned ten. Before that?" He cocked his brow. "If she wasn't ignoring me and Cade, she was screaming, calling us bastards, and throwing shit at us. She bolted with the first guy willing to take her ass away. She fucked around on Jack every second she got. He was no fucking saint either, but he didn't bring whores around us. She had no problem bringing men into her bed with Cade and I in the next room."

He didn't have to know her background to know Phoebe's life as a kid wasn't exposed to the shit he'd seen.

"You ever see her?"

"No."

"I'm sorry."

Kase shrugged and kept his gaze locked on her. She was feeling more for his situation than he was. It was the hand he was dealt, and he played it. Bitching and moaning about a past he couldn't change was a waste of his breath. He wouldn't give the cunt anything. He proved that years ago when she came looking for a handout. He'd refused to see her, even had her thrown out on her ass when she showed up at the clubhouse. He wasn't about to share that piece of information with her.

Phoebe pursed her lips together and tilted her head. "Your turn. Ask me anything What do ya wanna know?"

He caught the reeling in her eyes. She wanted to know more about him but was changing the subject. *This is what a good woman looks like.*

"Wanna know what the old man said to you to get ya to come for him with a bat."

She groaned, dropping her head against his chest and mumbling something he couldn't make out. He smiled and bit back a laugh.

"I fucking shared, don't pussy out on me." His tease got her attention, and she jolted up with a severe scowl.

She leaned closer with her nose inches from his. "I've never been a pussy a day in my life."

He raised his brows and sat up, resting his back on the headboard. He reached over for his cigarettes and eyed her carefully. He'd pissed her off with the comment. One of the best parts of Phoebe was her fiery personality. She sat and crossed her legs and pulled the sheet to cover her breasts. Her hair was a mess, her makeup smeared, and probably the sexiest she'd ever looked, at least in Kase's eyes. He lit his cigarette and watched as she drove her hand through her hair and flipped it over one shoulder.

When she remained silent, he nudged her knee with his leg,

and she glanced up through her lashes. She twisted her lips and sighed, allowing her shoulders to sag.

"It's a long story."

"Am I going somewhere?"

Phoebe shook her head.

"What?"

She glanced up and shrugged. "I just never talk about it."

"Then don't." He wouldn't pressure her into anything. He'd done most of his bidding for information by bullying his way to answers. For some reason, he couldn't bring himself to do that now. Not with her.

She watched him as if she was waiting on him to command her to answer him. He drew in a breath, keeping his eyes locked on hers. The corner of her mouth curled, and she leaned forward, pressing her lips to his in a soft lingering kiss. By all accounts, she was ending any further conversation. Then she pulled away, resting on her knees and waiting.

She licked her lips with hesitation. "I'll tell you."

He eyed her, and the silence dragged between them.

"Talk," he commanded with a smirk.

"He outed me."

Kase furrowed his brows.

Phoebe sighed. "When Jared died and everything came to light, the debt, the infidelity, all of it happened back in California. I spent nine months trying to sort out the financial shit and suffocating under all these new revelations. More women so early on in our marriage. The fact that most of our mutual friends knew about it for years. And no one told me. It was humiliating, embarrassing. I can't even put into words how it ripped me apart. It almost destroyed me." She drew in a deep breath. "My only saving grace was I had this little piece of heaven." She snorted and glanced around the room. "This shack on four acres where I could retreat and just be me without any baggage left behind by Jared. No one in Ghosttown was privy to any of the sordid scandalous bullshit of his death. They knew he died; they knew I was a widow. Without any details. And I never gave any."

Phoebe glanced up at the ceiling, and her shoulders bunched. "But Arnett did. A few months after I got back, I ran into him on Main Street. He was making a scene, as usual." She snorted. "He was complaining about the new benches and how they'd encourage loitering. Anyway, it was a Saturday afternoon, a lot of people around. I made a joke about his never ending need to complain." She rolled her eyes. "I stand behind that. We went back and forth, sharing insults and digs." She darted her eyes to Kase. "Can't remember exactly what I said to trigger it, but he lost his shit." She groaned shaking her head. "I swear, Arnett had all the info hidden away in some secret asshole vault of his and sat on it before exploding with it all." She sighed. "He started screaming about how we'd been so far in debt, I had to sell everything I owned just to pay it off, and how Jared had been cheating on me for years. Spewing shit about me not satisfying my husband so he was forced to seek out other women." She snorted and wiped her cheek. "As if that wasn't enough, then Arnett shared where Jared died. In the bed of his lover." She stared down at the sheets. "Even threw in how his mistress showed up at the funeral."

An icy blast filtered through his blood. Even a cold bastard such as himself could feel her pain through her words. The pain, the embarrassment, the hurt.

"You're fucking kidding me?"

She shook her head. "Wish I was. But no, she showed. The crazy bitch even had the balls to ask if she was named in his friggin' will."

"You beat her ass?"

Phoebe smirked and glanced up at him. "No. My dad and Carter wouldn't let me. I'm still shocked that I didn't go after her, but after all that happened, then all his debts I was left with, finding out he no longer paid the premiums on his life insurance so when he died, I got nothing. I sold the houses and took a loan from my father to pay off this place."

"I would have beat the fuck outta the old man too."

"I was actually walking away from him when Arnett delivered the final blow." She lost every ounce of ease, and her face paled. "He said he should have bought my property when he had the chance so he'd be rid of me. Apparently, Jared reached out to him, unbeknownst to me of course. Offered this place." She glanced up. Her voice lowered. "Real cheap for a quick sale. My guess is Jared recognized how far into debt he'd gotten himself into and was looking to cash in on anything he didn't deem his."

What the fuck? "The motherfucker was gonna sell without telling you?"

She nodded. "According to Arnett."

"Coulda been bullshitting you." He wouldn't put it past the old fucker to lie to her.

Phoebe snorted. "He wasn't. Before Jared died, I was getting calls from realtors wanting to list the house. When I mentioned it to him, he said it was probably cold calls. At the time I didn't question it, but when Arnett said that, it was like a whole new anger built inside me. Something snapped in me." She laughed without humor and curved her neck, staring back at him. "That's the man I chose to spend my entire life with. And he was trying to sell off this place to Arnett, told him he'd give it to him cheap just to get rid of it." Her cheeks flushed, and Kase could feel the anger radiating from her skin. He also sensed the hurt. He couldn't be sure which infuriated him more. The anger he could relate to; her hurt made him want to fucking strangle the old bastard across the street. He breathed heavily, keeping his emotions at bay. He was a master at the disconnect. Until now.

She grabbed her chest, and her eyes welled. "This was mine. I wanted this. I found it and used my money as the down payment with savings I had stockpiled away, and that son of a bitch was taking it from me." She gritted her teeth. "Behind my back?" She narrowed her gaze. "To anyone else this place is a shack in the woods." Tears welled in her eyes, and she whispered, "To me, it's everything."

His hand itched to touch her. Ease some of the pain some fucker laid on her. He didn't.

She drew in a deep breath. "And then I snapped, grabbed my bat from the truck, and made a beeline for him. Luckily for Arnett, Coop got to me first and grabbed it from me. My rage was so blind I didn't even care. I got three good shots before Coop could grab me and pull me off him. I was hellbent on making him feel every ounce of pain I was feeling."

"From what I hear, he did."

She chuckled and tilted her head. "Not one of my finest moments."

"That's why ya wouldn't sell last year, because this place is yours."

She clamped her lips with a short nod. She bowed her head and sniffled, discretely wiping her eyes. *Fucking hold her, asshole.*

He wasn't built to console. He wouldn't even know how. He eyed her, watching her break before his eyes.

"And Carter?"

Her shoulders slumped. "After I sold everything off, I was still forty grand in debt. My dad offered to loan the cash to me so I wouldn't have to sell this place. I took it. Been paying him back each month." Her cheeks pinkened, and he waited. Pushing her on anything right now wouldn't fare well for either of them. She licked her lips and sighed, deflating a bit on the mattress. "That's what I thought, but it turns out my dad was just a front. He borrowed the money from Carter. I guess he didn't have it, and knowing my relationship with my brother, he knew I wouldn't take it. And he was right."

"That's why you're selling now?"

"Yeah. When Carter slipped and told me, I made the immediate and rash decision to sell." She snorted. "Sometimes I'm impulsive."

"Can't take a loan?"

She cocked her brows. "With my credit? No bank would let me in the door." She shook her head. "Over a year later and Jared is still fucking me over." She sighed. "I love this place, but not enough to have Carter's money hanging over my head for the next couple of years."

He chuckled. "You and him always like this?"

"Since the day I was born. He's an asshole."

It was probably a verbatim response Caden would give if asked about him. He could relate to her with the discord, and he could relate to Carter with secretly having her back.

Kase shrugged. "Always been good and fair to me and the club."

She arched her brow. "So he has helped you out, huh?" She paused, and he read her curiosity. "Care to share, gimme something to hold over his head?"

"No."

She swatted his leg and smiled.

"Come here," Kase whispered.

She was too far away, and the fun and light mood that was usually involved with her was lost. He reached out, grasping her forearm and tugging her forward until she fell against his chest. Kase wrapped his arms around her back and smiled when she nestled closer in silence. She snuggled into his chest, and he felt the warmth of her body. It wasn't much, but he was willing to give her what he could. It was times like this he wished he'd been a different kind of man.

"Thank you." She whispered so low he wasn't sure he'd heard her right. Did she just thank him? She curled her fingers into his waist and nestled her face against his chest.

"For what?"

She sighed and he felt her weight bear down on him. "For this, Kase."

Chapter 13

Phoebe was waiting on the awkwardness to set in with Kase. She'd poured out all her history with Jared and then Arnett. *Hell, I cried in front of him.* Letting her guard down with anyone was something she tried her best not to do. She failed with Kase. It was odd since he didn't seem to be the heart to heart type, but he also didn't seem the type to judge.

She cracked two eggs in a bowl and was beating them when Kase exited her bedroom.

They had fallen asleep after her admission, and when she had woken, he was getting in her shower. It was the first time he'd done that, but she wasn't complaining. He wore the same clothes from last night, and his wet hair was slicked back and draped down his back. She'd never had a thing for long hair, but on Kase, everything worked.

"You heading out?" She watched as he eyed her counter. "Or do you want an omelet?"

He glanced up and smirked. "Three eggs."

She snorted and walked back to the fridge to grab more eggs.

"You working today?"

She turned, and he was resting against the wall.

"Yeah, I have a deadline."

"You do websites and shit?"

She nodded. "Graphic design. I used to work for a firm, but since moving here, I contract jobs. My old boss sets me up with some leads, which seem to be panning out."

"You reach out to Chey and Macy?"

She furrowed her brows. "For what?"

He shrugged, settling in on the stool at the counter. He clasped his hands and rested his elbows on the counter. "Set something up for their shop. I know they sell shit online." He glanced away. "The shop and the yard could use one. You set it up and bill me."

She rested her palms on the counter and leaned across, stopping a few inches from his hard face. "You trying to get me business? That's sweet, Kase."

"Don't need you starving. Don't like fucking bony women."

She dropped her head and snickered. "You are so fucking charming, Kase Reilly."

He reached out, cradling her jaw in his palm and pulling her closer. Her lips tingled against his, and she fell forward, rising on her toes.

A sharp knock had her stilled in his clutches. She turned her head toward the door. It was after nine but still fairly early for visitors. He released her, and she slid back onto her feet. She started around the counter.

"Probably one of my guys."

She halted mid step and spun around. "Does everyone know you're here?"

"I didn't hand out a fucking memo, but they usually know where I'm at."

"You told the club you're with me?"

He shrugged. "Why the fuck wouldn't I?"

Phoebe felt the heat rise up her neck and turned in hopes of concealing it from his eyes. She grabbed the door and opened it wide. It took her a brief second for her brain to grasp who was standing in front of her.

"Oh fuck."

The Enemy

"Nice fucking mouth, Phoebe."

Her brother Carter stood in front of her dressed in his usual uniform of dark pants with a matching jacket, white starched shirt, and tie. He took after their father with his looks. Many women considered him attractive. Phoebe couldn't see it. His asshole attitude blocked any nice features he might have.

"You can't just show up here, Carter."

"Why not? I own some of it."

She clamped her lips and stepped forward. It had been years since she'd hit her brother, but that streak was seconds from ending. To his credit, Carter didn't even flinch. Maybe it was years as a cop, but he showed no signs of backing down or concern for his own safety. She gritted her teeth and glared at him.

"Let him in," Kase commanded from behind her.

Carter's nostrils flared, and heat rose to his face. He darted his stare over her shoulder and then back down to Phoebe.

"Are you fucking kidding me?"

She may not have punched him, but this came as a close second. She grinned and stepped back into her house, pulling the door open wide to give Carter an unobstructed view of Kase, who remained seated at her counter.

Carter stalked inside and stopped a few feet away from Kase. He was burning mad, and Phoebe was in complete joy. She slammed the door closed and passed by Carter, who was set on sending death glares to Kase.

"I told you to stay away from her."

Phoebe laughed, prepared to use this moment for all its advantages. She strolled over to Kase, who had remained seated but turned to face Carter. She grasped his wrist, settling between his legs, and curled her back against his chest. Kase must have approved because he grabbed her hips, tugging her against him with his hand firmly holding her waist.

"He didn't listen, Carter. He'd didn't stay away." She rested her back into his chest and pressed her hand against his thigh. "In fact, Kase got close. *Real close.*" She smiled.

Carter twisted his lips in a disgusted snarl. "He's gonna use you, Phoebe." Carter pointed at Kase. "Is that what ya want, to be some random chick he fucks, then goes back to his house and fucks the club women?"

She hadn't given much thought to the women Kase had been sleeping with besides her. He was in her bed for almost a week. She fought against the anxious energy rising in her chest. It shouldn't matter, they were strictly casual. *Right?* She licked her lips.

She felt Kase stiffen against her back, but he didn't release her from his hold. His fingers dug into her hip, locking her in place. Her vengeful banter with Carter had turned to wondering if Kase was sleeping with other women. *Does it matter, it's casual, remember?*

"Get out, I wanna talk to her."

"No," Phoebe snapped. "You get out. I didn't invite you over, and I've got nothing to say and you've got nothing I want to hear." She lunged forward, but Kase's hand gripped her stomach, holding her back. His lips brushed against her hair, and she heard his soft whisper.

"Settle."

She was sure Carter couldn't hear, but he'd been watching them intently.

"Phoebe," Carter warned.

She shook her head, settling into Kase's embrace. He had nothing she wanted to hear, and apparently, Kase was prepared to back her up.

"You got two seconds to get out. Don't make me call the cops and have you arrested for trespassing, Carter." The corner of her mouth curled. "It would make Christmas at Dad's so awkward."

She expected a fight. Nothing surprised her more than when Carter turned and walked out the door without another word. They had always had a tumultuous relationship, something she wished had been different. She'd envied all her friends who were tight with their siblings. It was something she'd never have with Carter.

Kase nudged her forward, and she stepped from between his legs and off to the side. Breakfast had obviously been ruined. She skirted around the counter as he made his way back to her room. He was leaving. She could sense it. It was confirmed when he exited her room sliding his arms through his cut.

"You coming over tonight?" She hated the expectation in her tone.

He glanced over, eyed her for a brief second, and then scowled. "What the fuck is wrong?"

It was strange to be with a man who was so in tune when something was off with her. It was also annoying. She shrugged, content with playing it off.

He groaned. "Ah fuck me, don't play this nothing's wrong when something's wrong female bullshit. Fucking what, Phoebe?"

He wouldn't let it go. She inched closer to the counter and rested her elbow, glancing up at him. It was an awkward question, and one she wasn't sure she was prepared to hear the answer to.

"Am I the only one you're sleeping with?" She regretted speaking the words the second they left her lips. What did it matter? What they had was merely casual sex, right?

She waited and watched. From Kase, she could expect an immediate answer. It was either yes or no without explanation.

He pointed at her. "Get your ass over here."

She circled around the counter and stopped a foot away from him. He reached out, grasping her waist, and yanked her into his chest.

"Where the fuck did I sleep last night?"

She gulped. "My bed."

"Night before."

"Here."

He nodded. "Yeah, I fucking did. Gonna be here tonight too."

She cleared her throat. "Well, what about when you go on a run? Where will you sleep?"

He smirked and leaned closer. "In a bed thinking of your tight, wet pussy." His hand threaded through her hair, and his palm cupped her jaw. "Or I'll be thinking of this mouth, those fucking full lips," his thumb grazed her bottom lip, "sucking my cock." He leaned closer, pinning her in his stare. "And I'll do that shit while I'm fucking alone. You feel me?"

She nodded and couldn't resist the urge. She propelled on her feet, sealing her lips to his. If he had been offended by her questions, he wasn't reacting. His tongue slipped past her lips, and Kase took her for an amazing, passionate kiss.

God, this man.

KASE WALKED out her door and snickered to himself. Carter was leaning against the hood of his car with his arms folded. Kase had known him for years, and it came as no surprise he hadn't gone away. Like Kase, Carter didn't take orders well. He straightened as Kase approached, pulling out a cigarette and lighting it up. He didn't slow down.

"She ain't gonna let ya in, brother." Kase watched as Carter glared. Kase took a drag of his smoke and jerked his chin to the clubhouse. "Come on, get you some coffee and I'll listen to you tell me to stay the fuck away from her." He continued walking and was almost shocked when he heard the gravel crunch under Carter's boots. He remained silent and a step behind Kase.

He hopped the fence with one jump, and seconds later heard Carter do the same. He walked up to the door, holding it open behind him, and they walked through the darkened corridor. Being as early as it was, there were very few brothers in the house. He walked toward the bar, and Nadia glanced over her shoulder with a soft smile. Her gaze veered past him, and her lips curled into a bright grin. *What the fuck?* Kase turned back to Carter, who smiled at Nadia.

"Hey, Nadia."

Kase eyed the interaction. It wasn't the first meeting between these two, but he'd never caught anything other than a polite greeting. He pulled out a seat and watched as Nadia shifted closer to the bar, patting down her hair.

"Hello, Detective Ross." She giggled and rested her hands on the bar, jutting her breasts out of her low-cut shirt.

Carter would have to be blind to miss it. The bastard kept eye contact and never faltered.

"How are you?"

She smiled. "Good."

"Settling into Ghosttown, I see."

"Yeah." She sighed, and Kase noticed a slight break in her smile. It was an automatic response with no commitment.

He hadn't spent much time with her since the move. She had always been one of his favorites, but with the move came more work and less play. When Phoebe hit the scene, he'd abandoned all the club pussy for his sexy fiery blonde. He'd been completely honest with Phoebe. She was the only one sharing his bed, and he had no regrets.

"What are you doing here?" She turned, grabbing a mug and pouring a cup of coffee. Kase assumed it was for him. He was wrong. She placed the mug in front of Carter and leaned closer on the bar.

What the fuck?

Carter glanced down. "Thanks. I'm visiting my sister. She lives next door."

Nadia's eyes widened, and she glanced at Kase and then back to Carter. "Phoebe's your sister?"

Carter raised his brows, nodded, and then turned a darkened glare on Kase. He refrained from laughing. Carter should have known better than to think he could intimidate Kase.

"She's great."

Carter snorted. "You think so?"

Nadia nervously alternated her gaze between the men and locked eyes with Carter. "Yeah. Got to hang out a bit. She's really funny and sweet."

Kase glanced over at Carter, who tightened his grip on the mug. Phoebe had shared enough with Kase. He knew they weren't close. Seeing Phoebe through Nadia's eyes seemed to shift something in the detective.

Carter nodded with a smile directed at Nadia. "That's good."

Nadia obviously was feeling out the vibe and shifted away from the bar. "I'll leave you guys to talk." She walked away from the bar when Kase snapped his fingers. She jerked her head and stared back at him.

"Ya think I can get a fucking coffee?" He raised his brows and watched the pink drench her cheeks. It was almost comical, and Nadia, who always seemed cool and collected, shuffled around the bar. Kase kept his head angled in her direction though his eyes were on Carter. His eyes were planted on Nadia. She moved toward him and winked when she placed the mug in front of Kase.

She started to the end of the bar, and Kase heard her voice again. "It was nice seeing you, Detective Ross."

Kase smirked as Carter nodded. "Bye, Nadia."

The silence remained for a few minutes. Kase took a sip of his coffee, set the mug down, and folded his arms.

"What?" Carter asked.

Kase shrugged. "Known you a long time. Know the girls offered shit when you'd come by. Also know you didn't partake. Wondering why ya never took Nadia up on her offer?"

Carter settled into his seat with a sharp glare. "Not interested in club pussy."

Kase laughed. "You look interested, brother."

Carter sighed and glanced over his shoulder. "Nadia never offered." He shifted in his seat and pinned Kase in his stare. "Why, man, why her? Why Phoebe?"

Kase knew the subject had swiftly changed.

"Ain't doing nothing Phoebe's not okay with."

He sighed and circled his hand around his mug, shaking his head. "Look, me and her, water and fucking oil since the day she was born. I don't know why, but we've never been able to sit in a room together without it ending in a fight." Carter dragged his hand over his mouth. "Don't fuck with her, Kase." Carter turned his stare on Kase. "As a favor to me, who's done a lot for you and this club." He paused. "Don't fuck with her. She spent seven years devoting herself to an asshole who completely fucked her over, and she never saw it coming."

"Did you? See it coming?"

Carter sighed and folded his arms. "Like I said, we never got along. Didn't spend much time with them. When I did, saw some things I didn't like, but Phoebe wouldn't listen to me even if I tried."

"But you didn't? Try?"

Carter shrugged. "Figured she'd see it eventually. By the time she did, it was too late." He paused, and Kase was reading a side to Carter he hadn't before. Regret. "Don't hurt her, man. She's been through enough." He stood and straightened to full height, reminding Kase Carter was a massive motherfucker.

"Got no plans on hurting her, man."

"Good, 'cause as much she's a pain in my ass, she's a good girl who has lousy taste in men." Carter smirked and walked out the door.

Kase started out for the backroom and did a quick change. He had peeked in Jack's room to find him sleeping. He'd be going back to Caden and Marissa's tonight.

He returned a few calls and grabbed the deposit from the shop. He'd make a run to the bank before heading into the store. He started out the back door and rounded the clubhouse, catching two people on the edge of the property.

"Son of a bitch," he muttered, eyeing Carter and Nadia. She

was shifting on her feet while he stood tall, seemingly unaffected by the hot, half-dressed blonde making time with him.

Whatever happened there was none of his business, though he knew there were a few brothers who wouldn't take kindly to Nadia cozying up next to a detective. Carter had always had a good relationship with the club. They were on opposite sides of the law, but there was mutual respect. Most of his brothers had respected that, though there were a few who didn't take a liking to Carter. He was a pompous, arrogant asshole, very similar to Kase himself.

He started to his bike, eyeing the scene playing in front of him. Nadia reached out, caressing his arm, and Carter smiled but backed away heading toward Phoebe's property. Nadia watched him walk away and turned with her stare on the ground. He'd known her for years, both intimately and on a friend basis. There weren't too many Kase considered friends, but Nadia had been part of the small group. Something was changing with her. He made a mental note to have one of the women check up on her.

He sat on his bike with another woman plaguing his mind.

He pulled out his phone and sifted through his contacts until he found her name. It rang twice.

"Hey you, just thinking about my boys, how are you?"

Kase eased into his seat, tucking a hand under his armpit, and smiled off across the yard. "Good, everyone's good here. What about you?"

"Same shit different day, darlin'."

"Need a favor, from me not the club."

"Sure, what do ya need, Kase?"

"A property here."

She chuckled. "I thought you bought all the property in Ghosttown."

"This one just came on the market." He sighed. "Need you to reach out to the realtor, tell her you saw it online, you live out of the area so you'll buy sight unseen. Full asking."

"You want me to do it directly?"

It was a fair question, and he understood her confusion. Meg had been the front for the LLC when they purchased all the available property in town for the past five years. It was her name and signature only, and she rarely did any work.

"Like I said, it's not for the club. Need you to keep this between you and me."

"Okay, send me the info, and I'll make the call."

"Later." He ended the call, shoving the phone in his pocket.

It wasn't the conventional approach to keeping a woman close, but it was the only shot he had. If she needed to sell to pay back Carter, he wouldn't stand in her way. He also wouldn't let her lose the one thing that was hers.

Chapter 14

It was by pure chance she'd caught a glimpse of him through her kitchen window. He stood alone, centered in her yard. She'd waited before making her way outside.

He looked lost.

Phoebe started toward her back door, taking a brief second to watch him. She would have given anything to get inside his mind, see where he was at, know what he was thinking. She'd settle for being whatever he needed at the moment.

"Hey, Jack." She opened the screen, stepping out onto her back deck. He hadn't acknowledged her. He seemed too lost in his surroundings. Or maybe he was just lost.

She walked over to the steps and took a seat, waiting on Jack. She rested her elbows on her knees.

"Needed a breather," he muttered, glancing around her yard, focusing mainly on the woods.

"Yeah, I bet all the hot young women and free booze must be exhausting."

He chuckled and pointed at her, shaking his finger. "I like you."

"Yeah? Well, the feeling is mutual, so you ever need a breather, you're always welcome here, Jack."

He eyed her and squinted. "Ya got something with my boy, dontcha?"

It was a direct question. Phoebe did her best not to react. How was she supposed to answer him? Yes, she had something, which was most likely nothing that felt like everything when she was with him. It was a mind fuck even for her, who had a clear head. She clasped her hands and sighed. She was prepared to give her response when Jack turned his back and paced the yard.

"Never settled down after my ex-wife. Fucking evil, that one." He paused and glanced up at the sky. "Great pair of tits, though."

Phoebe chuckled. "They've been known to take down many a man, Jack."

He smiled with the sun shimmering over his face. "Shoulda picked better for my boys. Like Coll." She had no idea who he was referring to, but from the sweet tone when he said her name, she must have been special. He jerked his head to her, and she noticed the slight ease in his tense features. "Good to Cade, Trev, and the baby. I shoulda picked one like her," He nodded and jerked his chin in her direction. "Or you." He smirked. "You and me would have had a good time, I think."

She licked her lips. "You and me, two ex-cons on the open road? Woulda been a helluva good time."

He folded his arms, shaking his head with a grin. "Had a beauty. Chromed out Harley, huge, fast engine. No one could touch me. Good cushion for your sweet ass." He winked. "Wind in your hair, on your face, with nothing between you and the road but a piece of machinery, like a magic fucking carpet. Straightaways were the best, full throttle at Mach speed." His smile faltered, and he muttered, "Nothing like it."

She drew in a deep breath and willed away the tears welling in her eyes. Watching another person caught in a memory so strong, something they knew they'd never feel again, was heartbreaking. It was a physical ache in her chest listening and watching Jack.

"You miss it, huh?"

He drew in a deep breath and rested his head back on his shoulders. He closed his eyes with the sun beating against his hardened face.

"Every damn day."

We all have our time. It was the circle of life. Being born, childhood, adolescence, young adulthood, adulting, middle age, the golden years, and inevitably, the end. Phoebe was stuck somewhere in the middle, but for Jack, it would all be coming to an end. And the stabbing, heartbreaking truth was he knew it too.

Coming to an end doesn't mean it's over just yet.

"I got an idea." It wouldn't be a replacement for what Jack was missing, but it was something. Something she wanted him to have.

She shuffled up her back steps and hurried through her kitchen, opening the drawer. *I can't give you a bike, Jack, but this may be a close second.* She grabbed the keys and darted out the door. She found him standing in the same spot, staring at her in confusion. She jerked her head. "Come on. Let's go have some fun."

She didn't wait for him. She didn't doubt his curiosity and the promise of a good time would be enough to pique his interest. It did. She heard the gravel of the driveway crunch under his boots. She walked across the lawn to the shed in the corner. She opened the doors wide and glanced over at Jack, who poked his head around to get a look.

"Want to go for a ride?"

God, I wish I had my camera. She stared at him, training her mind to remember. Every angle of his features, studying the gleam in his eyes, the showcasing of his teeth. The purity of a joyous smile. *Remember this.*

He grinned, shaking his head, and she swore he was Benjamin-Buttoning before her very eyes.

"Ain't been on one of these in years." He walked up and slid his hand over the handlebars.

"Not scared, are ya, Jack?" She was teasing.

He scoffed, waving his hand with a sharp shake to his head. He turned back. "Let's go for a fucking ride, darlin'."

Between the two of them, they were able to pull both out in record time. She gave Jack first dibs. There was a slight burst of pride when he claimed hers, deeming it the faster of the two. Jack was right, it was. As much as Jared enjoyed the ATV's and was as much a thrill seeker as Phoebe, he was a little more reserved when it came to vehicles.

She ducked back into the shed, grabbing the helmets before turning to Jack.

"I ain't wearing one of those pussy hats."

Phoebe swung the key around her index finger. "Then *ya ain't getting the key, Jack.*" She smirked. "My house, my rules."

His nostrils flared. Stubborn man was going to fight her on this. She tilted her head and remained silent, staring at him. They could be standing there all day. Phoebe needed a new approach. She stepped closer, keeping the keys out of his reach. Jack was sly enough to grab the keys.

"Look at it this way. If I come to your clubhouse and decide I want to dance on your bar, you'd probably tell me I gotta lose my top. Am I right?"

The corner of Jack's mouth hiked up, and he slowly nodded. "House rule."

"Right. Your house, your rules, so I'd take off my top." *Bullshit, I just wouldn't get up there.* But Jack didn't need that piece of information. She raised her brows. "At my house, you want to ride my ATV's, you have to wear a helmet." She shrugged. "House rule, Jack."

He waited, squinting his eyes until he grabbed the helmet from her hand and started putting it on. He muttered under his breath, but she didn't catch it. Probably for the best. She got on her helmet, lifted her screen, and glanced over at Jack. He was waiting on her for the keys. She tossed them over, which he caught midair.

As they warmed up, she told Jack of the trails she'd made through her property. It had been a while since she'd ridden. They had most likely been overgrown.

"Wanna take the lead, and I'll follow?" It was probably the first time she'd uttered those words. Phoebe was always willing to be the first at everything, even the unknown. Today was different. It had been a long time since Jack had led a pack, something she knew he'd missed.

He nodded with a wide smile. He leaned closer and shouted over the engines. "Should take these down to Main Street, give the folks a real shit scare." His hearty laugh was contagious.

"We'll save that for next time." She jutted her chin toward the woods. "Let's go, Jack. Lead the way."

Jack gripped the handles tightly, sliding his hands over the steering. He paused, turning over to look back at her. She would have given anything to know what he was thinking. Something behind his dark eyes; she was seeing a deep sadness. *Oh shit, is this a bad idea?* She bit her lip, holding his gaze. He drew in a deep breath and slowly smiled, followed by a cheeky wink.

"Try to keep up, darlin'."

Jack ripped past her as if he was already going at a high rate of speed. He disappeared before she could grab her handles. She hurried and stormed through the woods, gaining on him. She'd always been an adrenaline junkie and thrived in situations like these. When she finally caught up, she kept a steady rate behind Jack.

KASE STOOD at the edge of the clubhouse and brought the cigarette up to his lips, taking a deep drag. The smoke burned his throat, and he glanced down. He'd smoked it to the filter. Again. He tossed it on the ground into the small pile by his feet.

He stood waiting until he heard them come back around. His

gaze followed the sound and watched the two of them rip through the path, as he had for the past hour.

"Hey, looking for you."

Kase glanced over his shoulder and lifted his chin, greeting Cade. Then he turned around, catching them whipping down the hill. It would be a few minutes before they came flying up the hill, dodging the large oak and circling the open flat spot. Then they'd disappear for ten minutes.

"What are ya looking at?"

Kase folded his arms and waited for Cade to stand next to him. He remained silent until the echo of the engines came closer. He saw from the corner of his eye Caden moved forward.

"Son of a bitch," Cade said in a whisper.

Kase glanced over and found his younger brother mirroring his own reaction. Caden smiled, shaking his head. Kase glanced back just as the ATV's came into full view. First Jack, then Phoebe close behind.

"How the hell did she get him to wear a helmet?"

Kase chuckled. "No damn clue."

Jack had broken the helmet law in countless states throughout his life. His Pop was dead set against them. Somehow, Phoebe had gotten him to wear one.

"Is that Jack?"

Kase hadn't heard her walk up. Marissa wound her arm around Caden's waist and curled into his side. His brother swung his arm over her shoulder as the two of them stared across the property. Kase expected Marissa to lose her shit. Not from anger, just concern. But instead, she watched, smiling. Once they disappeared into the woods, Marissa pulled out of Cade's hold and walked to the edge of the house, peeking around the side.

"How long they been at it?" Caden asked.

Kase shrugged. "Few hours, maybe."

One of the prospects had mentioned the ATV's earlier. When Kase heard there were two riders, one being a man with Phoebe, he immediately put out his cigarette and dropped his glass to the bar, storming out the back door. Jealousy was an evil and new bitch for Kase.

He'd waited to catch sight, and when he did, a warming of his ice-cold heart filtered over his chest. One look and he knew who the man was. Kase had ridden behind Jack most of his life. In his younger years when he was new to the club, he'd memorized everything about how his Pop handled his bike, from the way he grasped the handlebars to the small detail of how his feet pointed outward. There was no mistaking it was Jack.

He had a brief bout with concern. Jack wasn't the man he once was. He was more fragile and unsteady. A fall or even a minor crash could do major damage. Was it worth it? Kase had decided it was worth the risk when he caught the expression on Jack's face. His Pop didn't have much left, and he wasn't going to take it from him.

"Need to get him home?"

Kase's week with Jack had come to an end. They were there to pick him up. Cade glanced over, and then his eyes drew to Marissa, who was waiting on Jack and Phoebe's return.

"Riss?" Caden asked.

She didn't turn around, just shook her head. "When he's done." Her cheeks jutted up as she grinned with a soft chuckle. "And Jack isn't done."

The three of them watched as Jack and Phoebe made their way back into their line of view. For the next ten minutes, they watched in silence until they disappeared again.

"Where's the girl?"

Marissa settled back and started toward him, smiling. "Are you ever gonna use her name?"

Kase cocked a brow. He had nothing against her name, but when he thought of his niece, he immediately thought of her as baby girl. He sighed. "Cora, where's Cora?"

Marissa winked.

Caden reached out, taking her hand and tugging her against his chest.

"Probably in the middle of some ruthless tug-o-war between the women, but last I saw, she was in Nadia's arms."

Marissa laughed. "Yeah, but Meg was standing over her shoulder. She definitely could have swiped her by now."

"Not if Macy got in there."

Kase laughed and walked back into the clubhouse. The women had gone ape shit crazy over Cora. They started throwing their weight around, and somehow implemented the 'no smoking in the house when the baby was there' rule. He shook his head as they walked through the door.

"I'll see ya out there," he said as they walked toward the main bar and he headed toward his room. Kase took off his cut, laying it on his bed. He ripped off his shirt, tossed it into his bin, and grabbed a clean one. He made his way into his bathroom and washed his hands before putting on a clean T-shirt. By the time he made it back to the bar, everyone was crowded around the bar. He smirked, shaking his head. Macy was a pain in the ass, and stubborn as fuck. He wasn't surprised to see the baby in her arms. When she glanced up, she lost her smile and groaned.

"No, Kase, I just got her."

Nadia snorted. "Liar, you've had her the longest, Mace. You're a baby hog."

Macy gasped. "Not as bad as him." She jerked her chin to Kase as he walked straight for her.

He couldn't fucking deny it. He was, and when he came in, he trumped any motherfucker holding her. He reached out his hands, and Macy rolled her eyes before carefully slipping her into his hands. With the exception of Trevor, he had no experience with babies. He was a kid fucking magnet, which even he couldn't explain. Saint's daughter, Cia, Rourke's niece, Emme, and Hades' little girl, Allie, had a severe case of hero worship when it came to him. It was unexplainable to everyone around him.

He curved Cora in the curve of his arm and smirked. The talking commenced, and they spent the next two hours hanging out in the bar waiting. During which time, the women had backed off, knowing Kase would only give Cora up when he was damn ready, and it wouldn't be anytime soon.

Nadia placed a drink in front of him. He grabbed the glass and caught Caden's stare from across the bar. A small smiled played on his lips. It wasn't the first time he'd caught Caden watching him with his baby girl. There was an ease about Caden and his stare. Kase cocked his brow.

"Thank fuck she looks like Riss."

Caden shook his head, laughing. "Always gotta be the asshole, Kase."

Yes, he did. It was another hour before Jack came back. Kase watched as he made his way in, walking straight to Marissa. His clothes were dirt dusted and slightly disheveled. But all his focus on was the light in his father's eyes, the color in his cheeks, and the ease marking his features.

The past few months, his father's demise had been swift. Everyone was prepping for his death. It would be the end of an era for Jack Reilly. It never set well with Kase how his old man would go out. The strongest man he knew would fade as he had for the last few years. Kase pushed off the seat and ambled through the bar, making his way to his dad, who had his arm hooked over Marissa's shoulder.

"You had fun?"

His Pop sighed. "Haven't felt that free in ages."

Kase stopped mid-step. Phoebe gave his old man something no one else could. She gave him his old self. Marissa smiled as she caught sight of Kase. She maneuvered around Jack and came forward, smiling.

"Let me have her, baby-whisperer." Marissa winked. She reached over, taking the baby from his arms. She glanced over her shoulder at his dad. "You ready, Jack?"

Her jerked his head, still grinning. "Let me get my shit." He passed, and Kase watched his old man disappear down the hall. Would this be the last time? *Fuck!*

A warm hand rested on his wrist, and he glanced up to see

Marissa staring at him. Caden stood behind her, grasping her shoulders.

"We'll take him home, and next week I'll bring him back. That work for you?" Caden asked.

Kase jerked his chin. The two of them were making it easy on him. He was going to take it. Words were never his thing unless he was doling out orders.

Jack appeared, saying goodbye to the guys. Even the new prospects who never pledged under Jack's reign were showing respect. The way it should be. Jack made his way into their circle.

"Ready?" Marissa asked, curling the baby into her chest.

Jack nodded and then glanced up at Kase. His brows knitted. "Don't fuck it up, Kase."

What the fuck?

Jack pointed to the right, and he knew exactly who he was referring to. Kase bit back his retort. The last man he would be taking women advice from was his own father. He caught Caden covering his mouth, clearly amused. *Fucking asshole.*

"Hey!" Jack snapped, gaining his attention. His eyes perked, and he raised his brows. "You don't deserve her."

Caden snickered, and Jack turned on him. "What the fuck are you laughing about? Your ass doesn't deserve Coll. Ya tricked her, knocked her up, and now she has to stay with your sorry ass."

Kase smirked and eyed Caden, who was glaring at his Pop.

Jack slapped Kase on the chest, gaining his attention again. "You do what Cade did." Jack nodded. "Knock her up before she realizes she can do better than you." He pointed at Kase. "It's good advice. Fucking take it." Jack straightened his shoulders and shot up his arm. "See you bastards later."

Kase watched him walk through the room as though he was royalty. Motherfucker earned it. Marissa leaned close, kissing him on the cheek, and followed behind Jack. He didn't miss her amusement in the whole scene. She was thoroughly enjoying being Jack's golden child. *She earned it.*

Kase sighed and turned to Caden, who was laughing. "Still want him next week?"

Jack Reilly hadn't been a model father. But for Caden and Kase, he'd done right by them. He did the best he could. It was enough.

Kase slowly nodded. "Yeah, I want him."

Caden smiled, slapping him on the back. "See ya on Sunday."

Chapter 15

Phoebe stared out her back door at her yard with her phone against her ear. *This is good news.* If it was so good, then why was there a giant pit in her stomach? She rocked back on her feet, waiting for some of the excitement on the other line to rub off on her. Nothing.

"Why are you so quiet, this is amazing." Tory chuckled. "Full asking price, all cash, and a short close. God, why couldn't all my deals be as easy as this one?"

Phoebe cleared her throat. "It's great, I know. A little unexpected, though. I figured it would sit on the market for a while." It was all happening too fast. She had no plan for when it actually sold. Where would she go? Kase immediately popped in her head.

"Let's be thankful it didn't. Are you around in the next few days? I'll stop over, and you can sign the papers."

"Sounds good."

She hung up and started to the kitchen when she heard the bang.

The hard knock on her door could be only one person. She stared back at the wooden door, unwavering in her steps. It wasn't until after Jack left that she considered the possibility Kase would be upset with her for taking him out on the ride. She staggered forward, biting her lip. Indecision was the worst. Her best line of defense would be the playful approach. She strolled toward the door and opened it.

"Hmmmm..." She glanced up at the ceiling. "I don't remember requesting a booty call." She gazed down, taking in his solid stature. There was no way of telling what he was thinking. Kase proved to be the hardest person to read. She gripped the handle and opened the door completely, waving her hand in a grand gesture for him to enter. His scowl was locked in place as he walked through her door, narrowing his gaze as he passed.

When she closed the door, she found him staring at her. His heated gaze was causing a slight shiver down her spine. She hadn't thought of anyone else other than Jack when she suggested the ride. Not Kase or his brother or anyone else, just Jack.

She spread out her hands. "You're mad at me, I get it."

He seemed caught off guard, and his temple twitched. He folded his arms, which seemed to add height to his already empowering stance. "Do ya?"

His tone seemed off, and he lacked the menacing glare he usually sported when he was angry.

"He was fine, Kase. He didn't get hurt."

He remained silent. She would rather have him shouting. At least she'd know his level of anger. Was this the calm before he exploded?

"I'd rather live a short and full life than a long and unhappy one." She shrugged. "Quality over quantity."

"Is that your decision when it comes to my dad?"

"No," she whispered. "But it's not yours either, Kase."

He jerked his gaze, and she settled back a step. The usually angry Kase was easy to handle. However, this was personal, it was delicate. Humor and teasing weren't going to work, and this time, she didn't want it to. For all the time she'd spent with him, he only allowed small snippets of his emotion to show. Going against everything she said she wanted and thought she felt, she did want more with him. The little he did show her had her craving more.

"I stayed close to him, and if things got outta hand, I would have stepped in."

He snorted. "You think you woulda been able to settle his crazy ass?"

She raised her brows. "I did get him to wear a helmet."

Kase sighed. "I'll give ya that. Surprised the fucker knew how to put it on. Think that was the first time he'd ever put one on."

"I won't apologize," Phoebe said.

He slowly angled his head, reminding her of how intimidating and deadly Kase could appear. He circled the couch. Her heart leaped to her throat. It wasn't exactly fear, but anxiety of what he'd do next. *Unpredictable bastard.* She backed into the wall, not even realizing she had been moving. She may have come to an abrupt stop, but Kase didn't. He pressed his chest against her breasts, caging her in. He lowered his head, and she gazed at him.

This would be a good time to apologize. It probably was, but she couldn't bring herself to say it. She wasn't sorry. She flinched when his hand rose, gripping her neck. It was firm but not tight. His thumb strummed her throat, scratching against her skin.

"You gonna strangle me?"

"Should I?" He cocked his head, and the corner of his mouth curled.

"God, I can't tell if you're mad or not."

Kase shook his head. "Why would I be? Pop had a good time, and with his days numbered, I ain't gonna take anything away from him. When he came back to the house, he was on a high." He jerked his chin. "You gave him that."

Kase lowered his head only inches from her face. His nose skimmed the tip of hers, his hand spread across her neck, and the pads of his fingers dug into her skin, sending a sparked chill down her spine. His breath fanned over her face when he stepped closer, pressing her back into the wall even more.

When she jutted her chin, he clamped his hand, keeping her

from moving. His hand skated around her waist, under the back of her shirt. The coarse, rough skin grazed over her back, and she closed her eyes. They were so close, pressed against each other, she could feel her erratic heartbeat against his.

She flickered open her eyes to see him close as his lips skimmed her mouth softly and slowly. A warm heated rush prickled over her skin. The dominant, passionate Kase was what she had come to expect from him, and she loved it. But this, right here and now, his lips grazing over hers, gripped in his hold, which was firm but gentle, it was almost too much. Her efforts to deepen the kiss were combatted by him slowing it down. His fingers drew into the back of her hair, angling her head where he wanted her, and she obliged. She'd do anything he wanted as long as he didn't stop kissing her.

He hoisted her up, and her legs immediately wrapped around his waist. Her main focus had been the kiss, though she was aware they were moving. She flicked open her eyes when she felt herself being lowered. The mattress curved under her back as he lay her down. Kase angled himself over her, bringing his lips to hers again.

"Kase."

"No more talking," he whispered.

KASE STRETCHED his arms over his head cracking his back. The manual bullshit labor was better suited for the young prospects. His age was catching up with him. Or maybe it had to do with being up until two o'clock making Phoebe come. He rolled his neck and started inside the warehouse.

"Too fucking early," he muttered.

He'd left her place at seven, stopping by the clubhouse for a quick shower before coming down to the shop. Their business had really taken off, which meant more hours on his end. He wouldn't complain, but since the arrival of Phoebe, he'd been less eager to leave the sexy woman naked in bed.

He grabbed the inventory list, signing off before handing it to Dobbs, who was set to drive it in. The rotating schedule made it easier for the brothers to plan. Some took more jobs than others. Dobbs and Gage were on the higher end, whereas Trax had scaled back since Chey got pregnant.

Not only was the club business expanding, so were the families.

"Alright, I'm out. See you bastards in a few days," Dobbs said, slapping Kase on the back and heading out the door.

He glanced up at the clock. It was almost noon, which meant another few hours at the shop. He followed Gage through the back doors to the floor. Just as they breached the door, he heard the bell ring out from the front door. With Gage directly in front of him, Kase's view was blocked. He shifted to the right toward his office. As the boss, he had payroll to cover before the end of the day.

"Tell me you brought lunch, and I'll marry you right now. Swear on my life, I'll get ya on the back of my bike, and we'll drive over to city hall."

The familiar giggle had Kase backing his steps. He grasped tightly to the papers in his hand.

Phoebe stood center in the shop, her sundress skirted around her thighs and her long blonde locks pulled to one side with the strands dangling over her chest. *Fuck me.* She approached Gage, who was behind the counter, with an easy smile and her eyes glimmering. She hadn't seen him from where he stood.

"I do have lunch." She twitched her nose and pursed her lips. "For Kase."

Gage groaned and slammed his hand on the counter. It was all for show and had the intended effect. Phoebe laughed. She reached out, grasping his hand. "Next time, I'll bring you something, I promise."

Kase inched closer to the counter, and her gaze immediately locked on his with her lips twitching.

Gage turned around and glared at Kase. "This is bullshit." He arched his brow. "Next woman to walk into this town is mine. I'm calling fucking dibs now." He stalked around the counter, stopped next to Phoebe, and jerked his chin toward the bag in her hands. "At least tell me it's some vegan shit I would hate."

Phoebe scrunched her nose. "Cheesesteaks and onion rings." She bit back her smile.

Gage shook his head. "You're dead to me."

Kase, who usually held back his amusement, snickered. Watching the playful banter between them, her and his brother, affected him in a way he wasn't accustomed. She was relaxed in his element among his brothers.

Gage marched out the door but turned before reaching the doorway. "Bastard."

Kase grinned. *Yeah, motherfucker, this one is mine.*

Phoebe cleared her throat and held up the bag. "Hungry?"

He eyed her stance over the counter, and the corner of his mouth curved.

"Food, Kase. I mean the food."

He jerked his head toward the end of the counter and led her down the small hall to his office. This was a first in his life. Having a woman surprise him with lunch at his job? Never. He settled in his seat and watched as she pulled out the food, handing him the foil-wrapped sandwich. She pulled up the seat across from him and got situated before opening her sandwich and taking a bite. Meanwhile, Kase watched her. She chewed until realizing he was staring.

"What?" It was mumbled with a mouthful of food.

He snorted. "Surprise lunch date? It's a fucking first."

She slowly chewed and glanced around his small office before swallowing. "Is it weird?"

Was it? For him it was. If he wanted lunch delivered, he'd

order it. Having Phoebe stop in with lunch seemed unnatural and domesticated. It should bother him, unsettle him. Oddly, it didn't.

"No," he said, and unwrapped his sandwich.

They spent the next twenty minutes eating their lunch and bullshitting. He was struck by the easiness he had with her. With most women, Kase had an agenda, something he wanted from them, mostly sex. Sitting with Phoebe, listening to her talk about checking out the park and the prints, it all seemed easy. Maybe too easy? Something he could get used to, or even want.

The soft knock at the door was followed by its opening. Saint walked in and halted when he glanced over at Phoebe.

She waved and wiped her mouth. "Hey, Saint."

He gave her a warm smile and turned to Kase.

"What do you need?"

"Set up a meet with Mack. It's gonna have to be in a few weeks, but I got a date." It was a meeting Kase wasn't looking forward to. As much as he wanted Hades to be a part of the club, Mack of Ghosttown East had never been a favorite of his.

"Our clubhouse?"

Saint nodded and turned toward the door. "Nice seeing you, Phoebe." He closed the door, and Kase noticed his smirk.

Kase reached across the desk, grabbing his cigarettes when Phoebe stood up.

"Well, I gotta run. As committee chair, I gotta go make little kid dreams happen with this park." Her face said it all. The last thing she wanted to do was be in charge of the park, but she'd do it.

Kase stood and rounded the corner, grasping her hips and pulling her against his chest. A word of thanks was on his lips, but he'd always been better at showing his appreciation rather than saying it. He cupped her jaw in his hand, tilting her head for the perfect angle and kissing her.

She righted her top and started to the door. "I might have to bring you lunch more often, Kase."

He lifted his brow. "Yeah, you better."

Chapter 16

Phoebe pulled out the boxes and wrapping paper, setting it all up on her dining room table. She was giddy with excitement for the party. Not necessarily the gathering, but watching Bailey and Cheyenne opening their gifts. She had the gifts personally made, and they had come just in time.

She had gotten up earlier and finished some work, cleaned the house, and done a load of laundry. With Kase staying over almost nightly, she made a habit of a three-day minimum on sheets.

She set up the boxes and heard the creak in the porch steps before the door opened with Kase walking through. He didn't knock anymore. He'd made himself at home, which included a few changes of clothes tucked on the top shelf of her closest, a toothbrush in her bathroom, and his favorite beer stocked in her fridge.

Some days it seemed odd how they'd taken a very domestic turn in their casual sex relationship. Most people would want to define what they were doing. A part of her wondered how the two most anti-relationship people in existence were virtually having a relationship.

If she dwelled too much on what was happening, she might freak out. After all, she vowed never to commit again.

"Hurry up, I gotta get over there before this fucking party." He grunted, making a beeline for her fridge with a quick detour around the table to take her in for a quick kiss. She savored his tobacco taste and shook her head.

"Don't be so grumpy. Baby parties are adorable."

It had been dubbed a baby party because the idea of having a baby shower at the clubhouse was absurd. The irony wasn't lost on her, but she kept her mouth shut and went along with it.

Kase knocked the door closed, flicking off the bottle cap and taking a swig of beer. The ball of his throat bobbed, and she tightened her thighs. How could this man turn her on by just drinking beer? He dropped the bottle to his side, pinning her with his heated stare.

"We got time." His implication was all in his tone. As much as she would have loved rolling in bed with this man, there wasn't time.

She grinned and held up her hand. "No, we don't, and stop giving me those come-fuck-me eyes, Kase." She scowled and turned back to her wrapping project. She unraveled the paper taking up half her table.

"What did you get them as a gift?"

"I'm letting this shit happen at my clubhouse, that's gift enough," he snapped, and wandered closer to the table.

She peeked up and smirked. "Wanna see my gift?"

He didn't respond except to lift a disgusted lip at all the glittered paper lining her table.

She dug in her bag and pulled out Bailey's gift. She had found a personalized company in Lawry and special ordered the tiny little jackets. A while back she had snapped a picture of Kase's cut and forwarded it to the company with her order.

She pulled out the tiny leather jacket. On the back was an exact replica of the Ghosttown Rider patch, and on the front over the right chest she'd had it embroidered "Property of Bailey and Saint" in pink lettering. And "Property of Trax and Chey" in blue lettering on the other.

She held up the jackets, beaming with excitement. His eyes travelled over both jackets, and for a brief second, she caught the hitch of his mouth. He wasn't committing to saying they were adorable, but there was no doubt the president of the Ghosttown Riders approved.

"You love it, don't ya?" she teased.

He steeled his features. It was too late, she'd seen it. The small softening in his expression. On a man like Kase, it was rare, which made it all the more noticeable when it happened.

"How much that set ya back?"

She shrugged. "Not too bad." It was a lie. The custom jackets had been more than she anticipated, but they were worth it. Kase snorted, and she glanced up. He pulled out his wallet and tossed two hundred dollar bills down on the table.

"Kase, you don't have to."

He glared. "Put my name on the fucking card." He walked into her bedroom without another word.

It took her the next half hour to wrap the presents and get ready. It was more time than Kase would allow, but she won. She'd suggested he head over earlier, but he hung around waiting on her.

Once they made it over to the club, most people had arrived. She noticed the curious stare in their direction. It also wasn't lost on her how some of the women and men treated her. They were accommodating, and particularly interested. She was her usual friendly and cordial self, dodging intrusive questions about her and Kase. What did she expect? This was their first outing as a couple.

She was seated at the bar with Kase when Trax, Rourke, and Saint walked over.

Trax hooked his thumb over his shoulder. "Chey said to send ya back, they're opening presents."

Phoebe knitted her brows. "You don't want to see what ya got?"

Trax sighed and rolled his eyes. "I know Chey. We get home,

she's gonna wanna look at everything she got again." He arched his brow. "And she's gonna make me watch her. Trust me, I'm gonna see that live happening in my living room in a few hours."

Phoebe laughed along with the men. She slid off her stool and rounded Kase's back. His next move was unexpected. He grasped her wrist, pulling her against his chest and kissing her as though no one was watching. She gripped his shoulders and angled her head to deepen the kiss. If Kase didn't mind an audience, then why should she? He had the decency to do what she couldn't. He stopped the kiss.

She leaned closer and whispered in his ear, "Tease." Her teeth grazed his ear, and she pulled away. She rounded his back and glanced over the bar top.

"Nadia, come on, they're opening presents."

Nadia jerked her head up and blinked. "Oh, ummm..." She glanced around the bar.

"Nad." Kase jerked his chin toward Phoebe, and then Nadia's face lit up with a gleaming smile. She tossed the rag on the bar and made her way around to Phoebe. They started down the hall toward the back where the women had set up.

She didn't look back, but she had the distinct feeling soft brown eyes watched her as she disappeared around the corner.

THE PARTY WAS WINDING DOWN, and most of the women and a few brothers had started cleaning up. While the theme wasn't his choice, it had been a good party. He glanced over his shoulder, looking for Phoebe. She'd gone to help Meg put away the food. When he turned back, he caught a familiar smile. Kase snorted and rolled his eyes. *Go the fuck away.* She didn't.

Val sauntered up. He'd had her a few times, but she hadn't been one of his favorites. She hopped on the stool in front of him and smiled. He knew her angle, all the brothers did. However, she never pushed with Kase. She wanted old lady status, and as of now, none of the brothers were willing to give it to her.

"Is your friend gone?"

It had become known through the club Kase wasn't partaking in club pussy. Though a few women still tried their hand at flirting, they'd been shut down every time. Val was especially persistent. Young and fucking stupid. Her bullshit sweet routine might work on a prospect, but no other brother would fall for it. Especially not him.

He sharpened his scowl. "You mean my old lady?"

Val flinched and sat back. He knew why. It was an admission he'd never made before. He surprised himself with how easily it had flowed through his lips. It was as accurate as the definition. He wasn't with anyone else and hadn't planned on it. There was only one woman he wanted.

He pinned her in his stare and took a long sip of his beer before slamming it down on the counter. "Go."

Her reaction was exactly what he'd expected. She scurried away. He glanced around the room and noticed Nadia staring back at him with an amused grin.

Rourke sidled up to the bar with Macy under his arm. She was obviously feeling no pain and blustering a laugh. Kase eyed her and then glanced up at Rourke.

"Might wanna check on Phoebe."

Macy heaved forward and grasped his thigh. "I friggin' love her." Rourke shook his head and grabbed his old lady. He jutted his chin toward the back room.

"Comparing tits back there with Kelsey." Rourke raised his brows. "Thinking your woman is seconds away from showing hers."

Kase shot up from his stool and moved swiftly down the hall. The back room was packed with most members off on their own except a select few. He noticed Gage and Dobbs chatting with Phoebe in the corner. Kelsey was laughing and stood topless next to Phoebe. *Oh fuck.* While he had no problem with her hanging with his brothers, Phoebe's body was for his viewing pleasure only. He stalked forward, glaring at Gage, who seemed too entertained.

"Hey." It was the only word Phoebe got out before Kase bent down, slipping her body over his shoulder and storming out the door. He heard the faint groans of displeasure, and as expected, Gage's howling laugh. *Motherfucker.*

"Wait, Kase, the party's not over."

Kase rolled his eyes, making his way down the hall with Phoebe hanging over his shoulder. He pushed open his door, slamming it shut once they were inside. He bent down, placing her feet on the ground and leveling her shaky feet.

Her eyes were glazed over, and he wondered how much she'd had to drink. He'd seen Phoebe drunk, but this was a new level. She stumbled forward.

"I'm not ready for bed yet."

"Then get naked," he commanded.

"Wait." Her hand pressed against his chest. "Sixty-nine." The corner of her mouth curled, and she backed up into his bed, climbing on top. "The first time I saw you in the town meeting, I thought, 'this man sixty-nines'."

She lifted her dress off and tossed it on the floor. Her striptease wasn't very graceful as she fought against her bra snap, but he didn't need seduction.

When she slipped her panties down her legs, Kase licked his lips. There wasn't anything he wanted more than to be face first in her pussy while she sucked him off. The mere mention had him ripping off his shirt and tossing it on the floor next to him. He worked his zipper as he made his way to her at the edge of the bed. His bed. Finally, he was going to have her in his bed. All fucking night.

He'd had other women, but none of them had stayed the night. Overnight sleepovers were not welcome. Except Phoebe. He'd grown addicted to her warm sweet body pressed up against him as he slept. He shucked his jeans, taking in every sliver of her naked skin as she sprawled out in his bed. She leaned back, lying down and spreading her legs, giving him a teasing glimpse of her pussy.

Kase crossed the room, taking a spot next to her and angling her body up. Too much tequila had her wobbling over his mattress.

"You gonna pass out before I get my mouth on you?"

She twisted her lips. "I've had drunk sex before, Kase. I know what I'm doing. It's not like this is my first time. I had this one guy…"

He clasped her wrist and tugged her chest against his body. "Phoebe." His tone was menacing with a strong warning. He knew there were others before him, but there was no fucking way he wanted to hear about them. Phoebe smirked and pressed her lips against his mouth. He wasn't accustomed to women teasing him. Not many dared to try, and none pulled it off. Until her.

Her fucking kiss was intoxicating. It took everything he had to rip his mouth away. He gripped her waist and turned her body, guiding her legs to straddle his head. The second her pussy came into view, he locked his mouth over her pussy, teasing her clit and making her squirm.

"Kase." She moaned, her hot heavy breath over his cock. She hadn't even touched him yet, and he was on the verge of coming. She had that effect on him.

Kase grasped her ass cheeks, pressing her pussy against his lips and licking her until her body shivered against his. He was lost in her body, so it came as a shock when her lips wrapped around his cock. He pulsed in her mouth, shifting his hips and forcing her to take more of him. He was being greedy. Her tongue circled over the crown of his cock, and he tightened his grip on her ass.

He couldn't count how many blowjobs he'd gotten in his lifetime. He did know that none had ever felt as good. He flickered his tongue over her clit and dipped two fingers between her folds. It had gotten her attention, and she groaned against his cock. The vibration sent his hips jutting forward to take him deeper down her throat. Neither one of them would last much longer.

She suctioned over his cock, taking him completely down her throat, and moaned, sending him shooting into her mouth. Usually he had a build up to an orgasm, but he'd been too far gone to feel it. His length slipped from her lips, and his hands pressed against his hips. She swiveled her hips and screamed his name in a breathy groan as she came apart.

Fuck!

Chapter 17

She stretched her arms over her head, blinking her eyes open and tightening her brows. The ache was in the center of her forehead and crept over the top of her head in a slow throb.

Last night's festivities had been a blur. She remembered the party and hanging out at the bar with Kase, Gage, Dobbs, and a few others, but the details were foggy at best.

Tequila, I remember tequila.

She drew in a deep breath and curled to her side. She recalled doing plenty of shots, a round of darts where most of hers ended up in the wall. There were so many boobs she couldn't remember if any of them were hers. *Ugh....*

She slowly dragged herself up into a seated position, and the sheet dropped to her lap. A quick scan had her clothes scattered throughout the room. It definitely ended with a bang. She cracked her neck and sighed, glancing over to the naked figure next to her. Bits and pieces stared to emerge. Sixty-nine was only the beginning. He'd taken her twice, once bent over the bed on all fours and once with her on top. She curved her thighs and felt the glorious ache between her legs.

She pulled her shoulders down in hopes of relieving some

pressure in her head. It didn't. She needed water, aspirin, and coffee. She shifted forward but didn't get very far. His arm wrapped around her waist, pulling her against the bed and pinning her down against his soft mattress. His eyes weren't fully open, and he dropped his head, grazing his lips against her neck.

"Go back to sleep." His gruff tone resonated through the room.

"I need aspirin, babe." Her quick retort caught her off guard. *Babe?* She'd never referred to any man with that endearment.

His groggy moan didn't surprise her but his next move did. He released her body and ambled up from the bed. Her eyes followed him around the room and through the small doorway off to the left. She assumed it was his bathroom. She waited, keeping her stare glued to the open door. A minute later he emerged, gloriously naked and sporting morning wood. She bit back her smile and sat up as he approached the bed. When he extended his hand, she reached out her palm, and he placed two small white pills in the center. He jerked his chin to his side of the bed.

"Get some water," he said.

Phoebe watched as he skirted around the bed and walked toward the small chair in the corner. It took her a second to glance over and see the water bottle. She reached across the tangled sheets and grabbed the bottle. It was a simple task, yet the mere mention she needed aspirin and him getting it for her struck a chord in her heart. She took the pills followed by a large mouthful of water. She licked her lips, capped the bottle, and glanced up at Kase, who was zipping his jeans.

He walked toward a beat-up dresser and pulled the second drawer open.

"Gonna run to Cade's. Get dressed."

She sighed, shucking off the covers and gathering her clothes. She got dressed in silence and put on her shoes. She stood and waited on further instruction. Kase passed her and gestured toward the small door he disappeared into earlier. She followed to find exactly what she thought it would be. A bathroom.

He bent down toward the bottom drawer and pulled out a new toothbrush and set it on the counter.

She furrowed her brows. "That for me?"

He jerked his head. "Yeah. Gotta go check out a truck."

"I'll just head home. You coming by later?"

He scowled. "You're coming with me. Brush your teeth."

She was? She had yet to meet his brother. Marissa and Caden were supposed to come to the party yesterday, but the baby was running a fever. She eyed Kase and cocked her head. Meeting the family seemed to be a step, though he was treating it as if it wasn't a big deal.

"Meeting the family, huh? What's your brother like?"

Kase rolled his shoulders and gave her a bored stare. "You'll find out in twenty minutes if you hurry the fuck up."

She glanced down at her body. *This is not the best first impression.*

"Can I go get changed?"

"No." He turned toward the small closet.

"Kase, I'm unshowered, smelling like tequila, sweat, and sex. I can't go meet your brother like this."

He glanced over his shoulder with a small smirk. "Never brought anyone to Cade's. He's not gonna give a shit how you smell."

She tilted her head and arched her brow. *Never brought a woman to Cade's.* All the more reason to look half decent. Caden may not care, but she did. In a perfect scenario, she'd go home and get ready. From Kase's impatient scowl, she was sure it wasn't an option.

"Fine. Fucking take a shower, do what ya gotta do. We leave in twenty."

She chuckled and did what he said. She took a quick shower, washing off the sweat and makeup from the night before. She opted to ditch her panties and go commando. She sifted through her handbag for a hair tie and put on her shoes, emerging from the bathroom. Kase was on the phone and angled his head, watching her as she moved through the room. She may have exaggerated her moves for his eyes.

She leaned against the wall with his heated stare penetrating her body and sending a blazing heat over her skin. She smiled, and his scowl deepened.

"Next Saturday," he said into the phone without wavering his glance from her. "How many guys coming with ya?"

He nodded, which she assumed was a response to the person he was talking to. "Later," he snapped and got up, stalking to Phoebe. He grasped her neck, pulled her into his arms, and took her for a deep, heated kiss. She grasped his waist and moved closer. The seam of his jeans brushed up against her clit, and she gasped into his mouth. He pulled back an inch, eyeing her in confusion. Mentioning to Kase she wasn't wearing panties was probably not a good idea.

"C'mon." He stepped back and opened the door. She followed him down the long hall and breached the bar.

She wasn't sure why she did it, but she grasped his hand, clasping her palm against his and intertwining their fingers. If he minded, he didn't let on. They walked through the bar. It was empty except for Nadia rounding the bar and cleaning up last night's party. She smiled and glanced down at their hands. Her lips curled into a wide grin, and she glanced up at Phoebe.

"Good morning," Nadia said with more enthusiasm than an early morning called for.

"Morning," Phoebe said with a short wave of her free hand.

Kase led them outside and past a few bikes to his at the end. While she'd always found motorcycles intriguing and had been on a few in the past, she didn't know anything beyond their outward beauty. Kase's was especially sleek.

"Can I drive?" She smirked.

He angled his head slowly. A verbal answer was not needed. She bit back her smile.

"Where's my helmet?"

"No helmet law here."

She widened her eyes. "Kase, I need a helmet." She waved her hand in front of her face. "I like the way my face looks, don't you?"

He started back to the clubhouse without saying a word. She watched him walk in. It was quiet with only a few people filtering around the yard. When Dobbs rounded the back, he looked up. Phoebe shot up a quick wave. He grinned with a comical smile and headed her way.

"The prez taking you for a ride?"

"Going to Caden's."

He nodded and eyed her body, which seemed strange.

"How ya feeling?"

It wasn't so much what he said but how he said it. Details from last night were scattered and came in pieces. She squinted, watching his smile turn to a full all-knowing grin. She swallowed the lump in her throat, fighting back the blush rising from her chest. *What the hell did I do last night?*

She licked her lips, and Dobbs raised his brows. *Oh fuck.* Something definitely happened, and from the look on Dobbs' face, he had the details. She bowed her head and groaned.

"What did I do?" she asked, shaking her head and then peeking up when she heard him chuckle.

Dobbs laughed with a shrug.

"How bad was it?"

He snorted. "Fucking torture."

She gasped and widened her eyes. "What the hell did I do?"

Dobbs glanced over his shoulder with a sly smirk and then glanced back at Phoebe. "Kelsey was talking about your tits, saying they looked bigger than hers." He paused. "You offered to show them to her."

She could feel the blood drain from her face, and her mouth gaped opened. *Oh. My God.*

Dobbs snickered and held up his hand. "You were about to take off the dress when Kase put a stop to it. He threw you over her shoulder and took you to his room." Dobbs winked. "Never came back out after that, but uh…" He glanced up with a sexy smirk. "Mine and Kase's room share a wall."

She snorted. "You heard us?"

"The whole fucking club heard ya."

Phoebe shook her head and cocked her brow. "Am I gonna have to live this down?"

He snorted. "Gage will bust your balls, and the other brothers." He smirked. "We'll just hope Kase isn't around for the repeat performance." He chuckled and lifted his chin as he turned.

She rolled her eyes and shouted, "There won't be a repeat performance." Dobbs didn't look back, but from his hunched shoulders and his head shaking, she assumed he was laughing. She caught sight of Kase coming out of the house eyeing Dobbs. They spoke briefly in passing, but she was too far to hear what was being said. When Kase was a few feet away, she raised her brows.

"You neglected to tell me I was trying to flash my boobs last night." She narrowed her eyes and folded her arms.

Kase raised his brows, and the corner of his lip quirked. He remained silent as she glared at him. He mounted his bike, waiting for her to get on. She remained in her position.

"What the fuck are you waiting for?"

"How come you didn't tell me?"

He shook his head. "You didn't ask. Besides, do you give a shit? Everyone was partying, drinking, so you wanted to show your tits, big deal."

In her inebriated state she may have wanted to, but she never pulled it off, which had Phoebe cocking her hip and tilting her head, eyeing him.

"If it's no big deal, then why'd you stop me?"

He drew in a deep breath. "'Cause I don't share what's mine."

"That's a pretty bold statement, Kase, claiming me as yours."

"We gonna talk all day? Get your ass on the bike, we gotta go."

She smirked and paced forward. Her thigh brushed against his knee. She lowered her hand, pressing her palm against his leg, and leaned closer. He watched her through hooded lids, giving nothing from his admission.

"Phoebe," he growled in warning, but she refused to let it go. She swept her lips against his tense mouth.

"Do I get a 'Property of Kase' patch?"

He furrowed his brows and leaned back. "Would you wear it?"

She smiled, grasping his neck and kissing him again, and this time her tongue breached his lips. It was a kiss more suitable for the bedroom unless they were at the clubhouse, where apparently anything went. His hand reached around her waist, spreading across her ass and tugging her body to press against his side.

She broke off the kiss, staying close, and smiled. "Fuck no, I won't wear it." She winked and stepped onto the peg. Due to her panty-less dilemma, she carefully tucked her dress between her legs and took a seat.

Kase hadn't responded to her and handed her the helmet. He knew damn well she was messing with him about the property patch. He seemed genuinely shocked she might consider it. She wasn't sure of the whole meaning behind it. It didn't really matter either way. For her, she'd never wear anything identifying her as someone else's possession. She wrapped her hands around his waist and kissed his neck.

"I do like being yours, Kase," she whispered.

He started up the bike without a word, and they headed down the driveway. The ride was shorter than she liked. She caught a few stares, and some residents seemed a bit shocked when they recognized her on the bike. The rumor mill would be exploding today. She hugged his waist, pressing her chest to his back.

Let them talk.

FOR ALL HIS YEARS RIDING, he'd never enjoyed anyone at his back. Him and his bike was the only way Kase felt completely free. Somehow, Phoebe was changing shit for him. He grasped her thigh as she scooted closer. She'd obviously been a passenger in the past, though she did tend to lean too much into the turns.

The ride was short. Too short for his liking. He would have rather been taking her on a trip than going to his brother's house.

Kase pulled into Caden's driveway, riding up past the house and through the gates. He hadn't mentioned to Phoebe they'd be eating there too. He parked the bike near the units and shut down the bike.

His intention was to get her settled with Marissa and then check out the truck. The business had taken off, and they had bought three more trucks to add to their fleet. They were used and had to be checked, which was why Kase's attendance was needed.

"This is your brother's place?"

Kase got off the bike. "Yeah, c'mon."

He started through the yard and opened the back door, allowing her to pass through. He led her into the kitchen.

"Hey, Uncle Kase, how's it going?"

Kase smirked and lifted his chin, taking in his nephew Trevor. The kid was seconds away from manhood.

"Phoebe, this is Cade's kid, Trevor."

"Hi, Trevor, nice to meet you." She extended her hand, and Trevor moved closer with a sly grin. Kase didn't miss the obvious perusal of her body.

"Same here, Phoebe." Trevor smiled, eyeing her breasts. Kase cocked his head and glared at the kid who was about to turn eighteen. At this point he'd be lucky to see tomorrow if he didn't take his eyes off her tits.

Trevor must have felt his stare and jerked his head. It was a non-verbal warning his nephew heeded, and he ducked his head, walking around the table.

"You're here. I didn't hear the bike pull up," Marissa said at the doorway. Caden followed her in, walking up to Phoebe.

He extended his hand. "I'm Caden, nice to meet you."

"You too, heard a lot about you."

Caden furrowed his brows and snorted. "Half the shit he says about me is bullshit."

Phoebe laughed. "Same here." She winked, and Caden smiled back at her.

"This is the first time Uncle Kase ever brought a *friend* for dinner. You must be something special, Phoebe."

Kase sighed. "Let's check out this shit." He pinned his stare on Trevor. "Get up, your ass is coming with us."

Trevor leaned back on the chair. "Thought I'd stay here and get to know Phoebe." Trevor glanced over with a smile. Fucking kid was too damn good at the player card. Caden passed by his seat, gripping the back of his shirt.

Kase turned and grabbed Phoebe's waist, catching her completely off guard. She gasped but fell into his side. He pressed his lips to hers.

"So barbaric."

He arched his brow and smacked her ass before walking off with a grin. "Yeah."

It didn't take as long as they had thought it would to check over the trucks. Drake, Caden's best friend and main mechanic, had checked it thoroughly before they arrived. One of the trucks would stay with Caden and the other two would be used to make transfer of the parts and deliveries.

They were walking out of the warehouse when Caden glanced over suspiciously. "You settling down here, is that what I'm seeing?"

"You know me better than that, Cade. I don't do heart to fucking hearts with anyone."

"I know my kid's a pain in the ass, but he wasn't off on what he said."

Kase laughed. "One fucking dinner and ya got me married? What's next, a fucking kid too?"

"Missing out, Kase." He jerked his head to find Caden staring at him. "The domesticated shit, it's a good deal. Just sayin'."

"For you, brother."

It was a good deal for Caden. His brother got exactly what he wanted and deserved. But Kase wasn't Caden. They lived different lives. While Kase had managed to get the club on the right side of the law, for the most part, and making money to support the members, his life was far from traditional.

He had no intention of letting Phoebe go, but he did secretly struggle with a future. Even if he wanted it, was it fair to her? She was evoking new emotions and thoughts for him.

Kase could have ended their talk, but he continued. "You fucking forget our childhood, Cade? Pop was hardly around." He raised his brows. "And that bitch who calls herself a mother? I wouldn't wish her on a fucking enemy."

Cade knitted his brow. "You ain't Pop, and Phoebe, as far as I can tell, is nothing like our mother, Kase."

Both sentiments were true.

Kase started forward, but Caden gripped his arm. "Is that what you think? If you settle down, you'll be sealing the same fate as we had as kids?" Caden shook his head. "It's bullshit, Kase.

"Ain't looking to repeat the past for some poor fucking kid and a woman who deserves better."

Caden straightened his back, standing only an inch shorter than Kase. "You're a good guy, great president to the club, and when you're not being an asshole, a damn good brother. I don't tell you that shit 'cause your ego is already two fucking sizes too big, but it's true." Caden glanced across the lot. "Could Pop have been a better father? Fuck yeah, but he did the best *he* could for us. He ran a different club, Kase, he was a different kind of president than you. He was good."

Kase turned to find Caden staring back at him. "You're better. You pulled your guys out of the shit, made it better for them and their families. You did that." Caden shook his head and smiled. "Will you be a good husband? A good dad?" He shrugged. "Who the hell knows? You let them decide. Let *Phoebe* decide, man."

"Hey." The voice from the distance had both men looking at

the back of the house. Marissa stood on the porch. "Dinner's ready."

The conversation was done. Caden didn't know it, but he'd given Kase a new outlook, a much needed one. He'd always been the better of the two in Kase's eyes. Caden had proved him right tonight. His brother held the door open for him when they reached the porch. A verbal 'thank you' would have been best. Again, not Kase's style. He reached out, gripped Caden's shoulder, and gave him a sharp nod. It was the Reilly way. Caden returned the gesture, and they headed inside.

Kase settled in against the wall in the kitchen, watching the banter between Phoebe and his dad. It seemed Kase had competition, not only from the younger generation, but from the older. His Pop was fighting dirty giving some throwback stories, which Phoebe seemed to thoroughly enjoy.

The dinner lasted longer than any he'd ever had at Caden's, mostly with Jack holding court, Phoebe on one side and Marissa on the other. When the baby cried, it was Kase who left and got her, cradling her in his arm and sitting back down next to Phoebe.

"I call him the baby whisperer. I swear, she can be screaming her lungs out, and as soon as he picks her up, she's quiet," Marissa said, resting her elbows on the table and smiling at him.

Phoebe leaned closer, peeking over his forearm at Cora. She glanced up. "Wouldn't have pegged you being good with babies."

Kase ignored the comment and reached for his beer, feeling the stare from the end of the table. He glanced over at his Pop. It wasn't Kase he was looking at, it was them—him, Phoebe, and Cora. The corner of his mouth cocked.

When his dad sat back in his seat, his gaze travelled up to meet Kase's stare. He waited on his father's usual scowl or sharp tongue to lash out. Jack remained silent. He flattened his lips and sighed. It was a side to Jack that Kase hated. *Sadness.*

They sat around the table and bullshitted for the next hour. Whatever had been weighing Jack down earlier had been lifted, and he was back to telling tales of the good old days. It was after ten when Marissa and Phoebe started to clean up. Trevor had taken Cora back upstairs, and Kase was ready to get home.

"I'm heading up now." Jack stood and walked over to where Phoebe was leaning against the counter. He yanked her shoulders. Obviously surprised by his dad's maneuver, she fell into his chest. Jack wrapped his arms around her back for a tight hug.

"I'll see you next week. I'm coming over, don't make plans." He released her and stepped back. Phoebe's response was exactly what he'd expected. She grinned with a soft chuckle and nodded.

"Whiskey by the fire. I'm in, Jack."

His dad winked at her and glanced over his shoulder. His eyes scanned Kase and then Cade before landing on Marissa. "Night, darlin'"

"Goodnight, Jack."

Jack started toward the doorway.

Cade snorted. "Night, Pop."

Kase laughed. Jack usually ignored him and his brother in favor of the women. It was nothing new. Kase expected Jack to continue out the door without acknowledging them, but he didn't. He turned around and smirked, shifting his gaze between Caden and him. He drew in a deep breath and nodded.

"Night, boys."

Kase couldn't be sure of Caden's reaction; he was too focused on his Pop walking out of the room. He couldn't remember the last time he'd heard his father speak those words.

Night, boys.

IT WAS after eleven when he pulled up her driveway. He wouldn't be spending the night. He was set for a two-day run with Rourke and Gage. When he told her earlier, he sensed her disappointment. For some fucked up reason, he liked it. He wanted her missing him when he was gone.

He pulled to the end of her drive and waited for her to get off. She unclasped her helmet and shook out her hair.

"Here."

He glanced down at the helmet. It was a spare he'd had for years. "Hold onto it."

She stepped closer, wrapping her arms around his shoulders. "Are there more rides in my future?" She waggled her brows. Her innuendo had nothing to do with his motorcycle.

Her blue eyes softened, losing the glimmer of humor. "Gonna miss you."

While it may not have seemed like much of a declaration to most, Kase knew Phoebe. She didn't want a relationship, only out for a good time. The female version of himself. Her whispered words meant something. It was an admission. If he had to guess, a confession of sorts. He slid his hand over her cheek, grazing her neck lightly with the pads of his fingers.

"Two days, Phoebe." He swiped his mouth across her lips. "Miss you too." He almost didn't recognize his own voice saying the words.

Her arms tightened around his shoulders, and her lips meshed against his. Being sweet wasn't his thing, but she sure loved it. His hands roamed over her back, wanting her closer.

He couldn't remember the last time he made out with a woman only to prolong the night. He was the one who ended the kiss. If he had a choice, he wouldn't have. Only one place he wanted to be, and it was not on a two-day run. He lingered over her lips before setting her back a step.

He had about ten minutes before Rourke started blowing up his phone, asking where he was.

"Call me when you get there, okay?" She shrugged. "Just so I know you got there safe."

Never in his life had he checked in with a woman for any reason. He jerked his chin.

She gave him another quick kiss and started toward the house. He would wait until she got inside. Partially for her safety. He smirked, watching her hips sway. *And for the view.* She glanced over her shoulder, and then slowly turned and tilted her head.

"I have a confession." The corner of her mouth curled. "I was going commando the whole day."

What the fuck?

She laughed, probably prompted from his expression of disbelief. She slowly lifted her dress over her thighs, revealing she was very much telling the truth.

He growled and reached for her, but she backed away. A coy smile played on her lips. She lifted her hands and waved her fingers.

"You gotta go, Kase." She winked. "Try not to miss me too much." She walked back to her porch, and he smirked. Fucking tease. He'd remember this when he got home in a few days.

He waited until she was in the house before turning around and driving over to his place. They were leaving at midnight, driving through the night to cut out the traffic. He usually looked forward to runs, enjoyed the change of scenery. Not this time.

Two days. Too long.

Chapter 18

Two days. Forty-eight hours. Two thousand, eight hundred and eighty minutes.

It was slightly obsessive. She hadn't actually waited around for him. She kept herself busy, she worked, got shit done. As the two days closed in on her, she did feel the anxious excitement to see him. It felt foreign. She adapted to being immune to men until Kase. He'd changed it, and her father's words played in her head.

You gave your heart to the wrong man. He didn't deserve you. Someday, you will find someone who does. Maybe not now, but someday, this conversation will play back in your head and you'll say, 'The old man knew what he was talking about.'

And he did.

He'd texted her earlier, he'd be arriving around seven. When she heard the dual engines rumble at six-thirty, her heart skipped. A peek out her window confirmed it was Kase's and Rourke's arrival. Minutes later, she got the text.

Kase: Get your ass over here.

A few minutes later, she was out the door. Phoebe started across her yard, heading toward the clubhouse. *My man.* It was strange to hear her own thoughts. For a woman who had sworn off getting seriously involved with anyone ever again, she was the biggest hypocrite.

She caught Bailey at the edge of the fence waiting on her. Something was off. Her smile was forced.

"Hey, what's wrong?"

She shrugged. "Nothing."

"Bailey."

She sighed and glanced up through her lashes. "I was here yesterday, saw Tory leaving something in your mailbox, and I stopped to talk to her. Congratulations, I guess," she muttered.

Oh yeah. The offer. She had yet to touch the paperwork, opting to live in denial. Eventually, she'd get to it. Not now.

"Yeah, full asking, all cash, short close, deal of a lifetime." Phoebe repeated Tory's own words in hopes she'd sound convincing. She was failing. Phoebe cleared her throat. "Ironic too. A single me is moving out, and a single woman is moving in. Maybe she'll be the new Phoebe, a good replacement." She laughed and expected Bailey to join in. She didn't.

"No one can replace you."

"Well, then maybe this Megan can be a close second."

Bailey jerked her head. "Who?"

"The buyer, Megan McMillian."

It was strange to watch Bailey's features tighten and her face pale. When she swayed to the side, Phoebe reached out, grabbing her arm to steady her. "Are you okay? What's wrong, the baby?"

"Megan McMillian?"

Phoebe winced at the sharp tone. Bailey didn't raise her voice, but there was a spike in her tone, something Bailey rarely possessed. Anger.

"Son of a bitch." It was another rarity, to hear her curse. Phoebe rubbed her arm, unsure how to settle her friend. When she glanced past Bailey, she saw Saint a few feet away, concern marring his striking features.

"Sweetheart," Saint said.

Bailey whipped her head. "Did you know?"

Saint spread out his hands, clearly confused as much as Phoebe. "Know what?"

"That the club is buying Phoebe's property?"

Wait, what? Phoebe jerked her head to face Bailey and tightened her hold on her arm. *What the hell was she talking about?* Bailey shook her head and pointed at Saint. "If you knew about this, Saint…." Before she could finish her sentence, Saint stepped forward. "I didn't."

"Whoa, hold up, clue me in here. Bailey?"

She threw one last glare at her husband and turned to Phoebe. "When the club bought all the property in Ghosttown, they used someone else as a front, their LLC. They were concerned if the residents knew what they were planning, they would try to halt the purchases."

"Okay." It made sense on the club's part, and she wouldn't put it past a few of the townspeople such as Arnett to take issue and cause problems. She was familiar with the LLC as a few offers came in from them a year earlier. However, the last few were directly from the club. "What the hell does that have to do with my property?"

"They used Meg." She raised her brows. "It's short," Bailey gritted her teeth, "for Megan."

It took less than a second for it all to come together and sucker punch her in the belly. All the air released from her lungs.

Phoebe gaped open her mouth, completely blindsided with shock. Kase was behind the purchase of her property? Was it even possible? *Another example of trusting the wrong man.*

"That son of a bitch," she muttered under her breath. How could she have been so fucking stupid to have yet another man trick her? She staggered back, completely unaware of her surroundings, her mind in a complete fog. She blinked, trying to focus on anything around her. Her head was spinning, and the colors were fading in and out. A shooting pain stabbed her heart, and she pressed her knuckles between her breasts, trying to relive the ache.

"I can't believe I let this happen again." She shook her head and grasped her temples.

"Phoebe?" She heard Bailey's voice, but it seemed far away. It was then she realized she was moving. Her feet were pounding on the ground, and she was short on her breath. *I'm running.* Her front porch was only a few steps away when she heard another familiar voice. It wasn't Bailey's this time.

"Phoebe."

She darted up the steps and threw open the door with so much force it slammed against the wall, knocking down a glass frame. It crashed onto the wood floor and shattered. She paced through her small house until she sensed his presence.

Kase stood in the doorway.

Rage was strumming every inch of her body. Any lessons or tricks she may have learned in anger management wouldn't help her now. *Or him.* She stalked toward Kase, balling her fists. "You lying, manipulative motherfucker, son of a bitch, asshole, prick, bastard." She racked her brain for any insulting names she may have left out. "Jerkoff, douchebag, dickhead motherfucker." *You repeated motherfucker. He deserves it twice!*

She wasn't sure what enraged her more at the moment, what he'd done, or how he appeared completely unfazed.

"You ready to listen?"

She scoffed. "To you? Do you really think I wanna hear anything you have to say?"

Kase drew in a breath. "Calm the fuck down."

"Fuck you, Kase." She was streaming with rage. She darted forward, shouting, "Fuck you, fuck you, and *fuck you.*"

His jaw locked, and he scowled. "Listen."

"No, you shut up and answer my questions. Did you set up Meg to buy my house?" She was prepared to rebut his lies. She had a plan to pull out the paperwork. It wasn't necessary.

"Yeah."

She flinched. Phoebe was caught off guard by his honesty. She assumed he'd try and sugarcoat what he'd done, but instead he answered as though he saw nothing wrong with it.

"Why?"

"You fucking told me you wouldn't sell to me. I knew…"

She darted forward, refusing to let him finish. "So instead of respecting my wishes, you go behind my back, manipulate me into getting my property." She sucked in a harsh breath. "You are such an asshole."

"You were willing to sell to a fucking stranger after I had made a fuck ton of offers?" He dragged his hand through his hair as though she was being unreasonable. "Don't fucking talk to me about being manipulative when you, out of fucking spite, refused to sell to me. Nobody was gonna buy this goddamn shack from you anyway. I reached out…"

"Don't say another fucking word to me."

Her lips sputtered, but she couldn't finish her thought.

"I got shit to say, and *you will* fucking listen. You owe Carter, which seems to piss you off. I'm trying to save your ass here. A fucking thank you will do." He shook his head. "I got better fucking things to spend my money on, sweetheart, but here I am saving your ass."

She gasped. If his delivery hadn't sucked, she may have been able to see through it as a kind gesture. She hadn't. There were some things in Kase that set her off. His demanding, all-knowing bullshit was one of them.

"Stop being an asshole," she shouted. *Son of a bitch.* She didn't need him saving her. She wasn't a damsel in distress. She was an adult who could handle her shit.

"I don't need you to save me. I don't need anyone." She shook her head, completely consumed with her anger. "I'm perfectly capable of taking care of myself. You can't buy me, Kase."

"What the fuck are you talking about? I did this to help your ungrateful ass, and this how you fucking thank me?"

Thank him?

"I'm not thanking you 'cause I'm not accepting your offer. What?" She threw her hand over her head in pure frustration. She felt herself losing control, caught up in her own anger. "You buy my house, pay my bills, and then have access to free pussy whenever ya want? Is that the deal?" She gritted her teeth. "Fuck you, Kase. No man owns me."

He snarled. "I want free pussy, I can get it without putting up two hundred thousand dollars. You're good, but ya ain't that good, sweetheart."

It was a virtual slap in the face. He'd never even mentioned the women from the club, but now throwing it in her face had her heart racing and her anger raging.

She grabbed a pillow from the couch and whipped it across the room. He snagged it in one hand.

"What the fuck is wrong with you?" He raised his brows, and his eyes darkened. "Maybe the old man was right. You are fucking psychotic."

The dig was meant to hurt, and he'd succeeded. This was a new side to Kase, one she didn't love. She shook her head and tried to calm her breathing.

She drew in a deep breath. "I don't need you or anyone else bailing me out. You went behind my back, betrayed my trust." She gritted her teeth and muttered, "Same as Jared."

"You comparing me to that asshole?" He raised his brows and twisted his lips.

She was surviving on sheer emotion. Probably not the best at the moment. "I don't need your help!" she shouted. "I can do this on my own. I don't need you." It was as if she was speaking to Jared in the grave.

He snorted. "You've fucking lost your goddamn mind. You don't take what I'm offering, you ain't never getting the money for the house if you try selling to someone else. You have visions of cardboard boxes and eating cat food, fine, fucking do it." He leaned down, putting them at eye level. "Without me backing your ass, and cash, you're fucked. But you wanna do it on your own? Have it, sweetheart. Let me know how it fucking turns out for ya."

It was Jared all over again. Without him, she was nothing. It was how she felt for a long time. Had she been so wrong about Kase?

"I'll manage just fine."

He laughed with a nasty sneer. "Yeah, 'cause up until now, you've been doing a great job. Assault charge, arrested, a shit ton of debt from your husband who was fucking everything with two legs. Now you owe money to a brother who can't stand the sight of you. Yeah, you're fucking killing it, sweetheart."

She gasped and sucked in a harsh breath caught in her throat. Knowing it was one thing, hearing it from his mouth held more power. He was throwing her flaws in her face.

"Get out."

He snorted. "Yeah, I fucking will, 'cause my offer is off the table." He moved toward the door, opening it wide and never looking back before he slammed it shut. She was frozen, staring at the door. It wasn't until the first tear streamed down her cheek she drew in a breath.

His words played over in her head. *Assault charge, arrested, a shit ton of debt from your husband who was fucking everything with two legs. Now you owe money to a brother who can't stand the sight of you.*

She sniffled, wiping her cheeks. She wasn't sure what upset her more, Kase saying it, or knowing it was true.

The irony? I thought I loved this man.

MOTHERFUCKER.

Phoebe and her smart fucking mouth. Her inability to settle the fuck down set him at a new level of rage. If he hadn't walked out, he'd be enrolled in his own anger management class. His muscles bunched through his entire body as if he had a live wire streaming through his blood. His steps pounded through the yard, passing Saint a few feet away. Kase glared as he passed him but didn't say a word. Anything to come from his lips at the moment wouldn't be good.

This whole thing was beyond fucked up.

He had every intention of telling her when the deal went through. *Manipulative, my ass.* He was doing this for her ungrateful ass, and this is how she thanks him.

"Kase."

He'd been so blinded and deafened by his own anger, he hadn't heard Saint come up next to him. He ignored his most trusted brother and headed toward the clubhouse. Kase had always had a temper and did nothing to contain it. If people were smart, they shut their mouths and moved out of his way. Most sensed the changing vibe in the room as he barreled through the main room of the clubhouse.

"What's going on?" Gage asked, following him down the hall. "You good, man?"

He whipped his head and glared at Gage, who had the common sense to back up. Kase stalked to his room and slammed the door shut. As he paced around the room, he was looking for anything to throw, beat the shit out of, or kill. His anger for how everything with her went down was building a gut-curling rage.

He grabbed his phone from his pocket, dialing the familiar number.

"Hey, Kase, how are..."

"You call the realtor right now, and you back the fuck out of the deal."

The silence only lasted a few seconds, but it was too long for him. "Do it now, Meg."

"Okay," she whispered.

He ended the call, tossed the phone on his bed, and paced around the room. He was like a caged animal about to climb the walls. He needed to get the fuck out of there before he did something stupid, before he marched back over to her house and demanded she listen to the whole fucking story.

Fuck her.

"Need to get the hell out of here." He grabbed his keys, leaving his phone on the bed. If he brought it, he may be tempted to reach out to her ungrateful ass. He walked out the door and noticed the small group gathered at the end of the hallway. The conversation abruptly stopped when they looked over at him. He noticed the small redhead emerge past Rourke and Macy. She started toward him with a guilty concern.

Way to blow everything the fuck up, Bailey.

He'd caught the tail end of her rant with Phoebe. It was what started this whole shit show. He didn't even know how she knew. He was confident Meg wouldn't say anything, and no one else fucking knew.

She stopped in front of him and blocked his path.

Her bottom lip quivered, and she gulped. "Kase, I am..."

"Bailey." The deep warning had her glancing over her shoulder. Kase followed her gaze to Saint a few feet away. His VP stared back at her and slowly shook his head. It was a smart warning to give to his wife.

Kase always had a soft spot for her, but he was beyond capable of interacting with anything other than venom and rage. And Saint knew it.

Bailey ducked her head and maneuvered out of his way. As Kase passed, Saint nodded. Kase started through the main room, and the crowd separated, making a clear path for exit. He headed to his bike, resisting the urge to look over at Phoebe's place.

Fuck her.

He got on his bike and took off without a planned destination. He just needed to settle, and the open road was the only way he knew how.

Chapter 19

Three days.

There was only one place a person could truly lick their wounds and hide from the world. After her fight with Kase, she packed up her suitcase, blocked his number, and headed to her dad's house. To her childhood house. Her father had remained in the house long after her mother had passed a few years ago. He talked about moving but felt as though she was very much still part of the house.

Her room remained the same as when she was in college. It was bittersweet and slightly pathetic. She spent the first day rummaging through her old room and spending time with her dad. The next few days were filled with work and dodging calls from Ghosttown, mainly Bailey, who had been blowing up her phone.

By the third day, cabin fever had set in. For the last two hours, she'd been wandering around the house in search of a distraction from her boredom. She stopped in front of the fireplace mantel, noticing the thin film of dust on the picture frame. *Am I so bored I'm considering cleaning the house?* Pitiful. She reached up and grabbed the frame, wiping off some dust.

Oh the irony. She stared down at the photo. It was from her wedding.

"I loved that dress," she whispered.

Phoebe had destroyed everything from that day. Photos, favors, cards, every memento she had saved had landed in her fire pit. She donated her dress and sold her wedding rings. It was as though she was trying to erase her past. Unfortunately, she still had her memories.

Her father had several pictures from that day in frames all around the house for years. As of a year ago, only one remained. A family shot of her, her mom and dad, and Carter.

She sighed and put the frame back on the shelf. It was a great picture of the four of them. Everyone was happy, even Carter, it appeared.

Carter.

She wasn't sure exactly what prompted her to grab her keys and head out the door. Maybe the cabin fever had made her desperate. Whatever it was, an hour later she found herself parked in the lot of his condo complex.

Would he even be home? He'd probably slam the door in her face.

She sat in the car for the next few minutes. *Why am I even here?* She had never even been to his place, and he'd lived there for over five years. He would probably be pissed with her showing up unannounced. She snorted remembering he'd done it to her a few weeks ago. It gave her the push she needed to get out of the car. It was a short walk to his condo, and she found herself staring at his door.

"Why the hell am I here?" she muttered.

She drew in a deep breath and knocked.

She waited, and when she heard the footsteps padding toward the door, she straightened her shoulders.

Surprise, big brother!

When the door opened, it was Phoebe who got the surprise. Her breath caught in her throat, and her jaw fell open. *What the fuck?* It seemed she wasn't the only one shocked speechless. They probably mirrored one another with their facial expressions. Phoebe couldn't tell if she was turning a bright shade of red, but the familiar blonde in front of her certainly was.

The woman cleared her throat and smiled at her. "Hi, Phoebe."

Phoebe chuckled and grinned, pausing before she spoke. "Hey, Nadia."

Holy shit! What the hell was she doing at Carter's place? Phoebe gazed down Nadia's body, taking in her appearance. Nadia had a usual uniform for the club, and this wasn't it. She had a tee molded to her chest and tiny cotton shorts. Her hair, which was usually styled was a messy bun atop her head. While she wore a conservative amount of makeup, it was definitely downplaying how she looked at the club. Phoebe tilted her head. She'd always thought of Nadia as sexy and hot, but seeing her with a more relaxed look, she really was beautiful.

"My wallet is on the table."

The voice was shallowed coming from another room, but she recognized it as Carter's. Nadia jerked her head and then smiled back at Phoebe.

"Uh, we ordered takeout." She stepped back and waved her into the condo. "Come on in."

Phoebe slipped past Nadia and stood in the entry. The door closed behind her, and she glanced around the room. It was completely Carter. It was orderly and neat. There were some pictures on the wall, but none of people. They were mostly paintings. Typical Carter. She glanced around the area until a framed picture on the corner table caught her eye. She stepped closer, glanced down, and before she knew what she was doing, she gripped it and brought it closer to her.

She smiled, remembering the day. Carter's graduation from the police academy. She couldn't have been more than sixteen. It was them with their mom and dad.

"I swear you don't age, Phoebe."

She glanced up to find Nadia leaning against the couch, smiling. Phoebe snorted.

"Ah, to be sixteen again."

Nadia chuckled. "I was a late bloomer. Couldn't pay me to go back in time to sixteen."

Phoebe laughed and set the frame on the table. She opened her mouth but immediately clamped her lips when Carter came into the room. His focus was on Nadia, a smirk and a glint in his eye. When the hell had this happened? She half wondered if Kase and the club knew about it. Then the unsettling pit in her stomach grew just thinking his name. She drew in a breath and watched as Nadia glanced over at her. Carter followed her gaze, and his face hardened. *Not good.*

Before he had the opportunity to start yelling at her, she held up her hands. "I'm staying at Dad's and thought I'd stop by and say hi." She side-stepped toward the door. "Sorry to interrupt…"

Nadia reached for her arm as she passed. "You're not interrupting, Phoebe."

Phoebe snorted and glanced at her brother. His features seemed less stressed and more confused.

"I'm just gonna go." She stepped away until she realized Nadia was still holding her wrist.

"What's wrong?" Carter snapped, moving closer.

Phoebe shook her head. "Nothing."

He furrowed his brows. "Kase do something?"

This was the last thing she needed. She had no intention of opening up to anything that had happened with Kase to her brother.

She felt Nadia's stare bore into her, and she quickly glanced away, taking another step back. Her retreat was halted when Nadia tightened her grip.

"I just came home to visit Dad and thought I'd stop by. That's all, nothing's wrong." She hooked her thumb over her shoulder. "I'm just gonna go."

"Why didn't you call?"

Phoebe drew in a breath and shifted on her feet, glancing between her brother and Nadia. It was awkward. She shrugged and forced a smile. "I wasn't sure you'd let me come over." There, she said it. It was the truth. It was always better to ask for forgiveness than permission.

Carter dropped his arm from his hips, staring at her. *I shouldn't have come here.* She stepped back toward the door and hooked her thumb over her shoulder. "I'm just gonna…"

The buzzer rang, keeping her from finishing her sentence. Carter moved through the room, continually watching her. He grabbed the knob and turned back, pinning her with his stare.

"Sit. You're not fucking leaving." He disappeared through the door.

Nadia giggled. "Your brother's delivery sucks almost as much as Kase's, huh?"

Phoebe whipped her head around. "Does the club know you're here?" She widened her eyes, moving closer to Nadia and lowering her voice. "I won't say anything, I promise." She wasn't sure what the protocol was for women who stayed with the club. Would the members be upset to find out Nadia was spending time with a detective?

Nadia smiled. "They know. I'm visiting my sister who lives here. Came up a few days ago and reached out to Carter." She winked.

It was on the tip of her tongue to ask more, but Carter came through the door with two brown bags of food. He walked over to the breakfast bar, and Nadia released her hand. It was odd to watch the two of them as though there was a familiarity. It was sweet, and she couldn't help but smile. Nadia glanced over.

"Come on, make a plate, we've got tons. Carter always orders too much."

He grunted and scowled. "I like leftovers."

Nadia swiped her hand across his waist. "I know you do, baby."

What. The. Fuck. *Baby?* Phoebe remained frozen in the middle of the living room until her brother glanced up and jerked his chin toward the food.

The next two hours were surreal. They ate Thai food, drank beers until Nadia decided they should have margaritas, and she made a pitcher. The conversation was light, and lacked the awkwardness she expected. Nadia steered most of the conversation, keeping it light. She talked about her sister and moving closer to help her out. She didn't, however, sugarcoat anything with Carter.

"You got a handsome, sweet gentleman ask you over, you jump on the offer, am I right?"

Phoebe smiled and glanced up at Carter, who remained fixated on his food.

"Yeah. Carter's always been pretty smart. He knows a good woman when he sees one." It was meant to equally compliment Nadia, but she caught Carter's gaze and the small smile playing on his lips. Whatever was happening between them was a good thing.

It was a few minutes before Nadia excused herself, leaving brother and sister alone by themselves. Phoebe licked her lips and placed her plate on the table.

"I can go."

Carter glanced up and shrugged. "You got somewhere better to hang?"

She raised her brows. "Just Dad's, and after a couple days, the idea of going to bed at nine loses its luster."

He laughed and wiped his mouth. "You want the couch, it's yours."

She peeked up through her lashes. It was mind blowing to see Carter in another light. Not the perfect brother who was a detective. Just a guy. A nice guy.

"Thanks, Carter."

He nodded and lifted his bottle to his lips. He took a sip, eyeing her. "Not gonna tell me what went down with Kase, are you?"

The Enemy

No! She clasped her hands, stalling on answering him.

"What makes you think something happened?"

He settled into his chair and stared as though he was seconds from rolling his eyes. "Ya mean, besides the fact that you're hiding out at Dad's, and then coming over here?"

He had a point.

He jerked his chin to the bedroom. "Her phone has been blowing up since she got here. Caught some of the conversations." He raised his brows. "Got a lot of people looking for you." He folded his arms, and she wondered if this was an interrogation tactic.

Her heart sank. Her intent wasn't to have anyone worried about her; she just wasn't ready to deal with it.

"And..." When he paused, she glanced up. "I got Kase on my voicemail asking 'where the fuck you are'."

Nothing could have surprised her more. "He called you?"

"Yeah."

"W-what did you say?" She cleared her throat. The knowledge Kase had reached out to her brother looking for her made her anxious.

He shrugged. "Didn't return his calls." Carter smirked. "Kase Reilly doesn't like being ignored."

She laughed, envisioning how pissed off Kase would be. *Good.*

"Not gonna tell me?"

She flattened her lips and slowly shook her head. *If I talk about it, I'll lose it.* Even saying very little at the moment, her heart ached.

"Okay. You want me to play big brother and kick his ass, just say the word."

Phoebe laughed and rested against the couch.

FOUR FUCKING DAYS.

He spent them all rehashing how his night with Phoebe went

down. It was rare for him to have regrets. When the fuck did he become such a pussy? Everything he'd said to her had been accurate and honest. *And fucking nasty.*

"Uh, Kase?"

He spun around from the bay doors of the building to find a prospect hanging near the store entrance.

"Fucking speak, asshole."

Eddie blinked and stammered his words. "R-Rourke said he's a few miles out, so get the guys ready to unload."

Kase clenched his jaw and tightened his fists. He was seconds away from smacking the stupid out of his newest prospect. "What the fuck does it look like I'm doing?" He lunged forward, sending Eddie pacing back into the wall. "You think I'm just hanging here for the fresh fucking air?"

"N-no, I-I just..." The lump in his throat bobbed, and his gaze skirted around the room. This guy would never make it in the club if he couldn't hold his own.

"Kase, man. He was just relaying the message." Gage gripped his shoulder.

Kase jerked away from his hand and moved closer, towering over Eddie. "You back down like a little bitch ever again and you're done."

Kase turned and patted his pocket for his cigarettes. Something had to fucking giving soon before he started beating the shit out of people. Fucking Phoebe.

She had singlehandedly in a matter of minutes pissed him off and set him on a raging course of destruction. He'd been a bear ever since, snapping and yelling at every small thing. Even at the club, the women who usually made an effort to seek him out were rushing the other way when he walked in the room. It made no difference to him; he didn't want them. *Fuck!*

Gage chuckled, which was the last thing Kase wanted to hear. He turned, ready to unleash, when Caden and Rissa pulled up in the back lot with the new truck. Gage made his way out the door to greet them. Kase remained on the deck.

He watched as they got out of the truck. Kase was too far away to hear what Gage was saying, but if he had to guess, it was a warning.

Caden walked through the door with Gage and Marissa following.

"About fucking time," Kase barked and took a drag of his cigarette.

"Ten minutes late, asshole."

"Yeah, ten fucking minutes is money when these guys get delayed on deliveries. No wonder your company almost went under." It was a low blow, and Caden's jaw tightened. He stepped forward, but Gage shifted in front of him, grasping his arm.

"Kase is nursing a broken heart, so we all gotta cut him some slack."

Kase gritted his teeth and tossed his cigarette to the ground. "Shut the fuck up, Gage, before I beat the piss outta ya."

"Phoebe broke up with you? What did you do?" Marissa asked, which incensed him. What did he do? Offered to bail out her ungrateful ass, that's what he did, and she turned psychotic on him. He scowled and pinned his harsh glare directly at her.

"What makes you think I did something?"

Marissa tightened her lips in a flat line and shrugged.

"'Cause you're an asshole," Caden snapped.

Kase jerked his head. "Yeah, such a fucking asshole that I'm out here trying to buy her place, get her ass outta debt, and she turns into a raving lunatic bitch." His anger was getting the best of him.

Gage raised his brows in surprise, and Caden furrowed his brows, shifting around Gage.

"Wait, you're buying her property? For the club?"

"No, asshole, it's got nothing to do with the club. She put her house up 'cause she owed her brother. I was putting up my cash, not club money, to buy it. Then she goes off half-cocked about being free pussy for my taking, how I went behind her back and betrayed her, and some other bullshit." He dragged his hand through his hair. In his frustration, he ripped out a few strands.

"That's fucked," Gage said. "What's her problem?"

"Wait," Marissa stepped closer. "Did you tell her you were buying the house for her?"

"Knew she wouldn't go for it, so I had Meg make the offer."

"Oh fuck, Kase." Gage raised his brows and shook his head.

He gritted his teeth, taking in the expressions from the three in front of him. They all shared the same reaction. He'd fucked up.

"I was gonna fucking tell her, but the mayor beat me to it." For as much love as he had for Bailey, he wanted to strangle her. Had the deal just gone through, Phoebe would have the cash to pay Carter back and they'd work out something for her living at the house. Before his plan blew up, they had spent so much time together, the natural progression would have been living in the house, the two of them.

Marissa sighed. "She had a husband who screwed her over, right? Did awful things behind her back? Left her with all his debt and a broken heart. That much betrayal, it scars people, Kase. Makes it hard to put trust in anyone because they're afraid it will happen again." She gave him a sad smile. "I hear what you're saying, and I really believe your intentions were good, but you should have told her from the very beginning. Her finding out the way she did? From someone else? To Phoebe, I'm sure it felt like another betrayal from a man she trusted."

He stared back at Marissa in silence. He hadn't even considered what she had just said. It was new territory for him. He couldn't remember the last woman he shared an inkling of feelings for. It wasn't him; he had no desire for it until Phoebe showed up and changed his fucking world.

"Give her some time, Kase."

He scoffed. "Won't be hard since she's gone fucking AWOL." He needed everyone to stop fucking talking.

Marissa left, leaving Caden with Kase. His brother walked

over to him and sighed. Kase knew what was coming. Of the two, Caden was the voice of reason. Kase held up his hand.

"Not looking for advice."

Caden snorted. "Didn't think you were, man." Caden shook his head. "When she comes home, talk to her. Look, I did and said some shit to Riss when we were starting out." He shrugged. "It's like Riss said, your intention was good."

He stared off at the back lot. He'd spent his entire life being a stubborn prick. It took a day to fully grasp the magnitude of the fight. He figured she'd take time to cool off, see things his way, and reach out. She didn't. Four days and he hadn't heard a word from her.

"Look." Caden sighed. "Give her some time."

Kase snorted and shook his head. "I cut her too deep." He drew in a breath. He'd cut Phoebe to the core, throwing the shit with her dead husband and Carter into the mix. It was a low blow.

He'd fucked up with her. He knew it. Even if he found it in him to explain not seeing her side, his nasty comments would be hard to let go of.

"Kase, man..." Caden voice tapered off as he stalked through the warehouse when Rourke's truck pulled up. Kase needed to get away from everyone and all the talking. He made his way to his bike and caught Rourke's confused stare. Kase started up his bike and jerked his chin toward the open bay doors.

"Gage is inside, he'll help unload."

Rourke nodded and watched him. Kase pulled out of the lot. All he needed was to get on the road, drive to destinations unknown, and not think about anything or anyone.

Chapter 20

Phoebe shifted on the bed. *No, strike that, the couch.* She groaned, shoving her face into the pillow. Too much of everything last night. Too much liquor, too much sharing, too much of everything. She drew in a deep breath, which was constricted from the pillow being shoved against her face by her own doing.

"Coffee?"

Phoebe turned and squinted. Nadia was sitting on the coffee table facing the couch with a mug in her hands. Phoebe lifted onto her elbow and wiped the loose strands of hair away from her face.

"You're my favorite person on the planet right now."

Nadia smiled and offered her the mug, which she eagerly took.

She took a sip and peeked over the rim, noticing Nadia was dressed, and seemed to be ready to head out. With only one bedroom in the apartment, she knew where Nadia had slept. With her brother.

"So, you and Carter, huh?"

Nadia smirked and glanced over toward the hallway before turning back to Phoebe.

"We're just..." she paused. "I don't even know how to finish that sentence." She smiled and glanced down at the floor. "He's a good guy, ya know?" Nadia peeked up through her lashes. "He makes me feel special, which sounds like a total cliché." Nadia rolled her eyes and shrugged. "But I got this gorgeous, sexy guy who seems hellbent on making me happy."

While as brother and sister they'd never gotten along, she was finding a new appreciation for Carter. Up until last night, they'd been virtually strangers, and now? *I don't know what we are.* There was something, though. It would be small steps, ones she was willing to make.

"He does that, huh?"

Nadia glanced up, her eyes gleaming. "Yeah, your brother gives me butterflies in my stomach." Her cheeks blushed, and she ducked her head. "Stupid, right?"

Phoebe shifted upward. "No. I think it's sweet, and you deserve it, Nadia."

Nadia cocked her head. "You do too."

She was desperate to change the subject. She hadn't gone into detail with what happened, but both Nadia and her brother knew something was amiss. After Carter mentioned Nadia's phone blowing up, she was sure Nadia knew more than she was letting on.

"So, how does this work? I mean you and the club and Carter?"

"I haven't officially made the announcement, so please don't say anything, okay?"

Phoebe nodded.

"I'm actually leaving the club."

Phoebe jaw dropped. "Really? Why?"

"My sister lives up here. Her husband left her a few months back with three kids. She's struggling. That's why I came for the visit. I'm actually scoping out apartments. I'm gonna move back, help her out."

"But you'll come back to Ghosttown, right?"

Nadia sighed. "I love the club. I love the people, and I have for a long time. They're family." Her tone was endearing and genuine. There was no denying her love for the Ghosttown Riders. Nadia sighed, and her shoulders slouched as though something heavy was weighing on her. It wasn't just her stance, but the emotion in her features, almost sad. "But I'm ready to move on. Don't get me wrong, I love Ghosttown, but I miss the city. And…" She blushed. "I like Carter. I like the way I feel when I'm around him." Nadia smiled and her face lit up. "I'll miss the club, the girls, but ya know what I'll miss most? Watching the guys fall in love." She leaned forward, resting her elbows on her knees and pinning Phoebe with her stare. "Watching Kase fall for you has been my favorite."

"Nad…"

"I talked to Bailey."

Phoebe jerked her head and stared back at Nadia. She had figured it was Bailey when Carter mentioned people were looking for her.

She held up her hand. "She was worried about you. Told me what happened with you and Kase."

Phoebe straightened to a seated position. "Yeah? Did she share how he tried to buy my house from under me?"

"Actually, she said Saint told her Kase was buying it for you."

Phoebe jerked her eyes, landing on Nadia. "What?" She hushed.

Nadia nodded. "Yeah, said Saint told her Kase wanted to purchase it for you, knew you needed the cash buy out, and knew you wouldn't take a hand-out directly from him." Nadia leaned closer. "So yeah, he tried to trick you, but he was doing it for you." Nadia paused. "According to Saint, Kase just wanted you to get to keep your house."

Phoebe leaned back into the couch, processing everything Nadia had said. *No, he is the enemy.*

"Bullshit."

Nadia shrugged. "I'm just telling you what Bailey said. She also mentioned Kase being impossible since you left. Says he knows he fucked up, and without you taking his calls, he can't fix it. Best intentions, worst actions, I guess."

Phoebe shook her head.

"He claimed you as his old lady, Phoebe. And while that might not mean much to you, for Kase, in his world, it's everything."

She clamped her lips.

"I heard it with my own ears, girl." Nadia sighed. "Kase has been the president of the club for a long time. These members aren't just brothers, they're family to him. He takes responsibility over them and those around. He fixes the wrongs, Phoebe. He may have gone about it all wrong, but if I had to guess, Kase had you in mind when he did what he did. He wanted to make things okay for you because he loves you. I'm not saying what he did was right, but love makes us do crazy shit. It alters our way of thinking when we want the best for our other half."

"You really believe that?"

"I do. I know Kase, been around the man a long time." She pointed at Phoebe. "You changed the game for that man. Not much he wouldn't do for you, sweetie."

Phoebe laughed. "I was a bitch to him."

Nadia smirked. "And I'm sure he was an asshole. He's Kase." She chuckled. "I check back in thirty years? That man will still be an asshole. But I'm hoping he's got a good woman by his side to even that shit out." She winked. "You love him, don't ya?"

Did she? She slowly nodded.

"That's what I thought. We love Kase 'cause deep down he's a good guy. It's harder to see in him than the others. It takes a special eye to see past all those layers, and it takes superhuman strong strength to break down those walls he's spent the last thirty-eight years building. It takes you, Phoebe."

Phoebe slipped down into the couch, refusing to look at Nadia.

It took the next few hours to process everything Nadia had said. Kase was still at fault. He should have talked to her about his plan without going behind her back. However, if he had done it all for her?

Now what?

HIS CALLS HAD GONE UNANSWERED, and his texts didn't warrant a response. A face to face was what it was going to take. He'd spent the last few days watching her place with no activity in sight. He'd even put one of the prospects on her place. Nothing happening. It was as though she'd left town with no return in sight. He was battling with the reality of his fuck up.

He didn't understand women, or maybe it was just Phoebe. Either way, it had weighed on him. He was losing the only woman he'd ever deemed important to him. The only one who got inside. It was fucking karma.

He was twenty feet away from the clubhouse door when he got the call. He thought about ignoring it but answered anyway.

"What?"

"Need you to come here. Now, Kase," Caden said. His tone was enough for Kase to know why.

He halted mid-step and closed his eyes. Not tonight. He was scheduled to have his Pop dropped off tomorrow. Caden and Riss were going to swing by with him, and he'd spend the week there.

"Kase." Caden's voice was somber. No other words were needed.

"I'll be there in twenty." It was the exact time it took for him to get to Turnersville.

He turned around, walked to his bike, and dug into his pocket for the keys. It would be a long ride. Not time-wise, but in his head space, it would feel as though time was standing still. He knew it. Even without his little brother saying the words. Kase knew.

Pop was gone.

He got on his bike and started down the driveway, glancing

over to Phoebe's. The light on her porch was out. Kase never needed anyone in his life. His chest tightened, realizing he needed her right now.

The ride was as long as he'd expected. He pulled into Caden's driveway and faced off with the ambulance. There were no lights, no urgency of EMTs rushing around. It was quiet and somber. He drew in a deep breath and pulled around the van into a spot near the fence. A few residents of the compound lingered in the lot.

He dismounted and straightened as Drake approached. He'd known Caden's best friend since they were kids. A solid man who'd become a part of the family. His hands were tucked deep in his pockets, and his head was bowed slightly.

Drake stopped a foot away and glanced up. "I'm sorry, man."

Kase tightened his lips and nodded. He sighed and glanced over his shoulder. "They got him out?"

Drake cleared his throat. "Cade was waiting on you."

He started toward the front porch with Drake at his heels. This was a family matter. Drake needed to be there. He was family. Kase started up the stairs and could hear the infant cries before he made it to the door. He opened the screen and walked through the door with Drake following close behind.

It was in the air. The scent of Caden's home, once inviting and reminiscent, was stale and cold. He walked through the living room, noting the silence.

Pop was gone.

"They're upstairs." The solemn deep voice came from the kitchen. Kase turned his head. Trevor, his nephew, with his hand on the seated bouncer resting on the table with the baby. Kase walked through the oversized doorway to Trevor. He gripped his shoulder in a tight squeeze.

"Ya all right?"

Trevor nodded. The kid had grown up with Pop around his entire life. It wasn't just losing a grandparent. It was more. He was trying his best to do the manly thing, not show emotion. Trevor was failing. At seventeen, he was still a kid who just lost his grandfather. It was a hard loss. Especially a man like Jack Reilly.

Trevor blinked and shifted his shoulder, wiping his cheek.

"I gotcha, Trev." He tightened his grip and watched his nephew bow his head.

"Hey."

Kase turned to see Caden leaning against the doorframe. No tears, but enough grief to fill a room of mourners. They were built to never shed tears. It was how Jack had raised them. They wouldn't let him down when it counted. They would internally grieve, but on the outside, they'd show the hard exterior they were taught. His old man wouldn't want them crying. He'd want them celebrating. Neither brother was at that point just yet.

Kase lifted his chin, releasing Trevor's shoulder. He walked to his brother, reaching out and resting his hand on his shoulder.

"You good?"

Caden drew in a deep breath and flattened his lips. Reilly boys always bore through the pain. Cade gave a sharp nod. "Yeah."

"How?" Kase asked.

Caden sighed. "Went down for a nap, never woke up." He paused. "Riss was the one to find him."

"Fuck." Kase gripped his waist, bowing his head. His death would be hard enough on her, but to be the one who found him was gut wrenching.

The creaking of the steps caught his attention. He watched as the EMTs carried him down in the gurney. A sheet covered his face. Their steps were slow and precise, as though they were carrying precious cargo. They were. A lifetime of good times. Kase dropped his arm and turned, watching them roll the gurney through the living room and stop in front of him and Caden.

"We have all the information. He'll be released in the morning."

Kase walked over to the gurney and reached out, uncovering the sheet from his face. He looked like he was sleeping. Slightly pale, but all the makings of his father for the past thirty-eight years. His cheeks had hollowed with age, and his skin had taken a beating from the sun. But it was Pop, lying silently and content. Former President of the Ghosttown Riders. Kase pulled the sheet down a bit and grasped his hand, shifting his still warm skin and placing it over his heart.

Ride free and wild, Pop.

Kase stepped away and watched as they rolled his father out the door. The end of an era. The sniffling behind him caught his attention, but he allowed her the space. It would be hard on everyone. Ironically, it would hit Rissa the hardest, though she knew him the shortest amount of time. Some bonds couldn't be explained, just appreciated in their truest form. That was Jack and Riss.

When Kase turned, he watched his brother with his arm curled over his wife's shoulder and tucking her into his side. Caden walked them into the kitchen, kissing her head and rubbing her arm. His brother. A true man in every sense of the word.

Riss turned, glancing over her shoulder with tears welled in her eyes. "I'm sorry, Kase."

He nodded and mustered up a smile he knew she needed. "Lived a good life. You remember that, *Colleen*." Kase winked and she smiled.

It would take all the memories of Jack at a happier time for any them to get through this. They'd do it. They were fucking Reillys.

Kase spent the night at Caden's, sleeping in one of the open units. Marissa's old one. He lay in bed the next morning knowing what the day would bring. He rested his arm over his eyes. He was gone.

"Fuck," Kase muttered. He kicked off the sheets and started toward the shower. The day would be long with a multitude of planning. Their funerals were always large with outside charter support. This was different. Jack Reilly wasn't just a brother. He'd led many men as the president of the Ghosttown Riders. This loss would be felt at expansion.

The Enemy

He locked up the unit and walked through the yard. He noticed Saint's truck pulled up next to his bike. It came as no surprise his VP would be there for them. For him. He swung open the door and entered the house to whispered voices sounding from the kitchen. He inhaled a breath. No fucking tears. *Celebrate me, Kasen, don't you dare fucking mourn me. I didn't raise no pussy.* Kase snorted and shook his head. Even gone, he could still hear his voice in his head.

He entered and was immediately ambushed by Bailey. She wrapped her arms around his waist and whimpered. "I'm so sorry, Kase." He reached out, caressing her back. This was fucking Bailey, all sweetness and feelings. He accepted who he was, and he needed to let others be who they were. Bailey was an emotional, compassionate hugger. And Kase was going to allow it.

He glanced up to see Saint watching him. He dipped his chin. It was enough. He didn't need the words from his brother. They would all feel the loss.

Bailey released her hold but stayed close to him. Marissa glanced up from the table where she was seated with Cora in her arms.

Only two women in Jack's life he truly loved were those two. Kase stepped forward, leaning down. He reached for the baby, and Rissa handed her over without a word, but a small smile played on her lips. He curved Cora into his forearm. For a man as rough and hard as Kase, babies and kids had always come natural to him.

"Anything we need to do?" Marissa asked quietly.

He glanced away from Cora's beautiful dark brown eyes to Marissa, who shared the same gaze. He smirked and shook his head. "Got it covered. Lot of brothers gonna wanna come out for Pop. We'll make the calls and give it a day or two." He glanced up at Caden, who'd been watching him. "Give the old man a sendoff worthy of a president."

Caden snorted and forced a smile. "He'd like that."

He'd spent a few more hours at Caden's before heading out. He was just at his bike when Cade called out to him. Kase straddled his bike but waited to start the engine. His brother walked closer with an envelope gripped in his hand.

"You need help setting anything up, you call, all right?" Caden said.

Kase nodded. "Yeah. I'll reach out to the charters, set it up, and let ya know when, probably day after tomorrow." Kase lifted his chin. "He was a Ghosttown Rider, Cade."

"I know."

"But more than that, he was our Pop. Not forgetting that either."

The corner of Caden's mouth curled. "I know, Kase." He cleared his throat, glancing down at his hand. He jutted the envelope in Kase's direction. "This is for you."

Kase glared at the crumpled white paper. He reached out, flipped it over, and read the inscription. *Kasen*. It was written in his dad's handwriting. He jerked his gaze to Caden, who raised his brows and shrugged.

"I don't know, man. Riss was looking through his nightstand and found them."

Kase glanced down again. He couldn't remember a time his father ever wrote him a note.

"Leave one for all of us?" Her jerked his head toward the house.

"Yeah. Even Cora."

Old fucker took her advice. He'd overheard their conversation where Phoebe suggested he write them letters. Kase couldn't help but smile. Jack Reilly never took advice from anyone. Except maybe Phoebe.

"You read yours?"

Caden slowly shook his head. "Not yet."

Kase drew in a breath and tucked the envelope into the inside pocket of his cut. He rolled back the bike and then started up the engine. A shake of his head to his brother and he was heading down the steep driveway. He had intended on driving straight to the clubhouse, but his bike had other ideas.

He took the scenic route on the outskirts of Ghosttown leading him down to the river. It was Pop's run. He loved the ride, said it made him feel free riding through the trees and down the winding road to the river. It was a better view in the fall with the changing leaves, but it would do. He parked in the lot and made his way down the grassy hill.

He understood why his dad and Cade loved it so much. The quiet was tranquil, and even if it wasn't Kase's scene, he could understand it. He reached in his pocket and pulled out the envelope.

Kasen.

He snorted and slipped his finger inside, pulling out the white, lined sheet of paper.

His chest burned, and he forced the air into his lungs.

"Fuck."

Chapter 21

The past few days had been heartbreaking and rough to say the least. She had replayed everything Nadia had said to her, analyzing it word for word. It had only been a day since her return. It felt like a year.

She had tried to build enough courage to reach out to him, but like a coward, backed out each time. There was a part of her that had hoped he would reach out. He'd stopped as of two days ago.

When she finally made the decision to walk over to the clubhouse and talk to him, she changed her mind. The lot was jam packed with cars lined up on the driveway and the road. They must have been having a party, she assumed. It was not the time for a heart to heart with Kase.

She barely heard the soft knock at her door. She walked through the living room and wiped off her hands. She opened the door to find Bailey standing in a pretty, pink, flowing dress.

"Hey, I didn't know you were stopping by."

She had a tight smile, and after a closer inspection, she realized her eyes were red rimmed and glassy. She reached out and grasped Bailey's hand. "What's wrong?" She immediately glanced down at her swollen belly. "Are you okay?"

A tear slid down her cheek, and Phoebe reached out, pulling

her into her chest and ushering her inside the house. Bailey sobbed against her, and she wrapped her arms over her shoulders, slamming the door closed.

"Bailey, talk to me." Phoebe led her to the couch, reaching out and grabbing her unfolded laundry and tossing it on the floor. She'd worry about it later. Right now, nothing was more important than her best friend crying. She urged her to sit and followed her down to the couch, rubbing her back.

"I didn't know you were home until I saw your lights on." Bailey sniffled and wiped her eyes. "I was at the clubhouse."

Phoebe searched her face. "Did something happen? Where's Saint?"

"He's next door." She nodded.

Bailey turned, gazing up at Phoebe with tears streaming down her face. She smiled, though it didn't reach her eyes.

"Phoebe." Bailey gripped her hand tightly. "Jack died last night."

Phoebe sucked in a breath, though it didn't quite reach her lungs. It was caught in her throat. Her body froze, and all she could do was stare back at her friend. She just saw Jack last week at Caden's house. They had dinner together. *He's coming over this weekend.* She tilted her head and leaned closer. She shook her head and willed back her tears.

"I just saw Jack," she whispered as her vision blurred. *He's coming over, we're doing a fire.* She inhaled a deep breath through her nose. Her chest seized into a tight, gripping ache. It was a physical pain. Her heart was breaking.

Bailey clasped her hand over their intertwined embrace. Phoebe felt the heat brim at her eyes. She clamped her lips and stared down at the floor. Then her tears escaped, and she made no move to stop them. She couldn't be sure how long they sat in silence. Phoebe drew in a deep breath and glanced over at Bailey, who was watching her.

"What happened?"

Bailey sniffled. "He went down for a nap." She shrugged and wiped the tears from her cheeks. "He never woke up."

Phoebe tightly grasped Bailey's hand and cupped her mouth. For all the loss she was feeling, it paled in comparison to what Kase was going through. It only added to her guilt of overreacting with him.

"How are they?"

"Riss is taking it the hardest. Ya know they were super close." She swallowed. "Cade seemed," she paused, "okay, said Trevor was really torn up. They knew he was getting worse, but you never can fully prepare yourself for losing someone."

"Yeah," she whispered, her heart breaking for them all. Selfishly, it was breaking for herself. She cleared her throat. "And Kase?"

Bailey turned. "Quiet. Just very quiet."

Her heart ripped deeper for him. He would bottle it up and take it all on. He'd allow it to eat away at him before he showed anyone anything.

Phoebe wiped her cheeks. "Is there anything I can do?"

Bailey smiled with a shrug. "You can come over to the club if ya want?"

Would Kase even want her there? More than anything, she wanted to go to him. This wasn't about her, though. It was about Kase and what he needed. Phoebe twisted her lips. "I don't think I should."

"You're welcome if you change your mind, okay? Saint told me to tell you that. You are welcome there."

She smiled. "Okay."

Bailey drew in a breath and reached into her bag, pulling out an envelope. "So, um, Jack left them all notes in his nightstand."

She gasped, and her mouth fell open. It was a cross between shock and elation. Phoebe felt a burst in her chest, and she teared up once again. *Son of a bitch did it.* She couldn't contain her smile. After the night by the fire, they never spoke of it again. She had hoped he would but figured he'd forget. Jack took her advice.

"Caden wasn't sure when he wrote them. But um, he gave me this when Saint and I went over this morning."

It was the only saving grace to his death. She cupped her mouth and tried her best to hold back her tears. *Well done, Jack.* He'd left them all something behind. A piece of him. Her eyes welled. This would serve comfort for them. Maybe not right away, but down the road when they had rough days, Jack left them something of him. Just a little piece that would see them through the hardest of times. She glanced up through her tears with a small smile. *You did good, Jack.* She drew in a deep breath, which filled her lungs. She was almost giddy with pride.

She reached out and took Bailey's hand. "Bailey, he left you a part of him."

Although she didn't know the extent of Bailey's and Jack's relationship, it seemed fitting he would leave her a note. She may not be family by blood, but Jack obviously thought she was special enough to him to leave a part of him with her.

Bailey widened her eyes and stared back at Phoebe in confusion.

"The note." She gestured her chin to her hand, and smiled. "Jack left a piece of him with you. You'll always have something from him. It means you must have really meant something to Jack."

Bailey lips spread into a sweet smile with a slow nod. "It's for you, Phoebe."

What? No. She inched back and glanced down at Bailey's hands holding the white envelope. "What?"

Bailey nodded. "Caden asked me to give it to you. He had one for Riss, the baby, Trev, Cade, and Kase." Bailey leaned closer, smiling. "And you."

"But I-I, no. Are you sure?"

Bailey reached over, handing her the note. "Yes, I'm sure. Has your name on it."

It did. In a shaky scratch was her name. *Phoebe.* She slowly took the note as her heartbeat pounded.

"Are you okay?"

She stared down at the envelope. "I don't get it, why me? I hardly knew him."

"He knew you, Feebs, enough to consider you one of his people. Don't question it. Jack may have been losing it at the end, but he knew people, good people. He knew *you*. And it's like ya said, you must have really meant something to him, Phoebe."

Jack left me a note.

Bailey stayed a bit longer, and they shared coffee. The conversation lulled, so they sat in silence until Saint called. She offered to stay, but Phoebe was good with being alone, and Bailey was needed back at the house. She walked her to the door, giving her a long hug before stepping away.

Bailey turned halfway in the door and glanced over her shoulder.

"For Kase, quiet isn't good." She glanced at the floor and walked out the door.

Phoebe knew exactly what she was saying. However, she wasn't sure if seeing her was what he wanted right now. She decided to think on it. More than anything, she wanted to go to him. But it wasn't about her. It was about Kase.

She sat on the couch staring at the envelope. It took her a while to actually open it.

To Phoebe,

A smart, sexy woman with a great ass once said, ya got something to say, ya write it down. Well, here I am, darlin', writing shit down. Gonna make it short and it sure as hell ain't gonna be fucking poetic but here goes. I see something in you. My boy sees it. Now, he's an unworthy bastard who's gonna piss you off. Ya got my okay to shoot his ass if ya need to. Ya got my blessing to love him too. Kase ain't used to good women, his mom set the bar so fucking low, my boys never knew what they should be looking for. Hold that against the evil bitch and maybe me. Love him, darlin'.

Now you. I woulda taken ya on my bike, rode ya down to the river. Woulda had burgers and double the fries with your sweet ass every fucking chance I got. Woulda toasted sexy women and whiskey with ya. Woulda drove down Main Street on them ATV's. No fucking helmets! Woulda shared my life with you, the good raunchy shit 'cause there ain't many women wanna hear it but you ain't no regular woman. And I woulda listened to you, woulda wanted to hear about your life, your family. Woulda liked that a lot.

Forty years ago, I woulda made you mine.

Raise a glass to me darlin' and I'll raise mine to you.

Jack

She smiled through her tears. How could she not? Even through the tears dripping onto the paper, she smiled. Jack had left her a piece of him. She settled into the couch cushion, eyeing the shaky scribbling. It took time and thought for Jack to put his words on paper. *And he chose me.* She drew in a deep breath and sunk her head against the couch.

To bikers and whiskey, Jack.

POP WAS GONE.

He'd spent the whole afternoon making the calls. Every member, some from hundreds of miles away, would descend on Ghosttown tomorrow. He'd worked out the details with the brothers earlier in the day. Every member was onboard with giving Jack the sendoff he deserved. It was after eleven before he made his way back to his room. Alone. A few of the women offered to give him some company. He wasn't interested in anyone. At least no one in the club.

He'd poured himself a drink and settled on his bed. There wasn't any background noise, though the club was already filled with brothers. It was a quiet somber mood. After the ceremony, the club partying would pick up, but until then, they were mourning.

He sipped his drink and set it down on the table beside his bed. He slipped the paper between his fingers and opened it up. It was self-torture, but he did it again. This would mark the fifth time he'd read Jack's note.

To Kasen,

This was your woman's idea. I tend to listen to the sexy ones. Not 'cause they got something to say but 'cause a man's always got an agenda. But she was onto something. What the fuck would I have wanted us to do? Hell, boy, there ain't much we haven't done. But talking of the future, the one I ain't gonna be around to see. I got a few.

I woulda taken that ride up the coast, you by my side. Fuck the helmet laws, we woulda broken them in seven states. Woulda went back to that place we camped out at when you and Cade was little, the place in the mountains. Woulda taken you boys with me. Woulda liked to head down to the river, do some fishing with ya. You used to like that when you were a kid. Had your first sip a whiskey down by that river. Woulda liked to have gone back with ya. Woulda liked to see your sorry ass trick Phoebe into being your old lady. Woulda liked it even more to hold your kid in my arms. Think you woulda made a good dad, Kasen. Better than I ever was. Woulda liked to be face to face, when I finally told ya this...

No other man alive I would have handed my gavel to but you. You did right by the club, by all of us. Proud of you. And I know I ain't never told ya and I regret that, Kasen. You are a good man, a faithful and loyal brother, always have been. I made you hard, thought I was building a man. Forgot to show you the heart, most valuable piece of a true man. You take the long ride for me, you toast my name with a lowball of whiskey and you remember, you made your old man damn proud.

Ride free and wild, son.

Pop

Jack may never had said the words to Kase, but he'd left him with a reminder.

The knock at the door was light and hesitant. He ignored it. Anyone stupid enough to come to his door was leaving without a limb. He grabbed his glass, throwing back the whiskey and letting the slow burn taper down his throat.

The knock sounded again, timid and quiet.

"You knock again, and I'll put my boot through your fucking

ass!" he shouted. He needed the quiet and solitude, not some fucking asshole checking on him. When the door creaked, he tightened his grip on his glass.

"Kase," she whispered.

He closed his eyes. It was strange. She was the last person he wanted to see him this way, and the only person he wanted to set his eyes on. He remained silent while she padded quietly through his room.

She stopped a few feet away, and his gaze flickered to her sandals and her pink toenail polish. It was soft and pale, much like the woman he refused to look at.

"You want me to go?"

Kase flattened his lips and lifted his stare.

She clasped her hands in front of her. He couldn't recall ever seeing her as unsure of herself as she was standing in front of him. Her eyes were glassy and puffy as though she'd been crying. She fidgeted and glanced back at the door.

"Saint said it was all right for me to come back here." She bowed her head, staring at the floor. Her gaze lifted. "I just wanted to come by, make sure you're okay?"

He curved his brow, remaining silent.

"I'm so sorry about Jack." Her voice shook, and he watched her pretty blue eyes tear up. She inhaled, and her hands shook slightly. "Bailey told me." She stepped closer. "You all right?"

He lifted his chin. "He left you a letter." Caden had mentioned he gave it to Bailey to pass along. It didn't surprise him his Pop had left her a letter. She meant something to Jack. And to Kase.

She blinked, and he watched as her eyes welled up. She nodded with a slight shrug.

She forced a smile. "I'll leave you alone. But if you need something, anything, just call me, okay?"

She was leaving, and his chest seized. Asking her to stay wouldn't work. He couldn't form the words. It wasn't who he was. However, the last thing he wanted was to watch her walk out the door.

He snorted, lifting the glass to his mouth, taking a slow sip. "Done fucking hating me?"

She blushed, and he caught the raw pain filter over her features.

"I never hated you, Kase." She tucked her hands in her pockets. "My pride took a hit." She shrugged. "And right now, it seems small and petty compared to how you must feel."

"Wasn't a club deal." He watched, and she glanced up through her lashes. It wasn't the best time, if there even was one. If he'd learned anything with Jack's death, it was you never know when you might be looking at someone for the last time.

He clasped his hands. "Set it up, just me and Meg knew. Ain't club money, it was mine."

Phoebe's eyes widened, and her bottom lip fell open.

"Did it so you could stay there. Was gonna offer for you to live there, no fucking strings attached." He arched his brow. "But I know you, would have made sure you paid me back."

She licked her lip and bowed her head.

"You love that fucking hole of a house, it's yours." He growled. "I listened, Phoebe. I heard ya. It was yours." Her lips pursed. It seemed the truth was hard to take on, and maybe she was feeling regret. The silence lingered in the room. Too many emotions with Jack's death, the shit between them, and the distance.

"Kase." She slowly inched forward, and then stopped. It was rare for Phoebe to show signs of uncertainty. She'd always been so sure of herself in every encounter. Standing in the middle of his room, unsure whether he wanted her there, yet she fucking showed up. Even knowing what a bastard he could be at a time like this. Phoebe showed up.

She glanced down at the floor and seemed to be struggling with her next words. "I'll go, but if ya need me, just call, okay?" She hesitated. "Even if it's late." She licked her lips and peeked up through her lashes. Her gaze softened, and he felt it straight in his gut. "Whatever you need from me, Kase. It's yours."

I fucking need you.

He hadn't even realized it until she walked through his door. His chest tightened, and his blood heated at the thought of her leaving. He ground his teeth, scowling back at her, angry with himself.

Say the fucking words. He shot up his hand, dropping his glass on the floor, not even caring when it shattered. He grasped her wrist and pulled her onto his lap. She fell forward, and her legs instinctively straddled his lap. He wrapped an arm around her waist and drove the other hand through her long strands angling her neck.

"I need you," he growled. He pressed his lips against her mouth, and the sudden ache in his heart mellowed a bit. It was an admission he never thought he'd make to anyone. Kase had never needed anyone, but at the moment, he needed her. He slipped his hand under the back of her shirt, feeling her warm skin under his palms.

She curled her arms around his shoulders, and he leaned back on the bed, taking her with him. She hovered over him, her hair falling past her shoulders.

"You stay with me." It was a low command. It was an afterthought to ask, but Phoebe nodded as her eyes teared up. "We'll talk more later, ya hear me?"

She nodded.

Kase tightened his grasp on her bare back, pulling her closer. "Don't fucking leave again."

The corner of her lip jutted up, and she whispered, "I won't."

A lone tear fell past her cheek, and he adjusted her on his chest. His hand cupped her jaw with his thumb wiping away her tear.

"Pop would be pissed you're crying." His tone was graveled and rough but made her smile. She leaned closer.

"Crying is for pussies, he'd probably say."

The corner of his lips curled. Not many people knew the real Jack Reilly, but she did. It was something they'd always share.

"Yeah, and he'd say I was an asshole for letting you go."

She licked her lips. "Yeah, maybe. But he'd say I was the asshole for not seeing a man who wanted to take care of me, I think."

Kase smiled, gripping her jaw, sliding his mouth against hers. "Both assholes in Pop's eyes."

The corner of her mouth curled. "And yet, he loved us."

He did. Jack may not have said the words, but his last letter had. Kase tightened his grip and curled closer to Phoebe. "Yeah."

Their kiss would fade, and he'd find himself sleeping, no sex, with Phoebe curled against him. It was the only way he'd find peace. With the exception of her, he'd never slept next to someone he hadn't fucked. When he woke up, she was curled into his side with her head resting on his chest. It took time to untangle from her hold. He needed her close.

Eventually, Kase left her in bed. He walked through the quiet hall. He breeched the doorway leading to the main bar and glanced around, finding Dobbs, Gage, and Saint sitting at one of the tables.

"How's it going?" Gage asked.

Kase lifted his chin. "Gotta make the calls."

One of the prospects, Joe, came through the door, glancing around the room before landing his gaze on Kase. He seemed off; a bit nervous. It was understandable. On a regular day, Kase was scary as fuck. It seemed he set everyone on edge, especially after losing Jack.

"What?" he snapped.

"Uh." He was stalling and glanced over at Saint.

"Fucking speak, asshole." Kase had no patience on a good day.

"I-is uh, Phoebe here?"

He furrowed his brows. "Why?"

Joe hooked his thumb over his shoulder. Before he could say a word, Kase heard the rushed footsteps coming from the hall. He and the brothers turned to catch Phoebe walk in.

"What's wrong?" Kase asked.

She smiled, shook her head, and then glanced up at Joe. "They just pull in?"

"Yeah."

Kase watched the exchange and watched Phoebe, who was heading to the front door.

Kase darted up and walked to the door with the guys following close behind. When he opened the door, he saw an unfamiliar van parked near the steps. He recognized a few residents, Coop, Marty, and Carla huddled near the back where Phoebe was standing. The prospect was a foot behind her, almost in a guarding position.

"What's going on?" Dobbs asked.

Kase kept his eyes on the scene in front of him. "Don't know." He was going to find out. The last thing the club needed today was bullshit from the town. He walked down the steps a few feet away from the small group. His brothers had followed closely with Saint at his side.

Phoebe must have felt his presence because she glanced over her shoulder and smiled. "They brought food."

What? Who brought food? Kase was having a hard time following what she had said. The whole scene with the residents at the compound was strange on its own. And they brought food? What the fuck was happening?

Carla poked her head around the van and walked straight toward him. Marty and Coop followed behind. She smiled.

"We are so sorry to hear about Jack" Her eyes welled. "He was quite the character, and we're gonna miss him at the diner." She drew in a breath and waved her hand. "Anyway, a bunch of us got together early this morning and just prepared some things. Nothing fancy." She shrugged. "Just thought it might help if ya didn't have to worry about food."

When Kase remained silent, Saint stepped forward. "That was very thoughtful of you all."

Carla scoffed. "It's what we do here." She paused and glanced over at the members situated behind him and landed her stare on

Kase with a warm smile. "You're Ghosttown too, now." She rolled her eyes. "I mean, you always have been." She bit her lip and stared back at Kase, a warm glow lighting her cheeks. "You all are a part of us, that's all I'm saying."

As a club, they were never concerned with being accepted by anyone outside of the Ghosttown Riders. What Carla was saying, though, was resonating with him and his club. She turned to the van, and Kase stepped forward, finding his voice.

"Thanks. You send me the bill."

She scoffed. "There is no bill, no charge. Like I said, it's what we do here. We threw in some plates, napkins, and utensils. We weren't sure what you all needed."

"Joe will grab it."

Joe rounded the back of the van and halted when he looked inside. "Uh Kase, man, I'm gonna need some help."

He furrowed his brows and stepped closer, getting a glimpse. There had to have been over fifty foil trays of food. Who the fuck did they think they were feeding?

He eyed Carla. "You did all this?"

"We all did. Some came down to the diner to prepare the stuff, others did it at home." She glanced down the driveway, but from his view with the van blocking, he couldn't see who she was looking at. "And others will bring it themselves. Coop, go help her before she throws her hip out."

Kase walked around to Phoebe, who was standing near the edge of the van, smiling. Mary, from across the road, was slowly making her way up the hill pulling a small red wagon that held two large bags. Coop grabbed the wagon from her and kept at her pace until they made it to the van.

Carla shook her head. "Mary, you should have called me. I would have sent Coop for it."

Mary waved her hand. She inhaled a deep breath. It was a bitch of a hill for most people, but for an eighty-year-old pulling a wagon, it would be a beast. She released Coop's arm and smiled warmly at Kase and the members. A few more had shown up and were standing behind him.

"I want to give my condolences in person." She smiled and ambled up to stand in front of Kase, reaching out and taking his hand. "I didn't know Jack, but I've heard an awful lot about him from Bailey, and I wanted tell you how sorry I am."

"And bring food, I'm guessing." Phoebe chuckled and gripped his hand.

"It's my banana bread. I only had time to make fifteen loaves, hope it's enough." She smiled, tightening her frail hand on his before releasing him. She turned to Carla. "Anyone else think of desserts?"

Coop cleared his throat. "Marley sent over the cookies and brownies," Coop said. The man had been wary of the club. It struck Kase deeply that he and his wife would help them out.

Phoebe squeezed his waist. "Well, let's get everything inside."

Trax, Gage, and Dobbs stopped Carla when she grabbed a platter. "We'll unload, we appreciate this." Carla rested her hand on Gage's back and smiled.

"You'd all do the same for us, I believe."

Kase cleared his throat, gaining her attention. "We would."

She smiled with a slow nod and moved away, allowing the men to grab the food. It took two trips with all the guys helping. There was more than enough for the large crowd they were expecting.

The whole scene was more than Kase could comprehend. They had all lived their lives with a stigma on their backs. At times, it rang true. The club was all they had.

Until Ghosttown.

Chapter 22

The last two days had been a bittersweet, somber blur.

After the residents dropped off food, another truck came in with a few more trays and salads. Carla had said it best. *It was what they did.* She was surprised when the white Lexus pulled in, and she smiled when Elsa got out, heading to her trunk. She dressed up as though she was attending church and stuck out like a sore thumb. When Bailey started toward the car, Phoebe followed.

"Hi Elsa."

She poked her head from the trunk and scowled. "No one told me."

Phoebe blinked and glanced over at Bailey, who bit her lip. "Um, told you?"

She sighed heavily and rolled her eyes. "I didn't find out until a few hours ago."

Saint and Dobbs came over, probably from Elsa raising her voice at Bailey. As Phoebe moved closer, she saw the two boxes in the back of the truck. She stepped aside.

"I didn't have time to make anything. Luckily, I know people." She shrugged. "A twenty-pound turkey, farm raised, so it's the good kind, and a honey ham."

Phoebe bit back her laugh and watched as Elsa gestured for Saint and Dobbs to take the food. They thanked her and headed toward the door. Bailey spoke briefly while Phoebe stayed off to the side just watching. When Bailey walked away, Elsa rounded her car. She flicked her gaze to the backseat and then scanned around the lot, seemingly looking for someone. Her gaze locked on Phoebe, and she pursed her lips.

Phoebe raised her brows. Elsa was outspoken about her dislike for Phoebe, but it seemed she was the only option.

Elsa reluctantly waved her over, and Phoebe strolled toward her. When she rounded the back, Elsa was pulling out a large flower arrangement.

"There's no church service." It was a disgusted accusation. Considering Elsa's generosity, Phoebe would let the snarky comment slide.

"Nope."

Elsa shook her head. "Well, they can use it as a centerpiece."

Phoebe grabbed the multi-colored array of spring flowers. There was no doubt she'd spent a ridiculous amount of money on them. "It's very pretty."

Elsa's lips curved, though she seemed to be holding back. She jerked her head to the clubhouse. "And I'm gonna pray for all of them whether they like it or not."

Phoebe smirked. "Thank you for all of this, including those prayers, Elsa."

She didn't respond and got in her car. Phoebe, nor any of the members, would ever get an invite to Elsa's house, but even in small ways, the town had shown unity.

After bringing the flowers inside, much to the shock and amusement of many of the guys, she headed over to her place to take a shower.

"Do what ya gotta do, then get your ass back here. Pack your shit, you're staying here tonight."

. . .

KASE WAS HARSH AND HARD, demanding and spouting orders. She let him. They all did. It was what he needed. The turnout for Jack had been bigger than anything she'd ever seen. He would have loved it.

She spent her time at the clubhouse helping out, and while Kase seemed all over the place with prepping Jack's funeral, he was somehow always close by. Watching other people grieve was hard, watching Kase was heart wrenching. He was stoic and solid through the last two days. He never broke down. She hadn't expected him to. That wasn't Kase.

She wasn't sure what to expect from a biker funeral, but by the end of day two, she was convinced this was what she wanted when she died. It was a celebration of his life. It was drinking whiskey and sharing stories. Those were the best, especially from the older members. There were so many people, she couldn't be sure who was who, but they were all in agreement. Jack Reilly may not have been a model citizen, but he was a memorable and loyal brother.

The second night was winding down. Most of the visiting charters had headed out a few hours ago. She had finished cleaning up in the kitchen with the rest of the girls and took a seat at the bar.

"Can't believe you're leaving us, girl," Macy said, shaking her head.

The group had been in complete disbelief when Nadia made the announcement an hour ago. While many seemed shocked, she wasn't, and she noticed Kase wasn't either.

Nadia leaned on the bar. "I'll visit."

Meg snorted. "You better."

"Find a job yet?" Cheyenne asked.

Nadia glanced around the room. "Not yet, but I have a few leads bartending. It would work out 'cause then I can help my sister with the kids during the day."

Phoebe zoned out of the conversation but continued to watch Nadia. She was loved and would be missed. While she hadn't mentioned Carter to the other women, Phoebe had spoken to her brother earlier in the day. He called to extend his condolences to Kase. She only caught the tail end of the conversation when Kase said, "You take care of that one."

Phoebe smiled, knowing he was speaking of Nadia. Carter would, and if things worked out, she'd be seeing a lot more of Nadia.

After an hour, she started to the back through the halls. It had been a while since she'd last seen Kase, and she wanted to check on him. He continued to be the quiet, stoic leader, which worried her. He was bottling up his own grief. He would handle it however he saw fit. And Phoebe would be there when he needed her.

She walked to the doorway, eyeing the crowd. There were more people than she'd ever seen outside of a concert. She found Kase talking with Gage, who had a buxom blonde on his lap. She also caught Val's long hair swinging past her back as she made her way through the room.

Val sauntered up, and Phoebe smirked as she inched closer to Kase. She thought for sure Val would sidle up next to him. She didn't. She glanced up at Kase, who didn't pay her any mind, and then turned and continued her way through the room.

She walked through the crowds, sharing a few smiles with some familiar faces. It had been a long day for all of them. It may have been a party, but there was nothing wild about the scene. Small groups of brothers gathered, drinking and talking. A few games of pool were being played, along with darts. She weaved through the men and reached for Kase's back. His back stiffened under her hand. He jerked his head.

When she smiled up at him, he curled his arm over her shoulder and pulled her into his side. His nose skimmed hers, and she rose to her toes, taking his lips for a quick kiss.

"You good?" It was her main objective for the whole day. She gave him the space she figured he needed and gave him the time with his brothers. It didn't stop her from worrying. Kase wasn't the type of man to break down and share his feelings. He was a brick wall she'd have to chip at to get inside. It was a task she was willing to take on.

Jack's death, as tragic as it was, had become a turning point for them. Kase's walls were built so strong and high, yet she was getting in.

He lowered his head, grasping tight against her waist. "Checking on me, Phoebe?"

She curled her lips and angled her breasts against his chest. "Yes."

His gaze darkened, his brown eyes appearing almost black, and he leaned closer. His breath fanned over her face. "Acting like an old lady."

She knew the term; Bailey had explained it a while ago. It meant his woman, his one.

Her lips grazed his bearded chin, and she curled her face against his neck, whispering in his ear, "Does it bother ya, Kase?"

"No." His answer was immediate, and she turned her head. Within seconds, his mouth was on hers. She grasped his neck, pulling him deeper into the kiss. Public displays of affection had never been her thing. She wasn't necessarily opposed to it, but Jared was content with just hand holding. Kase was not. His tongue slipped past her lips, and she thrust her body against his, grabbing his neck and pulling him closer. She didn't bother looking at those who watched. She didn't care. All she wanted was Kase. His hand pressed against her back, his fingers trailing over her ass.

"Changed my mind." He glanced over his shoulder around the room. "Staying at your place tonight."

"Me or us?" she asked.

His hand tightened on her back, and his lips swept across her jaw. "Us."

Chapter 23

She stretched her arms over her head and curled her back to his side of the bed. She scooted her ass a few more inches and glanced over her shoulder, reaching behind her. She cocked up on her elbow, searching the empty room. Did he leave? He'd mentioned wanting to check out the site for Gage's new house. Construction was set to start in a few weeks.

She rolled out of bed and got dressed, staggering out into the kitchen. From her doorway, the entire house was visible with no sign of Kase. The only telltale sign he hadn't left was his cut hanging on the back of her chair. She wandered around her small space, peeking out the front door with no sign of him.

When she started back toward the kitchen, she noticed the back door open a crack. She made her way to the back and stopped at the door, peering down on her back steps. She had a small deck built off the back. There he was. She opened the door and made her way outside.

"Morning," she said.

He didn't look over at her and kept his stare on her backyard. She crept closer and stood a foot away behind him.

"You wanna be alone?"

"No." His answer was graveled and sharp, leading her to think maybe he was lying.

Kase hadn't spoken much about Jack. Even when all the members were sharing stories, while he listened and added a few comments, he never shared any of his.

She was prepared to go back inside when his hand shot out and grasped her ankle. She jerked her head downward to see him peering up at her. When he released her, she took a seat on the step, ignoring the moisture seeping through her shorts and drenching her butt. Her knee brushed against his leg, and he grasped her inner thigh, holding a tight grip with one hand and smoking a cigarette with the other.

She rested her palm over his hand and stared off into the yard. The last time she'd been out back was with Jack. The corner of her mouth quirked up.

"You wanna talk?"

He drew in a breath, staring out into the yard. "No."

She nodded, watching his profile. His hard face had lost some of the harshness and sharp edges usually reserved when he scowled, which seemed to be a usual uniform for Kase.

"According to Jack, I had a great ass," she whispered, pulling her hand from her leg and resting it on his back.

He smirked and turned his head, angling closer. "You do have a great ass."

She chuckled, resting her head on his shoulder. His grip tightened on her thigh. This was them. They worked without the words. She inhaled a breath and smiled. *Jack would like this.* Her and Kase sitting on the back porch with memories of him.

"You got shit to do." He raised his brows.

She did. Her deadline for her next contract had been extended, but she needed to get in about two hours before the end of the day. And he remembered. She rested her chin on his shoulder.

"It can wait."

He snorted. "Gonna sit out here all day with me?"

"If that's what ya need."

There was a pause in the silence, and then he grasped her jaw. She gazed up. His mouth dropped over hers in a soft, slow kiss.

"Whatever I need, huh?"

She nodded. "You'd do the same for me."

It was a statement, not a question. He answered anyway.

"Yeah, I would." She believed him.

It was over an hour of sitting on her back porch, mostly in silence, and while she was prepared to do it all day, she was relieved when he grabbed her hand and pulled her up from the stairs, leading them back into the house.

Kase had hung out, making calls while she worked. She'd overheard a tense discussion involving a member who wanted to switch charters. It seemed to put Kase on edge. When she asked him about it, she was almost surprised at how open he was with her. Apparently, Hades, who she'd met briefly at Jack's ceremony, was wanting to change over charters. Bailey had also mentioned Hades being Saint's brother. Kase downplayed the situation, but she was reading his stress level. The conversation abruptly ended when he mentioned going to Gage's property.

The ride to Gage's was a short one, and when they pulled up to the lot, she glanced around. She knew all of Ghosttown, but street names always threw her off, as did the development on the street. Three lots down, more construction had been started. She wasn't sure who owned the property, but she had a sneaking suspicion. When Gage mentioned the lot on Oakwood Drive, she hadn't put two and two together. Taking a look around the street, mainly across from Gage's, she smiled. She dismounted, waiting on Kase to park.

Gage and Dobbs were making their way down the hill.

"What do ya think?" Gage asked with his arms spread wide. There was no missing the pride written on his face.

The construction had been started, and the framework was done. The house, if she had to guess, would be a replica of the one across the street. A two-story smaller colonial. It seemed the design would coincide with the original construction. *Perfect.*

"All it needs is walls and you're set." Phoebe teased.

"Got my guys working round the clock. Should be done in the next month." Gage grinned and jerked his chin. "You know my new neighbors?"

She did. In fact, she'd been fairly close with the family before they moved. An original Ghosttown family. Karen and Charlie had lived there for over twenty years, raised their kids in the small town.

"Yeah. They're actually the reason I was bitching about apple turnovers at the meeting." She laughed and glanced over at the house. "They moved to California after Charlie retired, but Trista should be moving back soon." Phoebe smirked. "Their daughter. Twenty-four, I think. Just graduated college with her Masters."

Dobbs snorted. "She hot?"

She bit back her giggle. *Yes, she is, and with her beauty comes a whole lot of sass.* Even from a young age, Trista held a certain level of maturity usually reserved for adults. Until someone pissed her off. Her temper could rival Phoebe's. Of course, Trista lacked the patience of most adults. One strike and she'd bite back like a cobra.

Phoebe sighed and turned to face the men. "Gorgeous, actually." Phoebe cocked her head. It was only fair to give them a heads up. "Just a warning, boys. Trista may be young, but do not fuck with her." She arched her brow. "I'm serious. Not the neighbor you want to get on the bad side of."

Gage strolled closer with a slight gleam in his eye. "I like feisty women."

Phoebe chuckled and fell into Kase's side when he wrapped his arm around her shoulders. "Okay, Gage. Just don't underestimate her. With Trista comes the whole damn town. Don't mess with her."

Gage and Dobbs laughed it off, and Phoebe shrugged as they walked up the job site.

Don't say I didn't warn you.

The Enemy

KASE SAT at the end of the bar watching the door. He felt her hands curl around his waist and grip his stomach. Even without seeing her, he knew it was Phoebe. Only one woman alive would be so direct without asking. The only one he'd allow it from. She rested her chin on his shoulder, brushing her lips against his neck.

"Ditch your meeting and come play with me at my house." Her teeth grazed his neck, and it took great effort not to close his eyes. Her fingers tightened over his stomach. He turned his head glaring, but Phoebe stared back smiling.

"Can I tempt you with a blowjob?"

He smirked. "Try me." He growled, and she leaned closer for a kiss. The moment was fleeting.

Kase had been dreading the meeting. The other charter wouldn't let Hades go without something. He just didn't know what. He glanced over when he heard the voices.

Mack walked in flanked by two men. They were all members, but the meeting had all his brothers on high alert. Mack jutted his chin at Kase as his gaze filtered over to Phoebe. *Back the fuck off, man.*

Kase gripped her hand at his stomach and turned. "Head out now." It was a command. Phoebe leaned in kissing him and settled back, walking around the group and heading toward the door. He'd explained the meeting to her earlier, and she seemed to understand why he didn't want her around. Her safety was important.

Mack watched, as did his guys, as she sauntered out to the door. Kase jerked his chin toward her as he eyed the prospects. They followed her out as he knew they would. They'd also watch her house. He'd given instructions of Phoebe being watched while the other charter was in town. There was a mutual respect between the charters, but he wasn't taking any chances with her.

"Old lady?" Mack asked.

"Mine."

Mack's eyes crinkled. "We should trade sometime."

He'd known Mack since he started with the club at eighteen. He'd been a few years older, but also new to the club.

"No."

Mack smirked. "Don't blame ya, probably wouldn't be offering up mine if she looked like her."

Kase respected Mack as a president. As a husband, he was a piece of shit. It never bothered Kase in the past. A man did what he wanted. For some reason, it bothered him now.

"You want my guy, huh?"

Kase sipped his beer and raised his brows. "I don't fucking poach members. You know me better than that. Hades approached me. Told him we won't take him unless he's got the votes from you."

Mack sighed and rested back in his seat. They were in a stare down with neither man relenting. Kase had a feeling it would go down like this. He folded his arms. He'd do what he could to get Hades into the club, but Mack wasn't going to make it easy.

Nadia brought beers over and walked away. She was comfortable around most bikers, but he read the hesitation with Mack.

"All right, let's start the deal." He smirked and waggled his brows. "Start with you giving us two of your girls." He angled his head, staring back at Nadia, mainly her ass.

Kase slammed his bottle down on the bar, gaining attention from Mack and all the surrounding brothers from both charters.

"I don't peddle fucking human flesh, asshole. You want one of the girls, they wanna go with ya, that shit don't need my approval. You fuck with one of them, you'll have every one of my guys on your ass before you can even mount your bike. We straight?"

Mack snorted. "Getting soft on me, Kase."

Kase took the insult and banked it away. He'd never fallen for the name calling. Except when Phoebe called him a little bitch. Somehow her words got under his skin and festered. He made a mental note to paddle her ass next time he got her naked. He sighed, holding back the reaction Mack was dying to get.

"Gotta give me something. Losing my VP, need something from you."

"What?"

"Property."

Kase grinned. "Not on your fucking life. This is my town." He wouldn't barter with the Ghosttown property.

"Future marker, then."

Kase shook his head. "No."

Mack took a sip of his drink and set the bottle on the bar, swiping his lips with his sleeve. He glanced over at the men standing close by and gestured his guys to step back. Kase glanced up at Saint, who was scowling. When they locked eyes, Kase stared back at him. Whatever was about to be said, Mack wanted it to be private. So far, the negotiations on Hades weren't going in their favor. Saint and Kase, knowing each other for so long, had grown to read each other. Saint nodded slowly and backed away, setting the tone for the other members to do the same.

Kase turned back to Mack. "You give me a marker." He held up his hand before Kase had the chance to speak. "Nothing illegal. Just something I can call in, and you'll make good on it." He cocked his brow. "I need something, Kase. Hades is a big loss for the club, for my guys. Need something in the bank to pacify them." He paused and scowled. "You'd do the same in my position."

He would, and as president, Mack needed to show he had a strong hold on Hades leaving. It was more about saving face than anything else.

Kase nodded and stretched out his hand. "I'll give you a marker."

Mack clasped his hand. "Next meeting we'll vote him out."

Kase tightened his grip and pulled Mack toward him. The move had caught the Ghosttown East president off guard.

"Nothing illegal, you hear me?"

Mack smiled. "You have my word, brother."

Something didn't sit well with Kase, but only time would tell if Mack lived up to his word. The brothers from both sides congregated, and the party picked up. He stuck around for a while, mostly watching the charter. He'd given strict instruction to Trax, Dobbs, Rourke, and Gage to be on the watch for the charter. Keeping the peace was important, but so was the safety of his members, which included the women.

Chapter 24

"They loved it, Phoebe."

She smiled and tapped her feet on the floor in a celebratory dance. She'd been waiting on hearing back after submitting her project a few weeks back. After Jack's death, her life had been consumed with the club, and she'd almost forgotten about it.

"We have two other accounts we'd like you to take on."

"Absolutely."

"Great, I'll send you the contracts. If you need to negotiate terms, let me know, but they are high end and pay accordingly."

"I'll take a look and get back to you. Thanks."

She hung up and sighed in relief. It may have been a slow start, but she was getting back on her feet. She walked over to her table and powered up her computer. Her main focus was the pay.

When her phone rang again, she hadn't even bothered looking, assuming it was Jane.

"Hello."

"Mrs. Shaw?"

"Yes."

"Hi this is Vada Zink with Zink Realty Listing."

Shit! She had been avoiding the number for the past few

weeks. After speaking with the aggressively pushy rep, she'd decided the leasing company was out of the question. She'd been able to dodge the calls. Until now.

"Ms. Zink, listen..."

"Call me Vada."

She snorted, shaking her head. "Vada. As I told James, I'm not interested in leasing out my property."

"He said you were a maybe?"

Phoebe furrowed her brows. The utter defeat in her tone was evident. She was a far cry from the shark she'd first spoken to. Maybe she was new?

"I'm not, and I don't want to waste your time."

"I prepared a whole presentation." The hushed tone had Phoebe thinking Vada was talking to herself. *Why the hell do I feel bad?* No, she wasn't doing this.

"I could come to you, take you out to eat. I have a company card."

Phoebe laughed. "I'm pretty sure you aren't supposed to let on that you're trying to schmooze me, Vada."

"Oh, right."

"Look, I'm not interested, but I appreciate you reaching out."

"W-well, umm, if you change your mind, will you call me back?" There was a slight pause. "Please."

Phoebe smiled and cocked her head toward the door when she heard the knock. She started through the living room.

"Yes, if I change my mind, you'll be the first one I call, Vada."

"Thank you. Have a great day."

Phoebe clicked the phone and opened the door. She shifted back in surprise and then curled her mouth.

"Hey."

"How's it going?"

"Good."

Carter nodded awkwardly. "I'm picking up Nadia, but thought I'd swing by."

"Come on in." She opened the door, making room for him to

enter. They may be blood, but there was an awkward stranger vibe, always had been with Carter. For the first time, it felt different. Not completely comfortable and casual, but definitely better.

"Kase here?"

She snorted. "I got him tied to my headboard in the back."

Carter jerked his head and scowled when she laughed.

"Why are you always so fucking sarcastic, Phoebe?"

She laughed. "Same reason you're always so damn serious, Carter?" She shrugged. "You're you and I'm me, it's how we roll." She strolled to her couch and took a seat. "What's going on?"

He shifted awkwardly and searched the room.

"I shouldn't have told you about the money. It was fucked up, throwing that shit in your face. Pissing on ya when you were down." He straightened his back. "Not proud of how I acted. Should have told you that when you were at my place."

"It's okay."

"No, it's not, Phoebe. And you shouldn't think it is." He shook his head with a hushed curse. "You don't take that shit from me or Jared or any man, you hear me?"

Her bottom lip fell open, and she gasped quietly. In all her thirty-two years on Earth, her brother had never apologized to her for anything. It was surreal and hard to grasp his words.

"Well, I didn't technically take it. I mean, I did hang up on you, then kicked you outta my house."

"Yeah, and I deserved it." He raised his brows. "And you deserve my apology."

He walked over, taking a seat next to her on the opposite end of the couch. He clasped his hands and angled his head toward her. She righted herself on the couch and leaned closer.

She squinted her eyes. "Did Kase threaten you?"

Carter scoffed. "He's a mean motherfucker, I'll give him that. But I'm not afraid of Kase Reilly or any of the club." He paused, drawing in a breath and pinning her in his stare. "I'm apologizing because I was being a dick. Because I was wrong coming at you like that. You had a husband who was shit to you, you don't need that from me."

As small as it may seem to an outsider, it was the kindest thing her brother had ever said to her. She didn't quite know how to respond.

"Thanks, Carter." She glanced down at the floor.

There was a small gap of silence before he spoke.

"Got a proposition for you."

"What?"

He didn't respond immediately.

She chuckled. "What, Carter?"

"Don't sell. You keep doing the payments each month, send the checks directly to me, or you can go through Dad, whatever ya want."

She shook her head. "Carter, I just think…."

"Fuck Phoebe, let me do this." He glanced around the room and snorted. "For reasons I don't get, you love this place, and you should keep it. God knows you lost enough. You deserve this."

It was the nicest gesture he'd ever done for her. It tugged at something deep in her belly. Her eyes welled, and she drew in a deep breath, unable to speak.

"I've never done anything for you, let me do this."

She glanced up, and a tear escaped. "I've never done anything for you, either."

Carter smirked. "Then you'll owe me, I guess."

"Okay."

Carter nodded, and she saw the relief in his face. He wanted to do this, and he wanted her to let him. He shoved his hands into his pockets, seemingly nervous. She could relate. They'd spent their entire lives at odds. Their truce would take some time to get used to.

"Kase Reilly, huh?"

She glanced up and smirked. "Polar opposite of Jared."

He snorted and cocked a brow. "Not a bad thing when you put it that way."

"He's not a bad guy, Carter."

He smiled and sighed. "No, he's not." He angled his head. "Not with those he loves." He stood and walked toward the door. "Call Dad, he thinks you're still pissed at him."

She bolted up. "Going to get Nadia?"

"In an hour." He glanced over his shoulder. "Why? Gonna invite me for dinner?"

She shrugged, and for the first time in her life, she didn't want her brother to walk out of the room. "I'm not cooking for your ass, but I will let you buy me a burger at the diner."

He shook his head and laughed. "Get your shit before I change my mind."

THE VOTE WAS UNANIMOUS, as he knew it would be. Hades was officially a Ghosttown Rider.

"Welcome, brother," Kase said and rose from his seat. He walked over, extending his hand, and pulled him in for a hug. He'd had his reservations about Hades joining their charter. He'd always been loyal to the club, but he was coming from a different charter with illegal ties. If Hades could stay out of that shit and keep on with them, he was sure this decision wouldn't come to bite him in the ass.

Kase stepped back, allowing his brothers to welcome him. Kase watched from the corner of the room as Saint approached.

He stepped in line next to Kase and sighed. "I'll keep my eyes on him."

"Not concerned, Saint. He'll do the right thing, 'cause if he doesn't, he's out."

"He's got too much riding on this." Saint didn't elaborate. He didn't have to. *Allie.* He watched the men filter out the door, and followed behind with Saint at his side. The party would be the first since Jack's funeral. It was good. The club needed some good shit happening.

He breeched the door and found Meg leaned up against the wall. She smiled at the brothers as they passed by and pushed off the wall when Kase stopped next to her.

"What's going on, darlin'?" She would forever hold a soft spot for him and all the brothers. He usually didn't take outside help, but Meg stepped up when they needed it five years ago for the LLC to buy the property in Ghosttown. Not a woman he trusted more. Until Phoebe.

"Need a minute." She smiled, and he backed up, ushering her into the room again. Most of the brothers followed Hades to the bar except Saint, Trax, and Rourke, who came back into the room. Trax and Rourke were especially close to Meg, as was Kase.

Meg pulled out the seat and sat down. "Got a call last night. James Zink?"

Kase furrowed his brows. The name wasn't familiar.

"He's from a leasing company. Was interested in leasing out the land in Ghosttown for development. He gave some spiel about making money, sold it as if I could make crazy cash." Meg folded her hands at her waist and shifted in her seat. "I originally wrote it off as bullshit marketing, but then he mentioned he had a resident interested. A rep was setting up a meeting."

Kase furrowed his brows. "Who?"

She swallowed with an uneasy sigh. Her answer was going to piss him off, he could feel it. "Phoebe."

Kase felt the fire burn through his blood. "Bullshit." Meg flinched. *Fuck!* His intention wasn't to come after her. Saint rested his hand on his shoulder, and he jerked his glare to his brother.

What the fuck?

"Kase," Meg said, gaining his attention. Her face softened. "That's what he said, but I got my doubts. This morning I got a call from the rep. A mousy little thing who mentioned she'd be up in the area and wanted to set up a meeting. When I pushed, she basically confirmed she was trying to get a meeting with Phoebe." She raised her brows. "She didn't have one set up. Sweetheart, these are salespeople. It's what they do. Thinking Phoebe might not realize her name is being thrown around."

Kase eyed Saint. It was only a matter of time before they'd have to deal with people trying to come in. He thought it would be a few years while they opened up their businesses in Ghosttown, but he knew eventually the vultures would descend. This company was just one of many who would think they could make a go at Ghosttown. *No fucking way.* He needed to send a message. He gripped the chair and nodded to Saint, who read his mind. He smirked and jerked his chin. Kase turned to Meg.

"Call them back, set up a meeting. Need you to sell it like you're interested, Meg."

Her eyes widened, and she glanced up at Saint.

"What? Why?"

Kase stretched his back, eyeing his brothers. They'd known him long enough. They knew where his mind was at. Trax and Rourke nodded.

"You set it up, you let Saint know when, and make it at the town hall." He stalked around his brother. There was only one person he needed to see now, and she better hope to fucking God her answers didn't piss him the hell off.

Saint would handle Meg and explain the details. He walked through the bar, ignoring the naked women, and made a beeline for the door, tossing it open and hearing it slap against the building. He needed to calm himself. Meg's voice played over in his head, reminding him Phoebe hadn't betrayed him. His blood still boiled at the possibility. He hopped the fence and double timed to her door, not even bothering to knock as he swung open the door.

She jumped and gasped when he started toward her. She was smiling, but grew wary as the seconds passed. "I was just on my way over." She blinked. "Something wrong?"

He stood across the counter and rested his knuckles on it. "Did you fucking set up a meeting with the leasing company to buy your place?"

Her eyes widened, and she blushed. *Fuck.* It was not the response he wanted. She held up her hands. "Hear me out, Kase."

"What the fuck were you thinking?"

He should have known better. Phoebe wouldn't respond kindly to his harsh response. She squinted and cocked her head. The blush across her cheeks wasn't from anything other than fueled fire.

"You ain't selling to that motherfucker." He was losing his grip with her abashed reaction. No woman alive could get under his skin and do the fucking opposite of what he wanted like Phoebe.

Her lips pulled down. "Please, Kase. I don't want to do this again."

He scowled but knew exactly what she was referring to. He was starting an argument the same way he'd done before. It almost destroyed them. She glanced up through her lashes with a somber stare. She didn't want this and neither did he. He drew in a breath and clenched his fists. He needed to calm the fuck down before he did something stupid and he lost her again. Maybe for good this time.

"When I listed the house, I got some calls from leasing companies. Most backed off when I said I wasn't interested." She sighed and rolled her eyes. "Except for this.one. He's a pushy little bastard."

His brows furrowed, and the heat ran through his blood, but he remained silent.

"I spoke with James from Zink Realty Leasing, and once he explained how it worked, I knew it wasn't an option. I love Ghosttown. I'd never do that, Kase. You of all people know how much this town means to me. Do you really think I'd throw it under the bus and have them come in and put a strip mall on my land?" She raised her brows.

She had a point, and it was making sense beyond his anger.

"Why the fuck didn't you tell me?"

She shrugged. "The whole house fiasco was what almost

ruined us. Why bring up something that is a sore subject?" Her voice lowered, and she shook her head.

He dragged his hands through his hair. It was long overdue, but with everything, his dad's death, Hades coming in, he'd pushed it off. Her scowled, glaring across the counter and pinning her with his stare. "That fucking talk? It's happening now. I'll give you the loan. You pay back Carter."

She clenched her jaw, shaking her head. "Kase."

He raised his brows. "Non-negotiable."

She furrowed her brows and opened her mouth, but he held up his hand, and by a miracle she remained silent. "Same as a bank. Set up the loan with my lawyer. You pay each month; you work out a payment that works for you. No interest."

"Kase."

"No fucking interest, Phoebe."

Phoebe laughed and leaned forward, resting her elbows on the counter, jutting her ass back. *Fuck me.* Seeing her in the position alone was throwing off his train of thought. He tightened his lips, shooting her a harsh glare. It did nothing. Her irritating yet sexy smirk never wavered.

She tilted her head. "I'll think about it."

He ground his teeth, feeling the pressured sting in his molars. "What do ya need to think about? You got no other fucking choice." The second the words left his mouth, he regretted. It was talk like that which had her bolting. He balled his fists as he waited for her to lose her shit again.

She clucked her tongue. "Always got a choice, Kase." She lifted her brow. "Heard Gage is pushing for a strip club in town." She straightened her back and stood, mimicking his stance, except her arms cut into her breasts, causing her shirt to bunch and giving Kase a perfect view of her cleavage. It was a premeditated move. "If I got a side job…" Her blue eyes glimmered, and he drew in a breath. There was no doubt she knew how to work him. She skimmed her hands on the counter, making her way next to him. She stood next to him, inches from touching. It was calculated. She ducked under his arm, placing her body caged in his arms. She peered up through her lashes.

"I'm a great dancer. How different can it be without clothes?"

"You get off on pissing me off, dontcha?"

Her lips curled, and her blue eyes sparkled. "Maybe." She licked her lips.

He shook his head knowing Jack was probably looking down on him laughing his ass off. He was settling this shit with her now.

"I'll buy it, you pay Carter back, and we live here. Together."

"Wanna move in with me, huh?" She grinned and cocked her head. "You'd really do that, put the money up for me?"

"I'd do a lot for you."

She grinned. "Thank you."

He nodded and breathed a sigh of relief.

"I talked to Carter this morning. He wants to continue with the loan." She snorted. "I'll pay him directly."

"You want that?"

She shrugged. "I want to take the olive branch my brother is extending. It's more than just the money."

As much as he would have preferred to be the one helping her, he wouldn't push. She and Carter needed something, and this was a start. Sibling relationships were hard to maneuver sometimes. He knew from his own experience with Caden. He wouldn't come between them.

"Since we're sharing, maybe we should just put it all out there." She licked her lips; it was a nervous reaction to what she'd say next. "You said we'd live here together. You and me, Kase?"

"Yeah?"

She snorted, and her cheeks pinked. "Gonna make me say it?"

He'd have to, because he wasn't sure what she was getting at. "What?"

"You and me? The long haul? You see us together?"

"Do you?"

She clamped her lips and nodded.

He brushed his hand over her jaw, forcing her gaze to meet his. "You and me." He curled his lip. "Maybe even a kid or two, 'cause Riss is all over my ass about making her an aunt."

Phoebe grinned. "She'd make a good aunt, I think."

"Yeah." He smirked and wrapped his arm around her waist. He understood it. Actually, made him fall for her a little more. He cupped her jaw, yanking her body against his and taking her for a kiss. Even fired up and pissed off, he'd be no match for Phoebe. The enemy was his downfall.

She pulled away. "How'd you know about the leasing company?"

"They reached out offering us a deal, same as you."

She widened her eyes, and he caught the wariness.

"They wanna do this? Then let's fucking do it. Set up the meeting."

She widened her eyes. "What?"

"I want you to set it up, schedule it with Meg's. Make it for Town Hall, I'll arrange it with Bailey."

"Why?"

"Because this is my fucking town, and I'm gonna be very clear about it."

Chapter 25

Phoebe was the first to arrive, a few minutes before Bailey and Saint. Her friend opened the door and turned on the lights. It was strange to be in the town hall without all the residents. She dropped her bag in a chair and stretched her arms over her head. She wasn't one hundred percent on board with the plan. It had to be done; she understood Kase's reasoning. If they didn't put up a solid front for the developers coming in, it would only be a matter of time before more would come. While the club owned three quarters of the town, there were a few residents who owned large parcels of land. If they were sold with a high offer, it could be the beginning of the end for the quaint and quiet Ghosttown.

"Bailey." The deep warning had Phoebe turning around.

The tiny mayor sighed and rested her hands on her hips. There was no one cuter than a pregnant Bailey. It looked like someone had planted a giant Easter egg under her shirt.

"It's a folding chair, Saint. I can lift it." She blew out an exasperated breath and folded her arms. Saint had become quite possessive over Bailey. Well, more possessive. He started toward her, and she defiantly grabbed the chair, giving him her back. Phoebe covered her mouth, concealing her snicker.

"Feebs, tell him."

Oh shit. She clamped her lips and shrugged. "I'm on Saint's side with this one, Bails."

Saint glanced over his shoulder and smirked while Bailey frowned. Her soft murmur echoed through the empty room. "Traitor."

Phoebe kept her head down and helped Saint with the chairs, all the while feeling Bailey's scornful glare on her back. Meg arrived a few minutes later. Thank God. It was a slight distraction for Bailey. She unfolded a chair, set it down at the end of the row, and then sat down. Something felt off, she just couldn't place it.

"Hey, Saint?"

He glanced over from a few feet away and walked over to her.

"How hard will Kase go on this unsuspecting girl?"

He furrowed his brows. "What do you mean?"

She sighed and crossed her legs. "She sounded really young, ya know. She fumbled over her words and just seemed nervous as hell, and all we were doing was setting up a meeting." Phoebe shrugged. "I guess I'm feeling a little guilty, which is so unlike me, but I just think she's clueless, and I think Kase is out for blood."

Saint nodded with a half-smile. "He'll go hard. As you know, it's how Kase usually handles things. He wants to set a precedent for any future developers thinking they can come in." He paused. "Needs to be done."

"That's what I thought."

"I'm guessing if he needs to be reeled in?" He cocked his head. "You'll know how to handle him."

She snorted. "I was hoping you'd handle him."

Saint smiled and held up his hands. "No, he's all yours. I got my own spitfire to handle." He glanced up at Bailey, and she followed his gaze. Some couples were beyond perfect. That was Saint and Bailey.

There was a brief minute before the club descended on town hall. Kase led the pack into the old building. She was surprised to see as many brothers, but it made sense. The more backing, the deeper the intimidation. She stood, and was happily surprised when Kase made a beeline in her direction. They were official, though since the decision, she hadn't been around the members of the club. It was new territory for her. She had never been overly affectionate with Jared or any past lovers. It seemed Kase was the opposite. He stopped in front of her and lifted his chin. She was slightly unprepared when he grasped her neck and pulled her against his chest, but she went willingly. Why the hell wouldn't she?

She trailed her hands down his shirt and raised on her toes. The kiss was what she'd come to crave from him. Soft lips parting, inhaling his heated breath, and a sensual slip of his tongue. Nothing scandalous but enough for her to tighten her grip to keep him from backing away. Her arm wrapped around his waist, and she deepened the kiss.

"Missed you."

His gaze softened, and he leaned closer for another kiss. Then it was all business.

"Where is he?" Gage asked.

"Her," Kase responded, and stepped out of Phoebe's hold.

"What?"

Phoebe sighed. "Yeah, the developer set it up and sent a rep. Vada Zink."

Kase snorted. "Vada? That's her fucking name?"

Phoebe snorted and playfully slapped his stomach. "I think it's adorable, and she sounded very sweet on the phone. Nothing like the shark of a developer from last week. Right, Meg?"

"That man is an asshole. I can just sense it by his tone." Meg snorted. "But I gotta agree with Phoebe. Almost felt bad knowing it was a set up for her. She sounds young and innocent, like a lamb walking into the tiger's cage."

Kase snarled. "Don't go soft on me Meg. Already got my doubts about this one." He hooked his thumb over his shoulder, pointing at her.

"Hey." Phoebe sidled up next to Kase. She wrapped her arm around his waist and dug her fingers into his side. He didn't even flinch. His lip twitched. "I'm not soft. I'm an ex con, remember?"

The statement garnered a few chuckles from the men.

A soft voice echoed from the back door, and Phoebe turned. The little lamb had arrived. She looked exactly how she sounded. Young, naïve, and completely unprepared for what she was about to go up against. Phoebe and Meg both walked to the door.

"You must be Vada. I'm Phoebe." She extended her hand.

"So nice to meet you in person."

"I'm Meg."

Vada repeated the same enthusiastic phrase and shook Meg's hand. Then Meg dropped the bomb, making a quick introduction to the club. One by one, as she named the members, their scowls and intimidating stances were more than young Vada could seem to handle.

At least Phoebe wasn't the only soft one in the bunch. Meg grew increasingly uneasy as the men took seats, glaring at Vada. Bailey stepped forward with a bright smile, welcoming Vada, and guided her up to the desk to set up her presentation.

Phoebe walked down the aisle with Meg and whispered, "I feel like an asshole right now."

Meg sighed. "We are assholes. I'd be shocked if this sweet girl doesn't leave in tears." Meg placed her hand on Phoebe's back. "You heard Kase. If we don't make it known now, we'll be fielding calls every week from these companies."

Phoebe understood it, but she wished it had been the arrogant prick they were about to unleash on, not Vada. She took an open seat between Kase and Gage, who winked as she passed.

She watched as Vada set up her computer and screen and turned it around. She drew in a deep breath, and Phoebe could feel her nervous energy surge through the room.

"First, I just want to thank you for taking the time to come to the meeting. My name is Vada Zink, and I...

"What kind of name is Vada?" Gage asked. Phoebe glanced over, catching the smile playing on his lips.

Vada seemed caught off guard by the interruption. She fumbled with the small stack of papers she had in front of her. "Um," she cleared her throat when she croaked. Her cheeks blazed crimson, and Phoebe got an uneasy flip in her stomach. *Sympathetic embarrassment, is that a real thing?*

"It's German."

"Really?" Gage asked, amusement laced in his tone.

Vada nodded and smiled. She probably thought she may have found an ally in Gage. She hadn't. She drew in a breath. "My great grandparents came over from Germany. That's on my dad's side, but my mom has German descent too." She smiled. "I was named after my great, great-great grandmother. Vada means 'famous ruler'." Her smile reached her eyes, and Phoebe couldn't help but smile back.

The sweet moment was ruined by the loud snort from behind her. She turned her head to see Hades shaking his head.

"I actually went to Germany a few years back…" Vada continued, but Kase wasn't having any of it.

"Can we get on with this? Nobody in this room gives a shit about your fucking heritage."

Phoebe gritted her teeth and whipped her head in his direction. She clasped her hand over his thigh, digging her fingers into his thigh through his jeans, and sent Kase a harsh glare.

HE SIGHED and glanced over at Phoebe. She was trying to stab him with her nails. Unfortunately for her, it was a useless effort. He was being purposely rude. It seemed his woman didn't approve. He arched a brow. She leaned closer.

"I know you have to do what you have to do, but if you make her cry, I'm going to kick your ass when we get home."

He refrained from laughing, but his smirk couldn't be helped.

Her blue eyes squinted, and her lips pursed. She leaned closer, her lips brushing against his ear.

"We set up this meeting, Kase, and she drove all the way out here and prepared this presentation. We are knowingly wasting her time right now, so let's try to reel in the unnecessary cruelty. Just because life hands you the opportunity to be an asshole doesn't mean you have to take it."

She pushed off his thigh and turned in her seat, folding her arms. He'd pissed off his old lady. Usually he'd be amused by it. He wasn't, and as much as he had no problems being an asshole, it wasn't necessary with this one. He'd make his point, and he doubted she'd come back at him. He drew in a breath and eyed Vada, who looked as though she was seconds from running out of the room.

"Just get to the presentation."

She smiled, and her lower lips quivered. "Okay, um, I'm sorry."

It's like kicking a fucking puppy. He settled into his seat and listened for the next thirty minutes. She wasn't a natural. She fumbled over her explanation of how the company worked. At one point, he even got the impression she didn't wholeheartedly believe in it.

Halfway through, Saint asked a question. "Are there any restrictions? Let's say I have five acres, you can put up condos and a strip mall, am I right?"

She nodded with an eager smile. "Yes."

Saint sighed. "On any property?"

"Yes."

"If every land does this, we could have condos, strip malls on every street."

"It's very lucrative." She was missing the point of his question.

"I'm sure it is, but at what cost?"

She paused, furrowing her brows, and became quickly confused by the question. She flipped through her papers before glancing up when Saint called her name.

"We settled in Ghosttown to get away from all that. Have you been around town?"

She bit her lip and shook her head.

"It's quaint and quiet. That's how we'd like to keep it."

"But you can if you…"

Kase held up his hand, and she immediately clamped her lips. Phoebe jerked her head and again squeezed his thigh. He rolled his eyes, rewording his retort before he spoke.

"We sell off land to you, you'll over-build like every other fucking town in this country. Not in Ghosttown. Even if you get one or two, they don't have the acreage we do. You won't make money 'cause we'll fucking sabotage every advance you try to make. This is me being fucking honest and straight with you, so listen."

Her eyes widened in shock.

"There is no fucking chance, not even slim, sweetheart, you will be able to lease any property in this town. You need to go home or find somewhere else. You hear me?"

She gulped and peered around the room. While the women might be showing pity, he knew what she would be getting from the members. Confirmation she was not welcome in Ghosttown. Then she surprised the hell out of him.

Her shoulders straightened, and she took a second, gauging the group before turning to Meg. She smiled.

"As the owner of the land, I'd like to hear from you."

Kase snorted, shaking his head, and heard Phoebe's whispered groan, "Oh shit."

Meg sat up in her chair, eyeing Kase, who raised his brows and smirked. She inhaled a breath and turned to Vada.

"Actually, the Ghosttown Riders own the land, sweetheart."

"What?"

When she glanced at Kase, he grinned. "Yeah, we fucking own it, and ya know where we stand." He stood up and heard the members shift up from their chairs. "Don't come back." He walked through the room and out the door followed by his brothers.

Hades laughed and was the first to speak. "Thought for sure she was gonna lose it with the heritage comment."

Kase snorted.

They remained outside until Phoebe came outside, glaring at him. He held up his hands.

"She didn't fucking cry."

Phoebe squinted, and he was expecting a verbal assault. She remained quiet and circled in their group. He reached out, grasping her waist and pulling her into his side. She was reluctant but fell into his side. Her hand grazed his back.

"Think she'll head home, or will this be a problem, Phoebe?" Saint asked.

Phoebe shrugged. "Outside of the club, there are about thirty property owners in town, Saint. My guess? She'll reach out to them while she's here." She sighed. "There's a driving force with her, just don't know who is controlling it."

"Fuck," Kase snapped.

Phoebe squeezed his hand and he glanced down. "I've known these people a long time, and can't think of anyone who will take the deal, Kase. There's a reason why people move to Ghosttown and settle down." Phoebe and the club shared the same reason. The privacy and simplicity of their small town was a draw for most residents.

Only time would tell, he guessed. He and the club were prepared, if possible, to buy the land from anyone wanting to sell, but going up against the leasing company who could possibly offer more was weighing on them. Mainly Kase.

Chapter 26

She smiled, staring down at her phone.

Carter: Deposited your check. It didn't bounce.

Her relationship had taken an unlikely turn with her brother. In the past two weeks, they texted several times, and made plans for Kase and her to meet up with him and Nadia for dinner.

Phoebe: You trick Nadia into moving in with you yet?

Carter: I'm working on it.

Phoebe smiled. She clicked her phone, shoved it into her bag, and crossed the street. A quick scan of the road had her missing the curb, and she stumbled but caught herself. She flickered her gaze to the distraction which caused her mishap.

"Hey, Vada."

She spun around, and then smiled and rushed toward Phoebe. The eagerness was her downfall.

"Hi, Phoebe, it's so good to see you."

Phoebe held in her chuckle. "Still here, huh?"

Vada nodded. "Can't fail unless you quit."

Phoebe squinted her eyes. She didn't know Vada well enough to make assumptions. However, the urgent robotic tone led her to believe those weren't her words, but someone else's.

"That's true." She continued to pass her.

"Uh, u-umm…"

Phoebe turned.

"Can I buy you lunch?"

Phoebe smiled. *Ah, this kid.* That's what she was, just a kid, maybe fresh out of college, and not a clue how the real world worked. "You can." She shrugged. "And you can give me your whole spiel again, but it won't change my mind, sweetie, and I'm not gonna do that to you."

Her cheeks flushed, and she ducked her head. "I appreciate your honesty."

Phoebe eyed her and walked three steps, putting her closer to Vada. "Let me ask you something. Do you like your job?"

Vada cocked her head. "What do you mean?"

"Do you like it? Is this what you saw yourself doing ten years ago?"

Vada laughed and blushed. "Not even close. I actually have a Bachelor's in Education, got my Master's in Psychology." Vada sighed and gazed up at the sky. "But I uh, decided to work at the family business."

Phoebe chuckled, and Vada's blush darkened. Phoebe had a feeling the decision was not Vada's.

"You actually remind me of my first-grade teacher."

Her face lit up. "Yeah? That's funny because I always saw myself as teaching first or second. They're vital years." Vada rolled her eyes. "I know a lot of people think they aren't a big deal, ya know, crafts and games, but really, the earliest years set the tone for a student."

Phoebe felt her own excitement feeding off Vada's. She obviously had a passion for teaching. Why the hell was she working for a leasing company?

Phoebe nodded. "But you *decided* to work for your family?"

Vada lost the glimmer in her eyes and forced a smile. "My dad took over the company twenty-two years ago when my grandpa retired. It's completely family based, my brothers, my sister, her husband, my cousins, and their spouses. Everybody works there."

"It sounds like the job picked you, huh? That's a lot of pressure."

Vada didn't reply. She clamped her lips and offered Phoebe a smile. It was well rehearsed, something she practiced in the mirror. It was awkward. For both of them it seemed.

Kase caught her eyes, and his gaze narrowed when he glanced over at Vada. *Oh shit, girl.* Kase, along with Saint and Hades and a small girl holding his hand, started toward them. The last thing poor Vada needed was another encounter with the club.

"Can't take no for an answer?" As usual, Kase's tone was hostile.

Vada jerked her body and stumbled slightly, righting herself before she hit the curb. "Oh hi, how are you?"

Phoebe bit her lip. Much like their meeting from last week, it was painful to watch. Confidence came with time and experience. Something Vada was in dire need of. It would come, but not in the next five seconds when it was needed.

The men stood silent, glaring back at her. They had to; it's what would keep other developers from changing Ghosttown. Phoebe knew it was a necessary evil. *Oh hell, why do I feel bad?* There was something about Vada that was reminiscent of Bailey. The innocence. Obviously, Phoebe was the only one seeing it.

She remained silent and watched the small girl who couldn't be more than four swing her hand and wave.

"Hi."

Vada's gaze dropped, and her smile spread across her face. "Hi there. That is a very pretty dress."

Hades' daughter grinned. "It's new. It used to be Cia's, but she's too big now, so it's my brand-new dress. I'm Allie." Phoebe stifled her laugh. It was almost strange to see the bright-eyed innocence of Allie holding the hand of Hades. It was an anomaly.

Nothing shocked her more than when Vada bent at her knees, setting herself at eye level. She tilted her head with all her focus on Allie. It was a complete contrast to how she was with them. She rested her hands on her knees.

"It's nice to meet you, Allie. I'm Vada. That's super exciting." She cocked a brow. "Pink is definitely your color."

It was sweet, but not appreciated by the men.

"That's a weird name," Allie said with a smile.

"It's German."

"We know," Hades snapped.

Vada righted herself and smiled at Hades, who remained tight-lipped and scowling.

"Oh." Her eyes widened, catching Phoebe and the men off guard. She spun around and dug inside her large satchel thrown over her shoulder. She pulled out a small model of a building. She smiled down at Allie and reached out her arm.

"It's a stress ball." She licked her lips. "Well, not a ball, a building, but it's kinda fun."

Without a second thought, the small girl grabbed it. It was a sweet gesture, Phoebe thought. Apparently, she was the only one who thought so.

"You always give out shit to random kids on the street?"

Vada's mouth fell open, and her lips smacked together uneasily. "Oh, I-I don't..." She cleared her throat. "I mean, it's just a little freebie."

"I like it," Allie said, mesmerized with squeezing it. She giggled when it expanded in her hand.

Phoebe watched and felt her heart awkwardly pump.

"Nothing's free," Hades snapped.

"No, it is, it's just a marketing thing." She held up her hands. "No strings attached." She smiled and glanced at the group and ended with Phoebe. "It was actually my idea. Ya know, for the company."

"You specialize in manipulation?" Hades' accusation was harsh, and didn't go unnoticed by Vada, who shrunk in her stance.

Oh Christ.

Phoebe had enough. She stepped forward. "I think it's sweet, Vada. Allie seems to like it."

Vada bit her lip, eyeing the little girl. "Physical stimulants are imperative at her age." Vada glanced down at Allie. "I bet you're four, right?"

Allie lunged forward and grinned. "But I'm gonna be five in July."

Vada's face brightened, and she gasped, which was adorable as her interaction with Allie seemed so genuine.

"I bet that means you'll be starting kindergarten. You are going to have so much fun, Allie."

"I'm gonna be in class with Emme maybe."

Vada laughed. It ended quickly when Hades cleared his throat, and Phoebe watched the harsh glare he sent her. She bowed her head, backing up.

"I should go. Have a nice day," she said and turned. Vada glanced over her shoulder, and her smile brightened on Allie. She gave her a short wave.

Phoebe watched her walk away with her shoulders slouched and her hair sweeping past her neck as she bowed her head. She turned to the men. Kase and Saint were smirking while Hades was glancing over his shoulder watching Vada cross the street. When he turned and met her gaze, she raised her brows.

"See something ya like, Hades?"

The corner of his mouth curled. While he shared the same eyes and similar features with his brother, Saint, Hades had a ruthless and harsh demeanor. All the men of the club carried a certain rough exterior, some more pronounced than others. Kase and Rourke being the harshest. Hades surpassed them.

He winked and jerked his chin. "I'd break her, sweetheart."

"She might surprise you."

Kase snorted and shook his head.

She cocked her brow and curled her arm around Kase's waist. "Wasn't too long ago you referred to me as the enemy." Kase pulled her in for a kiss, which surprised her since his brothers were standing around watching. She blushed but gave in.

IT WAS LATER in the day when they started off. While his Pop had no instructions on how he wanted his ashes spread, both he and his brother knew, there was only one place where Jack could finally be home. They had made arrangements and decided to keep it just for them. Jack's life was Ghosttown Riders, but even beyond the club, he was their dad. When he mentioned it to his brothers, they were all in agreement, the last of Jack's life or death should be with Kase and Cade.

He took the ten-minute ride to the river. Jack's ride, and Mick's ride before that. It was symbolic to the older members. He parked at the edge of the path next to Cade's bike and Marissa's van. He gripped the jean-clad thigh of his old lady straddled against his back and glanced back at her. *Fucking beautiful. And mine.* Phoebe leaned closer, kissing his lips before maneuvering off the bike.

She removed her helmet, hanging it on his handlebar, and gripped his hand. It was strange. He'd never given much thought to hand holding, but it seemed to be a thing for Phoebe. He squeezed her hand and led them down to the river. Caden was by the water, looking out across the river. He was holding Cora in his arms and whispering something that made her smile.

Kase released her hand when Marissa started forward, wrapping her hand over his shoulders for a tight hug.

"Jack would have liked this, all of us coming here for him." She stepped back and turned, moving closer to Phoebe for a hug.

"I brought the whiskey," Phoebe said, and Marissa laughed.

"I don't drink, but for Jack, I'm making an exception." She sighed. "A small taste, that's all I can handle."

Kase snorted and glanced over his shoulder. The words were on the tip of his tongue with a retort, but he stopped, struck by

Marissa and Phoebe standing together. *Good women.* Probably better than what either Reilly brother deserved.

Phoebe stepped forward. "You okay, babe?"

The corner of his mouth twitched, and he nodded, turning and walking down by Caden and Trevor, who were standing at the water's edge.

He reached out, and immediately Cora reached for him, which made Caden laugh. He curled her against his chest and stared out at the water. So many fucking memories with his old man and brother. It was easy to focus on some of the shit Jack dealt them. The hardest part were the good times. The things he'd miss. He drew in a breath and turned to Trevor.

"Heard the news."

Trevor sighed and slowly turned to Kase. He nodded and remained silent. The kid had it all wrong.

Trevor been talking about joining the club since he was ten. Kase encouraged it, Caden not so much. It seemed he'd had a change of heart in the last year and would be heading off to college in the fall. He attributed that to Marissa.

"Proud of you, kid. First Reilly to go to college. That's fucking big." Kase glanced over to Caden. There was no hiding the man's pride. This was what he wanted for Trevor; to do better than he had.

"You pissed I'm not joining?"

Kase shook his head with a smile and then turned to Trevor. "Club would be happy to have you, but you gotta do what you want, Trev. You live this life on your terms." He pointed to Trevor. "Not mine, not your dad's. Club will be there you ever change your mind."

Trevor snorted. "Pop would be pissed."

"Yeah, no fucking doubt about that." He laughed, catching Caden smirk. Jack had always been pro club for his boys.

The spreading of the ashes wasn't ceremonial. It was mostly them standing around sharing stories. He and Caden sharing the most, though Riss and Phoebe chimed in a few times.

Trevor opened the canister and did the honors of spreading Jack's ashes in the river.

"Ride free and wild, Pop." It was a hushed tone only meant for Pop, but they all heard it. It was fucking perfect.

Marissa curled up to Caden, who wrapped his arms around her waist, dropping a kiss to her cheek before resting his chin on her head.

Kase pulled Phoebe closer, and her arm wrapped around his waist.

He could almost hear his Pop's voice.

You fuckers don't deserve them. He was probably right, but the Reilly boys were keeping them.

"Is this illegal? Spreading ashes in the river?" Marissa asked.

Kase snorted. "Yeah, it's fucking illegal, and the perfect send-off." He glanced over at Rissa and smirked. "Pop would have loved it."

She smiled with tears rimming her eyes.

There were a few moments of silence in what he assumed was their own personal way of honoring Jack. Kase drew in a breath, remembering the good shit. There was plenty. When he glanced over at Caden, his little brother smiled and nodded.

Jack Reilly may not have been perfect, but he was their Pop.

Trevor came forward with the bottle of whiskey, taking the first sip. The bottle was passed around. When it came to Phoebe, she held up the bottle and bit her lip. Tears formed in her eyes, and she drew in a deep breath.

"To bikers and whiskey, Jack."

She passed the bottle and curled into his side.

It was Cora who ended the ceremony when she started to get fussy. Caden had invited them back to their place for dinner. They would go. In fact, Kase had made a mental note to see them more often. They were family; he needed to be with them.

Kase and Phoebe stayed behind. He curled his hands over her stomach, drawing her back to his chest. She glanced up.

"I love you. And I'm not saying it because I want you to say it back." She shrugged with a small smile. "I just want you to know it." She paused. "And feel it."

It was the wasn't the first time he'd heard the words, but it was the first time he'd felt it from a woman.

He smirked, pulling her closer. "I do." He cocked his brow. "Do you?"

She slowly nodded.

In the end, the words meant nothing as long as they both knew what they felt.

Pure fucking love.

The End

About the Author

Amelia Shea writes contemporary romance. She released her debut novel in 2015 and has followed her passion for series romance ever since. Her writing style includes a little sweet, a little sassy, and lots of steam. She loves building stories with settings that become comfortable and familiar, and developing characters who feel real, and though they may be flawed, they learn and grow, and finally deserve a happy ending.

Born and raised a Jersey girl, she has settled down in the South with her amazingly supportive husband, her fabulous (most days) children, and her loyal, four-legged, furry sidekick, Bob.

Website: AmeliaShea.net

- facebook.com/AsheaWrites
- twitter.com/AsheaWrites
- instagram.com/Author_amelia_shea
- amazon.com/Author/Amelia-Shea
- goodreads.com/Amelia_Shea
- bookbub.com/authors/amelia-shea

Made in the USA
Columbia, SC
18 August 2024